ROCK STAR NATION

CHASING FAME, SUCCESS, GLORY, MONEY & FANS IN THE MUSIC INDUSTRY

BY NICK THOMAS

GUARDIAN EXPRESS MEDIA

Library of Congress Control Number: 2020911628
ISBN: 978-1735152301

Library of Congress Cataloging-in-Publication Data
Thomas, Nick

Rock Star Nation: Chasing Fame, Success,
Glory, Money and Fans in the Music Industry
Includes bibliographical references
ISBN 978-1735152301
1. Rock music – Music Business.
I. Title

We would like to thank the following individuals who offered their help in the creation of this book: John Mascolo, John Riley, Nick Regas, Mike Olszewski and Mary Ellen Huesken. Additionally, we are grateful to all of the individuals who consented to our interview requests.

Please contact the publisher to report any errors or omissions. Organizations and other groups interested in purchasing quantities of this book should contact the publisher. Additionally, this book is not affiliated with any sports drink maker, rock star, sports team, business entity or corporation.

Guardian Express Media
P.O. Box 205
Green, Ohio 44232

www.guardianexpress.com
Printed in the U.S.A.

▶ TABLE OF CONTENTS

▶ INTRODUCTION

Moments before the start of the sold-out concert, the restless members of the seasoned rock group are huddled together in the backstage area. As they wait for their cue to start the show, they exchange some small talk. They've done this pre-show ritual hundreds of times before and yet they're still jittery. Meanwhile, the level of anticipation in the dimmed arena increases by the minute.

Standing at either side of the stage, there's a number of insiders including the stage manager, a handful of record company execs, the local music press, a few balding deejays as well as various friends and colleagues. Proudly wearing their all-access passes, they're looking forward to the show. Meanwhile, a few roadies are still running around with tape and tools in their hands.

Finally, the house lights are turned down. A thunderous cacophony of stomping and applause erupts from the impatient fans, most of whom are holding their half-full plastic cups of overpriced beer and wearing their newly purchased concert t-shirts. The smiling musicians step out to their designated spots on the stage and are greeted by a roar of adulation. But no matter how many times the lead singer and his backing band have been running onto a stage, there is still an initial level of nervousness and uncertainly about how the night will go.

Glancing into the first few rows, the musicians spot a number of familiar faces – their wives and girlfriends, an assorted collection of superfans who follow the band from city to city and, of course, the filthy rich VIPs who paid ticket brokers more than a thousand dollars for the enviable privilege of watching the concert from the best seats in the house.

As the cavernous concrete-and-steel arena begins to shake and rumble, the leader of the group straps on his glistening vintage guitar and heads to the front of the stage. For the next two hours, 25,000 pairs of eyes are intensely focused on his most minuscule movements. He owns the room as he delivers a musical feast, from fist-shaking rockers to tender, syrupy power-ballads. His words are gospel and his melodies are sacred.

The rock concert is a momentous happening to be experienced in person, and is not just a straightforward performance of the group's hits. It is an opportunity to see, hear, feel and bask in the presence of the group's music and energy. And it is also an opportunity to join like-minded fans in sharing the near-spiritual experience. Throughout the packed venue, concertgoers are on their feet dancing and singing in a celebration of the good life. It certainly doesn't get much better than this moment.

As the concert is coming to its eventual close, the band trots off the stage. The lead singer soaks in the deafening chants of "We want more" from the animated fans who are waiting in anticipation of an additional encore or two. Wiping his sweaty face with a clean towel and resting for a minute or two, he can feel his heart racing as adrenaline is still rushing through his veins. Then, just as quickly, he leads his bandmates back onto the stage and returns to his spot behind the microphone stand. The banks of sizzling stage lights are switched back on and the grateful audience reacts as if the encore is a surprise bonus. Leaning forward into his microphone, he thanks his fans and strums the opening notes of the group's breakthrough hit, a sing-along crowd pleaser that the band saves for the end of the show.

With the last power chord echoing through the cheap seats in the deepest corner of the balcony, the drummer sets down his sticks and the audience is thanked for coming to the show. The house lights come on. The concert is over. The throngs of music fans head for the exits. Almost immediately, the fast-moving roadies have begun the backbreaking task of tearing down the stage and carting everything out to a waiting fleet of full-sized tractor-trailer trucks.

Running off the stage, the rock star has mastered his well-planned, end-of-concert routine and is protected by a wall of angry-looking, muscle-bound members of the security crew. Bypassing the usual line-up of fans, hangers-on and groupies, he decides to take a break from the post-concert festivities. After escaping into a stretch limo and returning to his hotel room, he is met with yet another circus of activities – an extravagant party with jumping music and newfound friends. Unable to help himself, the bone-weary and emotionally drained rocker decides to partake in the action. Why not? Everything is handed to him on a proverbial gilded platter – women, booze and drugs as well as a steady stream of adulation and flattery: "You were great tonight – really great!" However, this night is not much different from the night before. Or the one before that.

When you're a rock star, you can expect instant gratification, fan worship, physical pleasures as well as the public acceptance of your outlandish and lewd behavior. The commonly accepted Rules of Life do not apply to you. Did you break the law during a violent, public tantrum or get caught with a sizable quantity of unlawful powders or pills? Don't worry about it. The judge is more concerned about getting an autographed photo for his wife than in doling out justice.

In 1975, Billy Joel mused, "As you sign a record contract, you go through this change, because as soon as you put your name on the paper, you're an artist. The record contract says, 'Billy Joel, herein referred to as the artist,' and automatically you become an artist just by signing."

The *job* of being a rock star is occasionally the subject of a hit song such as "We're An American Band" by Grand Funk, "Have A Cigar" by Pink Floyd and "Into The Great Wide Open" by Tom Petty and the Heartbreakers, which follows the adventures of a budding rocker named Eddy. And when Joe Walsh gave us "Life's Been Good," he bragged about losing his driver's license, destroying hotel rooms and owning a mansion he's never visited.

Jon Bon Jovi called his hit "Wanted Dead Or Alive" an autobiographical story of the life of a touring rock star. Chronicling his daily routine on the road, he explained: "Take Nashville for example, we get in at 5 PM, I do a sound check, sing a couple of Elvis songs, now I'm doing an interview. I've got to meet contest winners and all this kind of thing. I'm busier than hell between now and the time I hit the stage. I hit the stage, I'm off the stage. I take a shower, get in the van, and I'm gone. It's like riding into town, robbing the bank, drinking the booze, stealing the women, and leaving before the sheriff gets here. It's really what I do for a living. I'm a cowboy."

Some musicians deal with the task of being a rock star fairly well. But most don't. There is no *Fame For Dummies* book. You can't go to Amazon and order a guidebook on navigating a bout of sudden rock stardom. There are no counselors who can offer detailed advice on dealing with the constant demands of adoring, obsessive or unbearable fans. There isn't a Cliff's Notes study guide on how to avoid becoming an arrogant, self-serving, pill-popping, abusive jerk once you reach the top. And there is no iTunes app that aids a musician in coping with the psychological consequences of having fans staring at you for hours every night. Keith Richards, in his tribute to George Harrison, wrote in *Rolling Stone*, "I think the other thing that runs between George and the Beatles and ourselves, the Stones, is that we're basically the same age and happened to find ourselves in this unique position without any training.... You can't go to star school."

In 1994, Kurt Cobain revealed his personal struggles with fame in the aftermath of the phenomenal success of the smash Nirvana album, *Nevermind*: "It was so fast and explosive. I didn't know how to deal with it. If there was a Rock Star 101 course, I would have liked to take it. It might have helped me." Likewise, when punk rocker Richard Hell was being courted by a record label, he did not know what to expect: "Like most unsigned young musicians, I knew nothing about the record business. I was not only naive but deluded. My idea of the recording artist's life came from *A Hard Day's Night* and *Don't Look Back*. I expected to travel in limousines for protection from screaming girls.... It's not that I felt entitled or power-hungry... [but] I assumed that the girls and cars just automatically accompanied record contracts."

After topping the charts in 1965 with their single, "I Got You Babe," Sonny & Cher emerged as both rock and media stars. Sonny Bono later recalled: "My goal had always been success. Cher's had been fame. Suddenly, overnight it seemed, we had both. On the one hand, we were no different than we had been just days earlier.... Yet we were different. The wave we caught was a monster. A commotion followed us around the clock. People knew us, gawked, asked for autographs.... There's no single prescription for coping with instant success. You just go with it. You try to keep your head, but it blows your psyche. No way about it. Confidence oozes. Your ego boomerangs."

And although New Wave singer Gary Numan was considered a one-hit-wonder in the U.S. – where his only top-40 success came with the single "Cars" – he was a significant star in his native England, scoring seven top-10 albums and more than twenty top-40 hits. Unfortunately, his fame and success happened practically overnight. He explained: "[In 1978] I was absolutely nothing. I think I'd done one little interview with a tiny little fanzine that sold about 200 copies, and then I was No. 1. It all happened in the space of three weeks, I think it was. Your whole world gets turned upside down. You're kind of expected to take it in stride, like you'd just got a new job. You just can't do that." Instantly, Numan became the focus of a media barrage: "All of a sudden everyone knows who you are. Some of them really love what you're doing to the degree that I found it frightening. People fainting when they meet you, screaming, wetting themselves. You'd shag a girl, then the next thing it's in the press. It's pretty weird."

However, in his autobiography, Charlie Daniels explained: "The truth about the music business is that there is no yellow brick road to get you there. There is no academic degree that guarantees the success you seek. There is no safety net to catch you when you fall. There's only you, your talent, your determination, your belief in yourself, and, most important of all, your attitude."

Recognizing both the perks and pitfalls of fame, hopeful musicians all over the world still attempt to achieve rock star status, whether through years of hard work in small gritty clubs or by jump-starting a career as a contestant on a television singing competition. Furthermore, a certain type of drive and motivation are needed to succeed in music. As *People* magazine reported: "The man who would become Freddie Mercury seemed depressed as he sat in a London pub one day in the late '60s. 'I'm not going to be a pop star,' he sighed glumly, as classmate Chris Smith would later recall. Then a smile spread across his face as he rose to his feet and threw his arms out in a heroic pose that would become familiar to millions of fans: 'I'm going to be a legend!' It was a laughable notion for an unknown art student barely into his 20s. But then it happened!"

Similarly, Bruce Springsteen admitted in his autobiography, "I didn't want to meet the Beatles, I wanted to *be* the Beatles." And in her 2004 high school yearbook, 18-year-old Lady Gaga (then known by her real name, Stefani Germanotta) stated in her personal profile that her dream was to one day be "headlining at Madison Square Garden." And taking his goal of achieving success to an extreme, Nine Inch Nails founder Trent Reznor told *The New York Times*, "I would stab my mother for a number one album, yes."

There are various personality types that are attracted to rock stardom: an artist who enjoys expressing and sharing his musical craft; an insecure, bullied teen who finds a bit of comfort in the positive reinforcement from others; the self-absorbed, egotistical, extrovert who craves constant attention; and the misfit and outcast with eight nose-rings and a myriad of bright tattoos who doubts he will ever find employment in a traditional workplace. Ultimately, being a rock star is equated with an artistic personality. This creativity manifests itself in the various aspects of a musician's life – from fashion and personality to morality and politics. Additionally, many musicians are attracted to the rock and roll lifestyle – at least in the beginning.

However, there are numerous occupational hazards when engaging in the rock star lifestyle, from drug and alcohol abuse to unintended pregnancies and STDs. Some would consider these the fringe benefits of fame; others would consider these to be unfortunate risks. Even worse, rock stardom often spawns a psychological malady known as

Lead Singer Disease – the unchecked desire for fame, ego-massaging, immediate gratification and debauchery.

Even if a recording artist does manage to achieve a hit album or number-one single, longterm success can be fleeting. In 1990, author Wayne Jancik wrote an entire book chronicling the history of one-hit-wonders during the rock era. From the Penguins ("Earth Angel") to Bobby McFerrin ("Don't Worry, Be Happy"), these artists learned that success can be fickle and short-lived. In the end, few singers and musicians are lucky enough – and luck is a major component – to cultivate a large and loyal fanbase and to enjoy a lengthy career. Only a small percentage of rockers ever headline large stadiums, are the subjects of multiple book biographies or get inducted into the Rock and Roll Hall of Fame. Conversely, the unlucky ones manage only a brief taste of stardom before quickly disappearing from the spotlight and returning to their ordinary, civilian lives.

▶ CHAPTER 1
MOTIVATIONS FOR BECOMING A ROCK STAR

There are a number of reasons why a person would be drawn to rock and roll as a profession. Some motives are noble and respectable, while others are rooted in hedonism and depravity; some are clear and obvious, while others are shielded secrets or not easily comprehended.

The list of common motivations includes the love of music, the desire for fame and the lure of wealth. As David Lee Roth once admitted, "I've been rich and I've been poor. Rich is better. Totally better." Other obvious motivations include the desire for constant praise, the need to be the center of attention, attracting romantic partners, attaining social stature, overcoming shyness, and even the idealistic notion of a carefree, bohemian existence. Some performers have expressed their own unique reasons for entering the music business. New Orleans pianist Dr. John revealed that he decided to pursue a career in music after experiencing a vivid dream in which he was ordered to follow in the path of jazz legend Louis Armstrong.

But motivations can also vary by age. Among teens, the incentives to join a rock band can include popularity among their peers, a few dollars of spending money, increased opportunities for dating and a guaranteed weekend party. During the classic MTV era of the 1980s, mainstream rock music had successfully formulated a suburban, adolescent, male fantasy. In music video after music video, guitar-slinging rockers were surrounded by long-legged, scantily-attired, big-haired, pouty-lipped women in revealing fishnet stockings who stretched out on the polished hoods of muscle cars or danced wildly in elevated cages. And it seemed that the only thing that a wide-eyed teen needed in order to achieve this goal was to grow his hair long, learn to play an electric guitar and find three or four other like-minded musicians to form a rock band.

Singer-songwriter Chris Isaak recalled his reaction to a performance by Roy Orbison: "I saw him on TV. I remember thinking, 'Look at this guy with dark glasses on, on TV, at night. He's an adult and he gets to do whatever he wants and he's singing this song and women are going crazy for him.' In my mind it was like 'This is as cool as it gets.'"

Similarly, Nikki Sixx of Mötley Crüe revealed what attracted him to the heavy metal lifestyle: "We're a rock 'n' roll band. We love the rock 'n' roll excess. And it's beautiful. Anybody that says that they wouldn't enjoy it is lying to themselves. It's the most exciting thing to happen since Christmas. You never really have to grow up. You really never have to make your own bed. You never ever have to worry about anything except rolling over and dialing room service and stumbling down the hall and doing what you love the best. That's playing rock 'n' roll. Then you have food, drink, and the party backstage with all the beautiful ladies and meetin' fans and it's a gas." However, Steven Tyler of Aerosmith argued: "Every kid on every block in every city in America wants to be a rock star. But if girls, money, fast cars, houses in Maui, and skybox seats to Red Sox games are your only motivation – and that's *a lot of motivation* – then you're in trouble."

Not all musicians were drawn to rock and roll for depraved or hedonistic reasons. John Fogerty explained in his autobiography, "I didn't get into music to get girls. Or to become famous. Or rich. Those things never occurred to me. I got into music because of *music*. I just loved it. It was (and is) a mystical, magical thing. I just wanted to write songs, good songs, *great* songs."

Similarly, Slim Jim Phantom, the drummer for the Stray Cats, recalled: "As far back as I can remember, I always wanted to be the guy in the band. I never gave anything else much thought. I didn't have the Beatles on Ed Sullivan moment. It was something I just knew early on in my life. It was more a slow burn. I always liked music on the radio, and anytime a band played on television, I watched with awe and curiosity. The musicians seemed to be mythic figures. It was a different world. The only thing I knew about it was that I wanted in."

Likewise, David A. Stewart of the Eurythmics explained how making music consumed him during his teenage years: "I was channeling... my feelings and energy into music. It's an amazing thing when you're on your own to be able to play an instrument; it provides solace. The bedroom isn't lonely when it becomes a place where imagination soars. My bedroom was a stage, a TV show, a recording studio. Anything I wanted it to be. I stood with my guitar and looked in the mirror, and I could visual myself as the next big folk singer." And British singer Kate Bush, who scored her breakthrough hit in 1978 with the track "Wuthering Heights," revealed: "Since I was 14, my only ambition was to get 10 songs on a piece of plastic. It couldn't have happened fast enough."

For some musicians, performing their art gave life a purpose. Bruce

Springsteen admitted: "When I was a child, and into my teens, I felt like a very, very empty vessel. And it wasn't until I began to fill it up with music that I began to feel my own personal power and my impact on my friends and the small world that I was in. I began to get some sense of myself. But it came out of a place of real emptiness."

Similarly, Dee Dee Ramone of the Ramones wrote in his autobiography: "Somehow, even at the age of twelve, I knew I was a loser. I couldn't see a future for myself.... Then I heard the Beatles for the first time. I got my first transistor radio, a Beatle haircut and a Beatle suit.... I had rock 'n' roll and it gave me a sense of my own identity." And, in 2019, while celebrating his 50th year as a professional musician, Elton John revealed: "I love to make records and I love to write songs, but the greatest thing for me, as a musician, is to play for another human being and get a response."

Conversely, a number of successful performers unwittingly got into music, from Marianne Faithfull to Macy Gray. And Ricky Nelson was a popular teenage actor on the television series, *The Adventures Of Ozzie And Harriet*, when he went on a life-changing date in 1957. He recalled: "I had never thought of singing on the show, but I went one night with this girl from Hollywood High, Arlene, and everything changed. We were driving over Laurel Canyon, and all of a sudden, Elvis's 'Blue Moon Of Kentucky' came on the radio. She went wild, and kept talking about how great he was, so I felt I had to say something. I told her I was going to make a record. She only laughed, so I said to myself, 'I have to do it.'"

Soon after, Nelson performed a rendition of Fats Domino's "I'm Walking" on television. Releasing the song as a single, Nelson would score his first of nearly three-dozen top-40 hits.

FINANCIAL REASONS FOR STARTING A ROCK BAND

Most musicians have traditional career and financial goals. While the short-term goal is to hold down a good day job while playing in a band on the weekends, the long-term objective is to be discovered and signed by a major record label. Despite the lofty and idealistic belief that money is not an important motivation when writing, recording and performing music, it certainly makes the process easier if you reside under a warm, dry roof with a comfortable bed and a well-stocked refrigerator. Success and the accompanying monetary rewards provide the opportunity to indulge in your musical artistry. As producer Giorgio Moroder observed: "Money is very important in a music career. The more you make, the more active you are, and the more you want to do good songs."

However, some musicians have modest financial goals. Dan Auerbach of the Black Keys remembered the duo's early objective when the Grammy-winning duo was considered a local act in Akron: "When we first decided to be a band, the goal was for us each to make about $150 a week, and we were able to do that within four months of our first show in March 2002." Similarly, for the first few years as a professional musician, bassist John Entwistle of the Who lived above a British pub with his mother. His ultimate goal at the time was to earn enough money to buy his own pub.

Conversely, Cat Stevens went into rock music because he saw it as an easy way to earn lots of money with minimal effort. His first success as a songwriter came in 1968 when the Tremeloes reached the top-10 with his composition, "Here Comes My Baby." Similarly, John Lennon, at age 25, told a reporter: "I want the money just to *be* rich. The only other way of getting it is to be born rich. If you have the money, that's power without having to be powerful." Likewise, Gene Simmons proclaimed: "You can never have too much money. If you disagree with that, you're delusional. Money isn't the root of evil – that's a lack of money. The less money one has, the more violent one becomes in pursuit of it. They say money doesn't buy you happiness – to that I say bullshit."

MUSIC AS A LEGITIMATE CAREER?

During a tour of Australia with Tom Petty and the Heartbreakers in 1986, folk-rock legend Bob Dylan was asked by a reporter: "Do you think you've passed the apex of your career?" A dry-humored Dylan responded, "What career? I've never had a career. I'm someone who doesn't work for a living."

The vast majority of people around the globe are employed in a 9-to-5 job, whether dressed in a workman's denim uniform or a tailored suit-and-tie. Most jobs tend to be repetitive with clearly established duties. Display some creativity or rebellious behavior and you'll probably get fired.

On the other hand, artistic types are not suited to the confined environment of a traditional workplace. They're attracted to careers that demand creativity and a touch of rebellious behavior. The required tasks vary from day to day, with little possibility of boredom. And an artist can usually choose his own work schedule and hours, whether morning or midnight.

British singer Robbie Williams once admitted: "I don't like to go to work every day. That's why I got into this business in the first place." Similarly, in the documentary *Mr. Blue Sky: The Story of Jeff Lynne & ELO*, Lynne fondly recalled the moment when he realized that he had finally attained the status as a full-time musician, without needing to hold down a *real* job. After several years of listening to his mother loudly stomp up the stairs every morning to reach his second-floor bedroom, he made a defiant announcement. Lynne recalled: "[My mother would shout] 'Hey! Come on you lazy booger, get up!' And this would be like at 7:30 or 8 o'clock in the morning. This one morning I said... 'Before you start, I'm not getting up today or ever again. I'm a professional musician now.' And you should've seen the look on her face."

However, in the 1950s and much of the '60s, a job in the music industry was not considered a lucrative or stable career choice. Few acts made it big and far fewer managed to score even one top-40 hit. Even if you made it onto the *Billboard* charts or the stage of *American Bandstand*, there were no guarantees of financial success. As singer Paul Anka recalled: "The idea of becoming a pop singer back in the mid-fifties was a truly fantastic thing to aspire to – it was literally like building a castle on air. A singer was a voice on the radio, on a record. Who knew how it even got there?"

*   *   *   *   *   *

Since the dawn of rock and roll, parents have attempted to steer their children away from joining a rock band and pursuing a career in the music industry. In the early-1970s, guitarist Brian May was finishing his Ph.D. at a college in London when he stepped aside to join a touring rock band called Queen, which was fronted by an outlandish lead singer with protruding teeth. Consequently, May's angry and bewildered father wouldn't talk to his son for more than a year. At around the same time, Jer Bulsara, the mother of Freddie Mercury, recalled, "My husband and I thought it was a phase he would grow out of and expected he would soon come back to his senses and return to proper studies. It didn't happen."

Similarly, Johnny Cash recalled how his father – an unpretentious, hard-working farmer – tried in vain to discourage his guitarist son from becoming a musical performer: "You're wasting your time, listening to them old records on the radio. That ain't real, you know. Those people ain't really there. That's just a guy sitting there playing records. Why d'you listen to that fake stuff? .... You're getting sucked in by all them people. That's going to keep you from making a living. You'll never do any good as long as you've got that music on the mind." Similarly, when Meat Loaf was in high school, his mother tried to deter him from pursuing a career in music by saying, "Good thing you're not going to be a singer, because you can't carry a tune in a bucket."

Even the members of the Beatles were targets of overbearing family members who were critical of their career pursuits. John Lennon was raised in his teen years by his Aunt Mimi who discouraged his artistic endeavors and often told him, "The guitar's all right for a hobby, John, but you'll never make a living at it." Similarly, Ringo Starr's friends and family considered him a fool for leaving his highly regarded position as an apprentice machinist in order to play the drums in a rock group. And Paul McCartney was the only member of the group who came from a musical background. But even though his father had once played the piano in a ragtime band, Paul was nearly deterred from working as a musician. George Harrison's mother was a little more tolerant of her son's musical aspirations when he announced his decision to leave home. She told him: "You go do it, but you'll be back in two or three weeks."

Likewise, Scottish singer KT Tunstall – best known for her 2005 hit, "Black Horse And The Cherry Tree" – came from a family of academics who were horrified by her decision to continue performing in indie rock bands after completing her college studies. She recalled: "No! How could that happen? My mum would say, 'Your friends are starting families, and I don't want you to be thirty-five, living up a hill with a smelly musician.'"

Similarly, before he co-founded the Cars in 1976, drummer David Robinson was constantly derided by his family for playing music with his band, the Modern Lovers. He recalled: "My mother thought I was crazy and then she realized you get paid for it. She thought you did it for fun. 'Cause I'd been doing it for free for so many years. That's why she was so against it. And then when the Modern Lovers got a record deal she said, 'Where did you get that money?' And I said, 'You get paid for it. The record company pays you.' 'They *do?*' It was okay after that."

However, even after an artist achieves a moderate level of success, some parents still aren't convinced. Dave Grohl recalled the reaction he got at home after Nirvana began attracting larger audiences: "When the first check came in, my dad said, 'You do realize this isn't gonna last, right?'"

Many musicians received the same career warnings from their teachers. As Neil Young recalled, "When I was in school, I was called into the principal's office – I was always getting into trouble – and he asked me what I wanted to do when I left. I said I wanted to be a musician and play in bars and clubs. He said, OK, but what do you want to do *then*? Like I had to stop sometime. I've never forgotten that. It's like I've always been kicking against it – like I have to carry on." Similarly, Steve Ferrone of Tom Petty's backing group, the Heartbreakers, was not encouraged to pursue a career in music by his teachers at Finsbury Road Board School: "I was told at school that being a drummer was not a real job."

Even though music education is offered at nearly all public schools in the United States and Britain, the curriculum is chiefly focused on classical music. Additionally, budding musicians in the U.S. are forced to join marching bands and are not encouraged to form small combos or groups. As Mark Knopfler of Dire Straits recalled: "Popular music was looked down upon by respectable society. There were no guitar lessons at school. It was frowned upon: 'Knopfler, I might have known you'd be involved in this... *rock and roll*, boy.'"

However, as rock and roll became big business, a growing number of parents encouraged their children to pursue their musical aspirations and offered up the garage or basement as a practice room. In 1980, as R.E.M. was building a strong fanbase in Athens, Georgia, the group's members sensed a potential career opportunity. Michael Stipe, the band's frontman, recalled what he told his parents: "I want to drop out of school for six months to see what this band will do. If nothing happens, I'll go back to school." Astonishingly, his parents agreed: "They were almost Buddhist in their reaction, so in the moment. They said, 'Pursue your dream; see where this goes. If you have to go back to school, you can go back to school.'" Stipe never had to go back to college.

Conversely, a few parents have pushed their young children into music careers. Brenda Lee and Loretta Lynn both began performing on stages at a very young age in order to help their financially struggling families. When Lynn appeared on a local television program in the late-1950s, her family didn't even own a television set. And in Gary, Indiana, family patriarch Joe Jackson drove his children to form a singing group in the early-1960s. Initially working with his three eldest sons – Jackie, Jermaine and Tito – the senior Jackson was infamously abusive in his quest to attain success and fortune. Even after the Jackson 5 emerged as pop stars in 1969 – following the release of the number-one single "I Want You Back" – Joe Jackson maintained a domineering reign over his musical offspring.

LEAVING YOUR DAY JOB

Although some musicians are willing to take the monumental risk and go all in, most are not. There are thousands of immensely talented singers and guitarists who never took their musical careers to the next level for fear of financial ruin. Knowing the pitfalls, dangers and great personal sacrifices required by the rock and roll road, most musicians would never choose to pursue a full-time career in the field. Therefore, it's no surprise that the vast majority treat their craft as a hobby or weekend venture.

While in his early 20s, drummer Woody Woodmansey – who would later find fame in a band led by David Bowie – suffered a great deal of ridicule for quitting his day job, shortly after he was promoted to assistant foreman at a manufacturing plant in England: "I went to the factory the next morning and told my boss that I didn't want the job, and also that I was leaving. Of course, he thought I was an idiot. 'So you're going to be a pop star, are you?' he said. I knew he was [mocking me], so I said nothing. Also, I could see his point. In an agricultural town like Driffield, no one went off and became a rock star. No one had ever done it, and there was no reason why anyone ever would. In his eyes it just wasn't going to happen. My parents' reaction was twice as bad. They went completely mad. My mum burst into tears and my dad shouted at me, 'Are you bloody mad? You've just been offered a foreman's job.'"

While some recording artists zoomed into the fast lane after their initial chart success, others were far more cautious. Tom Scholz, the founder of Boston, was afraid to leave his position as a product engineer at Polaroid, even though his group's first single, "More Than A Feeling," was frequently blaring from a table-top radio at his workplace. Although he went on extended, nationwide tours with Boston, he continued to request leaves of absence from his employer. Then after finally receiving his very first royalty check in the amount of $300,000, he realized he could finally afford to quit his day job.

Likewise, Frankie Valli, who enjoyed a string of top-40 hits with the Four Seasons beginning in 1962, admitted: "I was still living in a project, married with kids, for two years after we had success! I was afraid to leave. The first property I bought was a two-family house, because I said, 'Maybe this will go away, but at least I'll have a tenant who can help me pay the mortgage.' I had a job for the city of Newark as a maintenance repairman, and I took a leave of absence, through almost two years of hits! The guys in the band laughed at me. Everybody went out and bought Cadillacs. I was driving around in junk."

Meanwhile, in 1971, soul singer Bill Withers was working at an aircraft parts factory, where he made toilet seats, during the period he was recording his debut album. When his record company wanted to take some photos for the album's cover, Withers did not want to risk losing his job: "So it was funny because my first album cover picture was actually taken on my lunch break. Cause I didn't want to take time off, so I said, 'Send somebody up here.' You know, they can take my picture. So, I'm standing in the door with my actual lunch box."

Similarly, Paul Stanley of Kiss recalled his work schedule during the band's early days: "I was driving a cab at the time and sometimes I'd drive the cab to rehearsal, when I was supposed to be working, because it was cheaper than taking the subway. I also had two other jobs, one was punching holes in magnetic bulletin boards in a factory of women and the other in a kosher Orthodox Jewish food store, where I made sandwiches and wore a short-haired wig."

And by 1959, Dion DiMucci was financially comfortable after scoring hits such as "I Wonder Why" and "No One Knows." That year when he went on the ill-fated Winter Dance Party tour – headlined by Buddy Holly, the Big Bopper and Ritchie Valens – DiMucci decided against taking a plane ride between two stops on the tour – from Clear Lake, Iowa, to Moorhead, Minnesota – due to the specific price of the airfare. Despite the fact that Carl Bunch – the drummer for Buddy Holly – was stricken with frostbite while riding on the caravan's unheated, former school bus, DiMucci stayed behind. He later explained: "Buddy told us that the flight would cost $36. Thirty-six bucks. That figure set off an alarm in my brain. All my childhood I had listened to my parents argue about money and argue about the rent, and the figure kept coming up. So I could never forget how much they paid. It was thirty-six bucks. I couldn't bring myself to spend a month's rent on an hour flight to Minnesota.... I said to Ritchie, 'You go.'"

However, some acts had no interest in reaching the top of the *Billboard* chart mountain. According to Ron Wesiner, who co-managed the 1970s disco act Tavares, the group's members "didn't go to the next level because that wasn't their priority. They all had families and weren't willing to spend every waking hour touring and promoting, And I respected that. If your heart isn't into it 100 percent, you're not going to be happy, and if you're not happy, your music and concerts will reflect that, and you'll eventually go into the crapper. Tavares chose their fate, and for that, they get points."

*　　*　　*　　*　　*　　*

Although musicians are able get out of bed any time they choose, set their own hours and work on their own schedules, they rarely have the financial security of a 9-to-5 job. There are no pensions, no health insurance, no sick days, no paid vacations and no guarantees of a regular paycheck. Musicians are self-employed freelancers who are dependent on their own initiative and talent to survive.

▶ CHAPTER 2
EARLY STRUGGLES

Ever since Jim Denny – the talent manager at the Grand Ole Opry – told a young Elvis Presley in October 1954 that he should go back to driving a truck, countless performers in rock and roll have endured similar criticisms. Most gave up. A few did not.

Breaking out of San Francisco, Creedence Clearwater Revival epitomized the swamp-rock sound, which set them apart from their contemporaries like Janis Joplin and the Grateful Dead. CCR leader John Fogerty recalled: "It really came together after the first album [*Creedence Clearwater Revival*]. Because of 'Suzie-Q' being on the radio, we were invited to play more important places. We'd been a bar band, but after 'Suzie-Q,' there was a pivotal engagement at the Avalon in San Francisco. We were the opening act.... But something important happened. I plugged in to my amp and I started hearing an E7th chord with that swampy vibrato that I was making on my little Kustom amp. It just turned me on to be standing there – I was so excited that I was playing in front of a real audience in San Francisco; I was just *charged*. And suddenly, I was just inspired. I turned to the band and said 'just start playing E.' And I started screaming at the top of my range, just a melody and vowel sounds and consonants. By the way, this is exactly how I write songs. Then suddenly, right in the middle of having this burst of inspiration, it went silent. The stage manager had pulled the plug out of my amplifier. I looked at him and said, 'Why'd you do that?' And he said, 'Don't worry about that. You're not going anywhere.' That was June of 1968. I looked at him and said, 'Not going anywhere? You give me a year, pal, and I'll show ya who's not goin' somewhere!'"

Likewise, at one of their first-ever gigs, ZZ Top performed for only one paying customer. The band's singer Billy Gibbons recalled: "The curtain opened and there was just one guy. We shrugged and pressed onward. We took a break halfway through, went out and bought him a Coke." Bandmate Dusty Hill added: "We did an encore whether he wanted it or not."

The Electric Light Orchestra also had a slow start. The group's drummer Bev Bevan recalled a gig in the city of Sunderland, England, during ELO's first tour in 1972: "Just seven people turned up. We outnumbered them by one – and felt like applauding them. As I sat behind my drums that night I looked out at the backs of what were an unlikely collection of musicians fronting what seemed a totally empty hall. And hearing the bass and drums echoing around the emptiness, I thought: 'This is never going to work out in a million years.'"

Similarly, the Police failed to draw large audiences during their early shows across America while promoting their breakthrough 1978 single, "Roxanne." Drummer Stewart Copeland recalled one such gig: "We play the Last Chance in Poughkeepsie, and the only people in the place were the disc jockey and a journalist. It was a Monday night and it was freezing so everyone stayed home to watch the football game, apparently. We went out into the audience and talked to them for awhile, watched the game on television, then jumped on stage and did our set. It was strange. We introduced the members of the audience to each other. We had come 9,000 miles from home and made $12. But, hey, we got three encores."

Meanwhile, across the Atlantic, the Beatles were infamously rejected by nearly every label in England before EMI signed the quartet to a very limited contract. One of the rejecting labels, Decca Records, instead chose to sign Brian Poole and the Tremeloes. Even after the Beatles had scored a series of top-10 hits in Britain, they still couldn't get any respect – or radio airplay – in the U.S. Then on January 3, 1964, television talk-show host Jack Paar aired a BBC clip of the Beatles – just one month before the group's triumphal debut on *The Ed Sullivan Show*. Paar later admitted: "I didn't know they were going to change the culture of the country with music. I thought they were funny. I brought them here as a joke."

BOOED AS THE OPENING ACT

As a crucial part of "paying your dues," young performers hope to land a slot on a tour by an established act. However, headliners often have contentious relationships with their opening acts. At best, the opening act is personally invited onto a tour by the headlining artist. At worst, a record company or the local venue adds a little-known or emerging artist to the bill. When that happens, the openers are giving limited space to set up their gear on the stage, are often forced to forgo soundchecks, are given a limited amount of time they can perform and are barred from playing encores.

Unfortunately, rock history is packed with stories of opening acts greeted by hostile crowds. Led Zeppelin was taunted by audiences during their first U.S. shows as the opening act for headliners Vanilla Fudge. Similarly, just as Loverboy was enjoying airplay with their first U.S. hit, "Turn Me Loose," the Canadian group was hired as the opening act for blues rockers ZZ Top. Loverboy singer Mike Reno recalled: "The ZZ Top tour was tough, as their audiences were hardcore biker blues fans.... I remember one gig in Cape Cod when all hell broke loose so I put on a [baseball] batter's helmet while the audience threw cigarette lighters, bottles, ice cubes and coins – it all came raining down on us. We managed four songs before being booed off stage. That was a wake-up call, I can tell you."

And on July 17, 1982, a young Stevie Ray Vaughan was viciously booed by the audience at the prestigious Montreux Jazz Festival in Switzerland. Backed by his band, Double Trouble, the guitar virtuoso ignored the noisy outbursts – which continued throughout the entire performance – and finished his set as planned. Despite the negative reaction from the European audience, Vaughan attracted the attention of a pair of important admirers. Dazzled by Vaughan's prowess on the guitar, David Bowie hired him to play on the chart-topping album, *Let's Dance*. Equally impressed, singer-songwriter Jackson Browne offered Vaughan the use of a studio to record his debut album.

Oftentimes, the booing is the result of a mismatched line-up. In 1967, just after his brilliant performance at Monterey, a relatively unknown guitarist named Jimi Hendrix was hired as the opening act for the Monkees. At concert after concert, Hendrix was bombarded with screams of "we want the Monkees" or "we want Davy." After seven shows, a frustrated Hendrix flipped off the audience and stormed off the stage during the middle of his set at Forest Hills Stadium in New York. The promoters subsequently released Hendrix from his contract.

Other mismatched pairings included: James Taylor played an acoustic show as the opener for the Who in Cleveland during the early-1970s; New Wave act Blondie was booked as the opening act for both Rush and Genesis in the late-1970s; and in 1979, Kool and the Gang opened for the Charlie Daniels Band in Toronto. When Prince opened for the Rolling Stones in October 1981, he was met with scorn and insults. Hitting the stage in black bikini briefs and thigh-high boots, he was pelted with flying projectiles, many of which struck members of his backing band. Bill Graham, the tour's outspoken promoter, marched onto the stage but was unable to calm the crowd. A dejected Prince left the stage and reportedly cried upon reaching his dressing room.

On the other hand, if the opening artist outshines the main act, the situation can get ugly. During a British tour in 1977, an unknown Tom Petty and the Heartbreakers opened for headliner Nils Lofgren. But with Petty garnering strong audience response throughout the tour, Lofgren's roadies reacted by pushing the Heartbreakers' stage gear into a decreasingly smaller space on the stage.

In addition to outperforming the headlining artist, there are a number of ways for opening acts to get kicked off a tour. In 2006, Eric Church was fired from a Rascal Flatts tour for going beyond his allotted time, night after night. The Black Crowes were famously dropped from a ZZ Top tour after criticizing the tour's sponsor, Miller Beer. And in the early-1970s, the Gap Band made an unforgivable error. Lead singer Charlie Wilson recalled the unfortunate situation when his band opened for Rolling Stones: "We were in Kansas City; there must have been forty to fifty thousand people, and when we went on, I got so into the music that we rolled right into 'Jumpin' Jack Flash,' at the time one of the biggest hits on the radio and one we routinely played during our sets. I don't want to sound like an idiot, but honestly, I didn't know it was their song.... That was so disrespectful to a headliner, a fellow artist on a show, to perform his hit before he took the stage. But I wasn't thinking when I did it. I was so into the performance, so into the music, so in the moment, that I didn't notice. All I could see was everybody in the audience was on their feet with their hands waving in the air, screaming and cheering. Meanwhile, my brothers [in the band] were trying to get my attention by changing the notes to try to lead me into singing something else. Finally, I realized what I had done. The people backstage had to hold Mick Jagger back that night, he was so mad. After that, there was no more shows with the Rolling Stones."

▶ CHAPTER 3
THE FIRST SUCCESS

All musical artists have to start their careers somewhere, whether at an amateur talent show, a high school battle-of-the-bands or even a karaoke competition at a neighborhood tavern. Billy Joel recalled: "[I] remember doing an Elvis Presley impression when I was in the fourth grade. It was the first thing I ever did in front of people. I sang 'Hound Dog' and I was jiggling my hips like Elvis. I remember because the fifth-grade girls started screaming. I really dug the fifth-grade girls. I thought, 'Hey, this is pretty neat.' When the girls started screaming, the teacher pulled me off the stage."

As a teenager in 1952, Sonny Bono competed on a talent show at a Los Angeles television station. Although his entire body trembled in fear during the performance, he emerged as the winner. Bono recalled: "My prize was a transistor radio. But sweeter than the victory was standing and drinking up the rousing ovation my friends [in the studio audience] gave me. What a buzz. The rush rocketed straight to my head. It was like drinking 110-proof moonshine.... Sure, I was scared... of performing in front of people. But the recognition, the validation, the acceptance – they were overwhelming. I was instantly addicted."

Similarly, Steven Tyler of Aerosmith recalled his first experience on a rock and roll stage: "When I think about it now, forty-nine years later, I still have the same rush of feeling, that same energy and joy of endorphins flooding my brain. It's close to an addiction."

PRE-SUCCESS CONFIDENCE

Some musicians feel destined to make it big. Jerry Lee Lewis recounted his mindset as a child: "I was born to be on a stage. I couldn't wait to be on it. I dreamed about it. And I've been on one all my life. That's where I'm the happiest. That's where I'm almost satisfied."

A teenage John Lennon expressed a similar measure of confidence in conversations with his Aunt Mimi: "I used to say, 'Don't you destroy my papers.' I'd come home when I was fourteen and she'd rooted through all my things and thrown all my poetry out. I was saying, 'One day I'll be famous and you're going to regret it.'" Likewise, one of Bob Dylan's childhood friends recalled: "It was at summer camp in northern Wisconsin in 1953 that I first met Bobby Zimmerman from Hibbing. He was twelve years old and he had a guitar. He would go around telling everybody that he was going to be a rock and roll star. I was eleven and I believed him." And Bee Gees singer Barry Gibb detailed an incident from his teenage years: "I remember saying it to one of my first girlfriends at 14-years-old that if you dump me, you're making a mistake 'cause I was going to be famous."

Oftentimes, success seems predestined. Guitarist Mike Campbell of Tom Petty and the Heartbreakers explained: "I went and saw this play called *Jersey Boys*, about the Four Seasons, and at the end of the play, the actor that played Frankie Valli said something that rang true. They asked him the same question, what he considered the high point to be, and his answer was, 'The high point for me was when we were standing under the street lamp, and we found our sound, and we knew it was all ahead of us, and we knew what was going to happen.' And for me, I had that same feeling when we cut 'American Girl' in the studio, because we found a sound and a vibe that was ours, and I remember feeling that we had found something really special that no one else could do, and this can be us, this can identify our trip. I could feel it. It hadn't happened yet, but I could sense that, 'we've [got] something here.'"

However, confidence alone can't guarantee success. Stephen Pearcy of Ratt recalled: "Los Angeles was a town that ran on dreams. For a very long period of time, nearly everyone I met was an up-and-comer, convinced beyond doubt that they were destined to 'make it.'"

PAYING YOUR DUES

Rock stars almost always start at the very bottom rung. The process usually entails years of hard work, a great deal of practice, repeated failures and multiple setbacks. During his youth, Carlos Santana strummed his guitar for spare change at a park in San Rafael, California. Even after he joined a series of local bands, he still washed dishes in restaurants in order to pay his bills.

When an early version of the Beatles featuring Pete Best and Stuart Sutcliffe performed in a nightclub in Hamburg, Germany, the members of the band were treated poorly by the club manager. They lived in squalid conditions, earned very little and often had to endure hostile audiences. But by playing hundreds of grueling shows – night after night

– the budding performers sharpened their musical chops, cultivated the skills required to entertain audiences and learned the essential back-and-forth balance of a unified group.

And about two years before Garth Brooks released his first album, he had just moved to Nashville and was learning the rules of the music trade. As his bandmate Tom Skinner recalled, "I remember one lady, Wanda Collier from Warner Brothers Records, was talking to us about how it happened out there, which was basically keep your mouth shut, your ears open, your nose clean, stand in line, watch and learn and your turn will come. When she's done, Garth says – as sincere as he could be, and he meant it – he said, 'Wanda, surely there's got to be a shortcut.'"

Similarly, Steve Miller once offered advice to a budding songwriter on making it in the music industry. Max Marshall recalled: "He told me I'd need a routine. I'd need to master my songwriting voice: writing every day, charting other songs' chord progressions, feeling out the rhythms of words and the arcs of melodies. I'd need to tighten up my guitar voice: practicing scales every day, exploring tone in my fingers and through an amp. I'd need to find my singing voice: practicing scales, studying harmony, controlling my breath, learning to shape tones in my throat and phrase them through a line. I'd also need to find the right musicians, practice until we were a single organism, and figure out how to bring a song to life in a crappy venue with a bad P.A. Of course, we'd also need to develop an aesthetic and learn how to produce. Then, if we pulled all that off, we'd need to set up a publishing company and sign a contract that preserved our blood in an industry famous for leeches. After that, I'd really have to get to work."

But in the internet age, some rules have changed. A number of acts became recording stars, seemingly overnight, due to their YouTube videos. Others found sudden stardom by performing for the outspoken judges on television competitions such as *The Voice* or *American Idol*. Consequently, one-time contestants such as Kelly Clarkson, Chris Daughtry and Carrie Underwood became household names in a matter of months. However, a music writer for *The Cleveland Plain Dealer* wrote: "When Carrie Underwood won Season 4 of *American Idol*, it was pretty clear she had the voice that could set the world afire. Problem was, she had zero stage presence. The first time I saw her in concert, not long after that 2005 win, I thought, 'Wow, what a great singer, but the last time I saw a walk that stiff-legged, it was mops carrying buckets of water in the 'Sorcerer's Apprentice' segment of *Fantasia*.'"

Although musicians and singers may be born with a creative gift, they still need to polish, package and organize their abilities. Rod

Stewart has stated that as you pay your dues, "you learn the art of engaging the audience, which I don't think *The X Factor* can teach you."

RELEASING YOUR FIRST RECORD
AND HEARING YOUR SONG ON THE RADIO

Having your music released on a record or CD for the first time is a significant milestone. Mark Mothersbaugh of Devo described the experience of driving to a record plant in Cincinnati, where the quirky band had ordered 1,000 copies of their first single: "I remember looking at them out in the sun and thinking, 'This feels like we made art.... It had the feeling of, 'Nobody knows who you are; you could disappear and no one would know it.' Then we had this record... It was such a big deal."

Similarly, Tom Petty recalled his excitement upon releasing the first Heartbreakers album in late-1976: "We had gone back to Gainesville to rehearse for our first tour. While we were there, the record came out. We went to some chain store, and it was in one of the racks. It was the wildest feeling, like we had climbed Mount Everest."

The flip side of seeing your record in a store is listening to a deejay play your music. Doors drummer John Densmore recalled: "What a high: hearing one of your own songs on the radio while driving in your car! I rolled down the car window when I stopped at a traffic light to see if the car next to me was listening to the same station. They weren't, so I pumped up the song real loud. 'THAT'S ME!!!' I wanted to shout out to the world."

Similarly, as a member of the Squires in the early-1960s, Neil Young recalled his elation after hearing his first single on the radio when he was just 17-years-old: "Then the big moment came, and we heard [our song] 'The Sultan' on the radio! I was in my mother's car with my bandmate Ken Koblun, driving somewhere. I felt so good. I am sure I was walking on air for weeks.... My mother was telling everyone she knew. I could hear her on the phone calling all of her friends."

NEWFOUND FAME

Stardom can be fickle. One day a performer is a complete unknown and the next he's all over social media sites, on the pages of *Rolling Stone* and *Billboard*, climbing the iTunes chart and appearing on concert stages all over the world. Oftentimes a single performance can thrust a performer into the spotlight. Folk-pop singer Melanie recalled: "I can't tell you how terrified I was when I played Woodstock. I drove up with my mother. I had no clue. I didn't hear any of the hype or buildup or anything. We started driving, and we hit some traffic and then took a detour, made some phone calls – no cell phones or e-mails back then, of course – and I finally found my way to this little motel in Bethel. And there were all these media trucks and famous people. When I appeared at Woodstock, maybe a small percent, if that, had ever heard of me. I'd never been in a magazine or on TV or anything. I went up an unknown person and I walked off a celebrity."

Likewise, in the summer of 1977, Meat Loaf had just released the album, *Bat Out Of Hell*. Going on the road to promote the rock-opera-style project, the rotund performer was initially met by hostile audiences. Just days after he had been mercilessly heckled in Chicago, he headed to the East Coast. Arriving at a nightclub in New Jersey, he recalled seeing hundreds of people milling around the entrance: "I was wondering who they'd come to see. I go inside and everybody is staring at me. 'What do you have going on this afternoon?' I ask. 'Hell man... those kids are here to see you.' 'What?' They were lined up *in the afternoon*." Thanks to the heavy airplay of the track, "Paradise By The Dashboard Light," Meat Loaf was on his way to becoming a major star.

Similarly, singer Bob Geldof of the Boomtown Rats remembered his excited emotional state after scoring his first hit: "When 'Lookin' After No. 1' got to Number 17 [on the British pop charts], that would have been enough for me, honest to God. I couldn't believe it. One minute you're sitting at home... freezing. It's dark, there's no telly. Nothing good is going to happen in your life. Then suddenly, you're there.... The top 20! And you're Number 17! The Rolling Stones are just 10 above you! You can ring up your old man – of course it meant nothing to him but I think he understood what it meant to me."

And in the early-1990s, Alaska-born singer-songwriter Jewel was a struggling artist. She recalled: "Sleeping in my car and singing in [a] coffee shop seems like a really blessed time. I didn't think I would ever get signed to a label, but somehow I got a really big following going. I started with zero fans and ended up doing two shows a night. It was really awesome. I did five-hour shows, told the audience stories, and they'd tell me stories. Then labels started showing up, and it was suddenly surreal. It was like being Cinderella."

Clay Aiken, an *American Idol* finalist, recalled the exact moment he comprehended the scope of his success: "When I taped the *Primetime Live* interview with Diane Sawyer, I was struck for the first time with how significantly my life had changed. We were setting up in an old nightclub in New York City. There were arches, banquettes, and a curtained stage. The floor was checkered. It reminded me of the sort of place where Sinatra might have performed. When I arrived, there were bright lights and cameras everywhere. People scurried around with clipboards and cell phones. There were producers and management teams and makeup artists and camera operators and lighting experts and wardrobe consultants and assistants for assistants. I was stuck in the corner and I watched these masses of people rushing and bustling because of me. I wondered: *Why?* What had I really done? I sang. But I had always sung. Suddenly, people cared."

▶ CHAPTER 4
EARLY MONEY

Serious, goal-oriented bands will oftentimes begin their journeys as starving artists in order to achieve success. Pooling their financial resources, they will live together in the same cramped apartment or rundown house. They will spend their days writing music, practicing songs and formulating their own distinct sound.

While the Allman Brothers had set up shop in an old, well-worn Tudor mansion in Macon, Georgia, Tom Petty's first band, Mudcrutch, honed their musical craft in a decrepit farmhouse in Gainesville, Florida, which they nicknamed the Mudcrutch Farm. Meanwhile, the members of Lynyrd Skynyrd perfected their signature Southern rock sound by practicing for twelve-hours a day in blistering 100-degree summer weather inside a windowless shack they nicknamed the Hell House. Determined to make it big, they survived on peanut butter sandwiches in order to reach their collective goal.

However, some emerging bands don't have the luxury of a house or apartment. Although the hair-metal band Poison would eventually pack stadiums and sell millions of albums, the group had a humble start. Lead singer Bret Michaels admitted: "In the beginning... we spent three years sleeping in sleeping bags behind a dry cleaners in L.A."

And in the late-1960s, blues rocker Johnny Winter signed a lucrative contract with Columbia Records. His bandmate Tommy Shannon recalled: "It was weird how it happened. One night [we] were sleeping on the floor with our clothes in footlockers. The next day, we fly into the airport, where there were two beautiful girls waiting on us. We went from there to some mansions in upstate New York. We went from sleeping on the floor to living in mansions overnight."

Likewise, Blondie bassist Gary Valentine recalled the hardships during the group's first year: "We played a lot of small gigs in those early days – bachelor parties, weddings, forgettable dives with names like Brandy's and Broadway Charlie's. The idea was to get money to eat. Most people think a musician's life is about sex, drugs and rock 'n' roll, but most of the time it's about food." Similarly, Steven Tyler of

Aerosmith revealed the hand-to-mouth existence during the group's early days: "Like lots of bands, we lived in the same house, played. Got drunk, went to drug school together, stole to eat. We had no money... we were starving to death back then. I was stealing food from the Stop and Shop (rechristened the Stop and Steal). I'd go to the store and get some ground beef and shove it down my jeans to throw in with some rice.... And then the six of us would eat."

Not surprisingly, struggling rockers often date restaurant workers. As music writer Carl Gottlieb observed: "Most of the liaisons with waitresses were born out of man's two major drives, food and sex. A waitress who liked you might come home with you and if you didn't have a home she might have a place of her own that you could call home for a night. These same charitable goddesses of the night might even be persuaded to sneak a club sandwich out of the kitchen or make a 'mistake' on an order to a straight customer – that way there'd be a leftover sandwich or fruit-and-cheese plate to ease the pangs of... the ravenous, skinny folksinger in the small dressing room upstairs." And guitarist Bob Mothersbaugh of Devo recalled an incident after the group's first-ever concert in New York City: "Somebody from a record company approached us and said, 'I'd like to put you guys out on my label. Do you have girlfriends with jobs who can support you?' We said, 'Well, we think we'll wait for a better offer!'"

POOR AT FIRST

Rock and roll can offer a seemingly easy route out of poverty. The ability to write or perform music is a highly regarded and heavily rewarded talent in modern society. Scoring a top-40 record or hit album allows a performer to move from stark poverty to near-nobility. Consequently, many successful rockers had to deal with not only instant fame, but sudden wealth.

Countless singers and musicians have experienced a rags-to-riches transformation, reminiscent of a Horatio Alger novel. In his youth, Elvis Presley lived in public housing and wore second-hand clothing. At one point, his father was jailed for passing a bad check so that his family could eat. Far worse, Bob Marley grew up in a Third World slum. Raised by a single mother in the Trenchtown ghetto of Kingston, Jamaica, the teenage Marley lived in a shack made of corrugated sheet metal and discarded wood. His father, a white naval officer who was sent to Jamaica to oversee a plantation, never married his mother.

And as a child in the 1950s, Sammy Hagar lived in a series of dilapidated wooden shacks. Spending his summers in the blistering farm fields of California, he picked vegetables with his family. Hagar later recalled: "When my mom used to take us out on weekends, her idea of going out and doing something as a family was to take us four kids to the city dump and rummage. And we loved it. It was a blast, finding stuff. It was like a treasure hunt to us kids. My mom would find food, like rotting fruit and vegetables that grocery stores were dumping. She would find two or three good oranges and be so happy. 'Oh, look at these!' she would say."

Similarly, Billy Joel was raised by a single mother after his father abandoned the family and moved to Europe. Joel recalled, "We went hungry a lot. Sometimes it was scary not eating... Do you know what it's like to be the poor people on the poor people's block?... There was a lot of insecurity as a kid. It was a drag and I guess that it gave me the drive not to let it happen again. I'm not gonna be hungry again – ever!"

Likewise, Jack Bruce of the British power trio Cream admitted, "I'd never seen an indoor toilet until I started touring and staying in hotels. And of course I'd never been taught how to deal with money, so I just spent it." Likewise, Eric Clapton, Bruce's bandmate in Cream, recalled: "I grew up in an English village where we didn't even have a train station. Then I came to New York with Cream to play the Murray the K show, and I saw firsthand all this stuff I was hearing about all my life. To walk around Manhattan as a 20-year-old – it was magical. You would see someone with a biker jacket or cowboy boots, drinking malted milk. I was in heaven."

And in her autobiography, Pat Benatar discussed the financial struggles of her large, extended family: "Going to the grocery store with Mom was awful, because her choices always involved penny-saving decisions. She never bought anything extra, no backups, no luxuries – we were always on a strict budget. We never bought more than two rolls of toilet paper at a time. Not three, never four. Just two. You worried all the time that the toilet paper would run out before payday. I hate that. Seriously.... Seeing my pantry today, you'd think I have a Costco franchise.... I bet I own enough toilet paper to last a family of four for a year."

Similarly, Ozzy Osbourne was raised in an impoverished home: "I had a shirt, one pair of pants, one pair of socks, shoes, and a jacket.... I was always dirty and smelly, which the kids teased me about unmercifully, and which is why down the road I spent the first bit of money I earned from music on drugs and strong... cologne." By the mid-1970s, after scoring a series of top-10 albums as the frontman of Black

Sabbath, Osbourne was finally able to satisfy all of his materialistic desires. He recalled: "Everything I'd ever wanted as a kid, I had them deliver. I ended up with a whole shed full of Scalextric cars, jukeboxes, table football games, trampolines, pool tables, shotguns, crossbows, catapults, swords, arcade games, toy soldiers, fruit machines... Every single thing you could ever think to ask for, I asked for it. The guns were the most fun."

And although award-winning producer Quincy Jones had the financial means in 1986 to construct a 25,000-square-foot, hilltop mansion in the exclusive enclave of Bel Air, he was raised in abject poverty. In his autobiography, he recalled the bitter existence of his childhood: "I remember the cold. It was a stinging, backbreaking, bone-chilling Kentucky-winter cold, the kind of cold that makes you feel like you'll never be warm again. I had no music in me then, just sounds, the shrill noise the back door made when it creaked open, the funny grunts my little brother Lloyd made while we slept together, the tight, muffled squeals the rats made when the rat traps snapped them in half. My grandmother did not believe in wasting anything. She had nothing to waste. She cooked whatever she could get her hands on. Mustard greens, okra, possum, chickens, and rats, and me and Lloyd ate them all. We ate the fried rats because we were nine and seven years old and we did what we were told. We ate them because my grandma could cook them well. But most of all, we ate them because that's all there was to eat."

INITIAL WEALTH

With unexpected wealth comes important decisions – like what to buy. A successful, chart-topping musician quickly realizes that he has the ability to acquire nearly everything he desires. Ever since a young Elvis Presley began buying Cadillacs by the dozen, rock stars have been splurging on all sorts of extravagant purchases. Freddie Mercury – renowned for his decadent and lavish parties – once admitted: "I've always coped extremely well with wealth. I don't believe in hoarding money away in a bank. I love to spend, spend, spend. After all, that's what money is for. I'm not like some of those stars who are obsessed with counting their pennies." Likewise, Elton John once declared: "I really enjoy my money, and I don't feel any guilt about spending it. If I pay my taxes and I do my share of giving back, I have no qualms about what I do with my money."

Bob Dylan recounted the first expensive item he purchased: "A 1965 baby blue Mustang convertible. But a guy who worked for me rolled it down the hill in Woodstock and it smashed into a truck. I got twenty-five bucks for it." And Gene Simmons of Kiss recounted: "We started off 1976 on salaries of $85 per week. A few months later, we'd come off tour and the checks would hit us like meteorites. The first big one I got was for $1.5 million. After buying my mom a house, I had no idea what to do with the rest."

Not surprisingly, purchasing a large house in a nice neighborhood is a common practice among successful music stars. In 2016, Billy Joel revealed why he had purchased a specific home in Oyster Bay, Long Island: "I used to work on oyster boats and look up at this house and hate the guy who was living here with his inherited money, and now it's mine. Can you believe that? Oysters was all I was eating when I was on the boats. I had no money and had to get up at 5 a.m. in the middle of the winter."

But there was more to success than achieving financial security. Attaining wealth often meant gaining social status. An upward movement in the tax bracket also meant more cultivated tastes in food, furnishings, clothing and the rest. Suddenly, rockers sipped 20-year-old scotches and stocked their new wine cellars with bottles of 40-year-old French vintages. Michelle Phillips of the Mamas and the Papas recalled: "I do think I approached my new status with some intelligence, however, because with my first royalty check I went to the Farmers' Market and bought my first tin of caviar. I knew I would be expected to acquire a taste for it, and that happened, of course. It *was* expected.... Such indulgences are quickly learned."

In class-conscious Britain, becoming a rock star allowed musicians the opportunity to ascend beyond the working class and to be accepted into the affluent and elite classes. As journalist David Hepworth noted in *Word* magazine, "For every Bono, who married his childhood sweetheart, there's a hundred rock stars from similarly humble backgrounds who have ended up with somebody who didn't [have to] buy their own furniture. All the Beatles married 'up,' as did the Stones. John Lydon [of the Sex Pistols] from Finsbury Park married a German heiress. Jools Holland and his wife were invited to Prince Charles' wedding.... All successful rock stars are social climbers. It's part of what drives them."

However, some artists have a difficult time adjusting to their newfound wealth. Consequently, they tend to squander much of their fortunes. Bones Howe, a Los Angeles producer who worked with the Mamas and the Papas, revealed the spending habits of the group's members: "When the money started coming in they got into this thing among them, where they would have a contest every week to see who could spend the most money on a single item. I remember one week Cass won because she had bought a Mulberry Aston Martin." Another friend of the group recalled, "I'd never seen anybody spend more money than they did. It was party time and spending. Anything they saw that they wanted, they bought.... They were getting used to having their own way, and to having people kowtowing to them. And if they wanted something, they got it, no questions asked." Likewise, Duran Duran's longtime photographer Denis O'Regan recalled: "I remember Nick [Rhodes] and John [Taylor] having a discussion over which of them had the highest-ever hotel bill. One of them had run up a $30,000 bill – and this was [in 1988], an outrageous amount."

Similarly, boy-band singer Mark Wahlberg confessed to his reckless spending habits during his heyday in the 1990s: "Bro, I was spending money as quick as I could make it. Clothes, rented jets, a boat, going to the Palm and ordering 4½-pound lobsters, leaving $500 tips at bars – man, my credit-card bills ran from $70,000 to $150,000 a month!" And at the height of his career in the early-1990s, R&B singer Bobby Brown carried a briefcase containing hundreds of thousands of dollars of walking-around money. Acquiring a taste for fancy cars, he would approach total strangers and simply ask how much they wanted for their vehicles.

And in a real-life incident that mirrored the lyrics of his hit "Life's Been Good," Joe Walsh described one of his rock star extravagances: "I had a forty-one-foot sail boat and I lived in Santa Barbara, California, and I was in the Eagles. We came off a tour and I was on my boat, wishing I knew how to sail it or how it worked." Eventually, fellow rocker David Crosby gave Walsh some sailing lessons.

Some artists were notorious for their spending sprees. Jim Steinman, the songwriter and producer behind Meat Loaf's monster album *Bat Out Of Hell*, became a very wealthy man by the time he had reached his 30s. MTV veejay Mark Goodman recalled having dinner with Steinman at a fancy New York restaurant: "Steinman ordered the whole menu. He literally ordered everything on the menu – he was that rich, and that into the rock 'n' roll lifestyle. He didn't want to have to decide; he liked being able to sample from lots of different plates."

Some recording artists spend lavishly due to habit and public expectations. *The New York Post* reported: "On a hot, lazy Las Vegas day, Michael Jackson's eyes were glued to a catalog as he shopped from his hotel room for mundane but expensive trinkets such as Rolex watches, Barbie dolls and artwork. The 2002 shopping spree continued until Jacko exhausted his line of credit with the hotel. Frustrated, he reached in a duffel bag and handed his 4- and 3-year-old kids a stack of bills totaling $20,000 and ordered their nanny to 'take them out and buy them whatever they wanted.' He said, 'Go out and entertain yourselves,' recalled former pal Marc Schaffel."

Additionally, some hit artists were able to take their hobbies to new levels. John Dolmayan, the drummer for System Of A Down, plunked down $317,000 for an original copy of Action Comics No. 1 from 1938, which was the first comic book to feature Superman on the cover. Meanwhile, Phil Collins became a serious collector of historical artists from the Alamo in Texas. His collection eventually grew to $100 million in value and included a Bowie knife – which was used by Jim Bowie during the 1836 battle between the residents of Texas and the Mexican Army – and a pair of artifacts owned by Davy Crockett – a rifle and a fringed leather pouch. And Rod Stewart spent two-decades constructing a massive 124-by-23-foot train set – complete with rows of miniaturized skyscrapers and warehouses, toy-sized autos and wide streets packed with pedestrians.

Some artists are legendary for making esoteric and bizarre purchases. A reporter visiting Marilyn Manson's home in Hollywood Hills described some of the unusual items he spotted: "There's a stack of children's books (*This Little Piggy*, *Winnie The Pooh Meets Gopher*). An unused canister of Zyklon B., the poisonous gas Hitler used to exterminate Jews. A pistol and rifle on a coffee table. A prized clown painting done by rapist and serial killer John Wayne Gacy."

However, Noel Gallagher of the British band Oasis observed: "When you first get your royalties, you do stupid things with money. I do own a pair of Elvis' headphones. I bought them from Sotheby's, and I don't know what I was expecting to hear... And then you realize they're just a pair of crappy, old headphones." Likewise, in 1987, Johnny Cash's second wife, June Carter Cash, said of one purchase: "I am embarrassed to admit that my husband and son own a $5,000 dog. I know the world is crazy, but for $5,000, I would expect a dog to sing, dance, and tell funny stories."

WISELY INVESTING

Not all musicians are reckless with their earnings. In 1955, Chuck Berry was an emerging performer from St. Louis. With his career on the ascent, he joined an all-star rock and R&B tour. As Berry recalled: "Watching the other artists on the tour I began to wonder why they allowed themselves to waste money as I had observed many times. I was sure that some of my colleagues didn't realize the value of the money we were being paid for services we were rendering. They consumed too much in trifling purchases, gambling, and gifts to flatter girls, ordering foods that were outrageously priced only to impress a companion who tomorrow would not be remembered. When I questioned a certain high-earning artist about his real estate, he assured me he was comfortable in the elegant condo he was contemplating buying. At the time, I was in fear that [my first hit single] 'Maybellene' would catch pneumonia and die off the charts. The nearness of my not too distant past kept me frugal."

Likewise, singer-songwriter Moby could not escape the mindset he honed during his impoverished childhood. He admitted: "I go around and turn off all the lights and turn down the thermostat at my house. My friends make fun of me. Also, I still have a hard time drinking undiluted orange juice. We had to make orange juice last as long as possible, and I grew up drinking half water, half juice. It's hard to change your habits." Offering financial advice, he stated: "Don't buy stupid things like expensive cars and fur coats. The earning curve for most musicians is quite short, so when you make money you should save it and invest it."

And singer Robert Smith of the Cure recalled, "I'm not very materially minded. The first thing I bought when I had any money was a bed. I bought the biggest bed I could find. Then I bought a jeep, and after that there was nothing else I that wanted. As long as I've got enough money to buy books and eat, I'm not really bothered."

Similarly, despite her success, Chrissie Hynde maintained just two modest residences, an apartment in her hometown of Akron and a small two-bedroom apartment in London. At age 66 in 2018, she proclaimed: "I don't need a big house. I don't want one. And I only live in a couple of rooms, so what would be the point?"

Other rockers are simply cheap. Johnny Ramone was notoriously frugal with his money. Earning little during his stint with the Ramones, he squirreled away a portion of his earnings every month with a plan of amassing $1 million for his retirement. He achieved that goal shortly before the group disbanded in 1996. Ironically, he was earning *more* money after he retired, thanks to product licensing and album reissues, than during his grueling days on the road. Likewise, Rod Stewart is renowned for his penny-pinching behavior. As Carol Bodman, his personal housekeeper, revealed: "Rod doesn't carry money, doesn't tip and instructs his secretary to mark the levels on the bottle in his bar.... In 1974 Elton John bought Stewart a Rembrandt worth £10,000 and in return Rod bought him an ice bucket priced £27."

A number of artists became masters at wisely investing the proceeds from their music careers. When rocker Del Shannon disappeared from the charts in the 1970s, he was spending his time buying and selling property. And Paul McCartney acquired an impressive portfolio of music publishing rights to hundreds of hit songs. However, after McCartney shared his investment strategy with friend Michael Jackson, the King of Pop outbid McCartney on a catalogue of Beatles songs. (McCartney later lamented: "You know what doesn't feel very good? Going on tour and paying to sing all my songs. Every time I sing 'Hey Jude,' I gotta pay someone.")

Some rockers took more creative routes when investing. Jimmy Page recalled: "In the beginning of Zeppelin, I had this very small guitar arsenal: a Harmony acoustic, a Telecaster. Then, one day, I went to Eric Clapton's house, and every room had all these guitars in them. His whole house was like a guitar shrine. I was like 'Crikey!' Eric explained to me: 'They are all tax deductible!' So that's when I started buying more guitars."

Surprisingly, rock superstardom does not guarantee massive wealth. Elvis Presley was never a wealthy man during his lifetime. As Elvis biographer Joel Williamson explained: "Elvis did not... become rich. His performances grossed on average about $5 million a year during the last several years of his life, but at his death his total assets probably amounted to substantially less than $3 million. Like his parents, Elvis never thought about saving any money for a rainy day. He never bought stocks, corporate bonds, or rental property for investment or income. The final inventory of his possessions filed in the court records of Shelby County show that he did buy a $10,000 U.S. government bond. He probably forgot he had it. He practically never invested in anything he could not eat, wear, ride, or live in. Such scattered investments as he did make – for example, buying and selling airplanes – lost money. A large part of Elvis's income went toward keeping more than twenty people on his regular payroll, including a staff at Graceland, his 'guys,' and his father, Vernon, whom he eventually paid $75,000 a year.... Also, he was famous for his gifts to friends and strangers – new cars being a favored item. In all, he gave away about 275 'luxury cars' worth well over $3 million."

▶ CHAPTER 5
MUSICIANS AS BUSINESSMEN

Since the dawn of the music industry, songwriters and performers have been cheated, manipulated and deceived. Musical artists – both obscure and famous – have been harassed, threatened and blackmailed. The business of music is shady, corrupt and chronically unjust. As an unwritten rule, greed prevails over integrity.

The popular music industry in the United States emerged after the close of the Civil War. Stephen Foster, the country's first superstar songwriter, wrote some of the most cherished songs of the last half of the 19th century, including "Oh! Susanna," "Camptown Races" and "Old Folks At Home" (better known as "Swanee River"). But he was swindled out of his royalties and would die a destitute and broken man at the age of 37. The same fate befell many of Foster's successors in the 20th century – whether by unscrupulous managers, dishonest club owners or mob-controlled record companies.

In the 1940s, Frank Sinatra was the country's most popular artist in terms of both sales and airplay. And yet even he was bamboozled. As fellow pop crooner Rosemary Clooney observed, although Sinatra had sold millions and millions of records at Columbia Records, he would leave the label at the end of the 1950s with his contract unrenewed, still "owing six figures in advance royalties."

During the rock era, everyone from Elvis to the Beatles were victimized at some point in their careers. A brutal scene in the fictional 1991 film *The Five Heartbeats* was based on a real-life event. According to music journalist Robert Pruter: "A particular melodramatic moment takes place when a record company executive and his henchmen rough up a recalcitrant singer and then hang him by his feet out of a hotel window to force him to sign a contract. Insiders in the record business know this scene is a reference to the great Jackie Wilson, perhaps the most tragic figure in the history of rhythm 'n' blues."

Similarly, singer Jimmy Merchant recalled the sudden rise and fall of his group, Frankie Lymon & The Teenagers: "Our lives turned upside down overnight. We did three 90-day, one-night tours, went to Europe for a three-month tour, appeared on national TV several times and sang in two movies. But 18 months... after we started, it was over. At 17, I was broke and bussing tables at Shor's (a restaurant in New York City). The song I co-wrote, 'Why Do Fools Fall In Love,' was on the jukebox there, but I had nothing."

Meanwhile, Mark Mothersbaugh of Devo recalled how Warner Brothers Records openly fleeced the group in the 1980s, when cassette albums were on par with traditional vinyl LPs in terms of sales: "They were paying us less money for an audio cassette, but there were articles about how much cheaper it was to make an audio cassette than it was to press vinyl. So I went in and had a meeting with [Warner Brothers chief] Mo Ostin, and said, 'You know, Mo, I need to ask you something really important. Why is it that, in our deal, you have it so you're paying us substantially less money for every audio cassette that you sell than for every piece of vinyl, yet you make a bigger profit?' He just smiled and looked at me like I was his dense naive son. And he goes, 'Because that's the way it is'.... At least he was totally up-front about it. He was totally unashamed and that there was no justification except for power."

Likewise, Gladys Knight recalled her time at Motown Records, when company president Berry Gordy "and his managers tried to entice us by telling us they were going to buy us cars and houses, but we told them no thanks, we could take care of that ourselves, just give us our money. Anytime they tried to bill us for an expense or to 'give' us something, we demanded to know what the real cost was going to be to us. Our caution paid off. Once we noticed a deduction in our paychecks for some ridiculous amount for 'musical arrangements.' Now, those arrangements were nothing more than a few notes scrawled on a piece of paper by Motown's famed musicians. It was up to us to take those scrawls and make music out of them. When they billed us for that, we demanded they give us the piece of paper the arrangements had been written on. After all, we said, if we are going to pay for them, we want to have them. They couldn't come up with the goods, so the charge came off our tab at the company store. It wouldn't be the last time we questioned their accounting procedures."

Similarly, when Jerry Allison – a member of Buddy Holly and the Crickets and the co-composer of the track "Peggy Sue" – asked why the producer Norman Petty's name appeared on the song's credits, Allison was told: "The exact words I remember him saying were, 'Disc jockeys will remember me from the Norman Petty Trio, and so we'll get more airplay if my name is on it... but it won't really be on it.' Buddy said, 'Ay' because we just wanted to have a hit record. We really didn't understand royalties at the time. I really wanted credit for writing half the song instead of a third of it, but we ended up signing a power of attorney with Norman Petty, so we didn't have any say on what was going on."

Likewise, heavy metal vocalist Don Dokken learned an expensive lesson early in his career: "We thought we'd get rich once we were signed and selling records, but even the Elektra contracts were garbage. For every dollar they made, we made twenty cents split four ways. In Dokken, it was a four-way split, which came back to haunt me, because I wrote most of the hits. That's what started the war between [guitarist] George [Lynch] and I. When I signed that contract, we were at the airport ready to go to Japan for our first tour. The deal was still intact – that I owned 50 percent, and they divided 50 percent. They showed up at the airport with a contract that says it's a four-way split or we're not getting on the plane. I called [our manager] Cliff [Bernstein] and said, 'I can't sign this.' He said, 'Sign it and we'll work it out.' But it never did happen. He just wanted us to get on that plane. I was hijacked. We spent the next five years together getting famous, and I hated them, and they hated me."

And despite selling millions of records for Sam Phillips' Memphis-based label Sun Records, Jerry Lee Lewis never received a single royalty payment from the label for hits such as "Whole Lot Of Shakin' Going On" and "Great Balls Of Fire." In 2006, Lewis recalled: "Sam owed me millions. He told me he did. In front of several witnesses, yeah, I said, 'About how much do you owe me now?' This must have been about twenty-five years ago. He said, 'Well, a little over 8 million dollars.' I said, 'Why don't you pay me, Sam? It's my money, isn't it?' He said, 'I can't see it goin' for a bunch of houses and women and cars. I just can't let it go like that.' I said, 'In other words, you're not going to give me my money, are you?' He said, 'Nope. Not gonna do it. I know you shoulda gone after it. If you wanna do that, go ahead and sue me. But I'm not gonna pay you.'"

Similarly, Badfinger enjoyed a run of chart hits beginning in 1969. But the lack of financial stability was too much for Pete Ham, the group's singer, to handle. His bandmate Joey Molland speculated on Ham's decision in 1975 to take his own life: "This is all supposition, but I think Pete was really let down by the fact that our managers had put him in such a bad spot. Here's a guy who had written 'Without You,' 'Day After Day, 'Baby Blue,' 'No Matter What' and so on. By all accounts, he should have been fabulously wealthy. The reality of it was that he had been living in an attic for five years and drove a secondhand car. Nothing he did gained him anything.... The managers in New York were holding up all his money. His phone number was going to be cut off. His girlfriend was expecting a baby. He had no idea what to do."

NEEDING A LAWYER

At the start of the rock era, few artists bothered hiring a lawyer to protect their financial interests. Many budding rock and R&B performers were happy to sign away the rights to their music if there was a chance of hearing one of their songs on the radio. Most of these artists were young, inexperienced, ignorant of copyrights and publishing income, and would never consider seeking legal advice. And if they did hire an attorney, the record company would suddenly lose interest in signing the artist.

Independent labels frequently paid off their acts with a flashy car – often a Cadillac – and nothing more. "We used to go in and get paid, like, $69 per side, and that was it," claimed 1950s R&B star Ruth Brown, who didn't see her first royalty payment until 1988, when Atlantic Records belatedly wiped out the debts that many of the label's pioneering artists supposedly still owed to the label.

Hank Ballard, leader of the Midnighters and author of many early rock hits including "The Twist," recalled how King-Federal Records cheated him: "The company I was with... said there's no such thing as publishing rights. If you asked for publishing rights, they'd give you your contract back. I didn't know there was so much money involved in publishing. They would tell me, 'You've got to write a hundred songs before you can even get a BMI contract,' and I found out later all you had to do is write one song."

Jazz vocalist Jimmy Scott recalled: "In those days you never heard of an artist hiring an entertainment lawyer for protection. Maybe those guys existed, but I didn't know a single one, and neither did my buddies like Percy Sledge or Big Maybelle. When we all had our first little hits, there was no one to advise us. We went along with the booking agents and the record companies not because we were foolish, but because we had no choice. If you wanted to work, you signed on the dotted line."

Rock and roll pioneer Bo Diddley explained: "When I started to ask about royalty checks... my stuff started getting played less and less. And I didn't understand. And after a while it looked like it was set that I could plainly see it, that I was becoming a troublemaker because I started asking about royalty checks. That meant that I was going to cause problems, and the easiest way to shut you up was to pull your records off the airwaves. It's called blackball."

In the 1970s when Jimmy Buffett was launching his career, he learned a number of harsh lessons about the music industry: "It was indentured servitude, and it still is. If you apply supply and demand, there's always a supply of talent who's willing to do anything if you aren't." Likewise, Don McLean, of "American Pie" fame, observed: "Artists are very vulnerable. They'll just sign something and not realize that the person putting it in front of them is a smart guy who's thinking, 'Oh, I've got him locked up. He just wants the applause, wants the women, the money. And he's not thinking about what he's signing away to get it.'" And Ian McLagan, of the British band the Faces, proclaimed: "'Trust Me' and 'just sign it' are two phrases that should never be used in the same sentence, and what the hell is a 'standard contract' anyway?"

Meanwhile, Creedence Clearwater Revival's contract with Fantasy Records is legendary in the music business for its one-sidedness. CCR frontman John Fogerty recalled: "We signed a contract with the label in a very dark and noisy Italian restaurant. I couldn't read the menu, let alone the contract. I was underage anyway. All of us were, except [my brother] Tom." Fellow Creedence member Stu Cook remembered: "We sat in [Fantasy Records owner] Saul Zaentz's kitchen, and he told us, 'When you guys are successful, we'll tear up this contract and give you a real deal.' Well, we kept our side of the agreement. He didn't."

Likewise, James Taylor foolishly signed away the publishing rights to his first four albums – which included the hit songs "Fire and Rain" and "Don't Let Me Be Lonely Tonight." At 18-years-old, Taylor had been offered a recording contract, but only if he agreed to a publishing deal with April-Blackwood.

Similarly, in the mid-1970s, Bruce Springsteen was emerging as a star. However, in 1972, he had signed away his publishing rights and agreed to a five-album production deal in a contract with a company owned by his manager. The contract paid Springsteen a minuscule three-percent royalty on the retail price of his records! After a protracted and expensive lawsuit, Springsteen was finally able to free himself from the arrangement in 1977.

Likewise, Billy Joel's classic track "Piano Man" was the first single from his second album and his first with Columbia Records. What he didn't realize was that his previous contract with Family Records, which was signed in 1971, had bound him for life! Consequently, Joel would make sizable royalty payments to his former label for many years to come.

And Elvis Presley signed a contract that gave his manager, Col. Tom

Parker, a whopping 50-percent of his earnings as well as total control over the singer's career, which meant having to appear in dozens of cheesy movies. Parker subsequently lost millions of those dollars in the casinos of Las Vegas. And Beach Boys manager Murry Wilson foolishly sold the publishing rights to most of the group's hits in 1969 for a mere $75,000. Over the next several decades, the songs would earn tens of millions of dollars.

Even the members of the Fab Four were fleeced on multiple fronts. After signing a management contract with Brian Epstein that cost them 25-percent of their earnings, they were powerless as their inexperienced manager signed terrible licensing agreements, publishing deals and record contracts. And although Paul McCartney was worth a whopping $1.2 billion by 2019, he did not become wealthy until *after* leaving the Beatles. As his bandmate John Lennon admitted in 1969: "We earned millions and millions. The Beatles got very little of it. We've all got houses, we've managed to pay for them finally after all these years, and that only really happened since [new manager Alan] Klein came in. They used to tell Paul and I that we were millionaires. We never have been. We didn't get the money. George and Ringo are practically penniless."

Likewise, the members of the Rolling Stones were struggling financially – several years after the start of their hit run in 1963, when their breakthrough single, "Come On," landed on the British charts. A financial expert recalled a conversation he had with Mick Jagger in 1969 at the rocker's sparsely-decorated residence: "The essence of what he told me was 'I have no money. None of us have any money.' Given the success of the Stones, he could not understand why none of the money they were expecting was... trickling down to the band members. That was the key point, and explained the paucity of furniture in the house. He had nothing to buy any pieces with." Famed rock critic Joel Selvin verified Jagger's claims of impoverishment during this period: "They belonged to one of the most popular rock bands in the world and they led luxurious, glamorous, even decadent lives, but there is nothing more pathetic than rich people without money." During this period, it took Jagger eighteen-months to scrape together the down payment on a house in Chelsea.

By the 1970s and '80s, a growing number of singer-songwriters – from Paul McCartney to Tom Petty – established their own publishing companies and no longer had to split their songwriting royalties on a 50/50 basis. Singer-songwriter Tori Amos revealed: "I own my own publishing, meaning that I don't have a deal with an outside publisher. I hired my parents to collect the money for me. I generate the most income with songs I write, and this way I know where that money is. People want copyrights more than anything in this business – everybody wants your songs, and they want to pay as little as possible for them."

Eventually, entertainment law became big business. In the 1980s, most recording artists consulted with attorneys before signing recording contracts. As such, the business of music became more complicated. Greg and Suzy Shaw of the indie label Bomp Records were faced with the complexity of licensing one song to a large record company. Suzy Shaw recalled: "One of the paragraphs stated that the company would own the track 'in perpetuity, for the entire solar system and the known universe.' After we laughed ourselves silly at the very thought of them playing a song 2,000 years from now on Jupiter, [Greg] crossed out the phrase 'solar system' and wrote in, by hand, 'we reserve the right for Neptune,' and sent it back to the entirely humorless legal department of the company. A few days later we got the call. 'Mr. Shaw, we will be re-drafting the contract, we really need the rights for Neptune to be included, we cannot divide up the solar system in this manner!' Greg tried not to laugh and stood his ground, pretending to be very serious, and wanting to see how far they would go. The answer was, of course, all the way. They argued on and off for weeks, with Greg bargaining for perhaps retaining just one of the moons of Jupiter. They were not amused and were quite adamant about each and every moon and comet being included, and eventually Greg got tired of the game and signed off on Neptune."

THE PAYOLA GAME

When future R&B superstar James Brown began his recording career, he knew little about the inner-workings of the music business: "We got all dressed up and went to one particular deejay and talked to him really polite: 'Sir, we stopped in here today with a record of ours we hope you'll listen to and that you'll like enough to put on the air.' He sat through this little speech looking kind of bored, but he let us go on. When [we] had each said our piece, I handed him a copy of [the single 'Please, Please, Please.'] He pulled the record out of the sleeve and laid it to one side without even looking at it. Then he turned the sleeve upside down like he expected something to fall out of it. Nothing happened. He shook it. Nothing. Without a word he picked up the record and handed it back to me."

However, since the dawn of the music industry, payola has been the tried and proven method of manipulating radio airplay. In the pre-rock

43

era, pop singer Rosemary Clooney recounted that "the practice of buying or giving commercial favors was common. Whether it was called 'ice' or 'hot stives' or, more prosaically, a payoff or kickback, a gift to a DJ or to a power player at a record label could mean the difference between obscurity or renown. One music executive I knew had given his wish list to certain art galleries for the convenience of music publishers – something like the bridal registry at Tiffany's. When I visited his country house, it was like walking into a museum. On a smaller scale, a prominent DJ frankly described the greenback that came with a new record as no different from a headwaiter's tip for a good table."

In the 1950s, radio deejays became powerful gatekeepers who could break a new artist or a top-40 hit. Music journalist Bill DeMain observed: "Aware of their rising status, jocks established flat rate deals with labels and record distributors. A typical deal for a mid-level DJ was $50 a week, per record, to ensure a minimum amount of spins. More influential jocks commanded percentages of grosses for local concerts, lavish trips, free records by the boxful (some even opened their own record stores), plus all the time-honored swag.'"

The person most associated with payola was legendary deejay Alan Freed. Honing his craft in Cleveland before relocating to New York City in 1954, Freed once joked: "A man said to me, 'If somebody sent you a Cadillac, would you send it back?' I said, 'It depends on the color.'" In an era when individual deejays could select the records they played, the situation was ripe for abuse.

By the end of the 1950s, the government began targeting payola and staged a series of public hearings. Overnight, deejays were reined in by radio station owners who were fearful of losing their broadcast licenses. In the aftermath of the payola hearings, few people were actually prosecuted and even fewer lost their jobs. While Alan Freed took the brunt of the punishment, others such as Dick Clark received a slap on the wrist. In the process, Freed would lose his fortune, his fame, his reputation and his coveted position as the top deejay in the nation's largest radio market.

However, payola did not disappear from the music industry. In 1973, *Time* magazine declared: "The going prices for air play these days range from an occasional $50 in some regional stations to as much as $1,000 for a week of concentrated play in the big city rhythm-and-blues stations." And in 1977, Harry Wayne Casey – better known as "KC" in the disco group KC & The Sunshine Band – recalled how his single "Keep It Comin' Love" was kept out of the number-one spot on *Billboard* magazine: "It was number one on every radio station in the country for three or four weeks. Evidently, somebody paid more money for [Debby Boone's] 'You Light Up My Life'.... But in *Cashbox* and *Record World*... 'Keep It Comin' Love' was number one. It sold more than 'You Light Up My Life.' There were disappointing things like that happening out there. I realized this was a political game, like every other corporation or business, which was disappointing in a way, because growing up I didn't realize it was *that* political."

By the 1980s, the practice of payola was practically legit as the process was institutionalized by a powerful group of independent promoters who acted as the conduits between record labels and radio stations. But with the consolidation of the record and radio industries in the 1990s, an entirely new dynamic would emerge.

▶ CHAPTER 6
STAGE PRESENCE AND PUBLIC PERSONA

A successful rock and roll band is comprised of far more than just a collection of talented musicians who have the ability to craft and perform catchy songs. As rock became a visual medium, a musical act was forced to develop a distinctive image and memorable public persona. Looking like a rock star became a career enhancer.

In November 1961, when Brian Epstein first saw the Beatles at the Cavern Club in Liverpool, the members of the band looked scruffy and disorganized. They wore leather outfits, ate and drank onstage and frequently engaged in comedy routines. After Epstein was hired as their manager, he cleaned up the group's image – which meant tailored suits, bowing to the audience after every song, clean hairstyles, no more onstage eating and the elimination of comedy skits.

Conversely, the Rolling Stones were often viewed as the anti-Beatles. Originally a blues outfit, the Stones were fronted by a sneering, dangerous-looking, rubbery-lipped college dropout. Peter Noone, the lead singer of Herman's Hermits, observed: "I've always thought it would be so exhausting to be Mick Jagger. He's an extremely intelligent man and a good person to be around. But on cue he has to pretend to be a Cockney snob who hates everybody. Just to keep up that image."

Similarly, singer Peter Gabriel of Genesis attracted a great deal of attention in 1972, after he started wearing outrageous stage costumes. Portraying the various characters from the lyrics of the group's songs, Gabriel appeared as the Ageless Egyptian Prince, an alien visitor known as the Watcher of the Skies and the Biblical character Magog. Gabriel later discussed his motivation for infusing theatrics into the group's live shows: "I like some of the showmanship and gimmicks of rock and roll, whether it's Chuck Berry's duck walk, Pete Townshend's flailing arms, or the Sex Pistols' anti-promotion. I've heard TV producer Jack Good telling how excited he was when Gene Vincent first came to [Britain] to do his television show, and instead of this dark rock 'n' roll monster, coming off the plane was a very polite southern gentleman with a very slight limp. Good then persuaded him to dress in leather and exaggerate the limp. It struck me as an early example of rock 'n' roll myth-making, however contrived, but I like all that."

Meanwhile, Ramones co-founder Johnny Ramone devised the band's stage show and public image – short, high-octane songs; matching mop-top haircuts; the adoption of a common last name; and stage costumes consisting of biker-style leather jackets, t-shirts and cheap tennis shoes. And in concert, bassist Dee Dee Ramone began every song with a loud, rapid-fire shout of "one, two, three, four!"

Oftentimes, an artist's stage image was manufactured and groomed by the promotional department of a record company. In the 1960s, Motown was one of the most successful independent labels in the country. Wanting to establish a completely in-house operation, the label's founder Berry Gordy, Jr. launched a music publishing company and constructed a record-pressing plant. Wanting to promote his talented stable of young artists, Gordy booked a ten-week tour through the Deep South in 1962. However, with little experience on the concert road, young acts like the Supremes and the Miracles lacked the required polish and stage presence.

With the tour a near disaster, Gordy realized that his acts needed a great deal of refinement before they could achieve wider, mainstream success. Dubbing the process "Artist Development," all of Motown's acts were subsequently schooled in an assembly-line fashion. With former Moonglows leader Harvey Fuqua placed in charge of the effort, Cholly Atkins taught choreographed dance routines and Maxine Powell, the owner of a modeling school and agency, provided training in etiquette, poise and social skills. Lastly, the musical acts were taught personal grooming skills and were elegantly attired in matching stage costumes. Gordy had learned his lesson – in order to be pop music stars, Motown artists had to look and behave like pop music stars.

Most musical artists of the 1970s – especially more serious rock acts – did not expend much effort on their public personas. They let their music do the talking. But by the 1980s, MTV added a visual dynamic to popular music which favored performers who were young, attractive, thin and photogenic. In 1986, Frank Zappa quipped: "Today record companies don't even listen to your [demo] tape. They look at your publicity photo. They look at your hair. They look at your zippers.... And if you've got the look, then it really doesn't make a... bit of difference what's on the tape – they can always hire somebody to fix that. And they don't expect you to be around for twenty years. They want that fast buck because they realize that next week there's going to be another hairdo and another zipper. And they realize that the people are not listening, they're dancing, or they're driving, or something else. The business is more geared toward expendability today. That's because merchandising is so tied to 'visuals' now."

Similarly, Courtney Love observed: "It is really quite important in rock and roll to, like, just be skinny. You can be a crackhead, but you can't be fat. You can lose all your hair, but you can't be fat. You can, and I have done this, go to the Bowery Ballroom the day after getting arrested, have laryngitis, no voice at all, and get a pornographic review in *The New York Times*, even though not one noise came out of your larynx, but you can't be fat." And in an often-repeated story, the 1980s New Wave act Romeo Void lost the support of the promotional department of their record label after the band performed at an industry showcase. Realizing that the band's lead singer was overweight and did not possess the *proper* image of a young and modern rock star, Columbia Records soured on the group.

PUBLIC VS. PRIVATE PERSONA

Musical artists often wrestle with the conflict between their public and private personas. Treating his stage image like a film role, Ozzy Osbourne explained: "I like to sit in a bar to talk to local people. I don't like to talk about my job all the time when I'm not working. I forget who Ozzy Osbourne is. When I'm John Osbourne I totally blank him out. Then you get somebody who goes, 'It's him!' ... And then I have to be him for ten minutes and it gets tiring." Similarly, David Spero, the former manager for Joe Walsh, recalled: "Glenn [Frey] was always two people. When he was being an Eagle... let me put it this way, he used to wear a T-shirt that read 'That's Mr. Asshole to you.' But when he wasn't being an Eagle, he was pure fun. So funny and so much fun to be with."

Conversely, the Who's notorious drummer Keith Moon continually perpetuated his wildman public persona – at hotels, restaurants and bars – which contributed to his premature demise at age 32. Similarly, Doors frontman Jim Morrison maintained the same persona, both on and off the stage, and was known by both fans and intimate friends as an unpredictable, confrontational, risk-taking shaman. Fellow performer Alice Cooper (real name Vince Furnier) embraced a similar attitude during this period. Cooper recalled: "I was hanging out a lot with Jim Morrison. I really liked the guy but he had a negative effect on me. He believed that you had to live the role at all times, and I began to pick up on that. I started to go out in my leather, do outrageous stuff, get into fights in bars – all the things that I thought Alice should do. As the act grew and became a greater success, it became more and more difficult for Vince the person to find a place in the shadow of this Frankenstein monster. I began to be Alice 24 hours a day."

Likewise, avant-garde rocker Lou Reed once admitted: "Sometimes I need to be reminded who I am. Sometimes performing as Lou Reed and being Lou Reed are so close as to make one think they are one and the same person. I've hidden behind the myth of Lou Reed for years. I can blame anything outrageous on him. I make believe sometimes that I'm Lou Reed. I'm so easily seduced by the public image of Lou Reed that I'm in love with Lou Reed myself. I think he's wonderful."

However, art-rocker David Bowie was nearly consumed by one of the stage personas he created. As Bowie biographer Christopher Sandford chronicled: "By 1973 the character Bowie once described as 'total anarchy' had become a straitjacket. When he changed into Ziggy [Stardust] it was much more than just an act, it seemed like genuine possession. His weird make-up and space-age clothes were only reflections of his other-worldliness. The rumor went around, especially in teen magazines, that Bowie himself thought he was from another planet. In Los Angeles, he refused to go out during the day because, he said, quite solemnly, 'I'll melt.' Bowie stopped a concert in another city to harangue the audience about a spacecraft he was certain he had seen from his hotel window. He was intrigued, he told a journalist, 'to show how a nobody can become a god, and go bonkers in the process.' It was an ominous self-sketch if ever there was one." Bowie later claimed that the alter-ego "wouldn't leave me alone for years. That was when it all started to go sour... My whole personality was affected. It became very dangerous. I really did have doubts about my sanity."

Oftentimes, the concert stage provided shy and insecure artists the opportunity to project a measure of confidence. *Los Angeles Times* music writer Robert Hilburn recalled his first encounter with Janis Joplin, backstage before a concert: "Eventually, the door opened and I saw Janis leaning back on a sofa, appearing as drained and lifeless as she had sounded [the previous day] on the phone. Nothing about her suggested 'star.' This powerhouse of a woman seemed ordinary, almost anonymous.... As I watched her on the sofa, all the flamboyant attire and jewelry she wore on stage seemed her way of compensating for the beauty and personality that nature had failed to provide. Minus the camouflage or an audience to energize her, she seemed small and weak."

Some recording artists had their public images thrust upon them. After Black Sabbath released their debut album – with featured an inverted crucifix inside the gatefold cover – the group was greeted at early performances by fans dressed in satanic-styled black robes. Ozzy Osbourne and his bandmates had chosen the group's sinister-sounding name and adopted dark imagery after noticing that the public was drawn to horror films and paying money to be frightened. Tired of the misplaced attention, Ozzy eventually took the matter into his own hands: "I'd walk out of my hotel room in the morning, and they'd be right outside my door, sitting in a circle on the carpet, all dressed in black hooded capes, surrounded by candles. Eventually I couldn't take it anymore. So, one morning, instead of brushing past them as I usually did, I went up to them, sat down, took a deep breath, blew out their candles, and sang 'Happy Birthday.' They weren't too... happy about that, believe me."

Additionally, some musical acts found themselves forced into a role as society's spokesman and consciousness – whether they wanted the position or not. Writing in his autobiography, Bob Dylan recalled an incident from 1964: "Ronnie Gilbert, one of the Weavers, had introduced me at one of the Newport Folk Festivals saying, 'And here he is... take him, you know him, he's yours.' I had failed to sense the ominous forebodings in that introduction. Elvis had never even been introduced like that. 'Take him, he's yours!' What a crazy thing to say! Screw that. As far as I knew, I didn't belong to anybody then or now. I had a wife and children whom I loved more than anything else in the world. I was trying to provide for them, keep out of trouble, but the big bugs in the press kept promoting me as the mouthpiece, spokesman, or even conscience of a generation. That was funny. All I'd ever done was sing songs that were dead straight and expressed powerful new realities. I had very little in common with and knew even less about a generation that I was supposed to be the voice of."

Conversely, there was a downside to embracing anonymity and failing to develop a strong public persona. Rodger Hodgeson, the leader and chief vocalist of Supertramp, left the group in 1983 after a strong run of hits, which included "Give A Little Bit" and "The Logical Song." However, he encountered a significant problem after leaving the group to pursue a solo career. He recalled: "A little like Pink Floyd, Supertramp was a faceless band, and it was more about music than personalities. We rarely put the band on covers. But that created the difficulty I had initially in going out under my own name. I had to work to forge an identity."

THE BRAND

Formulating a brand is an integral part of establishing a public image. And one of the first tasks is to select a logo – which typically appears on album covers, t-shirts and the front of the drummer's bass drum. For the most part, successful rock bands tend to have easily identifiable logos. The Grateful Dead had multiple logos including a psychedelic skeleton, a dancing teddy bear and a red-and-blue skull highlighted by a lightning bolt. Other well-known logos include the red asterisk of the Red Hot Chili Peppers, the presidential seal of the Ramones, the stylized wings of Aerosmith, the royal crest of Queen and the cartoon-style exaggerated lips and tongue of the Rolling Stones.

Some rock acts have made fortunes with their brands. Early in the band's career, Kiss introduced a plethora of themed products. The band's guitarist Paul Stanley recalled: "It was during 1977 that we awoke to the possibilities of Kiss merchandising. That came out of listening to our fans rather than any marketing genius on our part. It was our fans who decided what would be cool, and we were happy to give it to them. It probably started out with Kiss belt buckles and the Kiss dolls. Then it took off from there... lunch-boxes, transistor radios, jeans, jackets, garbage pails, bubblegum cards, our own Marvel comic." During this period, Kiss was setting records in the rock world for merchandise sales. From 1977 to 1979 alone, the group sold an estimated $100 million in Kiss-related products. As Gene Simmons crowed in 2017: "Our licensing and merchandising dwarfs Elvis and the Beatles combined. If you go to Graceland, there's a Kiss exhibit – that's what people come to see."

Similarly, Jimmy Buffett established an immensely profitable empire built around his 1977 hit, "Margaritaville." And as Buffett's popularity grew, his concerts became Caribbean-themed events, with fans dressing in Hawaiian print shirts, beak masks and outlandish feather-adorned costumes. Touring nearly non-stop for five-decades, Buffett nurtured a loyal fanbase of Parrot Heads – a term coined by his devotees in Cincinnati. With his concert fees ballooning, he was singlehandedly pulling in Rolling Stones-level tour cash.

Additionally, Buffett launched a series of lucrative business ventures. This was a complete contrast to his financial state in the late-1970s, when he was living on a small boat which was docked on the shore of the Caribbean island of St. Barts. Buffett's business empire eventually grew to include tour bus rentals, a line of foods (including, of course, margarita mix), a chain of tropical-themed restaurants, hotels, a beer brand, an adult-living community and even a Broadway musical, *Escape To Margaritaville*. And in 1999, he launched his own label, Mailboat Records. By 2018, Buffett had 5,000 employees on his payroll as he had amassed a fortune worth more than half-a-billion dollars.

And in 1990, Sammy Hagar convinced his bandmates in Van Halen to invest in a nightclub in Cabo San Lucas, Mexico. After later buying out his partners, Hagar expanded the venture and launched his own line of tequila. In 2008, he sold an 80-percent interest in his company for a whopping $80 million.

PICKING A NAME

Many rock groups have struggled with the process of choosing a name. In the 1950s, it was a common practice for groups to name themselves after birds or automobiles. Some of the biggest rock hits of the decade were by the Orioles, Flamingos and Ravens or by the Cadillacs, Impalas and Edsels. And Buddy Holly's backing band, the Crickets, later inspired another insect name, the Beatles. Meanwhile, the Rolling Stones named themselves after a 1950 blues hit by Muddy Waters called "Rollin' Stone." During the psychedelic era of the late-1960s, rock bands adopted names such as the Chocolate Watchband, Strawberry Alarm Clock and the 13th Floor Elevators.

A stage name can send a powerful message, and picking a controversial moniker can have negative consequences for an artist's career. An offensive or controversial band name can even keep you off mainstream radio. Had the Butthole Surfers chosen a different name, it's likely their 1996 hit track, "Pepper," would have garnered far more airplay. Additionally, selecting a name that's difficult to pronounce or spell – like Hüsker Dü, deadmau5 or Enuff Z'nuff – can often hinder an artist's success. However, that was not the case with INXS, Gotye or Lynyrd Skynyrd.

Heavy metal and punk acts tend to choose combative, angry or sinister-sounding names, including Sid Vicious, Richard Hell, Rob Zombie and Cheetah Chrome. However, Iggy Pop – born James Osterberg, Jr. – had the nickname "Iggy" thrust upon him by his enemies, former bosses and one early concert reviewer. Eventually, he embraced the name's power: "I saw an opportunity there and never looked back. This name's catchy. People now knew me by this name, so I stuck with it. Then I thought I'd tag a good last name onto it, and because this sounded like show business, I came up with Pop.... When I begin a professional relationship with somebody, often I'm called Iggy.

When I met Jerry Moss, chairman of A&M Records, he called me Iggy. The president [of the label], however, always called me James. When my father's in a good mood, he calls me Iggy, just to hassle me. Occasionally my father calls me Jimbo. And sometimes my wife does, too. My audience calls me Iggy, but groupies always call me Jim, because Iggy's not a romantic name. It's a dangerous name. It's the kind of name, when shouted across a room, makes nice people wince. It's a dangerous game being called Iggy, no question about it."

Oftentimes musicians realize that their birth names are not suitable for rock stardom as was the case with the former Robert Zimmerman, who emerged as Bob Dylan. He later explained the decision to change his name: "Some people – you're born, you know, the wrong names, wrong parents. I mean, that happens. You call yourself what you want to call yourself. This is the land of the free."

Likewise, the former Farrokh Bulsara became Freddie Mercury; Saul Hudson of Guns N' Roses became Slash; Frank Castelluccio became Frankie Valli; Benjamin Orzechowski of the Cars became Ben Orr; Declan MacManus became Elvis Costello; Bret Sychak of Poison became Bret Michaels; Paul Hewson of U2 became Bono; and William Broad became Billy Idol.

Sometimes, a stage name is thrust upon a performer by their manager or record label. Lizzy Grant's management team helped the singer-songwriter emerged as Lana Del Rey. Similarly, Ernest Evans was rechristened Chubby Checker by the wife of *American Bandstand's* Dick Clark.

However, rock history is full of unflattering, odd or silly names. Some examples include Goo Goo Dolls, Archers of Loaf, Hoobastank, Milli Vanilli, Dead Kennedys, String Cheese Incident, Porno for Pyros and an all-white rap group called Young Black Teenagers. And years after the fact, Tom Petty admitted that he was not fond of the name of his 1970s band, Mudcrutch.

CLOTHING: LOOKING SPECIAL ON STAGE

Rock stars are often identified by their distinctive stage clothing: Jim Morrison's black leather pants, Roy Orbison's Ray Ban sunglasses, Angus Young's schoolboy uniform and Jimi Hendrix's psychedelic outfits. Conversely, some artists like David Bowie and Madonna had a knack for remaking their images during the various stages of their careers.

An artist's musical genre will often dictate how they will dress onstage. Shiny sharkskin suits? The act is an oldies doo-wop group or a Rat Pack, Vegas-style crooner. Well-worn bell-bottom jeans, a fringed leather vest, a peasant-style white shirt and sandals? Then probably a folk, country-rock or psychedelic-style rock band. Big hair, bare chests, Spandex pants and glam make-up? Likely a 1980s hair-metal band.

Not surprisingly, musicians have been setting fashion trends for generations. When bandleader Cab Calloway wore an oversized zoot suit in the 1930s, he spawned a fashion craze that was copied by other jazz artists. But when the clothing was worn in public instead of the stage, it was considered disruptive and became the frequent cause of violent street fights. Although the zoot suit trend did not survive into the 1950s, rebellious fashion statements became commonplace during the rock era.

Blue jeans – the item of clothing most associated with rock and roll – became the uniform of American youth in the last half of the 20th century. Beginning in 1853, gold-rush miners in California were the first to wear the thick, dark-colored denim pants, which were made by Bavarian immigrant Levi Strauss. The more famous indigo-blue denim pants were first produced in the 1860s. Blue jeans were later popularized by Western ranchers. The first Levi's pants made for women, Lady Levi's, were introduced in 1939. But Strauss refused to use the term "jeans," and they were initially known on the West Coast and among factory workers as dungarees or Californias. Then at the start of the rock era, actor James Dean defiantly wore blue jeans in public settings. Soon after, Elvis Presley was costumed in black denim for the film, *Jailhouse Rock*.

And when *American Bandstand* went on the air in 1957, the program inadvertently began influencing fashions. In addition to hearing the latest hit records and learning the newest dance steps, viewers were kept up to date on continually-changing youth fashions. Initially, the program maintained a strict dress code – boys wore suits and ties while girls donned dresses or long skirts. As author Marc Weingarten stated, some fashion trends on *Bandstand* "were born out of necessity. When girls from Philadelphia's West Catholic Parochial School wanted to conceal their starched uniforms for the television audience, they wore sweaters from which their stiff [round] shirt collars peaked through. That sparked the 'Philadelphia collar' craze which swept the Teenage Nation." Over time, the dress code on *Bandstand* was relaxed. Girls began wearing pants and increasingly short skirts, while boys abandoned their formal suits for sweaters or leisurely shirts. And thanks to rock and roll, teenagers began cultivating their own unique and, often, controversial fashions.

*   *   *   *   *   *

In the 1950s and early '60s, it was practically mandatory for rock groups to wear uniforms or matching stage outfits. As a rule, rock acts did not take the stage in their street clothes. The members of the Beatles had adopted a stage uniform of matching leather pants and jackets while playing in the nightclubs of Hamburg, Germany. Then, at the encouragement of Astrid Kirchherr, they wore similar mop-top hairstyles. Later, the group's new manager, Brian Epstein, took the group in a more mainstream direction with less-threatening, form-fitting, collarless suits. And when Ringo Starr joined the group as a replacement for Pete Best, he was forced to shave his beard. There would be no facial hair – at first – for any of the group's members.

However, the Rolling Stones singularly changed the rules of stage clothing. After their initial failure in 1963 to outdress the nattily-attired Beatles, Mick Jagger and his bandmates abandoned the strategy. Instead, they created a stir by taking the stage in street clothing or non-matching stage apparel. As designer Anna Sui observed: "You saw the scruffiness, the down-dressing that really didn't exist in the American vocabulary: the mismatched look, the leather jackets, adopting some of the traditional rhythm-and-blues style. And then, throwing in a pair of white shoes. It was just like, 'Wow, what is this?' That's how guys reacted. And to this day, you see guys dressing exactly that way."

Gene Simmons revealed the reason why the members of Kiss donned extravagant costumes and theatrical makeup: "When I used to go to the Fillmore East [theater in New York City], I'd see these guys onstage wearing jeans, and I would think, 'That's wrong. He should look bigger-than-life. He should look like a star.' When you see the guy, you should feel, 'Wow! Look at that!' He should blow your mind. When I first saw David Bowie, I thought it was the greatest thing in the world."

During the MTV era in the 1980s, musical acts were often identified by their stage clothing or visual image, whether Devo's yellow industrial suits, Adam and the Ants' pirate gear or the dramatic hairstyle of Mike Score, the lead singer of A Flock Of Seagulls. And while British-based New Wave acts typically wore bright, stylish suits with skinny ties or checkered t-shirts and plain tennis shoes, American heavy metal acts sported huge hair and wore gaudy make-up. While Madonna donned lacy wedding dresses and pointy bustiers, the members of the Go-Go's were spiffed up in bright, punky clothing and coiffed hair. Go-Go's guitarist Jane Wiedlin recalled: "Our signature thrift-store style became the rage across the country. Every night we'd be blinded by the sea of polka dots and stripes that our young female fans dressed up in. Our look became a mall staple."

By the 1990s, alternative and grunge bands avoided stage uniforms at all costs. But by the early-2000s, a number of alternative bands reintroduced uniforms to rock music. While the Killers wore black clothing and My Chemical Romance donned matching military-style jackets, Arcade Fire dressed in modern Nashville-style outfits and the White Stripes wore an amalgam of solid red, black and white attire.

However, some acts have intentionally disregarded audience expectations. In 1970, folk singer Phil Ochs provoked outrage at a Carnegie Hall concert when he appeared onstage in a shiny, gold lamé suit – similar to the outfit a young Elvis wore on the cover of the hit album, *50,000,000 Elvis Fans Can't Be Wrong*. And in 1983, Neil Young confounded his longtime fans by appearing onstage and in music videos as a rockabilly singer – with slicked-back hair, a shiny silk suit and a skinny, bright-pink tie – as he promoted the 1950s-style throwback album, *Everybody's Rockin'*. And in 2009, grunge-rock band Pearl Jam took the stage in Philadelphia, dressed in yellow Devo uniforms.

On the other hand, some artists avoid stage uniforms as a matter of practicality. Kim Deal, a member of both the Pixies and the Breeders, argued: "Why would anyone have stage clothes? It's just crazy. I have favorite t-shirts that I like. Ones I know the sleeves weren't too long and won't get in my way when I'm playing, stuff like that. Mainly it's about function. Like I know certain pants I can bend down and grab a beer if it's on the floor and it won't split or something."

LOOKING LIKE A ROCK STAR IN PUBLIC

Merely *looking* like a musician in public can elicit strong, positive reactions. Nightclub owner Manny Roth, the uncle of David Lee Roth, described the situation in New York City during the 1960s: "I was in the center of the scene there – all you had to do was carry an empty guitar case and girls would follow you."

Chris Cornell of Soundgarden recalled a similar experience in his youth: "Initially I was a drummer, and I remember standing somewhere in public with a pair of drumsticks, and these cute girls came up and started talking to me. We hadn't even played yet! It was actually uncomfortable. I thought, 'Is that all I have to do? Just hold drumsticks?' It immediately made me not like the girls." Likewise, years before he was a member of Motörhead, a teenage Lemmy was thinking about becoming a musician: "I took a guitar to school and was immediately surrounded by women. I couldn't play it, but with all due respect, you do have to learn a couple of chords eventually."

And in the 1990s, author Bob Greene joined the backing band of the surf-rock duo, Jan & Dean, for a series of concerts on the oldies circuit. Greene recalled: "I had been noticing something as I traveled: People seemed to feel compelled to come up to me and talk as I carried my guitar in its black case. I'd been lugging around standard business bags – carry-on suitcases, briefcases – for years. No one ever said a word. But as soon as I began carrying the Stratocaster, strangers appeared almost unable to help themselves. From the shape of the bag, there was clearly a guitar inside. People would approach to ask what kind it was, or to request that I unzip the case so they could have a look.... As I would lift it into overhead bins on airplanes, women – sometimes passengers, sometimes flight attendants – would occasionally run their hands over it. The reactions seemed impulsive, involuntary.... I'd lay the guitar case on a conveyer belt to go through the X-ray machine, would walk through the metal-detection portal to greet it on the other side, and find a security worker absentmindedly stroking it. I'd never encountered anyone stroking my canvas overnight bag."

Conversely, looking like a rock star can also elicit strong, *negative* reactions. Although Sonny and Cher were on top of the musical world in the mid-1960s due to their chart-topping hit "I Got You Babe," they were turned away from the posh American Hotel in New York City because of their oddball outfits. Surprisingly, their bohemian-style clothing was not a pre-planned gimmick. When the pair first began touring, Sonny usually wore a suit while Cher wore a simple blouse and skirt. But after losing their suitcases before a performance at the trendsetting Cow Palace in San Francisco, the duo was forced to hit the stage in their everyday, Southern California-style, hippie fashions. With the audience approving of their outfits, the duo wisely adopted the look at future shows.

And in the 1960s, male musicians with long hair were frequently the targets of scorn or violence. Led Zeppelin vocalist Robert Plant recalled: "I remember walking through Dearborn... with John Bonham in 1969, on a Sunday afternoon.... and some people went by in a big Lincoln Continental and they put the window down slowly and spat at us – because we were hippies. We were representing a challenge to the order." And when the Rolling Stones first toured the U.S. in the mid-1960s, they were harassed while traveling through Southern states, with the members of the band mockingly addressed as "miss" or "girl." Heartland rocker Bob Seger touched on the subject in the lyrics of his hit, "Turn The Page."

Slim Jim Phantom, the tattooed drummer of the Stray Cats, had a related problem when the retro rockabilly-style band first formed on Long Island, New York, in the late-1970s: "We loved dressing up and greasing our hair every day. We wound up being the local eccentrics who shocked everyone everywhere we went, and we embraced it. Every trip to 7-Eleven became a potential fight. There was no template for what we looked like. If we had dressed up like a classic rock 1970s front man with boas, sequined bell bottoms, and long hair or a Southern rock hippie, it would have been all right; the Saturday Night Fever disco-boy would have been pushing the envelope in our neighborhood but would've been accepted, but our look was totally foreign."

▶ CHAPTER 7
CRITICS VS. ROCKERS

Music critics tend to be arrogant, combative, opinionated and biased. More significantly, they have the ability to make or destroy careers. Consequently, musicians often have uneasy, adversarial relationships with music journalists. A writer for *The Hollywood Reporter* explained that in the music industry, "power and access came from three areas: you were the rock star; you were the drug dealer; or you were a powerful member of the press. Obviously, I was number three."

In the 1950s and much of the '60s, rock and roll was generally covered in the press by middle-aged journalists. These writers usually covered rock music as part of the teen section of a newspaper. Additionally, early rock magazines usually targeted female teens and featured a mish-mash of lightweight pieces with reporting that centered on a musician's clothing, personal tastes and dating aspirations. More serious rock journalism didn't emerge until the late-1960s with the arrival of magazines such as *Crawdaddy* and *Rolling Stone*.

To get hired as a newspaper or magazine reporter, a degree in journalism or English is usually required. However, in order to become a bonafide rock critic, a passion and understanding of the music scene were often the only requirements. Lester Bangs, the most notorious rock critic of the 1970s, had dropped out of community college after just one semester. Similarly, *Rolling Stone* founder Jann Wenner left college at age 20.

One rock critic revealed how he landed his coveted position at the young age of 22: "When I arrived at *The El Paso Times*... fresh from college [I was asked] would I like to be the paper's music critic? Of course I would. It was like being handed a license without having to take any exams, a license that granted me front-row tickets to all the big concerts, and phone interviews during which I could indulge in the fantasy that, for example, Edie Brickell and I really were pals.... [And] I was suddenly up to my eyeballs in free music. I could call any record company on earth and direct them to send me an album.... I should mention, mostly for my own embarrassment, that I was called upon to review many other genres about which I knew next to nothing, such as jazz and classical, the latter including a young harpist whom I inevitably compared to Harpo Marx."

With the maturing of rock and roll, writing about the genre became a serious business. In 1961, *New York Times* critic Robert Shelton announced the arrival of Bob Dylan with the headline "20-Year-Old Singer is Bright New Face at Gerde's Club." And in 1974, Jon Landau wrote: "I saw rock and roll future and its name is Bruce Springsteen." The following year, Springsteen appeared on the covers of both *Newsweek* and *Time*, and was heralded as "Rock's New Sensation."

However, rock critics sometimes completely blow it. Writing for *Rolling Stone*, Jon Landau trashed the debut album by Jimi Hendrix, which featured soon-to-be classic tracks such as "Purple Haze" and "Hey Joe." Landau wrote: "The poor quality of the songs and the inanity of the lyrics too often get in the way." Amazingly, critics at *Rolling Stone* would also pan the debut album by Led Zeppelin, *Harvest* by Neil Young, *Exile On Main Street* by the Rolling Stones and *Blood On The Tracks* by Bob Dylan.

Similarly, the Beatles were harshly lambasted by multiple critics in the 1960s. William F. Buckley, Jr. wrote: "The Beatles are not merely awful; I would consider it sacrilegious to say anything less than that they are god awful. They are so unbelievably [horrible], so appallingly unmusical, so dogmatically insensitive to the magic of the art that they qualify as crowned heads of anti-music." Similarly, a *Los Angeles Times* critic declared: "With their bizarre shrubbery, the Beatles are obviously a press agent's dream combo. Not even their mothers would claim that they sing well. But the hirsute thickets they affect make them rememberable, and they project a certain kittenish charm which drives the immature, shall we say, ape." And *The New York Times* offered: "The Beatles' vocal quality can be described as hoarsely incoherent, with the minimal enunciation necessary to communicate the schematic texts."

Oftentimes – as the cliche goes – music writers were attracted to careers in rock criticism because of their failed aspirations to be rock stars. But a number of music critics did in fact become hit rock artists. After Chrissie Hynde arrived in London in 1973, she wrote for *New Musical Express*. Likewise, before he was the frontman for the Smiths, singer Morrissey was the president of the New York Dolls fan club in England as well as a music writer for *Record Mirror*. And Mark Knopfler of Dire Straits worked as a music critic for *The Yorkshire Evening Post* while pursuing a bachelor's degree in English. In 1970,

Knopfler penned an obituary of Jimi Hendrix for the paper.

Some successful musicians became rock critics *after* finding chart success. In 1963, George Harrison was a columnist for the British newspaper, *The Daily Express*. In 1970, Pete Townshend began writing a monthly column for *Melody Maker*. And in 2010, Ozzy Osbourne was hired as a "health columnist" by *The Times of London*. Additionally, a few rock critics enjoyed success as songwriters: Richard Meltzer co-wrote the Blue Öyster Cult hit "Burnin' For You," while David Ritz co-wrote Marvin Gaye's 1982 comeback hit, "Sexual Healing."

*   *   *   *   *   *

There is a proper methodology for conducting an interview, and not all rock journalists have grasped the intricacies of the process. A Midwestern newspaper reporter offered some important pointers on the art of questioning entertainers: "Remember this: An interview is either explicitly or implicitly a negotiation. Both reporter and subject want something, the former looking for a good story, the latter for a favorable presentation about a person, a project or an issue. Each wants a measure of control over the conversation. Even before the interview begins, there may be discussions about what can and cannot be discussed; the interview itself can find reporter and subject steering the talk, and afterward there may be attempts to rephrase, reconfigure or simply erase something that was said." In the end, the journalists want to look good and sell more papers, while the artists also want to look good and to sell more albums and concert tickets.

Musical acts will often schedule media days when releasing a new album or starting a tour. Journalists make appointments to get their 10 or 15 minutes of questions over the phone. Before the interviews, most artists will make notes and are ready to offer preplanned answers for likely questions. Oftentimes, the artists will provide the same replies to the exact same questions, twenty times in a day.

And when an act tours, the local press will request access for interviews and photos. While major acts mostly ignore these requests, mid-level and emerging acts need all the free publicity they can muster. Before the rise of Clear Channel and other radio giants, locally-owned radio stations welcomed these touring bands into their studios for interviews and even on-air performances.

Of course, few artists actually enjoy giving interviews. Tom Petty lamented: "[Interviews] get brutal. They (the record companies) put in 15 a day and don't even think twice about it. After you've done that for about a week, you're really batty and you don't know what you think about anything. You're just talking and an hour later you've got an entirely different opinion than what you told this poor cat that's going to print it up. It's a real strange syndrome. It's like you're assuming a position of authority and I'm not. I'm not an authority on anything. And sometimes you just go so crazy you don't know what you're saying. I've had terrible troubles with interviews and it'll come back and I'll go 'Oh God! Did I really say that?'"

Noel Redding, the bassist for the Jimi Hendrix Experience, recalled: "We sometimes felt incapable of facing journalistic brain-pickers and trying again to come up with something fresh, witty, incisive, clever and intelligent. Jimi tended to play the spaced-out refugee from Planet X, leaving the interviewers to interpret it as they wished."

And while Frank Zappa despised members of the rock press, Bob Dylan often toyed with them. Robbie Robertson, the guitarist of the Band, recalled: "Very few artists have done more entertaining press conferences than Bob. Bizarre, quick, challenging answers were dished out faster than the reporters or music writers could digest. In the past he'd made entire rooms explode with laughter or frustration as he fielded pretentious questions." In the documentary *Don't Look Back*, Dylan viciously savaged a journalist in Newcastle, England, for asking inane questions. Dylan's disgust with journalists was laid bare in his 1965 track, "Ballad Of A Thin Man." Likewise, in 1977, Lou Reed downed half a bottle of scotch and then said to writer Allan Jones of *Melody Maker* magazine: "It's been a long time since I spoke to any journalists. This afternoon, I've been interviewed twice. Now I remember why I gave up speaking to journalists. They are a species of foul vermin. I wouldn't hire people like you to guard my sewer. Journalists are morons. They're idiots. They're ignorant and stupid."

Similarly, Ian Hunter declared in his autobiography: "My only beef, one that really gets me going, is the press. Those [guys] can ruin a beautiful day, I can never quite understand how a guy from a northern weekly paper can be brought down to London and suddenly transformed into a knowledgeable critic – qualified to knock, laud or misinterpret the work of someone like Hendrix or Morrison. Sometimes you find these guys have been in bands themselves and think they're ten times better than the musicians they're criticizing. Basically, all but a very few journalists are fans. They set stars up then wait for the next issue to pull them down. They have their favorite artists who can do no wrong, and they have dislikes which they continually air. I remember once reading an article in *Melody Maker* saying, '...The 700-strong crowd at Liverpool

Stadium went mad...' The stadium holds about 4,000 people, but the reviewer disguises this because he digs the band. Had it been a band he didn't like, he would have put, '... A three-quarter empty hall turned up to see so-and-so – are they on the way out?'" Likewise, former music journalist Neil Tennant recalled how his synth-pop duo, the Pet Shop Boys, was once ambushed by the press: "*The Sun* [newspaper] in England did an interview with us and asked us our views on all sorts of different subjects – pop stars and films and clothes and TV – and then they only printed everything nasty we'd said. And then they said we were the rudest men in rock."

A number of notable rock acts have been notoriously savaged by the press. Meat Loaf recalled the initial reactions from rock critics to his blockbuster album, *Bat Out Of Hell*: "When 'Bat' came out there was 10 people maybe that liked it; and out of hundreds of reviews, we got one good review from *The Cleveland Plain Dealer*." And British New Wave artist Gary Numan recalled the antagonism he faced at the start of his career: "The level of hostility was extreme. One newspaper said my mum and dad should have been sterilized. Really?" Likewise, Grand Funk Railroad were infamously abused by rock writers. Although the Detroit-based rock act reliably filled stadiums and received heavy radio airplay with rock anthems such as "We're An American Band" and "Some Kind Of Wonderful," they were dismissed by serious music scribes.

Similarly, decades before Freddie Mercury achieved near-sainthood with the release of the film biography *Bohemian Rhapsody*, Queen was habitually scorned by the press. In 1981, *Rolling Stone* writer Jim Henke said of the group: "The rhythm section is sloppy and sluggish; [Brian] May's guitar playing is limited to heavy-metal/hard-rock clichés and patented, though by now boring, harmonic lead breaks; Mercury's singing is lackadaisical and without conviction. 'They're not even up to the par of some third-rate New Jersey bar band,' another writer comments to me, and indeed, I'm somewhat mystified about what it is that makes this group so popular."

A number of hit artists have openly expressed hurt feelings over negative reviews. In the 1960s, pop singer Connie Francis was frequently targeted by critics. In her autobiography, she wrote: "No one mentions that, although certain questions shock and pierce your sensibilities, you must nevertheless remain gracious and sweet while you answer them. Nor do they tell you how harsh the words of critics, especially those you know don't like you very much, render you powerless, and how some of those words are forever written in your heart. Nor do they let you know that there are any number of people out there – some of whom you've never met – who are rooting for you to fall flat on your face." And late in life, Paul McCartney admitted, "I do albums and, like a fool, I listen to what people say about them. A *New York Times* critic damned *Sgt. Pepper* when it came out. The terrible thing is it puts you off your own stuff. It plays into your self-doubts, even though you overcame those self-doubts to write that song."

Even a sneering punk rocker like John Lydon – better known as Johnny Rotten – was rattled by the ugly barrages of music critics. In 2017, he revealed: "The things that hurt the most are when you get attacked verbally. Words can be incredibly damaging. They can hit you in the soul, in places you thought were private."

Major acts sometimes set ground rules before agreeing to speak with a journalist. In 1989, when Mick Jagger agreed to give an interview to ABC, the network had to abide by his strict terms. According to an insider, Jagger "wanted no unnecessary people at ABC while he was there. No secretaries, no receptionists, no cleaning ladies, no exceptions. He didn't want anyone asking for his autograph or talking to him. He was going to use the building's back entrance, slip into the radio studio around 10 a.m., conduct his one-hour taping, and leave. If anyone inside that building approached him with a camera or pen, he'd exit before doing the interview." Similarly, in 2016, Tom Jones declared that "there should be no questions concerning Tom's family, the recent death of his wife, Elvis or underwear." And it was no surprise that Axl Rose of Guns N' Roses required journalists to sign a lengthy contract before an interview was granted. The document demanded the complete control of the final, written article.

Sadly, a number of major artists – including Bruce Springsteen, Leonard Cohen, Neil Young, Joni Mitchell and Bob Dylan – rarely granted interviews in the latter portions of their careers. In 2017, the music critic for a large newspaper wrote: "Billy Joel isn't talking. Anthony Kiedis, Flea and Chad Smith wouldn't talk. Nor will Neil Diamond, Paul Simon, Dave Matthews, Tim McGraw, Faith Hill or even one of the darn New Kids on the Block. We in the media are dead to Bob Weir et al, had no chance with Chance the Rapper, were not allowed to be part of Queen's court, and Bono and the Edge still aren't giving the interview that we're looking for. The result is a growing disconnect between artists and their fans that in my mind is tantamount to a disregard for the people who have made them rich and famous."

However, Elton John has argued that refusing to grant media interviews actually helps artists cultivate a public persona: "Mystique is the greatest thing you could possibly have. People think they know me, but they just talk about the hair, the glasses, the spending. They didn't know anything about me. I never do interviews anymore. Your mystique is your biggest asset. It's what Prince had."

*   *   *   *   *   *

In the world of hip hop, a completely different ethos existed between performers and critics. Amazingly, music writers grew to fear rappers. In 1998, *The New York Times* reported: "Threats and assaults by rappers and others in the industry are becoming increasingly common, leaving some journalists operating in an atmosphere of intimidation and self-censorship. In a recent case, the editor in chief of *Blaze* [magazine]... was stomped in the face and struck with chairs by four men, two of whom he recognized as rap producers. The police say the assault, which took place last month in a conference room in the magazine's Manhattan office, left the 29-year-old editor, Jesse Washington, with head cuts and facial fractures. Mr. Washington, who said the beating was over a photograph of one artist/producer, has pressed charges against two of the men, who have denied beating Mr. Washington. 'When four guys have you on the ground kicking you in the head, it's for real,' said Mr. Washington, who is considering plastic surgery. 'My face got pretty wrecked. The fact that I didn't want my Mom to see me for a while tells you how serious it was.'"

Similarly, in 2017, when Eminem released his ninth studio album, *Revival*, the project was mostly skewered by music critics. In response, the rapper released a remix of one of the album's tracks, "Chloraseptic," which featured stinging attacks against the writers who knocked the project.

Conversely, in the rock world, physical attacks against members of the rock press are quite rare. However, in 1999, *Spin* editor Craig Marks was allegedly assaulted by members of Marilyn Manson's security team after the controversial rocker was not given a promised cover by the magazine. And notable British rock journalist Nick Kent was assaulted by Sid Vicious, who swung a motorcycle chain at the scribe during a Sex Pistols show at the 100 Club in London. But the most infamous attack on a rock journalist occurred in 1978 when Black Sabbath guitarist Tony Iommi viciously assaulted *Melody Maker* writer Allan Jones for penning an unflattering article. According to Jones, British rocker Alex Harvey subsequently offered to make Iommi "disappear." In the wake of the attack, music journalists avoided face-to-face interviews with Iommi for a number of years.

With the rise of social media in the internet age, the rules of music criticism were completely rewritten. Suddenly, everyone with a blog, podcast or Facebook account could be a critic with a sizable audience.

DEALING WITH PAPARAZZI

With the ascent of the 24-hour news cycle and the emergence of online gossip sites, the demand for celebrity news and photos has increased dramatically. The celebrity gossip machine gave rise to a new breed of aggressive photographers known as paparazzi. Mostly based in Los Angeles, New York and London, paparazzi will follow a target until they get their shots – regardless of the risks.

Not surprisingly, rockers resort to various means to counter intrusive photographers. In 2007, *Blender* magazine chronicled an attempt by Britney Spears to elude a team of paparazzi: "Britney drives like a rabbit being chased across a field. Trailed by 15 cars, she signals right, then turns left. Glides into a left-turn lane, makes a right. On Wilshire Boulevard, slows from 50 miles per hour down to 15, then bangs an illegal U-turn into brake-screeching traffic. The [paparazzi] driver in the lead mutters, 'bitch'.... The Britney chase feels like a video game where, every moment, you're sure you're going to die."

Most rockers rely on bodyguards to shield them from pushy photographers. Using another strategy, shock rocker Marilyn Manson once wrote a number of obscenities on his mouth and neck, shortly before arriving at a Los Angeles airport in 2002, in an attempt to devalue the photos taken by paparazzi. But the stunt backfired and the freakish shots of Manson appeared in numerous magazines and online forums. And in 2014, Steven Tyler revealed that he used high-tech thermal-imaging binoculars to ward off intruders: "[It] takes night vision one step further. I use it for paparazzi and shit around the house in Maui, just to check if they're lurking about."

However, the public treated celebrities far differently in the past. An entertainment writer remembered an afternoon in 1965 that she spent on the streets of Los Angeles with the members of the Supremes: "There we were walking along Hollywood Blvd. with no bodyguards or security. People recognized them and waved, but it was just fun. What an innocent time. No guns. No celebrity assassination, no stupid TMZ or the internet."

▶ CHAPTER 8
BAND POLITICS

There is a unique dynamic within every rock group. By default, the lead singer is the head of the band and the most difficult member to replace. Sometimes there are two strong personalities – usually the lead singer and the guitarist – and a co-leadership exists. Such was the case with Steven Tyler and Joe Perry; Axl Rose and Slash; and brothers Liam and Noel Gallagher. And while Mick Jagger and Keith Richards battled over control of the Rolling Stones, their bandmate Brian Jones – who was fired in 1969 – would publicly refer to himself as the leader of the group.

In the early years of the Beatles, reporters often asked who led the group. With both John Lennon and Paul McCartney co-writing nearly all of the group's material and providing the vast majority of lead vocals, the only obvious thing about the band's leadership was that Ringo and George were not in charge. Art Garfunkel of the 1960s hit duo Simon and Garfunkel recalled: "George [Harrison] came up to me at a party once and said 'my Paul is to me what your Paul is to you.' He meant that psychologically they had the same effect on us. The Pauls sidelined us. I think George felt suppressed by Paul and I think that's what he saw with me and my Paul. Here's the truth: McCartney was a helluva music man who gave the band its energy, but he also ran away with a lot of the glory."

And for better or worse, rock bands are usually described as "families." When you spend countless hours in cramped vans, motel rooms and restaurant booths with the same four or five people, the rock group unit begins to exhibit many of the same characteristics as a non-traditional blended family. Richie Furay, who co-founded the Buffalo Springfield in 1966, observed: "If you've ever been part of such a tight-knit team – in music or sports or any other endeavor – you know the power that is generated by that type of unity. You have to be a group player in those situations, and by understanding your strengths and weaknesses, the whole becomes stronger than the separate parts. The minute that bond starts to fail, though, everything begins to unravel, and before you know what's happening, you're beyond the point of rescue."

As a band grows in popularity and there's a need to hire new employees, the unit then resembles an extended family – like having uncles, in-laws, and cousins all living in the same household. With these changes, the members spend more time apart and the band dynamic evolves. As a rule, the more successful a band gets, the less time the members spend with each other.

Conversely, some bands resemble dysfunctional families whose members stay together for the sole purpose of working toward a common goal – becoming rich and successful. Roger Daltrey of the Who admitted in his autobiography: "Pete [Townshend] describes us as 'four people who should have never been in a band together.' Given our differences, given all the fighting and the fallings-out, it's a miracle we stuck it out through that first decade. Of course, there were many, many times when we almost didn't, but I'm not as surprised as everyone else that we survived. Even in the darkest days, I was never going to give up." And keyboardist Benmont Tench of Tom Petty and the Heartbreakers revealed: "I don't want to name names, but a lot of bands go out together and just don't like each other. They're making a lot of money and just checking in."

Likewise, in 1987, Roger Waters of Pink Floyd stated: "A band can only be a band if the people within it have some common ground, musically, politically, or philosophically. They need to have a certain amount of common ground in all those areas, just like in a marriage, and we no longer did. Sometimes you go on in a marriage because of the kids, and the bands go on longer than they should. Pink Floyd probably went on ten years longer that we should have."

However, the addition or loss of a band member can often change a band's dynamic – sometimes for the better, other times for the worse. As Beatles scholar Melissa Davis observed: "I think it's important to remember that the Beatles didn't *click* until they were John, Paul, George and Ringo. The lineup was important to their development at each step of the way, from the Quarry Men and the Silver Beatles to John, Paul, George, Stuart and Pete. But they only became the Beatles when all the pieces fell into place with that last change in August 1962."

BAND INFIGHTING

Much like traditional families, most rock bands tend to keep their dirty laundry out of the press. Revealing the details of an ugly squabble is never good for band morale. And yet these private disputes can become public if the lead singer or guitarist finds himself with a book contract – or after he is kicked out of the band.

There have been a number of legendary, internal spats in the world of rock and roll. When Beach Boys members Mike Love and Brian Wilson weren't trading barbs, they were battling each other in a courtroom. In Van Halen, there was quite a bit of bad blood, especially after David Lee Roth was fired by Eddie Van Halen. And British singer Morrissey publicly stated in 2006: "I would rather eat my own testicles than reform the Smiths, and that's saying something for a vegetarian." Even a manufactured band like the Monkees wasn't immune from hostile disagreements. During one such altercation, Peter Tork was head-butted by the group's diminutive singer Davy Jones. After Tork retaliated with a punch to Jones' face, both men had to be taken to the hospital.

However, the constant dustups between the Gallagher brothers in the Britpop band Oasis dominated the rock press during the band's entire 18-year run. Finally, on August 28, 2009, shortly before the band was about to take the stage at a music festival near Paris, Noel and Liam Gallagher were involved in a fracas that ended with the smashing of guitars. After Noel stormed out of the venue, the band's manager announced to the disappointed audience that Oasis "does not exist anymore." Soon after, Noel posted a message on the band's website: "I simply could not go on working with Liam a day longer."

Likewise, during the middle of a tour in 1973, the Everly Brothers had an onstage altercation. After Don Everly showed up inebriated and then botched the lyrics of the duo's hit "Cathy's Clown," the brothers began quarreling. Eventually, Phil chucked his guitar and shouted: "I'm through with being an Everly Brother." At a subsequent show, his brother Don attempted to perform on his own and was met with heckling from the audience. Responding to the hecklers, Don shouted: "The Everly Brothers died ten years ago." And with that declaration, the duo would remain estranged for the next decade.

Similarly, brothers John and Tom Fogerty of Creedence Clearwater Revival maintained a very public war of words until Tom's death in 1990. John Fogerty recalled the origins of the power struggle within the swamp-rock group: "We went into RCA studio and knocked out most of *Bayou County*. The difficulty came when we started to do overdubs.... Doug [Clifford] clearly couldn't keep the rhythm. But the real [issue] was vocalizing. The guys wanted to sing the backgrounds on 'Proud Mary.' I knew it was a pretty good song; I wanted it to be as good as it could be. From the day I had gotten my tape recorder in 1962, I had been harmonizing with myself. I knew how to do that like tying your shoe. There was a big fight in the studio. I think I made a speech in the studio and again at dinner. I said, 'It doesn't matter who plays what. What matters is it's us against the rest of the world.' We gotta make the best record this band can make. The logic of that kept the guys in the band quiet for a while. But it was a time bomb. Eventually, they couldn't swallow that. They didn't want the band to make the best record it could make. They wanted to have access to the glory.... So the last years of the band was me listening to three guys who were jealous, and full of negativity."

Meanwhile, Linda Ramone was often called "the Yoko Ono of punk rock" for breaking up with Joey Ramone and then subsequently dating his bandmate, Johnny Ramone. Except for an occasional word in their crowded touring van, the two men would rarely speak to each other afterwards. But tensions within the band were nothing new. Chris Frantz of Talking Heads recalled watching a performance by the Ramones at CBGB in the late-1970s: "They were crazy. They'd be on stage playing and then they'd just stop and start fighting."

Similarly, soul superstars Sam & Dave may have been a powerful twosome on the stage, but in 1968 Sam Moore turned against Dave Prater. That year, Moore watched his musical partner shoot his wife in the face during an argument. Over the next twelve-years, the two men would continue to tour without uttering a single word to each other after leaving the stage.

And after a series of well-publicized conflicts among the members of the Eagles, the hit group imploded in July 1980 during a fundraising concert for presidential hopeful, Senator Alan Cranston. While performing their hit "The Best Of My Love," Glenn Frey walked over to Don Felder and allegedly made a threat: "I'm going to kick your ass when we get off the stage." Felder later recalled: "As the night progressed, we both grew angrier and began hissing at each other under our breaths. In the sound booth, the technicians feared the audience might actually hear our outbursts, so they lowered Glenn's microphone until he had to sing. He continued to approach me after every song to rant, rave, curse, and let me know how many songs remained before our fight. 'That's three more, pal, Glenn said. 'Get Ready.'" After the show, an enraged Frey chased after Felder's limo. In the aftermath of the altercation, the frazzled members of the Eagles realized it was time to disband.

However, public conflicts are sometimes unavoidable. Neil Young called the annual Rock and Roll Hall of Fame induction ceremonies the perfect forum for airing dirty laundry and revisiting festering disputes: "You never knew what to expect.... People spoke off the top of their heads or from a little cheat sheet of paper. People cried and laughed and settled scores. A lot of them settled scores. There was a lot to say for some of them and this was their best chance." In 2006, Debbie Harry traded barbs with two former members of Blondie who had unsuccessfully sued to rejoin the band. And in 2012, Creedence Clearwater Revival drummer Doug Clifford and bassist Stu Cook were livid with John Fogerty for refusing to perform with his former bandmates.

Likewise, Guns N' Roses singer Axl Rose, who was feuding at the time with former bandmates Duff McKagan and Slash, refused to attend the group's induction. He explained his position in a letter to *The Los Angeles Times*: "I strongly request that I not be inducted in absentia and please know that no one is authorized nor may anyone be permitted to accept any induction for me or speak on my behalf. Neither former members, label representatives nor the Rock And Roll Hall Of Fame should imply whether directly, indirectly or by omission that I am included in any purported induction of 'Guns N' Roses.'"

Meanwhile, the advent of the rock supergroup usually resulted in clashes of bloated egos. As a result, many of these outfits collapsed after just a single album or tour. For every Traveling Wilburys who sold millions of albums, there were a dozen all-star projects that fared poorly. Similarly, during the sessions for the all-star charity single, "We Are The World" by USA For Africa, the performers were told to check their egos at the door. Paul Simon remembered that he "expected to see more ego – you know, 'The Gloved One' meets 'The Boss' and things like that – but it didn't happen."

Superstar acts also suffer similar ego conflicts, whether Fleetwood Mac, Van Halen or the Eagles. David Spero, the former manager of Joe Walsh, described the unbearable hostility during the Eagles' Hell Freezes Over reunion tour in 1994: "You had five guys with five different assistants. They arrived at the hotel from the airport in five different vans. In the hotel, they had rooms on five different floors. At the show, they stayed in five different dressing rooms. Nobody hung out. No cameras were allowed anywhere. Everyone was guarded and tense."

Worse yet, violence is commonplace within certain bands. In Lynyrd Skynyrd, vocalist Ronnie Van Zant – who in his youth had aspired to be a boxer – was clearly the leader and authoritarian enforcer. If his bandmates made a mistake during a performance, they knew to expect consequences after the show, including vicious words and an angry punch or two. On one occasion, Van Zant struck keyboardist Billy Powell in the face, knocking out several teeth. Similarly, drummer John French claimed he was "screamed at, beaten up, drugged, ridiculed, humiliated, arrested, starved, stolen from, and thrown down a half-flight of stairs" by his eccentric musical boss of many years, Captain Beefheart.

And although brothers Ray and Dave Davies of the Kinks engaged in a number of legendary violent exchanges, the group's drummer Mick Avory infamously attacked Dave Davies in May 1965 during a concert in Cardiff, Wales. Believing he had killed Davies, Avory fled the theater and went into hiding. Injured but alive, Davies was rushed to a hospital where he received sixteen stitches for a deep gash in his head.

Even a former Beatle had the capacity to get violent. At a 1976 Paul McCartney and Wings concert in Boston, guitarist Jimmy McCulloch refused to return to the stage for an encore. McCartney subsequently chased McCulloch into the band's dressing room and reportedly "smacked" him. McCulloch reconsidered his decision and returned to the stage. And Mick Jagger was notoriously punched in the face by bandmate Charlie Watts for referring to him as "my drummer."

GETTING KICKED OUT OF YOUR OWN BAND

Getting fired from your band can happen for a variety of reasons: musical differences, personality conflicts, inadequate musical skills, missed rehearsals and – most commonly – substance abuse. In the early-1950s, the Dominoes were one of the top R&B groups in the nation. Formed by manager Billy Ward – an overbearing miser – he fired lead singer Clyde McPhatter for the offense of asking for a small increase in his meager wages. And in 1962, drummer Pete Best was infamously booted from the Beatles and replaced by Ringo Starr shortly after the group signed a recording contract with EMI.

The Rolling Stones booted two members in the 1960s. Founding member Ian Stewart was fired because his image was considered wrong for the group; later, Brian Jones was fired due to his unreliability and worsening drug use. The same thing happened to Syd Barrett in Pink Floyd, whose excessive use of LSD had diminished his skills as a musician. Similarly, guitarist Pete Willis of Def Leppard was fired during the middle of the *Pyromania* sessions and was replaced by Phil Collen; as vocalist Joe Elliott recalled: "We all drank, don't get me wrong, but when we drank we just told dirtier jokes a little louder. Pete caused problems. He was disruptive and negative. The band had to come first." And Ozzy Osbourne was booted from Black Sabbath in 1979 due to chronic substance abuse. The last straw came when a drunken Ozzy was passed out in a hotel room while his bandmates were forced to perform a concert without their lead singer.

Some expulsions were for far more unusual reasons. Bass player Doug Bogie was fired from an early lineup of Queen for jumping around the stage too much during performances. And in 1991, Poison guitarist C.C. DeVille played the wrong song during a performance at the annual MTV Video Music Awards. Afterwards, he was involved in an ugly backstage fistfight with bandmate Bret Michaels and was fired. Five years later, DeVille rejoined the group.

Like DeVille, a few ousted musicians were able to return to their bands. In early-1966, singer Roger Daltrey was fired from the Who after punching Keith Moon and flushing the eccentric drummer's drugs down the toilet. After briefly recruiting Boz Burrell as a replacement singer, the Who agreed to rehire Daltrey on the condition he refrained from brawling with his bandmates.

And following the firing of Michelle Phillips from the Mamas and the Papas on her 22nd birthday in 1966, she subsequently attended the group's concerts – often sitting in the front row and staring at her replacement, Jill Gibson. Eventually, the group relented and Phillips was asked to return.

David Ruffin of the Temptations was not as fortunate. Abusing drugs and regularly missing shows, he was booted from the hit Motown vocal group in 1968 and replaced by Dennis Edwards. But Ruffin would not accept his dismissal. Showing up at the group's concerts, he would climb onto the stage. Temptations biographer Mark Ribowsky recalled the awkward scene at a concert in Valley Forge, Pennsylvania: "Just as Edwards was breaking into lead vocal of 'Ain't Too Proud To Beg'... Ruffin took the microphone from his hand" and began singing. "For a split second, no one knew what to do. The Temptations shuffled on, tried to act nonchalantly. [The Temptations' business manager Don] Foster began frantically calling security. Then as the audience recognized the shadowy figure as David Ruffin, a festive mood grew in the hall. What no one knew was that Ruffin had bought his way into the arena" as a paying customer. Eventually, the Temptations resorted to hiring extra security guards to keep Ruffin from jumping onto the stage. Although Ruffin was later offered a second chance with the group, he failed to show up for his first scheduled concert and was fired for good.

More often, performers simply want to move on after a respectable run of success. Bob Welch amicably left Fleetwood Mac at the end of

1974 and even stuck around to teach his replacement, Lindsey Buckingham, the guitar parts to the group's songs. (Buckingham wouldn't be as fortunate when he was unceremoniously fired from the group in 2018.) However, Steven Van Zandt regretted walking away from Bruce Springsteen's backing band in 1984: "It's the one defining moment of my life. It was a mistake I've never recovered from. Financially, it was apocalyptic. That said, we did take years off the life of the South African government [Van Zandt created Artists United Against Apartheid in 1985]. But is that worth losing all of my friends, all of my power base, all my juice, all my celebrity capital, to save a few lives? And you've got to say, 'Yeah, sure. It was.' But I look back and think, 'Jeez, if only I could've done those things and stayed.' I would've had the perfect life."

Unluckily, some musicians leave shortly before their band makes it big. Such was the misfortune of Duran Duran singer Stephen Duffy, bassist Andy Nicholson of the Arctic Monkeys, guitarist John Berry of the Beastie Boys, drummer John Kiffmeyer of Green Day and guitarist Tracii Guns of Guns N' Roses. And although Dave Mustaine was forced out of an early lineup of Metallica in 1983, he went on to form another noteworthy metal band, Megadeth.

REPLACEMENT LEAD SINGERS

While some bands continued to thrive after replacing their lead singers, most did not. Rock bands with replacement lead singers tend to fare poorly and are often relegated to oldies status or second-tier venues. Released in 1996, a Talking Heads album without frontman David Byrne was panned by both fans and critics. And when J. Geils' vocalist Peter Wolf quit in 1983 after a 16-year stint, the group ended its long, hit run on the charts. Likewise, Mötley Crüe without Vince Neil as the lead singer struggled to fill venues in the mid-1990s.

And although Van Halen has had three different lead singers – David Lee Roth, Sammy Hagar and Gary Cherone – it was Roth who remained the face of the band, even after he left in 1985. While the Hagar-fronted version of the group sold more records and had more chart hits, it was Roth who provided the band with its personality and swagger. (Surprisingly, Hagar and Roth went on a double-headlining tour in 2002. Although the "Sam and Dave" tour began on friendly terms, the final two tour dates were cancelled due to growing animosity between the two rock stars.)

Most often, the sudden death of a lead singer quickly finishes off a band. After the passing of Jim Morrison, the remaining members of the Doors auditioned several singers. In the end, the band soldiered on with Ray Manzarek and Robby Krieger sharing the lead vocal duties. The pared-down trio would record two poorly-selling albums, including the aptly titled, *Other Voices*, before disbanding in 1973. However, three decades after the Lizard King had overdosed in Paris, Manzarek and Krieger hired British rocker Ian Astbury of the Cult to perform as the Doors of the 21st Century. After a number of concerts, Doors drummer John Densmore won a permanent injunction barring the group from performing as the Doors. Ultimately, the group was billed as Riders On The Storm. Similarly, following the death of Queen legend Freddie Mercury, a number of guest vocalists – including Paul Rodgers – would front the group for a series of tours.

More typically, lead singers voluntarily leave their own bands as was the case when Steve Perry quit Journey in 1987. Eventually, Journey would find a replacement singer on YouTube, Filipino-based Arnel Pineda. (When Journey was inducted into the Rock and Roll Hall of Fame in 2018, it was Pineda who took the stage to perform the group's signature hit, "Don't Stop Believin'.")

Similarly, Judas Priest found a replacement singer in an unconventional manner. After leather-clad frontman Rob Halford left the group in 1992, he was replaced by Tim Owens, a young singer who headed a Judas Priest cover band in Ohio. Although the other members of Judas Priest were thrilled with Owens' vocal delivery and stage presence, there was an unfortunate downside. As guitarist K.K. Downing recalled: "Despite all the positivity, we still had that age-old problem when, the moment we came offstage, the first thing some fans would say wouldn't be, 'Hey, guys, what a great show...' Instead we'd get, 'Hey K.K., when's Rob coming back?' There was a lot of that." (Upon Rob Halford's decision to rejoin Judas Priest in 2003, Owens was dismissed from the group.)

On rare occasions, hit bands find greater success with their replacement singers. Australian heavy metal act AC/DC continued to thrive after Brian Johnson replaced Bon Scott, and subsequently enjoyed a strong run on rock radio in the 1980s. Similarly, after Peter Gabriel's departure from Genesis, drummer Phil Collins did a commendable job as the group's new singer, with the new lineup garnering a great deal of chart success.

MULTIPLE VERSIONS OF THE SAME BAND

When a rock band splits up or an important member leaves, there are often ugly words and expensive lawsuits. Additionally, these conflicts can also lead to competing versions of the same group. There were two touring versions of the classic rock group Foghat from 1990 to 1993. Similarly, there were multiple versions of the British ska band, the English Beat. And in 2008, UB40 singer Ali Campbell left the pop-reggae group to form his own lineup of the act. In turn, the original version of UB40 hired Ali's brother, Duncan, as his replacement. Consequently, the siblings stopped speaking with one another.

Similarly, the constant infighting among the members of Jefferson Airplane/Starship resulted in the splintering of the group and a series of subsequent lawsuits over ownership of the band's name; the same thing occurred with the Byrds as numerous incarnations of the folk-rock group hit the concert road in the 1970s and '80s. And during a turbulent period of the Bee Gees history in the early-1970s, one of the backing musicians attempted to take over the group!

Meanwhile, the Black Crowes were plagued by bouts of sibling rivalry during their entire run. When brothers Chris and Rich Robinson had a serious falling out in 2013, both men formed competing groups. While one band was called the Magpie Salute, the other was known as the Crow Flies. In another case of intense sibling rivalry, brothers Tom and John Fogerty of Creedence Clearwater Revival frequently battled over the direction of the band, which culminated with the departure of Tom Fogerty in 1971. And in the 1980s when two members of CCR – drummer Doug Clifford and bassist Stu Cook – began to tour as Creedence Clearwater Revisited, they were unsuccessfully sued by John Fogerty.

FRICTION BETWEEN ARTISTS

Oftentimes, there is friction between major artists during a tour, especially when determining who gets the top billing and closes out the show. In the 1950s, Chuck Berry and Jerry Lee Lewis nearly came to blows on numerous occasions over the issue. In an often-repeated story, Lewis once lost an argument and agreed to let Berry close a show. Lewis gave the performance of a lifetime, during which he set his piano on fire. As he left the stage, a particularly satisfied Lewis said to Berry, "Top that."

In 1963, when the Beatles were still unknown in America, they went on a tour across Britain with visiting American singer Roy Orbison as the headlining act. Early in the tour, John Lennon and Beatles manager Brian Epstein demanded a reversal in the billing – with the Beatles closing the shows as the headliner. Orbison graciously consented: "I agreed because I was singing ballads and they were singing songs like 'Twist And Shout,' so it all made sense. Anyway, I was making four or five times as much money as they were, so I gave them a break. As you can see, it was the right move."

And at the Philadelphia portion of the Live Aid spectacle in 1985, promoters Bob Geldof and Bill Graham worked hard to make sure things went smoothly, with each act given an allotted amount of stage time. But with dozens of major musical acts performing at the event, backstage disputes and high-strung antics were commonplace. As Graham recalled: "Some of the artists were very cooperative and congenial and some of them acted like stars. Jimmy Page, Roger Plant, and Eric Clapton were standing in the backstage area when Madonna got out of her limousine with her entourage. They started walking through and her advance guys were saying 'Move, *please. Move*, please. *Madonna's coming.*' One of them touched Eric's arm and told him to move over. Eric said, 'What's this?' The guy said, You got to look out. Madonna's *coming*. And Eric said, You must be [joking]!'"

* * * * * *

Although feuds and beefs are commonplace in the world of hip hop, they tend to be infrequent in rock and roll. Nonetheless, there have been a number of legendary quarrels, grudges and disputes. Some were brief, while others lasted decades.

Despite press reports, the much-publicized feud between the Beatles and Rolling Stones in the 1960s was essentially a friendly competition. The two bands even agreed to schedule their single and album releases at different times. And when Neil Young criticized Lynyrd Skynyrd in the lyrics of the songs, "Southern Man" and "Alabama," the Florida-rooted classic-rock band responded by mocking Young in the lyrics of their anthem, "Sweet Home Alabama." But despite the perceived friction, there was little actual animosity between the two rock acts.

One legendary dispute occurred in front of 400,000 spectators at the US Festival in 1983. An inebriated David Lee Roth took a swig of whiskey and then insulted another act at the festival: "I wanna take this time to say that this is real whiskey here. The only people who put iced tea in Jack Daniel's bottles is the Clash, baby!" The previous day, Roth had been involved in a verbal altercation with the Clash's frontman Joe Strummer. The two men had argued over Van Halen's reported $1.5 million payday for their performance versus the Clash's relatively paltry fee of $500,000, which they were donating to charity. It didn't help that one of the Clash's associates had previously referred to Van Halen's recorded output as "hamburger music."

However, a number of rock acts have engaged in long-term hostilities. A pair of Britpop groups – Oasis and Blur – had unkind words for each other throughout the 1990s. The rivalry began when their respective singles – "Roll With It" and "Country House" – were released on the same day. While Blur scored the bigger hit, Oasis would become far more successful in the long run. The spat was punctuated by Noel Gallagher of Oasis, who stated that he hoped that Blur members Damon Albarn and Alex James would "catch AIDS and die." Gallagher would later apologize for his outburst.

Oftentimes, rockers fight over women as was the case between rap-rocker Kid Rock and heavy metal drummer Tommy Lee of Mötley Crüe – both of whom were previously married to *Baywatch* actress Pamela Anderson. Their war of words came to a head at the 2007 MTV Video Music Awards when a cigar-smoking Rock punched Lee. Rock would later deny that the fight had anything to do with Anderson.

And in a battle of Midwest blues-rock duos, Jack White of the White Stripes repeatedly accused the Black Keys of pirating his sound. Additionally, White also got into a physical altercation with Jason Stollsteimer of the indie rock outfit, the Von Bondies. Although both men accused the other of starting the fight, White eventually pleaded guilty to assault and battery and got off with a $500 fine and mandatory anger-management classes.

Sometimes feuds appear out of nowhere. Folk singer Joni Mitchell, once a huge devotee of Bob Dylan, told *The Los Angeles Times* in 2010: "We are like night and day, he and I. Bob is not authentic at all. He's a plagiarist, and his name and voice are fake. Everything about Bob is a deception." She also criticized Grace Slick and Janis Joplin for "[sleeping with] their whole bands and falling down drunk." Mitchell would later backpedal from her remarks, blaming the interviewer for misrepresenting her statements.

▶ CHAPTER 9
THE RELATIONSHIP BETWEEN FANS AND MUSICIANS

Successful musical artists have fans. Rock stars have millions of fans. Music fans will regularly buy or stream music. They will also attend hundreds of concerts over a lifetime, usually spending a small fortune on tickets, travel expenses and artist merchandise.

Fans express their devotion to a musical artist through various means, such as attending a concert dressed like the object of their fandom. In general, audiences tend to copy visually conscious artists such as David Bowie, Cher, Lady Gaga and even Bob Marley. In the 1980s, Madonna fans would don wedding dresses and lacy clothing. And at Nirvana shows, venues would be inundated with men in plaid flannel shirts, thrift store cardigan sweaters, torn-up jeans and Jackie Onassis-style sunglasses. On the other hand, looking too much like a musical artist can also come with a price. At a 2012 Kenny Chesney concert, a fan was booted from a concert in Nashville after he was accused of causing a commotion by "looking too much" like Chesney. The fan was told by a security guard: "You are purposely trying to impersonate a celebrity, so we're kicking you out." The fan later received an apology.

Some fans make pilgrimages to the birthplaces of their musical idols, whether Tupelo or Liverpool. And of course, these same fans name their children after famous performers. Others will launch fan websites filled with valuable historical data on recording sessions or song-by-song setlists of past concerts. And serious collectors will pay big bucks for bootleg recordings, whether rare alternate takes of well-known tracks or live performances that were clandestinely taped by a member of the audience.

Superfans will go to much further lengths. In 2010, a 37-year-old British man decided he wanted to show his passion for Miley Cyrus by getting a tattoo of her face. Then over the next five years, he added 28 more Cyrus tattoos on his body, including three large head shots. But when Cyrus disparaged the superfan on Twitter – calling the tattoos "creepy" and "ugly" – the man announced he was removing them.

A growing number of superfans endure plastic surgery to look like their favorite performer. In 2013, a 33-year-old man from Los Angeles admitted to spending more than $100,000 on surgery with the ultimate goal of looking like Justin Bieber. The fan declared: "Once Justin shot to fame his face was everywhere and all I kept thinking when I saw his picture was, 'I want to look like him.'"

When asked about "obsessive" superfans, Rod Stewart compared them to sports enthusiasts: "I'm a great Glasgow Celtic fan. I wouldn't say I'm obsessed, but I get a great deal of pleasure out of collecting the programs and watching the games. It's entertainment. It's what gives them happiness. So, yes, I can identify with them. It's almost like an identity of sorts. People need another identity other than their own, something that they can latch on to – something that takes away the tedium."

Some bands have managed to create a subculture or lifestyle. The Grateful Dead, Phish and Insane Clown Posse each spawned legions of loyal devotees who would follow them around the country from concert to concert. In 1991, a newspaper writer in Florida described a typical Grateful Dead gathering: "Rainbow waves of tie-dye ripple past beat-up VW vans. People are buzzing about ecology and peace, playing bongo drums and juggling. Marijuana smoke hangs in the air like widely scattered clouds. Vendors sell woven friendship bracelets, vegetarian hot dogs and peanut butter sandwiches. There's music everywhere.... It's just the Deadheads holding one of their parking lot festivals – a scene that replays itself in every city where the Grateful Dead perform."

AGGRESSIVE AND DEMANDING FANS

What exactly does a musical artist owe to his music-buying, song-streaming, concert-going fans? Does he have any responsibility other than recording music and touring? And what is the proper etiquette when a performer is confronted by a fan in a public setting – whether walking on a city sidewalk, eating dinner in a restaurant or pushing a cart full of groceries at Trader Joe's? Oftentimes, a fan who runs into a celebrity is star-struck – wide-eyed, overexcited and unable to speak coherently – and will attempt to capture a memento of the inadvertent encounter, whether with a photographic selfie or an autograph.

Gospel singer BeBe Winans revealed a story about an aggressive fan who confronted R&B crooner Luther Vandross: "He was riding an escalator up and a lady who was headed on the down escalator recognized him. She made a big fuss when Luther didn't stop and sign something, blurting out, 'I'm never going to buy another one of your albums again!' Though Luther couldn't stop – he was on an escalator! – when he reached the top, he immediately hopped the *down* escalator. Upon catching up to the woman, he asked, 'How many of my records do you own?' The lady quickly rattled off several titles. Luther then reached in his pocket and paid her a couple hundred dollars and said, 'There, that should cover it. I never want you to buy my records again. You don't own me.'"

Similarly, Simon Le Bon of Duran Duran has complained about how fans treat celebrities as communal props: "The public property thing can get too much. When everybody thinks that they know you personally, they can get really fresh and forward with you. I mean, I know I do this for a living and I go out and give a lot of myself on stage and on the record, but I don't give *that* much. It's very disconcerting when somebody comes up to you and grabs your ass or something. I may be public property but there are some parts of me which aren't, and that's one of them."

And in 1992, Mark Wahlberg – then known as Marky Mark – griped: "I've met a lot of 25- and 30-year-old women who have seen me on MTV. They want to rub my chest and all this nonsense. I always say to them, 'You want me to take off my shirt?' How would I sound coming up to you and saying, 'Take off your shirt?' They're trying to exploit me to the fullest."

Likewise, Tanya Donelly – of the alternative rock bands Throwing Muses, Belly and the Breeders – explained how she reacts when a fan requests a hug: "Sometimes I say, 'I don't like to be touched.' That's a way of getting out of it.... I'm getting less and less polite as the years wear on." Similarly, in 2016, pop singer Justin Bieber declared in an online post that he was finished taking photos with fans: "It has gotten to the point that people won't even recognize me as a human, I feel like a zoo animal, and I wanna be able to keep my sanity. I realize people will be disappointed but I don't owe anybody a picture."

And in 1970, John Lennon angrily protested: "I'm sick of all these aggressive hippies or whatever they are – the now generation – sort of being very uptight with me. Just either on the street or anywhere, on the phone or demanding my attention, as if I owe them something.... They come to the door with a... peace symbol and expect to just march around the house or something, like an old Beatle fan. They're under a delusion of awareness by having long hair. And that's what I'm sick of. They frighten me."

Fans can be especially irrational or aggressive in large groups when a mob mentality takes over. Keith Richards revealed: "I was never more in fear of my life than I was from teenage girls. The ones that choked me, tore me to shreds, if you got caught in a frenzied crowd of them – it's hard to express how frightening they could be. You'd rather be in a trench fighting the enemy." Similarly, Michael Nesmith of the Monkees recalled a frightening situation at a Midwestern hotel during the band's heyday in the 1960s: "We had come down in the elevator and as a prank, I pushed the wrong floor and it opened into a wide open hallway of teenagers. They took one look and said, 'Can this be real?' When they saw the twinkle in Davy [Jones'] eye, they screamed and came running. If you've ever seen 50 or 100 teenage girls running and screaming at something, you could see what World War III might be like. It's terrifying beyond description. We took off running, but we were caught in the bowels of this hotel. I was running for open portals. I thought we were screwed. They didn't want souvenirs. They were going to tear us apart. We ran outside and I saw a patrol car sitting parked.... I grabbed the back door. The police turned around like, 'Who the hell are you?' We were all in costume, all the way to the green hats and the red velvet suits. I said, 'We're the Monkees.'"

Likewise, British radio host Bob Harris recalled the pandemonium after a concert by T. Rex frontman Marc Bolan in 1971: "The local police formed a cordon to get us into the cars, but I remember coming out of the stage and the first thing I was aware of was stainless steel, because all these girls were holding scissors, or even knives, to try to get themselves a lock of Marc's corkscrew hair. He was a little bit shorter than me, so all these scissors were coming straight for me at eye level."

Fan worship can also be physically dangerous for the fans themselves. According to an account in *The Saturday Evening Post*, the Beatles "toured New Zealand and Australia [in 1964], where as many as 300,000 people not only howled greetings but sometimes trampled one another underfoot. In Australia the Beatles left behind an estimated 1,000 casualties. One girl burst a blood vessel in her throat from screaming. About a dozen fans were kicked by police horses. Another girl suffered carbon monoxide poisoning when she was knocked down near the exhaust pipe of an automobile hemmed in by the mob. When she tried to get up, she was pinned there by several other girls, who had climbed on her back to get a view of the Beatles."

Similarly, in October 1964, the Animals made their first trip to the U.S. on the heels of their chart-topping hit, "The House Of The Rising Sun." After five nights of performances in New York City at the Paramount Theater in Times Square, the Animals were scheduled to appear on *The Ed Sullivan Show*. But while running through the throngs of hysterical young fans enroute to the CBS television studios, tragedy struck. As the group's roadie James "Tappy" Wright recalled, "Arriving for Ed Sullivan, we were mobbed, the girls surging forward and grabbing at our hair and clothes. A security guard pulled us through the back entrance and slammed the door closed behind us. I turned and three fingers fell at my feet. We stood there, horror struck, and stared down at the three painted fingernails on their fleshy stubs, just laying there on the concrete floor. [Animals drummer] John Steel wretched the door back open and pulled the injured girl into the building. We tried to comfort her while she ran off for an ambulance, but the girl, apparently oblivious to her severed fingers and bleeding hand, just seemed delighted to meet the band."

FLEECING THE SUPERFAN

Most artists have legions of superfans. These fans take artist worship to a higher level. It's common for devotees of Elvis Presley to build shrines in their homes or to even devote entire rooms to Presley memorabilia – whether photos, books, trinkets or the occasional pricey artifact. Many hardcore Beatles fans have an irrational desire to own every variation of every album that the Fab Four recorded. Whether mono, stereo, remastered, colored vinyl, 180-gram audiophile disc or U.K. import, they *need* to possess a copy – preferably in sealed, mint condition.

In describing his large CD collection, rock journalist Chuck Klosterman lamented: "I would say that I've owned at least 500 of these albums twice (once on cassette and once on compact disc) and that I've owned a few of them three times (for example, I bought all 26 Kiss releases in tape, and then I bought them all on disc, and then I bought them on disc *again* when they were remastered in 1999, which really just means somebody went back into the studio and made them louder)."

Repackaging previously-released albums as fancy, elaborate boxed sets became an important source of income for veteran rock acts. In 2018 when Guns N' Roses released a 30th anniversary edition of the group's landmark album *Appetite For Destruction*, there were three different versions. In addition to a basic version, there was a "Super Deluxe Edition" with four CDs, a blu-ray disc, a hardcover book and loads of memorabilia. But for the ultimate fan, there was a $999 "Locked N' Loaded" edition which was housed in a faux leather and wood cabinet, and included bonus items such as rare photos, patches, posters and guitar picks.

Kiss frontman Gene Simmons eclipsed all of his competition. In 2017, the tongue-wagging media star released a comprehensive $2,000 box set. Weighing 38-pounds, it featured a Simmons action figure and 150 new tracks. For the ultimate superfan, premium packages ranged from $25,000 to $50,000, and included an executive producer credit on the project as well as a two-hour visit to your home by Simmons.

THE COST OF CONCERT TICKETS

In 2002, Tom Petty reignited his longstanding battle with the music industry when he released the concept album, *The Last DJ*. The project was tentatively titled *The Golden Circle*, a reference to high-priced concert tickets, which became commonplace after the reunited Eagles began charging $100 for admission to their shows in 1994. Just one year earlier in 1993, top-level acts such as Paul McCartney and Bruce Springsteen were charging between $26 and $32.50 per seat, with little in the way of additional, tacked-on service charges.

Not every rock act opposed higher ticket prices. At the time, David Crosby created a storm of controversy when he said in the press: "What they do in terms of the gigs and the pricing and the rest of it is completely out of our hands. Anybody who thinks it's too much money shouldn't come." However, Petty admitted, "I would feel embarrassed charging 200 bucks" for a ticket.

The question remains – should a musical artist worth millions of dollars charge the maximum that the market will bear? If they don't charge top dollar, then the secondary market – dominated by scalpers – will take a $50 concert ticket and mark it up by a few hundred dollars. Paul McCartney, who grossed an average of $4.4 million per concert in 2019, defended the cost of tickets to his concerts: "I always say to my promoter: What does Madonna charge? Ding! What does Elton charge? Ding! What does U2 charge? Ding! And they always give me a ballpark figure. And that's what I charge.... We're not trying to take advantage."

With growing complaints over the rising costs of concert tickets, in 2007 Ozzy Osbourne launched the Ozzfest tour, which instituted a novel strategy – free admission for fans and no salary for the bands. The production costs were instead underwritten by sponsors, parking fees, concession sales and merchandise. However, the rock world took a very dim view toward the arrangement. Gary Bongiovanni, editor-in-chief of *Pollstar*, insisted: "People in the industry don't like that it's a free show, because it sends the wrong message. This is a show that's worth money, and people should pay for it. It's cheapening the product by giving it away." But Ozzy's outspoken wife Sharon Osbourne countered: "The Stones played for two million people for free [in Brazil]. Did that devalue them? Obviously not." (In the end, most of the "free" Ozzfest tickets were resold on the internet for an average of $25.)

However, many top-tier artists discovered an innovative method to increase their concert revenues – the premium VIP package. Becoming commonplace in the 2010s, VIP passes included various perks such as meet-and-greet sessions with the bands, limited-edition tour merchandise, autographs, backstage parties and even karaoke sessions. In 2011, a premium ticket to see Bon Jovi cost a whopping $1,750, while Roger Waters' most loyal fans paid a *mere* $755. In 2018, VIP packages cost $1,400 for Guns N' Roses, $2,250 for Ozzy Osbourne and $2,500 for Metallica. And during Avril Lavigne's 2014 tour, fans dished out $400 for a post-concert picture with the singer. But with the attendees barred from touching the Canadian rock singer, photo after photo captured Lavigne awkwardly standing a few feet from her fans.

Eventually, *Rolling Stone* asked in a headline: "Are VIPs Ruining Festivals?" The magazine lamented the fact that there were two distinct levels of admission to the Coachella festival. Either you bought a general admission ticket and sweltered in the sun along with tens of thousands of other working-class music fans "or you could've paid $3,250 to get shuttled to the side of the stage from the nearby air-conditioned safari tent, which has a couch with throw pillows, wooden flooring, a queen-size bed and electrical outlets. You'd be able to drink from a private bar, use a private restroom, swim in a private pool and get advice on the next band to check out from a personal concierge."

Additionally, many artists utilize their websites to increase profits. As *Rolling Stone* reported: "Joining an artist's online fan club was turned into another stream of income. In exchange for paying $100 to join the Police or Rolling Stones fan club, concertgoers had the first chance to purchase concert tickets. But with demand great for some tours, even the $100 fee guaranteed nothing as was the case for the 2007 Police reunion, with the group earning in excess of $2 million just in fan club fees." Additionally, "fan clubs often don't even give their members first crack at presales. American Express cardholders regularly get even earlier access, as do season-ticket holders at venues."

And in 2020, a newspaper columnist in the Midwest complained about the cost of the tacked-on fees when purchasing concert tickets: "Buying really good tickets to a big show is almost like buying a yacht – if you have to ask how much, you can't afford it." When he looked into the price of two seats for an upcoming Rolling Stones show,

Ticketmaster was charging $666 per ticket – plus an additional $105 service fee. That came to $1,542 for two seats. Although the columnist was willing to shell out the enormous cost for the two tickets, he wasn't willing to pay the exorbitant service fees and chose not to see Mick and the boys.

Limited edition, autographed, coffee-table autobiographies can also provide a nice income bump. Jimmy Page published a lavish hardcover book costing an astonishing £445. However, a Traveling Wilburys biography personally signed by Jeff Lynne went for a more reasonable £245.

In the hip hop and R&B communities, musical artists often tap into an unlikely revenue source – the "after party." After the end of a concert, independent promoters distribute flyers to fans as they leave the venue, promising that the headlining performer will be visiting a local nightclub. Charging fans anywhere from $10 to $25 for the privilege of drinking or dancing in the same room as Drake or 50 Cent, local promoters typically pay the artists anywhere from $10,000 to $25,000. Sometimes the artist might perform a song or two, but usually not. Often, liquor companies pick up a portion of the nightclub's booking fee.

SIGNING AUTOGRAPHS

British New Wave rocker Elvis Costello recalled: "The first time somebody asked for my autograph, I actually argued with them. I said, 'Why do you think you want my signature?'" On the other extreme, country superstar Garth Brooks set a record at the 1996 CMA Music Fest when he signed his name for 23-hours straight, with only a few bathroom breaks.

Autograph collectors have been around since the dawn of the celebrity. From Elvis to Fabian, the 1950s were an innocent time of collecting autographs just for the sake of enjoying a souvenir or memento. Teenage girls often carried around dime-store autograph books that were signed by touring performers. Actress Debbie Reynolds, who scored a number-one pop hit in 1957 with the ballad "Tammy," recalled: "I would stand by the stage door for a couple of hours after every show, signing special pictures the studio had made for us. In those days you were *taught* to give an autograph to everybody. I pass that along to all the new stars who are aloof and think that fans are an imposition. It takes longer to say no than it does to sign an autograph."

In 1966, Mick Jagger explained his reaction to fans who ask for autographs: "I get used to it. 'It's not for me, it's for my son in the hospital with a hole in his head.' Or. 'Do it for Johnny, he's a cripple and his sister's got leukemia.' If my kids had leukemia I wouldn't go and tell everybody. It's amazing how many people's children are cripples. I sound hard saying that but I'm not. I'd sign my autograph anyway."

Soul singer Gladys Knight recounted: "Over the years, I've become accustomed to being asked for autographs and to being photographed with people. Most of the time, I am glad to do it. I did draw the line a few years ago, though, when I was in a restroom stall in an airport and a woman's hand appeared at my feet holding a pen and a paper. 'Would you mind autographing this?' she asked from the adjoining stall. 'When I've finished my business,' I said as I stared in disbelief at the strange but well-manicured hand that had invaded my space."

Unfortunately, by the 1980s, signing autographs had evolved from the simple act of bonding with fans. In the age of the internet auction, signatures of music stars increased in value and could bring hundreds of dollars. While most musicians continued to sign autographs *for free*, sports figures were far more likely to charge big money for their John Hancocks. For a number of years, retired baseball legend Pete Rose made a full-time living by signing his name, over and over again, for visiting tourists inside a Las Vegas storefront. In his best year, he earned a whopping $3.6 million by sitting at a table and doing nothing else but autographing objects such as jerseys and baseball bats.

Consequently, many recording artists have severely curtailed the once-cherished custom of signing autographs. Neil Young observed: "Now when I arrive at an airport, there are professional autograph people all over me. I don't know how the hell they know what I am doing seemingly before I do, but there they are, bugging me in the security line and at the curb. It costs me to avoid them but so be it. They bother me. They pose as real fans and try to make me feel guilty if I don't sign something. They are so devious and deceptive, feeding on my love for real fans." And in 2011, Doors drummer John Densmore posted a message on his website: "The last several years I have been so flooded with [autograph] requests that it is interfering with my personal life, and I am going to have to stop. Fans (or opportunists from Ebay) track me when I land at any airport, follow me into the bathroom, and hang around my hotel, looking for my John Henry. It is unfortunate, but I have to draw the line." Similarly, when R&B singer Solomon Burke was asked by fans to sign some photos and records after an appearance at the Rock and Roll Hall of Fame, he rebuffed the disappointed autograph seekers with the comment, "Why do you want my autograph? So you can sell it on Ebay?"

Chuck Berry, a member of rock royalty, took an entirely different approach. If he was fond of a particular album, he would neatly sign his name on the cover. If he didn't like the record, he would either sign his name upside-down or on a dark spot of the cover. On the other hand, in 1999, when an autograph hunter handed Keith Richards a guitar to sign near the Russian Tea Room in New York City, the legendary performer simply walked off with the instrument.

Most musical artists have realized the financial value of their signatures and began peddling autographed CDs and other collectibles on their own websites. Hundreds of acts – including Chris Isaak, REO Speedwagon, Jewel, Scotty Moore, Bon Jovi, Yngwie Malmsteen and Ace Frehley – offered signed goodies. Conversely, the members of Def Leppard came up with a creative solution for dealing with the hordes of autograph hounds – they charge $5 per signature and donate all of the proceeds to charity.

However, some artists still genuinely enjoy meeting fans and autographing items – free of charge. Singer-songwriter Gary Wright revealed: "The real reward for me came when I would finish a show and afterward, while signing autographs, was able to listen to many stories fans related to me about how 'Dream Weaver' played an important part in their lives – stories like 'that was the song we played at our wedding' and 'I was going through a very tough time in my life, and listening to your song inspired me not to end my life.' I was moved – many times profoundly so – by these experiences I was hearing. Inwardly, I would thank God for the privilege of helping these souls in my own humble way, while trying not to let the ego get in the way."

ROCK ARTIFACTS

The serious fan wants a genuine piece of rock and roll history. However, during the early years of the rock era, many irreplaceable artifacts were unwittingly discarded, donated to charity thrift shops or even stolen. Immediately after the untimely deaths of Jimi Hendrix, Mama Cass and Marc Bolan, scavengers broke into their residences and pilfered their personal possessions. And in the weeks after the death of Kurt Cobain, his widow Courtney Love gifted much of his personal belongings to visitors who came to pay their respects. One of the items, Cobain's cigarette-burned sweater he wore during Nirvana's *Unplugged* session in 1993, later sold at auction for a whopping $334,000.

When Elvis Presley became a Las Vegas lounge singer in the 1970s, he gave away hundreds and hundreds of sweat-stained handkerchiefs. At the time, few fans in attendance realized the potential collector's value of these souvenirs. And no one could have imagined that the guitar Duane Allman used on the track "Layla" by Derek and the Dominoes would sell for $1.25 million in 2019.

A significant number of historical pieces of rock and roll history have made their way to pop-culture auctions. At these public sales, institutions like the Hard Rock Cafe often trade bids with wealthy private buyers who view music artifacts as solid financial investments. And at times, rockers attend these auctions to buy back their own history. Before the formation of the Rolling Stones, blues enthusiasts Mick Jagger and Keith Richards made their first recordings with a group of friends in 1961. The informal sessions took place at an acquaintance's house and were captured on a reel-to-reel tape player. Many years later, Jagger was able to acquire the recordings at a London auction with a high bid of $80,000.

Music historian Jim Henke – who spent a great deal of time searching for important historical memorabilia in his role as the VP of exhibitions for the Rock and Roll Hall of Fame – revealed: "One thing I've noticed is that the bands are becoming more aware of the value of this stuff. A couple bands even have an archivist on staff. There's more awareness in general of the value of this stuff."

However, not everyone sees dollar signs when collecting music memorabilia. Nashville-based performer Marty Stuart, a self-described country music historian, noticed in the late-1970s that celebrity-owned instruments, stage costumes, set lists and related one-of-a-kind items were finding their way to the city's pawn shops, second-hand outlets and guitar stores. Motivated by his appreciation of music history, Stuart regularly scoured the city for these castoffs. Initially storing the memorabilia in his bedroom, the collection eventually grew to 20,000 items and filled a 5,000-square-foot warehouse.

*   *   *   *   *   *

Music fans desperate for memorabilia will go to extreme lengths. Before a concert in Gainesville, Florida, Pat Benatar noticed some unusual activity near the venue. Benatar recalled, "Eventually one of our crew members went outside for a smoke and noticed a tent that was set up in the parking lot with a sign that read, 'Pat Benatar Souvenirs'.... It turned out that some college kids bribed the front desk at our cheap hotel to find out what room we'd stay in. They unscrewed the windows, snuck in, and stole our bedding and our trash. They had cut up the sheets and pillowcases we'd slept on into little squares and they were selling them. They were also selling our garbage – old Kleenex, used Q-tips, and razors."

Similarly, British performer Adam Ant recalled the surreal scene in the late-1960s when his mother worked at the home of Paul McCartney: "The hardest part of the job was having to fight her way through hordes of girls waiting outside, many of whom had come from abroad and camped there for days or weeks at a time. They would beg her for a souvenir, or sometimes just a touch, believing she may have rubbed shoulders with Paul. Mum would sometimes bring something out with her when she left, a bar of soap, maybe, or even an old comb or newspaper. They would grab these bits of trash wide-eyed. Unable to control the tears that came flooding out, receiving each item as if they had been given some kind of holy relic."

Tom Petty had a similar problem when he resided in Encino: "[People] would steal my garbage cans. They'd steal my whole mailbox. Take it right off the post. I went through three mailboxes. And the garbage. I used to worry about what I was putting in the garbage. Finally, I said, 'Look, man, if you want to dig through the garbage for it, you're welcome to it.'"

Some rockers were not as generous with their trash. Neil Tennant of the Pet Shop Boys lamented: "They go through your rubbish.... One girl came up to me and said to me, 'My friend's got all your old razor blades stuck on her bedroom wall.' Or, 'She's got all your Christmas cards, you know you threw them out last Tuesday,' and, at that point, I got a shredder.... In fact, that's my only commandment. When you get famous, you do need a shredder."

New York City-based writer A.J. Weberman was rock music's most notorious trash thief. A self-described Dylanologist, Weberman frequently rifled through Bob Dylan's garbage cans in the early-1970s and then discussed the finds on a local radio program. *Rolling Stone* magazine chronicled one of Weberman's forays into Dylan's trash: "After a good half-hour of picking, some potentially valuable bits of Dylan memorabilia begin to emerge. Included in the haul is a fund-raising letter from a rather artsy-craftsy Greenwich Village private school attended by one of Bob's children, a false start to a letter to Johnny and June Cash, shredded remains of various fan letters, Polaroid negatives of Dylan and his brood, and empty granola and cookie mix boxes. Also found in the trashmine is a medical report from a veterinarian on the condition of [Dylan's pet dog] Sacha, some torn-up drawings of Bob a la the *Self Portrait* cover, notes on the out-takes to *Self Portrait*, an original poem, and a note from Mama Zimmerman:

'Fort Lauderdale is great. Enjoy the candy!' Underneath all this trivia is a pile of rock and music magazines, including *Rolling Stone* and *Crawdaddy*."

And when trash is unavailable, fans will settle for more esoteric paraphernalia. After Kanye West's 2019 performance at the Coachella Festival, attendees of the concert sold bags of the turf from the venue.

*   *   *   *   *   *

In general, recording artists don't tend to save the collateral pieces of their own musical history. When you're struggling to get from one gig to another, the last thing you're concerned about is carefully preserving items that seem unimportant at the time. Dealing with pushy reporters, finding an open late-night restaurant and washing your clothes between gigs are the priorities at hand. And when you're touring across the country in a crowded van that's packed with musical instruments, space is a precious commodity.

Conversely, a few artists are hoarders who save everything. When David Bowie died in 2016, he had accumulated a treasure trove of 80,000 items from his lengthy and prolific career. A few years before his death, some of the artifacts were displayed in a touring exhibition.

*   *   *   *   *   *

There is an often-repeated story in the Midwest about a serious record collector who was given an ultimatum by his exasperated wife – "it's either me or the records." Years later, he would half-seriously lament, "I sure miss her." As author Nick Hornby suggested in *High Fidelity*, hardcore male record collectors – the passionate buyers who are experts in the genre they compulsively accumulate – have trouble maintaining traditional relationships with women. And among themselves, they tend to argue about music-related topics – vinyl records versus compact discs, which rockers sold out, was Ringo a good drummer, the best version of a particular song, which inductees don't belong in the Rock and Roll Hall of Fame and why Britain seems to produce better rock magazines than the United State.

However, it's these collectors who help fund the lifestyles of musical performers as well as everyone else who works in the music industry. Without dedicated fans, there would be no rock stars.

▶ CHAPTER 10
THE FAME AND POWER OF ROCK STARDOM

Rock stars are celebrated at various music award shows, whether the Grammys, American Music Awards or Brit Awards. Arriving at a ceremony, a rock star is greeted by outstretched microphones, flashing cameras and giddy screams. Emerging from his stretch limo with a glass of champagne in his hand, he's wearing dark sunglasses and a rocker's outfit of black leather and gold bling. He is accompanied by a bevy of long-haired beauties who appear as if they walked right out of a music video from the decadent '80s. As he confidently saunters down the red carpet, the assembled crowd holds its collective breath to see if he will engage in some sort of outlandish behavior that only a rock star can get away with.

So you wanna be a rock star? Everyone does. Or it just seems that way. As long as there's the demand and the machinery to manufacture fame, there's never a shortage of rock stars or the fans who adore them. While most chart-topping acts possess intrinsic talent, clearly some do not and have been aided in their ascent to stardom.

By the 1990s, "rock star" had evolved to mean someone who had achieved the American dream – on steroids. Although the term originated in the pop music field, it has been appropriated by Hollywood, professional sports, the business world and even the political realm. It's the ultimate achievement in a celebrity-obsessed society – Rock Star Status. Oh sure, Bruce Springsteen is a rock star as is Bono of U2. But actor Dwayne Johnson – appropriately nicknamed the Rock – is also considered a rock star. And golfer Tiger Woods is a rock star. And even a computer geek like Bill Gates is a rock star. With rock star prestige comes fame, celebrity worship and various ancillary benefits. Suddenly, your face is everywhere. You have millions of followers on Twitter, tribute websites pop up on the internet, and journalists – professional and otherwise – chronicle your public and personal life.

At the 2018 dedication of his star on the Hollywood Walk of Fame, former *American Idol* judge Simon Cowell crowed: "If anyone says fame is a bad thing, I don't know what you're talking about. It's the best thing in the world." But not everyone in the entertainment world would agree. In 1999, Whitney Houston lamented: "Picture this. You wake up every day with a magnifying glass over you. Someone [is always] looking for something – somebody, somewhere is speaking your name every five seconds of the day, whether it's positive or negative."

Is fame in itself a goal of some musical artists – or is it just a necessary part of achieving success in their chosen field? And once rock stars have attained fame, is it an addiction which must be fed with constant praise and attention?

*   *   *   *   *   *

Rock and roll certainly did not invent the musical celebrity. In Germany and Austria, classical composers such as Mozart and Bach were the rock stars of the 18th century. And across Europe, composer and pianist Franz Liszt was greeted at sold-out concerts by large crowds of infatuated female fans. At the close of his performances, well-coiffed society women would rush the stage and fight over scraps of anything he had left behind.

In the United States, the popular music industry emerged at the end of the Civil War. But even before then, European opera singer Jenny Lind had taken America by storm. Nicknamed the Swedish Nightingale, she was brought to the U.S. by showman P.T. Barnum. According to a report, when she arrived in 1850 on a trans-Atlantic ship, "30,000 screaming, waving New Yorkers had assembled. West Street for a dozen blocks was clogged by crowds; and when the ship drew near the wharf, the mob surged forward.... The gangplank had been specially carpeted. When Jenny appeared and began to descend, the enthusiasm of the crowd burst all bounds. Dock gates crashed before the rush; men and women were trampled underfoot and injured. Strong lines of police formed to protect the Swedish Nightingale." The press dubbed the phenomena "Lind Mania." Over the next two years, Lind staged 150 sold-out performances before returning to her native Sweden.

At the turn of the 20th century, Italian opera star Enrico Caruso was the most revered and highest-paid performer of his time. He was described by *The New York Times* as "the first blockbuster recording artist, at a time when relatively few people even owned record players and a record cost more than a ticket to the opera.... Caruso had the first modern opera career, because of the role recordings played in it – in making him a superstar and in documenting the voice for posterity."

By the early-1940s, Frank Sinatra solidified the archetype of the solo vocalist as a pop culture icon. Oozing charisma and good looks, the rail-thin Italian-American performer enjoyed his initial success as a vocalist in the Harry James Orchestra and, later, the Tommy Dorsey Orchestra. But with swooning teenagers deluging Sinatra's early performances at the Paramount Theater in New York City, bandleader Tommy Dorsey grew resentful. After quitting Dorsey's band in 1942, Sinatra stayed on at the Paramount as a solo attraction for an extended stint.

The bold and cocky Sinatra was the first pop singer to evoke frenzied screaming from impassioned female fans. Nicknamed "bobbysoxers," Sinatra's legion of devotees were distinguished by the ankle-high white socks they wore. At one Sinatra appearance in New York City – the Columbus Day Riot of 1944 – more than 700 police officers were needed to restore order among a mass of 30,000 unruly, mostly female fans. When the audience inside the theater refused to leave at the end of the first show of the day, the frustrated crowd waiting outside went berserk. While the crooner era barely lasted into the 1950s, rock and roll would soon breed the modern-day teenage singing idol.

DEALING WITH FAME

Coping with newfound fame and becoming the focus of attention are not easy tasks. Counting Crows singer Adam Duritz had a difficult time adjusting to his status as a rock star. He recalled, "They're looking at you all the time, and they don't even talk *to* you anymore. They talk *at* you. You become more a souvenir of yourself. I wasn't ready for people to look at me that way.... Suddenly I found myself in a situation where everyone wanted to take my picture. That alone nearly caused a nervous breakdown." Likewise, Jack White of the White Stripes observed: "A lot of people who go through fame, even a small taste of it, are going through experiences that probably no human being should ever go through. I've walked into a room and felt like I'm intimidating people. You don't know what you're supposed to do." However, some artists have unrealistic notions about fame. British singer Lily Allen admitted: "I did want to be famous, but I didn't realize what famous was. I thought fame just meant 'Everyone will love me.'"

Some artists readily embrace celebrity status. Before Nirvana had achieved notoriety outside of Seattle, Kurt Cobain recalled an incident he witnessed during an early tour: "We were in Detroit, playing at this club, and about 10 people showed up. And next door, there was this bar, and Axl Rose came in with 10 or 15 bodyguards. It was this huge extravaganza; all these people were fawning over him. If he'd just walked in by himself, it would have been no big deal. But he wanted that. You create attention to attract attention." And in his autobiography, Tom Jones revealed his reaction to his first taste of fame in the 1960s: "[I] can't get enough of the attention and the praise and the whirling, in-and-out-of-cars glamour of it all, and the ability I suddenly seem to have to change the atmosphere in a room just by walking into it. I get the impression very early on that I'm not going to struggle with this stuff."

Conversely, as pop singer Tony Orlando observed: "Elvis was not comfortable with his celebrity status, if you will. In fact, I suspect it almost embarrassed Elvis that he had the power to walk into a room and immediately become the focal point." And bass player Noel Redding of the Jimi Hendrix Experience declared: "Adulation in particular sets you apart from reality and, more devastatingly, from the relaxed sincerity of close friendships. No one sympathizes because you are envied, not liked."

Meanwhile, award-winning rock journalist Chuck Klosterman contrasted a pair of encounters he had with the same performer – before and then after achieving fame: "The first time I spoke with Marilyn [Manson], he was among the most interesting and insightful musicians I've ever encountered. When we talked a year later, he was surly and consciously outrageous. In that second conversation, Marilyn even feigned stupidity – he claimed he didn't know where North Dakota was, and he said he was unfamiliar with the name 'Newt Gingrich.' By the time he released *Antichrist Superstar* in 1996, Manson was so popular he would only respond to media requests from major press outlets; when he did talk to the media, he usually said stuff that was totally insane, sometimes mentioning how he enjoyed cutting into his flesh with razor blades and pouring drugs into the open wounds. Like every shock rocker before him, his weirdness was directly proportional to his fame."

Performers also understand that their fame grants them power and influence. Pioneering 1950s rocker Dion DiMucci admitted: "Dick Clark was almost like a secular pastor to me – a father figure.... He told me that fame had given me more authority with kids than any of their teachers had, so I should be very careful of the choice I made. People would believe whatever I said, just because I was their favorite singer. If I said a certain kind of hairstyle made girls look pretty, girls would run out and get it, and their boyfriends would want them to. If I said I liked a particular make and model of automobile, it would become the cool car to have. Dick Clark wanted me to know... with great power comes great responsibility."

LEAD SINGER DISEASE

Rock stars are prone to Lead Singer Disease, a term coined by Eddie Van Halen to describe the behavior of *both* David Lee Roth and Sammy Hagar. After Roth left Van Halen in 1985, Eddie Van Halen proclaimed: "Dave is not a rock and roller. He wants to be a movie star." Noel E. Monk, the group's road manager, said of Roth: "He had always been, as they say, a legend in his own mind, and when legitimate stardom and success came his way, he devoured it like a drug. Increasingly, I would see David posing at every opportunity, not just in the dressing room before going onstage but every time he passed a mirror or window. I'd catch him pausing and vamping, tossing his hair and sucking his cheeks like a model."

Rock vocalists who are stricken by Lead Singer Disease tend be spoiled, thin-skinned, self-centered and overbearing. The spotlight must be firmly fixed in just one position – aimed at the lead vocalist who's strutting around on the stage. That also means a separate dressing room, his own limo and a swarm of assistants and gofers. Public tantrums are commonplace and encouraged by the press.

Elton John recalled how difficult and unreasonable he became at the height of his fame in the 1970s: "I could be unbelievably horrible and stupid. On tours I'd get on a plane, then get off it, maybe six or eight times. I'd walk out of a hotel suite because I didn't like the color of the bedspread. I remember looking out of my room at the Inn on the Park one day and saying, 'It's too windy. Can someone please do something about it?'"

Female vocalists who are afflicted with Lead Singer Disease are known as divas. R&B singer Sheila E. – best known for her work with Prince – recalled how success had turned her into a monster in the mid-1980s: "The sky was the limit – I could have anything I wanted – and, in that environment, I became increasingly impatient for that 'anything' to come to me *now*.... I became mean, demanding, and angry. I stopped asking and started telling. I began to see my team as a group of people working *for* me, rather than as individuals who worked *with* me. I didn't give them the acknowledgment and appreciation they deserved. I didn't say 'please' and 'thank you.' I was becoming a nightmare. I turned into a diva, I was a million miles away from the Sheila Escovedo my parents raised me to be." Similarly, author Randy Tarraborrelli said of Diana Ross: "She would demand that people call her Miss Ross and that everybody diverted their eyes from her when she entered a room. She would insist her dressing rooms have the same color scheme as the color of her eyes." And when Madonna appeared on a German television program in 1995, she refused to use the studio's bathroom facilities and instead demanded a customized toilet, sink and shower be brought in with a crane and installed adjacent to the building.

However, singer Annabella Lwin, who fronted the 1980s British band Bow Wow Wow, offered another explanation: "When bands have a lead singer, they seem to get upset or, dare I say, jealous that the lead singer gets all the attention. The truth is, of course the lead singer will get a degree of attention, because that's who connects with the audience. It's the only human element in the equation. The bass player plugs in his bass, the drummer bashes away on the drums. With all due respect, I'm not demeaning them; I'm just stating a fact. Every lead singer since time immortal will always get more attention."

THE PITFALLS AND PRICE OF FAME

Ultimately, fame can be a two-edged sword. Achieving success in the music world often comes at a huge cost. Francis Whately, who oversaw a David Bowie documentary in 2017, said of the Thin White Duke: "In the '60s, he was very driven and wanted to be famous at all costs. He tried on musical styles just to be famous, (and) would move from one group of friends to another in order to advance himself. When he became Ziggy Stardust and the fame started, he welcomed it. But very quickly, it became tiresome for him.... The idea that he couldn't walk down the street, particularly in London, was an awful thing for him." Bowie would later lament: "Fame itself, of course, doesn't really afford you anything more than a good seat in a restaurant. That must be pretty well known by now. I'm just amazed how fame is being posited as the be-all and end-all, and how many of these young kids who are being foisted on the public have been talked into this idea that anything necessary to be famous is all right. It's a sad state of affairs. However arrogant and ambitious I think we were in my generation. I think the idea was that if you do something really good, you'll become famous. The emphasis on fame itself is something new. It's not the same thing at all. And it will leave many of them with this empty feeling."

Similarly, Barry Gibb of the Bee Gees recalled how in 1978, the *Saturday Night Fever* soundtrack "was No. 1 every week. It wasn't just like a hit album. It was No. 1 every single week for 25 weeks. It was just an extraordinary time. I remember not being able to answer the phone, and I remember people climbing over my walls. I was quite grateful when it stopped. It was too unreal. In the long run, your life is better if it's not like that on a constant basis."

Fame also can lead to self-imposed isolation. When asked how success had affected him, singer Isaac Slade of the Fray admitted: "I have wrestled with a lot of loneliness in this band, especially as we've gotten more successful. I guess it's a cliche, the lonely lead singer in the band, but it's hard explaining to people how isolating it is."

Fame can also lead to unforeseen problems. In 1975, when Yoko Ono was pregnant with her son, Sean, an angry John Lennon recalled the nearly tragic scene inside a hospital emergency room: "Somebody had made a transfusion of the wrong blood type into Yoko. I was there when it happened, and she starts to go rigid, and then shake, from the pain and the trauma. I run up to this nurse and say, 'Go get the doctor!' I'm holding on tight to Yoko while this guy gets to the hospital room. He walks in, hardly notices that Yoko is going through... convulsions, goes straight for me, smiles, shakes my hand and says, 'I've always wanted to meet you, Mr. Lennon, I always enjoyed your music.' I start screaming: 'My wife's dying and you wanna talk about my music!'"

And singer-songwriter Janis Ian complained: "Imagine living like this. You can't drive yourself, because of the liability – twice, people in other vehicles recognized you and deliberately tried to cause an accident so they could collect a settlement from your insurance company. You take limousines instead, and only with drivers you know, because you worry about being kidnapped and held for ransom.... You keep the windows up all the time, grateful that they're dark.... You can't go shopping without attracting a crowd; they grab at you and your clothes until security comes and hauls you away in tears. And you keep thinking to yourself, 'This is what I wanted. This is what I worked for.'"

Similarly, Axl Rose of Guns N' Roses revealed: "People are always trying to provoke some kind of fight so they can sue me. I'm scared of thrashing an asshole and going to jail for it. For some reason I can walk into a room and someone will pick a fight. That's always happened with me."

UNCHANGED BY FAME

Gary Rossington of Lynyrd Skynyrd once remarked: "Being a rock star doesn't really mean anything. To me, stars are things up in the sky. Being a good person is what really matters. Spending time with family and friends, and enjoying good old Southern hospitality are what brings me happiness now. There is something special about living down South. People are real down here. All my friends, no matter what they do for a living – truck drivers, gardeners, construction workers – are proud of who they are. People look you in the eye down here. The community is in your heart."

Upon achieving fame and accumulating wealth, some artists barely alter their lifestyles. Queen bassist John Deacon purchased a modest home in South London with his first sizable royalty check but never relocated because he did not want to disrupt the lives of his six children. And Noel Gallagher of the British hit group Oasis recalled: "Even in the Nineties, when it was mad and there were photographers all around the house, it never occurred to me to send someone else out to get cigarettes. It took me five minutes – went for a walk, gave a wave, went back inside."

Similarly, former *Britain's Got Talent* contestant Susan Boyle was relatively unaffected by her massive success. As *The Philadelphia Inquirer* reported: "The 51-year-old singer who entered the TV talent contest to make her late mother proud is remarkably unchanged. She's still a bit frumpy, though she's acquired a new hairdo, more expensive clothes and a makeover.... Boyle now has a car and chauffeur to take her to appointments, but she sticks close to familiar places and routines. She has bought a new house, a modern four-bedroom two-story in Blackburn that cost $480,000, but locals say she often stays in the modest row house she grew up in."

And in 2005, Bono made a remarkable admission: "In the Nineties, I started a journey out of self-consciousness toward where I am now, where I wake up and forget that I am in a band. I will not let that thing called fame change my mood anymore. I don't travel with security. I don't mind getting turned away at restaurants."

THE SUPERNATURAL POWERS OF ROCK & ROLL

Western society tends to view celebrities as mystical or superhuman beings. Rock critic Allan Jones described a meeting with David Bowie at a luxurious hotel in 1977: "I'm walking through the doors into the main suite which, when I get there, is empty. No trace anywhere of Bowie. I look around and notice the windows to the balcony are open and that the lace curtains are billowing into the room, sunlight streaming through them. And then, surrounded by a glowing halo of light that can only be described as celestial, David Bowie is standing in the doorway to the balcony and all that's missing from the scene is a choir of angels and their booming blissful harmonies. I'm momentarily dazzled, rooted to the spot like a slack-jaw hillbilly. And now I realize he's talking to me."

Rock music is oftentimes viewed within a religious framework. Listening to a cherished song or favorite artist can bring joy and exhilaration, which is sometimes interpreted as a spiritual experience. In 1970, Little Richard – an ordained preacher – told *Rolling Stone* magazine, "I believe that my music is healin' music. Just like Oral Roberts says he's a divine healer, I believe my music can make the blind see, the lame walk, the deaf and dumb hear and talk, because it inspires and uplifts people." Likewise, fans of Bob Marley often regarded the reggae superstar as a holy man. Although the central theme of Marley's musical output was the veneration of the Rastafarian faith and its spiritual leader Haile Selassie, Marley was treated as a semi-deity following his untimely death at age 36 in 1981. And on ABC's *20/20*, LaToya Jackson described her late brother, Michael, in devout terms: "He wasn't God, but he was certainly God-like. He was the closest thing to a god that I knew."

And not surprisingly, fans often expect their musical heroes to possess supernatural abilities. Beatles press officer Derek Taylor said of the group in 1964: "It was as if a savior had arrived and all of these people were happy and relieved, as if things somehow were going to be better now. The only thing left for the Beatles is to go on a healing tour." Unfortunately, he wasn't the only one who believed that the Fab Four possessed divine powers.

Ringo Starr recalled a distressing situation that the Beatles regularly faced during the peak of their popularity: "Crippled people were constantly being brought backstage to be touched by a 'Beatle,' and it was very strange." Peter Brown, a Beatles insider, wrote about the group's first trek across America: "Everywhere the Beatles turned, they seemed surrounded by the unfortunate; children crippled by various diseases, blind children, the retarded, the terminally ill. It was the crippled children who sat in the first five rows of every concert, so the Beatles looked out over a sea of wheelchairs. And it was inevitably the afflicted who got backstage passes. Desperate parents would present these children to the boys, and one of John's primary memories of touring was the twisted hands reaching out for him." And according to one Beatles biographer, "In Australia, a woman threw her disabled six-year-old at Paul, who was riding in an open truck. When Paul handed the child back the woman wept. 'He's better. Oh, he's better!' she exclaimed."

George Harrison later declared: "We were only trying to play rock 'n' roll and they'd be wheeling them in, not just in wheelchairs but sometimes in oxygen tanks. What did they think that we were able to do? I don't know." Likewise, John Lennon would later argue: "I'm not claiming divinity. I've never claimed purity of soul. I've never claimed to have the answers to life. I only put out songs and answer questions as honestly as I can – no more, no less. I cannot live up to other people's expectations of me because they're illusionary."

Nonetheless, music does possess a number of unique healing properties. Playing the drums repairs the brain after a stroke, music therapy aids social functioning among those suffering from schizophrenia and merely listening to music has the ability to alleviate anxiety, depression and chronic pain. Tom Petty explained: "Music is a real magic: It affects human beings, it can heal, it can do wonderful things. I've had two people contact me in my life about coming out of comas [while their families played] a song... of mine, that they had liked before they were injured."

*   *   *   *   *   *

Beatles insider Ray Connolly once wrote: "There's an unwritten rule in entertainment that says you should never meet your idols – because nine times out of ten they will disappoint you." One 14-year-old fan who won a radio station prize to attend a Beatles news conference in 1964 recounted his reaction when the four Mop Tops walked into the room: "You know, for so long, you built them up into some larger-than-life beings. And they were just regular human beings. They looked small. I was expecting giants." And the wizard behind the curtain was a mere mortal, too.

▶ CHAPTER 11
ROCK STARS & PRIVACY

Soon after scoring their first big hit, rockers quickly realize they have lost their privacy. Not surprisingly, successful performers have to hire full-time guards, install tall fences and employ high-end security systems. And stars like Bob Dylan and Whitney Houston were forced to purchase the properties adjacent to their homes for the purpose of ensuring some level of seclusion and personal safety. Additionally, both George Harrison and Zac Brown fought local zoning boards to close walkways near their homes in order to discourage prying eyes. Brown explained: "I'm not interested in the public coming up to my home, people snooping, walking up to my windows. I've had to sell property for this reason."

In 2018, *The New York Times* offered an example of what typically occurs when a famous rocker is spotted in public: "On the back patio of a Greek restaurant, a white-haired man making his way to the exit paused for a second look at one of his fellow diners, a man with a prominent nose who wore his dark hair in a modest pompadour. 'You look a lot like Steve Perry,' the white-haired man said. 'I used to be Steve Perry,' Steve Perry said. This is how it goes when you are Steve Perry. Everyone is excited to see you, and no one can quite believe it." Likewise, Steven Tyler of Aerosmith revealed: "Sometimes you're in the gym at 7:30 in the morning, and you haven't had your coffee and everyone you meet is like, 'Oh, my God!' It's like getting pecked to death by chickens."

Some superstars such as Elvis Presley were prisoners of their own stardom. As one Presley biographer wrote: "[Elvis] achieved the material riches of the American Dream, but what he earned was suffocating fame. Unable to go out to the movies, he rented theaters and arranged private screenings in the middle of the night for himself and his entourage. Unable to treat his daughter to a day at an amusement park, he paid a full-day's profits so he and his child could ride a Ferris wheel without being pestered. Unable to develop real friendships, he filled his payroll with the hired yes-men of the 'Memphis Mafia.'"

Singer Paul Anka, who became good friends with Presley during the 1970s, recalled: "You wouldn't see Elvis in a public restaurant... holding forth at a table full of friends.... Elvis was scared to death to do that.... His social terror was extreme. I'd say. 'Elvis why don't we just go out for dinner, go for a walk? 'On, no!' He was too terrified of that. You'd go over to his hotel – we both worked for the Hilton – and he'd have aluminum foil on the windows; he never wanted to see the daylight."

According to *The New York Post*, in the last years of Elvis' life, fame had transformed him into a captive inside his own home: "At Graceland, he spent most of his days and nights upstairs in his pajamas, rarely venturing beyond his bedroom or adjoining office.... [His fiancee Ginger Alden] never saw him eat at a table. Meals were delivered to them in bed. To spruce up, Elvis might throw on a jeweled blue bathrobe. Or if there was a need to leave the house, he would pull a jumpsuit over his pajamas."

The members of the Beatles suffered many of the same problems. George Harrison's former producer Ken Scott recalled that "George grew tired of fame and adulation faster than the others. He was always kind and polite, but he did his best to downplay who he was as much as possible.... When someone would come up to him and say, 'Aren't you George Harrison?' he would come back with 'You know, I've been told I look like him by other people but I don't see it. I think I'm much better looking, don't you?' Very rarely did anyone pursue it further." In a 2004 interview, Paul McCartney recalled: "George once said that fame cost him his nervous system. I can understand that. Fame happened to us all when we were just kids, really. Being recognized wherever we went, that came really quick.... Until the whole world knew who we were. So there was nowhere, absolutely nowhere, we could go where we weren't instantly recognizable. And, whatever we did, even if we never made another record, we could never be *un*famous again. So it's sink or swim." Similarly, in 2008, when Ringo Starr was asked about "the last place" he had "visited where nobody recognized" him, he responded, "I don't believe it's happened yet. Walking along the streets, you'll see the nudges. I've been to Nepal, and they wave at me. It's just how it is." And John Lennon once complained about the constant attention: "I see these hungry eyes, these people, it's like they want to eat a part of me."

Kurt Cobain, who also struggled with the reverberations of fame, said of Lennon: "I just felt really sorry for him. To be locked up in that apartment. Although he was totally in love with Yoko and his child, his life was a prison. He was imprisoned. It's not fair. That's the crux of the problem that I've had with becoming a celebrity – the way people deal with celebrities. It needs to be changed; it really does."

Jeff Lynne, who openly idolized the Fab Four, once admitted: "Would I have liked to have been a Beatle? I don't know. It wasn't all beer and Skittles being a Beatle. To have been under so much pressure, to not have been able to walk down the street? I'm a very private person. I would have found that very tough. So maybe no."

Conversely, when former Guns N' Roses guitarist Slash was asked about the "price of fame," he explained: "I guess there are certain sacrifices, like losing a sense of anonymity. But you just sort of knew what you were getting into, so why whine about it?"

Beyond losing their privacy in public settings, rockers also undergo an intrusive examination of their lives for the entire world to see. At the dawn of his career, Johnny Cash stated: "I was well aware of the fact that the private lives of entertainers are anything but private. The public knows or will soon know the moral and spiritual position of any entertainer who comes on the scene.... There is no better light to read what is really on a person's face than a spotlight."

Additionally, when you're famous, everyone you come into contact with on a daily basis will later talk about the interaction. However, some will do far more. Steven Tyler of Aerosmith explained: "Everyone you work with, buy a car from, hire as a babysitter; everyone who fixes your computer. Each become, overnight, a writer of short stories, a chronicler of mouth-watering scandal.... Anyone who's worked for Paul McCartney, believe me, has a story to tell."

As a result, hundreds of books have been written by people who knew, dated, married or were employed by the Beatles or Elvis. In 1976, Elvis felt betrayed when two of his former bodyguards – cousins Sonny and Red West – signed a lucrative contract to write a book about their time with the King. The resulting biography would sell in excess of three-million copies. Similarly, Elvis' ex-wife Priscilla dated a number of men later in life, including Tom Jones. But two of her ex-boyfriends would ultimately write books after ending their relationships with the former Mrs. Presley.

DINING IN PUBLIC

A simple activity like eating a meal in a restaurant can be a major hassle for a rock star. Nick Rhodes of Duran Duran recalled how, in 2015, he watched in horror as a mob swarmed around pop singer Justin Bieber at a charity dinner: "I felt so bad for him. All night, non-stop, no-one would leave him alone, even when he was eating.... Everyone coming up to Justin had a phone, wanting a picture – guys who were 50 or 60, who really should have known better, demanding a selfie for their god-daughter. I just thought 'Let the guy eat!'"

Similarly, when the album *Pyromania* became a worldwide smash, Def Leppard singer Joe Elliott recalled: "In four months, I went from no one bothering me at breakfast to having 400 people watch me eat steak and eggs. You become a prisoner in your own room. This is what makes people in bands totally weird."

And singer-songwriter Janis Ian recalled the experience of eating in a small diner after a concert: "I noticed one older man staring at me out of the corner of his eye.... He kept gawking, and it became irritating. It's hard to relax when someone actually turns around on their counter stool and stares at you without pretense, occasionally whispering something to the person next to him and laughing. I felt like a zoo animal."

Likewise, when Axl Rose and his entourage would visit an all-night restaurant in the early-1990s, there was a predictable reaction. According to Rose's touring assistant Craig Duswalt: "When we arrived at one of these fine establishments, it was virtually empty. One disheveled waitress, one male cook with a hairnet, half asleep, and a manager reading the daily newspaper for probably the fifteenth time with a cup of coffee. It was always interesting to see the looks on their faces when they saw who just got out of the stretch limo and walked into their little restaurant. The manager would always sit us in the 'nicest' booth and usually ask for an autograph. Axl obliged. The waitress would take our order and fumble her words while explaining the 'specials.' We were fully aware that Denny's never had specials, but Axl was there, the waitress always wanted to spend as much time as possible at our table. So she made up some specials. Happened all the time. A once empty restaurant would somehow fill with people within fifteen minutes. It only took one phone call from an employee for the word to get out. And in small towns around the world, news spreads quickly. And remember, this is long before everyone had social media on their cell phones."

And on an episode of *The Dick Cavett Show* in 1971, John Lennon complained that he couldn't get a meal at a restaurant because the waiters would be shocked to see him in person, and then would babble instead of paying attention to what he ordered. Conversely, J.J. Cale – best known for writing the classics "After Midnight," "Call Me The Breeze" and "Cocaine" – recalled going to a restaurant with Eric Clapton during the middle of a recording session: "The minute we walked in, everybody went 'That's Eric Clapton!' And we couldn't eat! What Eric says is, 'Well, that's part of show business.' It just rolls off him. He likes it."

NOT ALL ROCK STARS ARE SPOTTED IN PUBLIC

In the first decade of the rock era, it was still possible for a hit rock and rock star to remain relatively anonymous. Even in the 1970s, the members of Pink Floyd boasted about how they were able to walk to their concerts from nearby hotels and no one would recognize them. Similarly, Jimmy Buffett admitted that he is rarely recognized when venturing out in public: "No one bothers me. It's amazing. I'm not on television and that's the big difference. I can walk around with shocking anonymity. People don't know who I am. I went to Disney World walking around the other day and was stopped twice."

Likewise, drummer Graeme Edge of the Moody Blues explained why his bandmates wanted to remain anonymous during their early years: "There were no photographs of any of us [on the hit album *Days Of Futures Past*], except the tops of our heads sitting at a meeting [on the back cover]; it was all very low key. The reason for that was we had just come back from a Beatles tour. We just saw what a life they led. We said, 'No, no, no... That's not for us.' They couldn't do anything. They couldn't get out of their hotel. They couldn't go to a pub or club. They were trapped in their hotel room every day. It was a bit scary. I'd step out of the hotel, and just because I was short with long hair.... I'd be chased up the street, and I wasn't even one of 'em."

Some musicians are known by their stage costumes and become virtual unknowns when they aren't wearing their signature gear. According to a profile in *The New Yorker*, "George Strait has discovered that when he isn't wearing a cowboy hat people often don't realize that he is George Strait. In San Antonio, where he lives, he can usually visit restaurants unmolested, so long as he doesn't smile too widely – he is famous for his smile, which is bright and crooked."

Similarly, in 2012 when Frank Beard of ZZ Top leisurely walked down the red carpet at the Rock and Roll Hall of Fame induction ceremony in Cleveland, he went completely unnoticed. No one screamed, no one shouted his name and only one or two spectators took his photo. Despite the thousands of music fans in attendance, he was essentially incognito without his trademark bandana and sunglasses.

However, many artists are forced to wear disguises when venturing out in public. Alice Cooper admitted: "If I go to a baseball game, I tie my hair back and try to disguise myself so I don't have to sit there and sign autographs for eight hours." When David Bowie walked around New York City in his latter years, he carried a Greek newspaper to convince bystanders that he was a foreign tourist who just happened to resemble the Thin White Duke. And at their last-ever paid concert in Britain, the Beatles had to sneak into the large venue. Reporter Derek Johnson recalled: "I was waiting for the Beatles at the back door of Wembley Stadium, where the kitchens were, when this big van drew up and four chefs got out, with the proper white hats and aprons, carrying trays of goodies in their hands. As they walked towards me, I realized that it was the Beatles. They frequently adopted disguises to avoid being mobbed by screaming girls. They got in without being spotted and were running across the kitchen when Ringo tripped and his tray of cakes went everywhere, followed by the other three landing in a heap on top of him like a Marx Brothers routine. It was an awful mess, but they were so pleased to have got in with no trouble that they all thought it was hilariously funny."

NOT KNOWN IN PUBLIC

On some occasions, musical artists have suffered negative consequences when they *aren't* recognized. Early in the career of Connie Francis, she had difficulty convincing a security guard to let her into the *American Bandstand* studio, where she was scheduled to perform her first hit, "Who's Sorry Now." Francis recalled, "'I'm a singer, sir,' I whispered meekly, 'and I'm doin' the Dick Clark Show.'' 'Yeah I know, kid. Me, too. Only, I'm a ballerina' .... 'No, honest-to-goodness, mister,' I whined plaintively. 'I really am a singer. My name is Connie Francis'.... 'No kiddin'?' the guard answered. 'Well, my name is Geronimo.'"

And in December 1967, Jim Morrison was making out with a female fan – backstage, before a concert in New Haven, Connecticut – when a police officer told the couple to leave. The officer did not recognize Morrison. Ignoring the officer's orders, Morrison was maced. Later, during the performance of "Back Door Man," Morrison taunted the police officers in attendance and told the audience what had occurred backstage. Drawing the ire of the police, Morrison was arrested for indecency, inciting a riot and public obscenity.

And singer Cher experienced an episode of mistaken identity during an early Sonny & Cher concert: "The craziest it ever got was at the Cow Palace in San Francisco, where the kids kept running onto the stage. The promoter got afraid that the stage would collapse, and he stopped the concert several times. [Sonny] sat tight, even when it got hairy, but I'd run off at the first sign that kids might break through. At one point I was running between the stage and the car parked offstage, which was a vulnerable, open area. A security guard mistook me for a crazed Cher lookalike – one of those girls who were ironing their hair straight and dying it black, to go with their vests and bell-bottoms. This big Neanderthal grabbed me by the throat and put me in a hammerlock. I couldn't breathe and was starting to pass out when our managers jumped on top of him and almost killed him."

▶ CHAPTER 12
BAD AND ILLEGAL
BEHAVIOR EXCUSED

Standing at the podium of the Rock and Roll Hall of Fame induction ceremony in 1989, a tuxedoed Mick Jagger mused: "It's slightly ironic that tonight you see us on our best behavior, but we're being rewarded for 25 years of bad behavior.... Americans are funny people. First you shock them and then they put you in a museum."

Having a hit record can change a musician's life in unexpected ways. Not only are rockers unchained from following society's rules and norms, but they routinely get away with breaking the law as well. Singer Grace Slick admitted: "If you were in a rock 'n' roll band in the '60s, the only thing you couldn't do was kill people. Everything else was acceptable."

In his autobiography, Sammy Hagar revealed how his 1984 hit "I Can't Drive 55" substantially impacted his life: "That song changed my relationship with the California Highway Patrol. At that point in my life, I'd had thirty-six tickets. My license taken away three times. I was paying $125,000 a year for car insurance, because I had all these hot cars. I'd been to traffic school. I hired attorneys, I erased as much as I possibly could, legally and financially, and I was still in bad shape. 'I Can't Drive 55' changed everything. Since I wrote that song, I've maybe had two citations. I've been pulled over at least forty times, stopped and let go."

However, at the start of the rock era, performers were under greater scrutiny in a futile attempt to stamp out what was then considered a dangerous, corrupting form of music. Consequently, early rockers had to be on their best behavior. In 1956, Elvis Presley was threatened with arrest by Judge Marion Gooding – over the issue of "impairing the morals of minors" – if he was caught shaking his hips during a concert in Jacksonville, Florida. Heeding the warning, Elvis shook only his pinkie finger during his entire performance.

But eventually, the public face of the rock star would dramatically change as outlandish displays of recklessness became the norm. While Pete Townshend smashed his guitar onstage, his bandmate Keith Moon marched around in Third Reich uniforms and drove cars into swimming pools.

Eventually, even novice rockers felt the need to act out in public. In the mid-1960s, future Aerosmith members Joe Perry and Steven Tyler regularly crossed paths in a New Hampshire resort town, Sunapee Harbor. At the time, Tyler was the frontman of a pair of teenage bands that were popular in the area. Perry, who was a restaurant grill cook at the time, recalled: "Steven would come in with his bands and they'd act like they figured rock stars are supposed to, throwing food, real loud and obnoxious, wearing Carnaby Street outfits, the whole trip in this little town that looked up to them as the local rock stars." After Tyler and his bandmates left the restaurant in shambles, it was Perry's job to clean up the mess.

ROCK STARS AS SPOILED CELEBRITIES

Not only is rock star behavior excused, it's expected and encouraged. A young Bobby Darin once told Connie Francis: "There are rules in life for everyone, right? But if you're a star, they just don't apply to you. Stars make their own rules. They're the royalty of this country. Signs say 'Do this,' or 'Don't do this,' and you know the signs were meant for the rest of the world, but not for you."

Eric Clapton admitted that in the 1970s, "it was my normal thing when I was angry to contest authority, so a customs official, or a policeman, or a concierge, or anyone else with a uniform would get the sharp end of my tongue, and then it would be left for someone... to clean up the mess, or bail me out, make apologies, pay the bill, or do whatever it might take to redress the situation."

Similarly, Meat Loaf admitted: "I was out of control. I would have tantrums – nightly! I would rage in my cage before going on. I would throw chairs, demolish dressing rooms. I threw microphone stands at the band. I was throwing microphone stands at the *audience*. I was a perfect monster. The band would give me a wide berth as if I were some beast in captivity about to be exhibited to the public."

And according to drummer Skip Alan, the members of Led Zeppelin "would get red carpet treatment wherever they went. As soon as they got into a club – they'd start picking up everything off the table and chucking food around. There'd be Dover soles going all round the restaurant. They were just insane. [The group's tour manager Richard] Cole would always sort out the aggro. He'd drop a few hundred quid to the manager and say, 'Sorry about that, mate.'"

And rapper Kanye West established a reputation for his public outbursts during the early years of his career. In 2007, when he failed to win a prize at the MTV Music Video Awards, he launched an angry tirade. Then two years later, he rushed the stage and grabbed Taylor Swift's award as she was about to thank the audience.

SPECIAL TREATMENT BY THE LAW

Prisons have been the subject of a number of rock hits from "I Fought The Law" and "Chain Gang" to "Jailhouse Rock" and "Thirty Days In The Hole." But curiously, rockers are far more likely to sing about prison than to spend time behind bars. As a rule, celebrities of all stripes receive favorable treatment in the court system due to their fame. What judge wants to be responsible for locking up a popular entertainer?

British keyboard player Rick Wakeman recalled how he frequently accompanied Keith Moon and his entourage on a number of drinking sessions in the 1970s: "Most evenings ended with us being brought home in a police car. But we all had a fantastic relationship with the police in those days, because it was also entertainment for them. As long as no one got hurt and we paid for the damages."

Even Johnny Cash was frequently in trouble with the law. Despite briefly landing in jail seven times on misdemeanor charges, he never served any prison time. In one instance, he accidentally started a large fire in California which charred 500-acres.

More often, rockers found themselves in trouble for using illicit drugs. Although the dramatic drug convictions of Keith Richards and Mick Jagger made the front pages around the globe in 1967, the charges against Richards were later dropped and Jagger's six-month sentence was commuted. Even when they're found guilty in a court of law, musicians caught with drugs are usually sentenced to rehab rather than prison time.

And although some countries have strict drug laws, a rock superstar can still expect a slap on the wrist. In 1980, when Paul McCartney was caught with nearly half a pound of marijuana upon entering Japan for an 11-date tour, he faced a sentence of seven-years behind bars. Instead, after spending just nine-days in the Tokyo Narcotics Detention Center, he was released and subsequently deported from the country – without ever having to make a single court appearance.

Some crimes are far less likely to be excused. Decades before O.J. Simpson led police on a slow chase down a Los Angeles freeway, singer Jerry Lee Lewis earned the nickname "The Killer." Whether or not Lewis played a role in the mysterious deaths of two of his seven wives is still debated. Lewis wasn't as lucky in 1976 when he was ordered to pay damages of $125,000 for accidentally shooting his bass player in the chest.

Not all rockers have been as fortunate when dealing with the justice system. Rick Stevens of Tower Of Power and former Eric Clapton sideman Jim Gordon were both convicted of murder. And Sid Vicious was infamously accused of murdering his girlfriend Nancy Spungen, but fatally overdosed before the start of his trial. And the eccentric producer Phil Spector was also not spared. Convicted in 2009 of murdering an actress at his home, Spector was sentenced to a minimum of 19-years in prison.

QUESTIONING ROCK STAR EXCESS

Few musicians have been critical of rock star excess. Simon LeBon, the lead singer of Duran Duran, declared: "I don't have a lot of sympathy for people who are fabulously wealthy and are treated like royalty and behave badly. But I also think we've facilitated their being famous for doing nothing, and in so doing we've said, 'Well, make it interesting then.' So they live their lives in public, and they lead more and more extreme lives. And really, it's happening because the public demands to see it."

Similarly, Yannis Philipakis of the British indie rock band, Foals, insisted: "When stuff is going well in your life don't forget that it could be very different. I find it repellent seeing people who have acquired success treat people badly. Always treat a waiter well, always treat bar staff well, treat your cab driver well, treat anyone performing a service for you well."

And late in his career, British rockabilly singer Shakin' Stevens warned: "The most important lesson I've learnt during my career is that, yes, talent is important, but equally, so is the way you conduct yourself with other people – and always remember, that the people you meet on the way up, are the same ones you're gonna meet somewhere back down the line."

Additionally, Millennials are less tolerant of rock excess than previous generations. In 2017, rock singer Matt Healy observed: "The days of being a rock star without any kind of self-awareness are dead. The days of being able to get away with anything and be glorified for it are dead. Thanks to the internet, everybody's got everybody else's number. How can you go out and be... Jim Morrison? The world isn't gonna allow for that."

ROCK STARS GETTING FREE THINGS

Payola takes many forms in the entertainment industry. Over the years, hit rock acts were the targets of instrument makers who hoped to see their gear used onstage or featured on album covers. But the swag in rock and roll was not limited to musical equipment. Even when there is no formal arrangement between a corporation and a rock star, companies will deluge a hit act with free stuff – whether or not the artist actually uses the gear, wears the clothing or drinks the particular brand of whisky.

Tom Petty recalled a situation in 1979, just after the release of his commercial breakthrough, *Damn The Torpedoes*. At the time, the members of the group were finally selling huge numbers of albums but had yet to reap the financial rewards of their hard work. As a result, they were quite happy to receive whatever promotional gifts they were given. As Petty explained in 1981, "[Nike had] seen that we wear their wrestling shoes... so they said we could come over and get some stuff for free. When we got there they just started piling stuff on us: 'Oh, I like that one.' 'Great, what size would you like?' After we had more than I could carry, they said, 'Don't forget, we've still gotta go over to the sportswear.' Then when we were all finished, they looked at this enormous pile and said, 'We better give you something to carry it all in,' and brought out these huge leather equipment bags.... You know, when you're broke, nobody gives you nothin' – nothin'. But as soon as you can afford it, it's 'Sure, go ahead, take whatever you want.' It's ab-so-lutely backwards."

Additionally, trendy restaurants will offer free meals or drinks to stars in exchange for attracting customers who hope to get a glimpse of a celebrity. Led Zeppelin's tour manager Richard Cole explained, "I'll tell you how much we used to drink. I think we bankrupted Steve Paul's Scene [nightclub] in New York because we *never* paid our bar bills."

However, being accustomed to special treatment can result in embarrassing situations. Pattie Boyd, the first wife of George Harrison, recalled an evening out with her husband and friends at a small town in England: "That night we went into Bangor in search of a restaurant and found the only one that was open late, the Chinese. Fine. In we went. A couple hours and many bottles of wine later, we discovered that none of us had enough money to pay the bill. We weren't used to paying restaurant bills. Or any others, for that matter."

Similarly, there are monetary risks when hard-drinking musicians get together for a night out. As Nick Mason of Pink Floyd explained: "If you go out without a promoter or record exec on hand to pick up the bill, an outing involving drinking can easily become a terrifying financial experience as the more experienced participants make their excuses and slip away early, leaving the luckless victim holding the tab, and filled with a grim determination never to socialize again, certainly not in an overpriced bar."

Fame and stardom can also mean free admission to rock concerts. And if you're a big enough star, you're invited to watch the show from the side of the stage. Steve Ferrone – who replaced Stan Lynch in Tom Petty and the Heartbreakers – recalled the time he was invited by George Harrison to attend a Prince concert at Wembley Arena: "We didn't have any tickets or anything. We got into this limousine to Wembley and George said to the driver, 'Just drive around to the back.' We slowly pull up to the two security guards at the gate, and they ask for credentials. George rolls down the window and says, 'It's okay, it's me.' And they say, 'Oh, okay, fine, park over there!' He looked at us with a little grin and said, 'It's good to play that Beatle card sometimes.' He didn't take it terribly seriously, but he was aware of the clout."

Additionally, some musical acts make unreasonable demands of host cities when touring. In 2004, Knight-Ridder reported: "The national promoters of the Michael Jackson tour have asked the city of Philadelphia to agree to arrange free hotel rooms and free use of JFK Stadium and to relinquish the city's usual cut of stadium food and beverage sales before the Jacksons will set foot on stage in Philadelphia. Taxpayers, in effect, would be subsidizing the Jackson 'Victory' tour." Although Philadelphia balked at most of the demands, other cities offered generous concessions to the Jacksons.

Not all rock stars take advantage of their fame. Graham "Suggs" McPherson, the lead singer of Madness, stated: "I have never said, 'Do you know who I am?' to get in somewhere. But I do remember being outside a nightclub once and hearing Billy Idol say exactly that. Everyone around him was rolling around on the floor laughing. So I've always been wary of that sort of outcome."

Additionally, fans will often shower rock artists with gifts. When news spread that Jack White's favorite guitar – a hard-to-find "J.B. Hutto" Montgomery Ward Airline model from 1964 – was falling apart, a fan paid $3,000 for a mint-condition instrument on an online auction site and shipped it to a very grateful White. Nonetheless, White felt awkward accepting the gift: "It was very nice of him, very generous. I don't know – a lot of people have given me guitars in the last year or two, and I don't know what to say. I hate to take them. I feel bad taking presents like that." And in 2019, when a bidder at a charity auction paid $243,200 for Olivia Newton-John's iconic black leather jacket from the hit film *Grease*, the superfan gifted it back to the singer. However, some gifts are downright creepy. Jared Leto, the lead singer of 30 Seconds To Mars, once received a human ear from a fan. Instead of disposing of the body part, Leto "poked a hole in it and wore it as a necklace."

Nonetheless, although a rocker may be accustomed to getting free drinks and complimentary steak dinners, the same cannot be said for any work he needs done to his home, car or business. Suddenly a $20,000 swimming pool costs twice that amount, and a $300 visit from a plumber might cost far more than that.

▶ CHAPTER 13
THE SPECIAL FANS:
THE GROUPIES

Money and fame are powerful aphrodisiacs. The rich, famous and powerful have always had their choice of partners. Whether politicians, NBA stars or chart-topping singers, there's a certain allure attached to encounters with well-known public figures.

Amazingly, the simple process of strumming a guitar or singing into a microphone can make someone desirable. Punk rocker Richard Hell once remarked: "It was interesting how playing rock and roll made a person attractive. I hadn't been handsome before."

Consequently, some music fans want more than an autograph, a selfie photo or a quick handshake. Devotees who act on those impulses and offer themselves to musicians are known as groupies, a term reportedly coined by Bill Wyman in 1965 during a Rolling Stones tour of Australia.

Although groupies did not start with rock and roll, they are an omnipresent part of the seamier side of the music industry. In the 1970s, the members of Led Zeppelin were legendary for their episodes of groupie abuse. The Cameron Crowe film, *Almost Famous*, featured a number of groupie characters. Similarly, the Mötley Crüe biographical film, *The Dirt*, exposed the extreme debauchery of the rock and roll lifestyle.

Pioneering rocker Jerry Lee Lewis admitted: "It seemed like women fell out of trees. Playing in the clubs... you just do it. They just lay it on you. It was just about impossible to resist. And I just had to pick one out. It just kind of seemed like a dream. It just seemed like 'The Impossible Dream,' as Elvis would say. I'd see these girls walking by the bandstand, mouthing 'I love you,' and I'm sixteen, seventeen, and I see these girls, and I just try to turn my head and do my songs and get off stage. And, son, it was good. As long as I wanted them."

Many rockers have kept tallies or written chronicles of the women they met. Gene Simmons of Kiss, on the other hand, took thousands of Polaroid pictures of the women he encountered on the concert road. (However, after Simmons married model Shannon Tweed, he publicly swore off groupies.) Similarly, singer Stephen Pearcy of Ratt admitted to bedding three women a day while on tour: "Back in the day, I used to keep my itineraries to keep track of every single chick I ever met.... I kept them my whole adult life. Had stacks and stacks of them. They got burned by my super-pissed girlfriends. I'd just write the girl's name, her phone number, the city I met her in, and a rating. You know, seven, eight, maybe a nine. Once in a while, a true ten."

Some rockers seem to have a psychological hold over their fans. The first time that singer-songwriter Carly Simon met Mick Jagger, she observed: "Right away, I could tell that for Mick Jagger, all women, including me, were his, by divine right. Women existed to frame him, impress him, shimmer for him, illuminate him, jog themselves helpfully into his peripheral vision: a fast-click snapshot Mick might take out of the corner of one eye for future purposes and dalliances."

However, not all rock bands were able to attract groupies. Ozzy Osbourne recalled his early years on the road with Black Sabbath: "Even after our first album went gold, I never got good-looking chicks. Black Sabbath is a blokes' band. We'd get [cigarette butts] and beer bottles thrown at us, not frilly underwear."

Some groupies became celebrities in their own right. One notable groupie, Connie Hamzy, was immortalized in the lyrics of Grand Funk's 1973 hit, "We're An American Band." Nancy Spungen, another legendary groupie, had traveled to England to follow Johnny Thunders' band before ending up as the tragic junkie girlfriend of Sid Vicious.

However, it was Pamela Des Barres who made a career out of penning revealing books about her proclivities in the rock world. As the world's best-known groupie, she was intimate with a who's who of musical royalty. Asked by Jimmy Page to accompany him on a Led Zeppelin tour, she recalled: "One time I was on the side of the stage as Jimmy entranced 80,000 fans with his guitar playing. From my vantage point, sitting on Jimmy's amp, I almost felt like one of the group. Girls in the audience looked up at me and wondered which one I was sleeping with, and I was so proud. I was exactly who I'd aspired to be – the girlfriend of the lead guitar player in the world's biggest rock and roll band."

Amazingly, even celebrities were not immune to acting like infatuated groupies. Noted producer Ted Perlman recalled the odd scene, backstage at a Martin Luther King, Jr. tribute concert in 1986: "We were sitting in the green room and I had Liz Taylor on one side of me and Bob [Dylan] on the other side and Elizabeth saw Bob and just hit on him. She got all giddy over him. Bob was wearing this flannel shirt outside his dirty jeans and he's got work boots on. He's got dirt under his fingernails. His hair hasn't been washed for three days.... He's skinny and he's grungy and his personal hygiene – he has no hygiene. That's just the way he is... But women don't care. He has that kind of power over them."

APPROACHING GROUPIES

Rock bands typically employ roadies and stage hands to deliver backstage passes to the women in the audience whom the musicians would like to *meet* after the concert. Some bands devised complex codes to communicate the location of their selections during the course of a concert. More often, women simply make themselves available by hanging out by the stage doors or finding out where the band is staying.

R&B vocalist Gladys Knight recalled the exploits she witnessed while touring in the 1960s: "It seemed like the tour-bus driver always knew which corner they'd be waiting on as we came into town to pick up groupies who wanted to hitch to a star for a brief ride. Often the guys in the other bands would mistreat these groupies terribly. I remember one horrible time on the road. I think it was in Alabama, when one of these girls fell asleep on the bus with her mouth open and a few musicians amused themselves by flicking cigarette ashes in her mouth."

On the other hand, Art Garfunkel was far more sophisticated when he wanted to meet a female fan. He once admitted: "I had it down to an art form. When you sign autographs after a show, you see the real pretty one and make sure you get to her last. Then you ask, ever so casually, 'Have you had dinner?'"

Female rockers weren't excluded from the hedonistic rock and roll lifestyle. However, the relationship between the female artists and their groupies tended to be far different. In 1986, singer Aimee Mann of 'Til Tuesday discussed her encounters with potential groupies: "I have male fans. I don't know what they want to do with me. I certainly don't inquire. They're pretty young and odd. They're really cute. They're usually under 20, outsider kinds of guys who have funny haircuts, dress differently."

Conversely, Chrissie Hynde claimed that she has never been approached by male fans offering themselves up after a concert. She explained: "It doesn't work like that for women. A guy might see a pretty girl saying, 'Let's go,' but it doesn't work the other way around." Similarly, Stevie Nicks described what it was like to be on the road with Fleetwood Mac in the 1970s: "[We were] very cloistered.... Christine [McVie] and I didn't go out. We didn't pick up guys. We'd hang out, play cards, and watch movies. It wasn't that much fun." In fact, when the group began recording *Rumours*, the studio provided a small house for the band. However, as Nicks recalled, "that house was like the riot house. There were girls everywhere and everybody was completely drunk the whole time. Me and Chris [McVie] decided we couldn't be there. The next day we moved out and got two matching apartments next to each other."

In the wake of the "Me Too" movement – epitomized by the alleged exploits of Harvey Weinstein and Bill Cosby – many in the entertainment industry have openly pondered why so few musicians have been tarnished by similar allegations. There are, of course, a few highly publicized cases involving Michael Jackson and R. Kelly, but they certainly are the exceptions.

However, Van Halen road manager Noel E. Monk detailed an exchange he witnessed between Alex Van Halen and a female worker, backstage in the early-1980s: "As a young, attractive member of the catering staff puts a plate of chicken wings on the buffet table, Alex ceases drumming and playfully grabs one of the woman's thighs. He smiles; she giggles and swats his hand away, and goes on with her work, seemingly unfazed. But I have a feeling she has a pretty good poker face – or maybe she is simply used to unwanted attention that comes with catering for rock bands. What can you say? Sexual harassment in one walk of life is merely harmless banter in the world of rock. Times have changed, of course, but thirty-five years ago? Well, you had to expect a little caveman from your rock star. These guys were conditioned to believe that just about every female who crossed their paths was a potential – and potentially eager – playmate. That's rock 'n' roll, baby. It's not just about the music. It's about sliding back down the slippery slope of evolution."

Conversely, Roger Daltrey of the Who told an interviewer: "Why would any rock star need to push themselves on women? Usually it's the other way around. I'd like to have £1 for every woman who squeezed my ass. Mick Jagger would be a billionaire out of it."

THE DOWNSIDE OF CAVORTING WITH GROUPIES

There are a number of moral, financial and health risks when cavorting with complete strangers. Rockers have sex with fans. Lots of sex. Lots of unprotected sex. As a result, STDs are a common problem, more so now than in the past. And not surprisingly, unexpected pregnancies can result from these serial, random encounters.

Consequently, musicians tend to have many offspring. Ray Charles had twelve children with ten different women. Blues legend B.B. King had fifteen children with fifteen different women. And amazingly, pioneering R&B star Screamin' Jay Hawkins – best known for the hit "I Put A Spell On You" – was married six times and had hundreds of lovers as he sired an estimated 75 children during his lengthy musical career. And when Hawkins died at age 70, he left behind a 31-year-old widow. At one point, the Rock and Roll Hall of Fame attempted to organize a "family reunion" for his offspring at the museum in Cleveland.

And before he became a soul music legend, Sam Cooke led the nation's most popular gospel act of the era, the Soul Stirrers. Cooke was hired in 1950 as a replacement for R.H. Harris, who was unable to travel with the group after becoming the target of numerous paternity lawsuits in multiple cities around the country. (Likewise, Cooke would father at least three children out of wedlock.)

*   *   *   *   *   *

Many rockers have refused to undergo genetic tests to prove or disprove paternity. In 1987, Tom Jones had a three-day fling with model Katherine Berkery during the middle of a U.S. tour. When she became pregnant, Jones denied the child was his. Ordered to take a DNA test, Jones was declared the boy's father in 1989. Nearly twenty-years later, Jones – then worth an estimated $300 million – finally acknowledged the existence of his son.

And after the death of David Cassidy, a 44-year-old woman publicly claimed she was his daughter. Despite previous denials by Cassidy and members of his family, the woman proved his paternity by testing DNA taken from a water bottle she had purchased on an auction website, which contained a small amount of the late singer's saliva.

Oftentimes, rockers may acknowledge their out-of-wedlock offspring but refuse to be involved in their upbringing. In 2018, Oasis co-founder Liam Gallagher met with his 21-year-old daughter for the first time in 19 years. Conversely, Steven Tyler has maintained a close relationship with actress Liv Tyler, since learning she was his daughter.

However, not all paternity claims are legitimate. In 1984, a German court dismissed a paternity suit against Paul McCartney that was filed by a 21-year-old German hairdresser. And Pete Townshend explained: "Imagine three or four girls coming along and saying, 'I had sex with Pete in the Sixties, when he was 25 and I was 12.' I know it didn't happen, but when you're a pop star people say all kinds of things.... I get

lots of pictures of children with big noses who claim I'm their dad."
Similarly, in 2011, then 17-year-old teen idol Justin Bieber was slapped
with a claim of paternity by a 20-year-old California woman. With his
reputation – and material wealth – at stake, he angrily denied the charges
and agreed to a paternity test. More significantly, in order to prevent
future claims, Bieber's legal team threatened litigation against the
woman, including a defamation lawsuit.

*　　　*　　　*　　　*　　　*　　　*

Musical performers also risk becoming the target of violence when
cavorting with fans. After the Beatles became a popular act in Liverpool,
a growing number of women openly flirted with members of the band.
Consequently, jealous boyfriends were often eager to start fights. During
one such post-concert skirmish in January 1961, John Lennon broke a
finger and Stuart Sutcliffe suffered a head injury.

Similarly, James "Tappy" Wright, a roadie with British Invasion act,
the Animals, recalled an incident at a New York City hotel in 1964,
while he was having breakfast with the group's guitarist, Hilton
Valentine. Wright recalled: "Out of the corner of my eye [I] saw a huge
hand descend onto Hilton's shoulder. 'Which one of you Animals is
sleeping with my sister?' The hand belonged to Cassius Clay, one of the
greatest boxers who ever lived, now known as Muhammad Ali. Under
Clay's hand, Hilton was shaking. We both knew immediately it would
be Eric [Burdon], but there was no way we were going to throw him to
the mercy of a furious Clay. We played dumb – what else could we do?"

TURNED OFF BY GROUPIES

Not all rockers appreciate the attention from eager groupies. Noel
Redding of the Jimi Hendrix Experience recalled: "I, for one, had
overdosed on sex. Not bad enough to say 'no' but still... so much and so
easy. No fun. No chase. After the shows, we'd scan the crowd of girls,
'OK, you and you (and you?) Come with me.' I didn't think it'd ever be
possible, but I just got fed up.... Every part of my body was showing
wearing and tear."

And Pete Townshend explained: "My take on groupies had nothing
to do with morality; I just didn't understand what they really wanted....
If you got to spend a few nights with Daltrey or Clapton, what did you
go on to do that would make it mean something? Tell your friends? Put
notches on your high heels? One woman, who often slept with Eric, was

never anything but beautiful, elegant and impressively intelligent. What made her follow bands around and hang around backstage, waiting for crumbs?"

Similarly, Alice Cooper explained in 1980: "Groupies were fun, especially at first. It was a status thing to have a groupie one day that had been with a big band the night before. I mean, you're on your way up and you're with this chick who had spent the night before with the Rolling Stones... After a while it gets odd, though, waking up and not knowing who the chick is next to you. It gets so you can't stand it.... I mean it actually does kind of get you sick. I'm really a romantic guy."

And ELO drummer Bev Bevan said of groupies: "Those girls seemed, after a time, to be a particular type. Often well-heeled, living on Daddy's money, a solid educational background – but they were living for kicks, taking any drug, any drink and sleeping with anyone to try to make life as exciting as possible. I suppose a groupie's all-time ambition is to marry a rock star – but most have to settle for a t-shirt."

Some rock artists were psychologically overwhelmed by the prospect of having to deal with aggressive groupies. Duggie Fields, a close friend of original Pink Floyd frontman Syd Barrett, described the pandemonium at the group's concerts: "Some of the girls were stunning, and they would literally throw themselves at Syd. He was the most attractive one; Syd was a very physically attractive person – I think he had problems with that. I saw it even when he was out of the group (by the beginning of 1969). People kept coming around and he would actually lock himself in his room. Like if he made the mistake of answering the front door before he'd locked himself in his room, he found it very difficult to say no. He'd have these girls pounding on his bedroom door all night, literally, and he'd be locked inside, trapped."

*   *   *   *   *   *

There's a saying among stars in the music and sports worlds – what happens on tour stays on tour. However, with the popularity of smart phone cameras, that is no longer the case. What used to be a private encounter can suddenly be streamed over the internet to the entire world. As Alex Kapranos, the lead singer of Franz Ferdinand, observed: "Some guys in bands still act as if it is still [the pre-internet era]. Then they see the pictures on Instagram, Facebook, Twitter, etc. Then their wife sees them. Then they can't tour any more. Or they get a divorce."

HANGERS ON: THE POSSE

In the music world, hit artists relentlessly find themselves the targets of con artists, yes-men, shady businessmen, opportunistic characters and various other hangers-on whose goals are to somehow finagle their way into the star's action, wealth or fame. While younger artists on the ascent are easy prey, veteran artists are glaringly aware of the hazards that accompany stardom and subsequently try to steer clear of these scammers.

Dave Wakelin of the (English) Beat observed: "You're always getting people trying to con you. People say, 'I can do this for you or that,' and after you've been talking to them for five minutes, you realize they're making it up as they go along. And what they actually mean is, 'Can I stand by your side and empty your pockets while you're doing something else?' Usually, the more wicked they are, the more they'll keep at you; the more you swear at them, the more they smile and try to be 'a real help.'" Likewise, Noel Redding of the Jimi Hendrix Experience recalled: "As we became famous, people began to hassle me, sometimes heavily, for money. I was regularly asked to guarantee loans, make investments, give handouts. Sometimes I was able to help friends, but mostly I didn't have what they wanted, and I was glad to escape the viciousness that followed some refusals."

Nevertheless, the bigger the musical act, the more likely there's a bloated entourage of paid assistants, who often do little work outside of massaging the artist's ego. Singer-songwriter Moby once warned: "Avoid people who just want to make you feel good about yourself. They're called sycophants, and they're the most dangerous people that any musician can be surrounded by." Rockabilly performer Ronnie Hawkins recalled an incident, backstage after a Bob Dylan concert in 1990: "He had about a hundred and fifty yes-men in his room. If he had reached for a cigarette, so many lighters would have come out that it would turn the sprinkler system on."

However, some musical acts avoid accumulating oversized entourages. Tom Petty explained: "I have never surrounded myself with [a] posse. I've seen artists go really wrong by having a lot of people around them to keep the myth inflated. I've always tried to stay with people who treat me fairly normally. It's really a drag not to be treated normally. I guess there's people who love that and really come to life in those kinds of situations."

The most legendary legion of yes-men were Elvis Presley's constant companions and sidekicks, informally dubbed the Memphis Mafia. The group of associates – close friends and relatives – were either on salary or regularly received lavish gifts. Among their duties were to protect the singer from fans, help with setting up tours, keep daily schedules and always be available to fulfill any of Elvis' whims. Pop singer Andy Williams recalled his first encounter with Elvis and the Memphis Mafia, backstage at the Caesars Palace casino in Las Vegas: "We talked about music and a few other things, and after a few minutes I noticed that every time Elvis said something mildly funny, his entourage would burst out laughing as if it was the funniest thing any of them had ever heard. Every time I said something halfway funny in response, my group would do the same thing. It was like two rival gangs meeting."

Not surprisingly, amassing a large entourage can be financially draining. Michelle Phillips of the Mamas and Papas recalled: "A lot of times it was hardly worth going out on the road because it cost us so much; we were big spenders. We liked having a lot of people with us. Even though some were incompetent, they were all good company. (I don't know of any band of real stature that had so many unorthodox and useless assistants on the road.)"

And according to documentary maker Nick Broomfield, R&B singer Whitney Houston "had all of these people who [were financially dependent on her], whether she was performing or not, right to the end, which was really why her $250 million fortune disappeared to nothing. All her friends and family had cars and houses, and she basically was paying for it all."

However, in the world of hip hop, a performer's success is gauged by the size of his posse. And as beefs arose between rappers, their posses would settle the scores.

STALKERS

There are always fans who are eager to enter into the worshipper/worshipee relationship, with both sides seemingly getting something out of the arrangement. However, when fans take that worship up another notch and become obsessive, they are potential stalkers. A number of pop songs have dealt with stalking including "Every Breath You Take" by the Police, "One Way Or Another" by Blondie and "Stan" by Eminem.

According to experts, stalkers tend to be male, in their late-30s to late-40s, have above-average intelligence, are either unemployed or employed on a part-time basis, and are often delusional. About 50-percent make threats against the targets of their stalking and about two-percent murder them. In 1990, California became the first state to make stalking a crime. Eventually, all fifty states enacted similar legislation.

Shockingly, stalking is commonplace in the music industry. Teen heartthrob Justin Bieber was the target of a grotesque plot to kill and then castrate him after a concert at Madison Square Garden. A fan of Icelandic singer Bjork mailed her an acid-spraying package, which was intercepted by police in London. The fan filmed himself making the device and committed suicide shortly afterwards. And when Miley Cyrus starred on *Hannah Montana*, a 53-year-old man was arrested for stalking the actress. He claimed she was personally sending him love messages on her television show. As he was dragged away from her production studio in Georgia, he cried out that he and Cyrus "will always be together."

Adam Ant warned: "If you're not famous, you can't understand it. At first it's fine, but what does 'fan' mean? It means 'fanatic.' So then you get the stalkers. You start to realize that any one of those people could have a gun." In his autobiography, Ant described one of his many stalkers: "She told me that the antenna I'd had planted in her head was working, that she could hear me talking to her, calling her to see me. She also put notes through my letterbox saying that we were married, including wedding rings and photographs in the envelope. For months she made my life hell."

An equally odd episode occurred at Michael Jackson's Neverland Ranch in the early-1980s. Jackson's longtime producer Quincy Jones recalled: "According to Michael, 'Billy Jean' was about a girl that climbed over [his] wall. He woke up one morning and she was laying out by the pool, bathing suit on. Just invaded the place, a stalker almost. And Michael says she had accused him of being the father of one of her twins!"

The members of the Beatles also had to deal with dangerous stalkers. In December 1999, George Harrison had few security measures in place at his Friar Park estate when an intruder broke into his home and entered his bedroom. During a subsequent brawl, Harrison was stabbed numerous times. After recovering from the near-fatal attack, he installed fences and implemented a number of other protective measures. Meanwhile, at around the same time, another stalker broke into Harrison's second residence in Hawaii. While inside, the intruder made herself a meal, did her laundry and telephoned her mother.

Likewise, when John Lennon resided at the Tittenhust Park estate near London in the early-1970s, he neglected to install any security systems on the premises. Instead, every morning a few of his employees would walk the grounds to evict the uninvited intruders. Tragically, it was Lennon's public accessibility on the streets of New York City that made him the target of a crazed publicity-seeker in 1980.

However, the most unusual music-related stalking case occurred in Scandinavia. A 300-pound forklift driver from the Netherlands was accused of stalking ABBA singer Agnetha Fältskog for a two-year period. According to *The New York Post*, the fan was "obsessed with ABBA in general and Agnetha in particular, [and] moved into a ramshackle cabin a short distance from her home in rural Sweden. He decorated his home from floor to ceiling with glossy color photos of Agnetha – and then began hanging out around her house." In 1997, she unexpectedly began a two-year relationship with her superfan. However, following their breakup in 2000, she sought a restraining order after he kept showing up at her home.

While most musical artists resort to traditional means when dealing with stalkers – like calling the police – Tanya Donelly of Belly once took the matter into her own hands: "The way he was harassing me was so typical and unimaginative. I ended up doing something in retrospect that was probably dumb. I wrote him a threatening letter saying, 'I will hire someone to hurt you if you contact me again.'" Amazingly, the stalker backed off.

*   *   *   *   *   *

It was revealed in 2018 that pop superstar Taylor Swift employed facial recognition technology at her concerts to identify known stalkers. With a virtual army of fanatics hounding her, she was forced to take extreme action. One of her stalkers had been sentenced to six-months in prison for breaking into her home, taking a shower and then falling asleep on her bed. And in 2018, another fan of the singer tried to demonstrate his affection by robbing a bank and then showering the stolen cash on the front lawn of her $17 million home in Rhode Island.

▶ CHAPTER 14
HOME LIFE:
FAMILY AND FRIENDS OF ROCK STARS

A career in music usually means a life as a wandering nomad. In 1974, Mick Jagger offered some insider advice: "If you're a musician I think it's very good not to be with anybody, and just live on your own. Domesticity is death. You see, the trouble with most musicians is that they're too domesticated. A musician doesn't spend too much time at home; he's on the road living out of a suitcase. Then, when he gets back home, he tends to become very domesticated.... It's taken me years to start buying furniture – I still don't hardly have anything and what I've got is falling to pieces. I can't stay in one place for too long."

Additionally, decompressing and returning to civilian life after a long concert tour are not easy tasks. Country singer June Carter Cash, the second wife of Johnny Cash, once told her musician daughter, Carlene: "You've got to always remember that when you're out on the road, everyone is telling you you're fantastic. Then you go home and you've got to be normal again. It's really hard to adjust, and you get the blues real bad. You get depressed because you come home after all this adrenaline's been going and the one you love isn't going, 'yeah' ... all the time. And they shouldn't, because you have to come back to normal." Similarly, Paul Stanley of Kiss observed: "After being on the road, being home takes some getting used to. When I'm on the road, I know that any time I can ring one of fifteen rooms and have company.... On the road, I can get yeses from everybody, but when you're home, you get nos."

Additionally, rock stars often resent the damage that their careers have caused to their relationships with friends and family members. Freddie Mercury of Queen admitted to a confidant: "For each step that you go up the ladder of success, you have to leave something behind that you love. You will lose friends, you will maybe even lose family, that's the price you have to pay." Similarly, Shirley Bassey, who entered show business at age 17, admitted: "Leaving [home] was the worst thing I ever did. I've found happiness in my work, but not in my private life. I had to take from my private life to make my public life successful. I had to make a lot of sacrifices.... I was happy until success entered my life, and then it was all downhill. Success spoilt me. It took away my happiness. My success became a barrier with my family. They couldn't relate to me, and I couldn't relate to them."

HELPING OUT FAMILY MEMBERS

Successful musicians tend to be financially generous with members of their families. Beginning in 1980, George Harrison sent his sister, Louise, a monthly "allowance" of $2,000. However, the payments stopped a year after his death in November 2001, despite the fact the former Beatle had amassed an estimated $300 million estate. Not a wealthy woman, she continued to work into her 80s and, ironically, managed a Beatles cover band.

And Marvin Isley recalled a phone call his family in Cincinnati received from his three older siblings in the Isley Brothers, who had spent a year on the road promoting their hit single, "Shout" – "One day in 1960, they called home and said, 'Ma, get really close to the phone. Listen and tell me what this is.' Then they shook something against the phone. She said, 'C'mon, guys, tell me what y'all are doing.' Finally they told her: 'Mama, these are the keys to your new house. It's in New Jersey. There's a plane leaving Cincinnati at six o'clock in the morning. You and Ernie and Marvin be on that plane. And don't bring anything. No clothes, no furniture. Call the relatives and tell them to take what they want. We're gonna buy everything new.' Sure enough, that next morning we were gone."

Likewise, Graham Nash, a co-founder of the Hollies, recalled that in 1967, "we got a check from Columbia for $250,000. A quarter million big ones! That made an impression on me. In retrospect, I handled it pretty well.... I tried to help my family as much as I could. One of my mother's dreams was to have her own pub, so I bought her one, the Unicorn in Pendleton. She ran the place and sat at the end of the bar regally, like Queen Elizabeth."

However, Tom Jones had some difficulty convincing his father to leave his coal mining job in the late-1960s: "I say to him, 'Well, why don't you work out what you would earn between now and retirement and I'll write a check for that now.'" That did the trick and his father agreed to retire. Similarly, after Adam Ant scored several top-10 British hits in the early-1980s, he begged his mother to leave her job at a laundromat. She finally decided to quit after her workplace was inundated by fans demanding autographs and mementoes.

Conversely, having a famous and wealthy family member can also cause personal strife. Pop singer B.J. Thomas recalled: "As my success increased, life never got better at home, except that our roles had changed. Even though my success as a singer was minor [in the mid-1960s], I became the head of the family. Dad was still alive, but everyone came to me. Mom even asked me about what to do with [my sister] Judy when she came in late. The family had unconsciously made me the authority, because I was getting recognized as a singer. I was also making money. I felt like a rich uncle the family didn't like. Just having the money somehow gave me a special position."

Similarly, Paul Simon's father had trouble dealing with his son's enormous success. As the younger Simon explained: "All of a sudden, in my mid-twenties, I was the richest person in the family and the one with the most power.... When my father retired, I gave him money to move out of his house and get a new place, a better place. My mother had no problem with it, but I think my father may have been confused; maybe he even felt usurped. He was an unusually smart guy, maybe the smartest guy I've ever known, but I was famous, and that put something between us that wasn't necessary. He did say at one point, 'I'm not going to compete with you because I know I'm going to lose.'"

Some hit artists are also generous with their friends. In 2005, Peter Tork of the Monkees admitted: "I gave a lot of my money away when I was younger – just left it in bowls around the house and people would help themselves to handfuls of it. I wasn't thinking too clearly at the time and it might have been my low self-esteem, thinking that I didn't deserve to keep the money."

However, friends and family members of successful stars – whether in sports, film or music – often *expect* a financial payday. While most stars are willing to share their good fortune, some are not.

FAMILY MEMBERS DEALING WITH FANS

Having a celebrity in your family can create a host of problems. When interviewed in 1971, the exasperated mother of Bob Dylan revealed: "You just don't know. This past winter in Florida, I'd go to a party or reception or a wedding, *anything*, and sooner or later it would happen. Someone would find out I was Bob Dylan's mother, and I wouldn't have a moment's peace from there on in. People would form *receiving lines* to talk to me. Most places now, I don't even say my name is Zimmerman. And the reporters... they call me from all over the country, at all hours of the day and night... to ask the most absurd things."

Similarly, in 2000, George Harrison recalled: "My mother was a nice person, but she was naive, as we all were in Liverpool in those days. She used to write to anybody who'd written to us, answering the fan mail. She'd answer letters from people saying, 'Dear Mr. Harrison, can you give us one of Paul McCartney's toenails?' Still, to this day, people come up to me brandishing letters that my mother once wrote to them."

However, some rock star parents refrained from openly discussing their celebrity children. Eva Jagger, mother of Mick, explained: "It was just a feeling I got. I suppose you didn't want to feel big-headed, so you went in the opposite direction. You didn't want people to think you were puffed up."

Meanwhile, some hit artists have attempted to distance themselves from their families. After arriving in the Greenwich Village district of New York City in January 1961, Bob Dylan initially claimed he was an orphan. Likewise, Sting told an interviewer in 1980, "I suppose part of my egocentric drive is an attempt to transcend my family. I come from a family of losers – I'm the eldest of four – and I've rejected my family as something I don't want to be like. My father delivered milk for a living and my mother was a hairdresser." (Sting would later regret making the comments.)

NEGATIVE OR DESTRUCTIVE INFLUENCE ON CHILDREN AND FAMILY

When parents work in the music industry, their offspring rarely enjoy a normal childhood. Decades before marrying Ozzy Osbourne, the former Sharon Levy grew up in a musical household. Her father, Don Arden, was an artist manager and concert promoter in Britain. She recalled the difficulties she experienced with her schoolmates during her childhood: "The first thing I did was tell them my father was a policeman. I couldn't possibly have explained what he really did – it was far too embarrassing. The last thing you want as a child is to stand out. And I stood out enough anyway, because I wasn't at school regularly, because my parents didn't participate in school life at all. We never mixed with anybody who wasn't connected with the industry, other than kids at school, and we weren't even supposed to bring them back home." Similarly, Aimee Osbourne, the daughter of Ozzy Osbourne, had a chaotic upbringing due to her father's celebrity status and often-embarrassing antics. As *The Independent* reported: "She found it hard to [bring] schoolfriends home for playdates given that her father was once reputed to have bitten the head off a bat."

And for better or worse, the children of rock stars are also treated as celebrities. By extension, these children are considered fair game by both fans and the media, and pixelating their faces in media photos does little to protect them from the intrusive spotlight. Consequently, Michael Jackson went as far as placing masks on his young children whenever they ventured out in public.

At age 15 in 2008, Francis Bean – the daughter of Kurt Cobain and Courtney Love – admitted: "People are fascinated by me, but I haven't done anything. I'm famous by default. I came out of the womb and people wanted to know who I was because of my parents. If you're a big Nirvana fan, a big Hole fan, then I understand why you would want to get to know me, but I'm not my parents. People need to wait until I've done something valid with my life."

Additionally, the children of rock stars are frequently raised in an adult world and are exposed to the debauchery of the music industry. Mackenzie Phillips, the daughter of Mamas and Papas leader John Phillips, recalled: "My father was always surrounded by a noisy, outrageous, wild party. Rock 'n' roll stars, aristocracy, and Hollywood trash streamed in and out of his homes. He lived beyond his means. There were eight Rolls-Royces in the driveway and two Ferraris. The house was full of priceless antiques, but if something broke, it never got fixed.... There was a cook, but nobody shopped for food. The house was complete chaos, a bizarre mix of excess and oblivion, luxury and incompetence."

Oftentimes, rockers do not have sufficient time to nurture personal relationships. Guitarist Mick Jones of Foreigner – who was married and divorced three times – explained: "While I believe that marriage is a great institution, it doesn't really work if you're spending more time with your guitar than with your wife and family. I refer to music as my mistress, because it's got such a hold on me."

Likewise, Charlie Daniels admitted: "By far the hardest thing about being a professional road musician is being away from your family.... When [my son] Little Charlie was about six months old, I was gone from home for sixteen weeks, and when I finally walked through the door and picked him up, he started crying. He didn't know who I was, and that hurt.... I missed my son's first steps, his first words, grammar school plays, and high school football games. There is a price to be paid for following the path I chose."

But even when an artist isn't touring or recording an album, home life is rarely routine. Being a musician is typically a nocturnal activity which might start in the evening and end at 3 or 4 a.m. in the morning. In 1986, Tom Petty admitted: "My family acknowledges I'm sort of a Martian. It still cracks [my daughter] Adria up that I'm just waking up when she's coming home from school."

Similarly, Chris Entwistle, the son of Who bassist John Entwistle, recalled: "I wouldn't see dad in the mornings. He wouldn't get up till midday because he'd have been in the studio or wherever playing or rehearsing all night. On Sundays, we used to sit together and watch old movies.... Those were the only times that I really spent with him when I was very young."

Not surprisingly, musicians sometimes step back from their stardom in order to focus on their families. With John Lennon lamenting that he was an absentee father with his first son, Julian, the former Beatle decided to abandon his music career after the birth of his second son, Sean, to become a self-described "house husband." And after scoring 18 number-one hits on the country chart, superstar Garth Brooks abandoned his music career in 2000. Instead of performing for tens of thousands of fans in packed concert halls, he would spend the next thirteen-years raising a family. Waiting until the last of his three daughters had finished high school, Brooks belatedly restarted his music career and recorded a new album in 2013. Brooks explained, "People said, 'How could you walk away from music?' But being a dad – there's nothing that can touch that."

Similarly, at the age of 59 in 2010, Phil Collins was more concerned with being a family man, which included a daily routine of driving his young children to school. When asked about his next record, Collins replied, "I don't anticipate making any more records. The last thing I want to do is light a fuse that leads to all this other stuff.... It's something that takes you away from home, ultimately, and I've spent all my life away from home."

And disturbingly, there's an inherent risk to being the child of a famous rock star. Following the violent murder of John Lennon in front of the Dakota building in New York City, Yoko Ono feared for the safety of their young son. Sean Lennon later revealed: "When I was going to school, I had bodyguards. Come to class. Come to the bathroom. Go to the gym. Every day. Two big bodyguards packing guns. I was definitely aware of why they were there."

CHILDREN AND OTHER FAMILY MEMBERS OF ROCK STARS
FOLLOWING IN THEIR MUSICAL FOOTSTEPS

Countless sons and daughters of famous musicians have followed in their parents' career paths and tested the rock and roll waters. While most failed miserably, there were some exceptions. Elvis Presley's only daughter, Lisa Marie, spent decades working in the music field. She recounted: "In my situation, people are either gunning for you or rooting for you, really dramatically. They think, 'Oh, you've got a silver spoon, you're born into this, and it's all because of your father.' But if you get a door opened, it's up to you to walk through it, and through to the next door and the next door."

Meanwhile, the twin sons of Ricky Nelson – Matthew and Gunnar – enjoyed a career in rock music that produced several hits, including the chart-topping single, "Love And Affection." (Ricky Nelson, himself, had been the son of popular bandleader Ozzie Nelson and his singer wife Harriet.) Also, Bob Dylan's son, Jakob, had a respectable amount of success in the 1990s as the leader of the Wallflowers. Likewise, Ozzy Osbourne's daughter, Kelly, scored several pop hits in the U.K. Additionally, the son and namesake of honky-tonk legend Hank Williams, Sr. has done very well for himself in the country music field.

Not surprisingly, musical families often push their children to pursue careers outside of the field. Although Yoko Ono was hoping that Sean would become an anthropologist, that was not to be. He explained: "What am I going to do? Be a lawyer or a stockbroker? I'm from a family of artists. And I have faith that my body of work will speak for itself." However, the only Beatles offspring who achieved any real success in the rock world were Julian Lennon, the son of John and Cynthia, who scored several hits in the 1980s beginning with "Valotte," and drummer Zak Starkey, the son of Ringo and Maureen Starr, who has toured with a number of bands including the Who and Oasis.

Some rock star children try to make it on their own merits instead of riding on a famous parent's coattails. Renee Stewart – the daughter of Rod Stewart and model Rachel Hunter – explained: "When I was at school in L.A., if people asked me what my dad did I'd say, 'Oh he's in entertainment.' No disrespect to him, but you want to make your own life. You want to be your own person. Trading off it can really screw you up and it kind of makes people cringe." And when the daughter of country music superstar Garth Brooks pursued a career as a singer, she purposely tried to distance herself from her father. Calling herself Allie Colleen, she wanted respect as a performer in her own right. Similarly,

Norah Jones – the daughter of sitar legend Ravi Shanker – barred the mention of her famous father on early press releases.

However, a number of rockers invited their children to join their bands. In the 1970s, rockabilly pioneer Carl Perkins toured with sons, Stan and Greg. And at age 15 in 2006, Wolfgang Van Halen (the son of Eddie Van Halen and Valerie Bertinelli) replaced Michael Anthony in Van Halen. In 2019, Nicholas Collins toured with his famous father, Phil. And when Led Zeppelin hit the stage in 2007, it was the late John Bonham's son, Jason, who took over on drums. (The younger Bonham also enjoyed a successful solo career as the leader of the metal band, Bonham.) Rick Wakeman's son, Oliver, replaced his father as the keyboardist in two groups, Yes and the Strawbs, and Deacon Frey replaced his father, Glenn, in the Eagles. And Frank Zappa's son, Dweezil Zappa, eventually launched a tribute act that was dubbed Zappa Plays Zappa.

Siblings have also attempted to follow their rock star brothers or sisters into the music industry. Pete Townshend's brother, Simon, recorded a number of solo albums before joining the Who as a backing guitarist. Similarly, Mick Jagger's brother, Chris, had a respectable career in the 1970s. And years after Michael Jackson and his brothers landed their first chart hit in 1969, their sisters Rebbie and Janet both enjoyed commercial success in the 1980s.

On rare occasions, a parent of a rock star will attempt to pursue a career in music. When John Lennon's estranged father, Alfred, released a single in 1965, "That's My Life," it received airplay on the BBC. But when John heard the track, he angrily ordered Beatles manager Brian Epstein to pressure the BBC to drop the single, which they did. Conversely, after the Black Keys won multiple Grammy awards, the father of Dan Auerbach decided to record an album. In 2018, Chuck Auerbach – a 68-year-old antiques dealer – released *Remember Me*, which was produced by his son.

Even dating a rock singer made someone a potential performer. Mick Jagger's shy, model girlfriend Marianne Faithfull became an unlikely singing star in the 1960s. Both Yoko Ono and Linda McCartney performed with their Beatle husbands. And following the tragic death of Ritchie Valens in 1959, his teenage girlfriend Donna Ludwig – the subject of his ballad hit "Donna" – was pressured by her father to enter a recording studio and record the single, "Now That You're Gone."

TRYING TO GO HOME

When a rock star performs in his hometown, there are usually complications. Family members and friends will deluge the performer with requests for free tickets or backstage passes. Local politicians and the media will turn the event into a circus. And at the concert, the artist will tone down his onstage antics and language out of respect for his parents, who are sitting in the front row.

In 2006, when Tom Petty was scheduled to perform a hometown concert in Gainesville, Florida, he had hoped to visit longtime friends, members of his extended family and a number of old hangouts around the city. Unfortunately, his plans went awry. He stated at the time: "It spooked me, really. It was nice but it was also overwhelming. You can't really walk down the street or talk to anybody because everybody was talking at once. At the concert I just hid in the bus until it was time to play."

And John Lennon's first wife, Cynthia, was distressed by how her Beatle husband was treated in July 1964, during his triumphant return to Liverpool for the premier of the film, *A Hard Day's Night*. She recalled: "[He] found it strange that although he'd grown up in Liverpool, he could no longer walk down the streets, drop in on old friends or pop into one of the clubs to hear the latest sounds. He could never again be ordinary in Liverpool, and he hated that. From now on he could return only as a big celebrity, one of the most famous in the world."

Similarly, Belinda Carlisle, the lead singer of the 1980s group the Go-Go's, described how her sudden fame had changed the way her old friends treated her: "The hardest part of our success in those days, at least for me, was going back home.... Whenever I got there I found myself feeling sad, lonely, and isolated. I didn't fit easily back into our scene. My old haunts and old friends weren't that accepting; no one wanted to have anything to do with me. I didn't feel that I had changed, but everyone else did."

Likewise, in 1969, Bob Dylan returned to Hibbing, Minnesota, for his ten-year high school reunion. Arriving late to the event, which was held at the local Moose Lodge, the former Bobby Zimmerman was accompanied by his wife, Sara. As Dylan biographer Toby Thompson wrote: "As soon as he walked in, people clustered about... they wanted *autographs*, here ten years later, they actually wanted autographs!... Bob stayed for an hour, but then some guy... tried to pick a fight with Bob, so he left." It would be the last time Dylan would attend a school reunion.

DATING AND MARRYING A ROCK STAR

Dating or marrying a rock star is not an easy task. Rockers are very rarely monogamous, a fact that can cause all sorts of strife. Staying in a relationship with a rock musician usually means voluntarily accepting that your partner will engage in multiple flings and affairs. Marianne Faithfull, who dated Mick Jagger in the mid-1960s, observed: "I had a very cool attitude towards Mick and his infidelities. They hurt me, but I never showed it. I just pretended not to notice, it was too painful. I loved him." And Tom Jones, though married to the same woman for more than 50 years, was a well-known serial cheater. On one occasion, his wife physically attacked him after reading a newspaper account about one of his many paramours.

Likewise, at the same time that Paul McCartney was dating Jane Asher in the mid-1960s, he was also seeing actress Peggy Lipton – shortly before she became a star on the television series, *Mod Squad*. In her autobiography, she wrote about her first encounter with the Beatle: "During our lovemaking, I caught myself... thinking, how was this making me feel? Special? Connected in any way? I didn't have to pretend how attracted to Paul I was.... I liked absolutely everything about him, yet when we walked down stairs together I wasn't feeling too good. I saw myself as just a young girl he had taken to bed and that was it."

And at the cusp of his fame in the early-1970s, Bruce Springsteen dated a Kent State University student. Years later, she put their relationship in perspective: "To date somebody in the music industry is very, very difficult. There's a thousand girls in the world and they all have an ulterior motive. You didn't know who really was your friend and who just was trying to get close to you to get close to him.... I said to him a long time ago that I wish he had decided to become a writer and not a musician so I didn't have to share him with the rest of the world."

Some rockers actually enjoy marriage a little *too* much. In Tommy Lee's autobiography, *Tommyland*, the heavy metal drummer exposed the proclivities of one of his unnamed Mötley Crüe bandmates: "There was one guy in the band who was married but couldn't seem to get enough of matrimony. This guy had more than what I'd call a mistress – in fact, he had more than one of them. He'd set these girls up with apartments, jewelry, clothes – all of it.... A girl would come rushing into our dressing room backstage and show off her engagement ring to the rest of the band. We'd be totally silent, like, 'Oh... right on.' It always ended up bad, of course, because he was already married! Duh! It was just a matter of time before the girls would rush into our dressing room again, asking us all what happened and wondering why he broke it off."

Surprisingly, some rockers complain about the type of women they tend to meet in their chosen profession. Singer-songwriter Ed Sheeran admitted: "I've gotten more attention from the wrong sort of women. Like, the sort of women I wouldn't have wanted to date anyway show attention now – the ones that are kind of driven by money and fame and want to be taken out to nice restaurants and bought nice things." Likewise, Marilyn Manson, who has dated actresses such as Rose McGowen and Rachel Evan Wood as well as porn stars such as Jenna Jameson and Stoya, declared: "I am flypaper for damaged women."

And Gregg Allman admitted in his autobiography, "Every woman I've ever had a relationship with has loved me for who they thought I was. Maybe they were in love with whatever was onstage, but when the lights are out and the sound goes off, you're left with this dude, and that's me. Obviously, that's the person they didn't get to know."

Simply finding potential romantic partners can be a problem when you're a famous rock star. Adam Ant recalled his quandary during the height of his career in the 1980s: "Meeting new people, especially women, became difficult because I had no idea if they were going to sell their 'story' about me to a newspaper as soon as I left them."

Likewise, in 2013, Stevie Nicks griped: "Like, I'm gonna go to a bar? And hang out? I mean, where am I gonna meet somebody?" Joking about filming a matchmaking video, she mused: "Hi! My name is Stevie Nicks, and I'm looking for somebody that is no more than five years older than me. Please no health problems, no diabetes, no heart disease, no gout, please, no bipolar; if you're on an antidepressant, not good" [or] "Hi! You know, I'm in a band called Fleetwood Mac, and, you know, I'm looking for, like, a guy who's, like, tall, and, like, you know, anywhere from... well, I don't really date younger men, so, you know, anywhere, from, I guess I could go as young as 58. And as old as 68. Not 70. Just 68. And, um, I like to travel, but I have an assistant, and she always has to come with me because I really gave up packing a long time ago."

MODELS AND ROCKERS

Def Leppard guitarist Phil Collen explained how his dating life changed dramatically after his sudden stardom in the early-1980s: "When I was younger, I'd driven an old beat-up Ford Cortina. When *Pyromania* blew up, I replaced my old Ford Cortina with a black Porsche, and within a week of my owning this car, a beautiful South

African model knocked on my window as I was sitting in traffic on Blackfrairs Bridge in London and gave me her number. Funny, that never happened in my Ford Cortina."

Similarly, at age 19, Mick Jagger was a college student as well as a budding musician. At the time, he was dating Chrissie Shrimpton, a very attractive 17-year-old who was the younger sister of famed British model Jean Shrimpton. As Chrissie Shrimpton later recalled, "I used to hear them whispering, 'Poor Chrissie, her boyfriend's so ugly.'" Just a few years later when he was topping the charts on both sides of the Atlantic, Jagger's physical features were suddenly deemed unimportant.

Not surprisingly, rockers often find themselves dating models. While Billy Joel, David Bowie and Ric Ocasek all married fashion models, Chubby Checker was wedded to a former Miss World from the Netherlands. Rod Stewart was a serial model man – as long as they had blond hair and hot legs. And how many rockers have dated or married the eye candy actresses in their music videos? Plenty.

Billy Joel has defended his preference for attractive spouses: "People are just interested in you because you're a rock star. O.K. Some guys use a car. Some guys have a cute dog. I'm a rock star. That's who I am, what I do. What's wrong with that?.... I was married to some beautiful women. I always get compared to how beautiful they are and how not beautiful I am, and it's kind of funny, it's like *Beauty and the Beast*. I don't mind being the beast, I want them to be good-looking, and if they don't mind me looking like me, why should I care?"

However, both sides get something out of a rocker/model relationship. A writer for *Spin* magazine suggested that "rock stars like [models] because they're beautiful to look at. They're tall, thin, and don't eat much. They have their own money. They get most of their clothes for free.... Rock stars go out with them because they give birth to beautiful and talented children. Children from their previous marriages like them because they know about beauty and hair care;" and conversely, "models go out with [rockers] because they're as close to royalty as they will get. Models can't marry Kennedys or Rockefellers. Models like [rockers] because they wear tight pants and have long hair. They get into most clubs for free, sit at the best tables, and don't pay for their drinks. Models go out with them because they pay alimony and palimony."

Oftentimes, successful musicians will date or marry someone who is significantly younger – simply because they can. In 2012, 53-year-old Madonna dated 24-year-old French dancer Brahim Zaibat. She told ABC News: "I didn't choose to, you know, I didn't, like, write down on a piece of paper I'm now going to have a relationship with a younger man. That's just what happened. You see, that's the romantic in me."

Likewise, at age 45, Rod Stewart would marry 20-year-old Rachel Hunter. Billy Joel, age 55, married Katie Lee, age 23. In 1989, 52-year-old Bill Wyman of the Rolling Stones would marry 18-year-old Mandy Smith. (Ironically, Wyman's eldest son would later marry Smith's mother, a union that would last just two years.) And even pre-rock musical stars played the same game. In 1966, Frank Sinatra married Mia Farrow when he was 51 and she was 21. And at 54, Bing Crosby married a 24-year-old actress.

FAN RELATIONSHIPS WITH ROCKER WIVES

Simply being married can cause a number of career problems for musicians. When pop singer Rick Springfield announced his engagement, many of his female fans went berserk. Springfield revealed: "I've received some nasty 'fan' letters containing charming things like drawings of gravestones with [my wife's] and my names written on them in what appears to be blood. Apparently these sweet people now want us both dead."

Consequently, a number of rockers were married in secret, for fear of hurting their careers. A single, unattached rock star is much more popular and desirable than one with a spouse at his side. According to Jim Morrison biographer Patricia Bulter, Morrison's girlfriend Pamela Courson "stated that she and Jim did agree to a common-law arrangement during a Doors tour in Colorado in 1967. 'Jim and I had discussed marriage on several occasions before this trip... but felt, as did his managers, that the... publicity [of] a publicly registered marriage would have a detrimental effect upon the image they were trying to develop for him.' Apparently it was one thing for [bandmates] Ray, Robby, and John to get married, but for the band's sex symbol to do anything as seemingly safe and normal as taking a wife was deemed potentially harmful for the group." Likewise, few music fans realized that Bob Dylan was married to Sara Lowndes for 12 years – until the couple eventually divorced in 1977.

And when John Lennon became the first Beatle to marry, the group's manager Brian Epstein was aghast and hid the marriage from the press for as long as possible. Every member of the Beatles, he believed, should be viewed as romantically available to their fans. Lennon's first wife, Cynthia, recalled: "I was still a secret, and I hated it: I wanted to be acknowledged as John's wife. Of course, some of the Liverpool fans knew, but to the rest of the country he was young, free and single... I had to play up to the role I'd been assigned." In 2005, she discussed her marriage and subsequent divorce from John: "Someone asked me recently whether, if I'd known at the beginning what lay ahead, I would have gone through with it. I had to say no. Of course I could never regret having my wonderful son. But the truth is that if I'd known as a teenager what falling for John Lennon would lead to, I would have turned round right then and walked away."

Oftentimes, the wife or girlfriend of a rock star is considered a muse – a source of inspiration during the creative process. And unfortunately, they are often the uncredited co-writers of some of music's best-known hits. There have been a number of notable muses in the world of rock and roll: Erin Everly was the musical inspiration for Axl Rose, Linda Eastman for Paul McCartney, Anita Pallenberg for Keith Richards, and Pattie Boyd for both George Harrison and Eric Clapton. Boyd later explained: "I find the concept of being a muse understandable when you think of all the great painters, poets, and photographers who usually have had one or two. The artist absorbs an element from their muse that has nothing to do with words, just the purity of their essence... In my case both George and Eric had an inability to communicate their feelings through normal conversation. I became a reflection for them."

Also, there's the girl in the song, the real-life women who were the inspirations for hit songs – whether Sharona (The Knack), Sherrie (Steve Perry), Carol (Neil Sedaka), Sara (Hall & Oates) or Suzanne (Leonard Cohen). And in 1956, when a shy Canadian teenager developed a schoolboy crush, he expressed his affection through a song. After "Diana" became a smash top-10 hit, suddenly the world discovered that young Paul Anka had written the song about his sister's babysitter. The real-life Diana later recalled how the press hounded her all around town: "I had reporters waiting for me when I graduated from high school. Guys wouldn't ask me out because their picture would be in the newspaper the next day."

Marrying a member of your own band can also breed a host of problems. Fleetwood Mac became a musical soap opera during the 1970s as couples married, divorced and had various affairs. Christine McVie revealed the challenges of remaining married to husband John McVie: "We were very happy for three years and then the strain of me being in the same band started to take its toll. When you're in the same band as somebody, you're seeing them 24 hours a day and you start to see an awful lot of the bad side."

Similarly, even though they were divorced, Jack and Meg White continued to perform as the White Stripes. Other notable divorces within the same musical act include: John and Michelle Phillips of the Mamas and the Papas; Ike and Tina Turner; Sonny and Cher; the Captain and Tennille; Thurston Moore and Kim Gordon (Sonic Youth); and both couples in ABBA.

However, a few same-band rock marriages have endured despite the pressures. Such was the case with Paul and Linda McCartney; Tina Weymouth and Chris Frantz (Talking Heads); Lux Interior and Poison Ivy (The Cramps); Win Butler and Régine Chassagne (Arcade Fire); and Pat Benatar and Neil Giraldo.

▶ CHAPTER 15
THE MIND OF A ROCK STAR

Entertainers – particularly actors, comedians and musicians – tend to have extreme personalities. There are several distinct personality types that are drawn to the world of rock and roll. Whether narcissists and risk takers or social outcasts and sociopaths or nonconformists and artisans, the music industry has always attracted the fringes of society.

Rockers also tend to be creative types who view the world in their own idiosyncratic, non-traditional perspectives. Dave Grohl has argued: "I think some people are born with a restless creative spirit.... A gene, and I've always been that way."

Oftentimes, rock artists are complex, tortured souls who make a living baring their intimate, emotional struggles to complete strangers. Stevie Nicks has admitted that Fleetwood Mac made its finest music when the group's members were battling their personal demons.

ARTISTS, BEATNIKS & NONCONFORMISTS

In the last half of the 20th century, America experienced a dramatic shift in cultural norms, as nonconformity became mainstream. Rebellious behavior – especially among the post-war Baby Boomers – was expressed through clothing, art, politics, drug use and, of course, popular music.

Emerging in the 1950s out of the urban, artist communities on the East and West Coasts, the Beat Generation challenged many of the hallmarks of Americanism: consumer materialism, organized religion, traditional values and structured employment with a preset 9-to-5 schedule. The Beat movement had emerged from the Bohemian tradition, the philosophy launched in Paris around 1850 following the publication of Henri Murger's *La Vie De Bohéme*. Political poet Allen Ginsberg gave the Beat Generation a contemporary voice in 1955, when he gave public readings of his controversial book, *Howl*, at an art gallery in San Francisco. Other influential beatnik works included *Go* by John Clellon Holmes, *Naked Lunch* by William S. Burroughs and *On The Road* by Jack Kerouac.

Across America's college campuses, like-minded bohemians were drawn to underground clubs and coffeehouses, where they absorbed abstract poetry, politically charged folk music and modern bebop-style jazz. It was the folk music scene at the University of Minnesota that lured a restless Bob Dylan away from his rock and roll roots in 1959. A year later, Dylan read the Woody Guthrie autobiography, *Bound For Glory*, and became obsessed with the outspoken folk singer. Soon, the Bohemian movement transformed San Francisco's North Beach into a beatnik community, which would give rise to the "hippie" archetype.

Soon, rock and roll followed the lead of modern folk and jazz, and began promoting similar counterculture ideologies. The war in Vietnam also fed an anti-authoritarian sentiment among youth, most of whom had no interest in fighting a war in far-off Asia. As rock music created its own subculture and adopted libertine values, disaffected youth embraced messages such as "make love, not war" and "tune in and drop out." The Summer of Love in 1967 was the culmination of the decade's dramatic societal and political upheaval.

SOCIAL OUTCASTS

Outcasts, misfits and loners often find refuge in music – especially fringe and non-mainstream genres like punk, death metal, emo and avant-garde rock. In the late-1960s, cult leader Charles Manson wanted to spread his Helter Skelter doctrine by becoming a pop singing star. Even Sting has admitted that had he not been a successful rock singer, "without a doubt, I'd be a criminal or some social deviant."

Over the years, numerous musicians have revealed that they were unpopular students who were bullied by their peers. Don Henley of the Eagles recalled meeting Janis Joplin in the 1960s: "She was just another one who wanted to show the people back home [in Texas]. Janis had been bullied in high school. They'd made fun of her because she was different. She was looking for acceptance, which is why a lot of us went to California: to find our tribe. I think all of us were misfits in our own way, which is why we go into the business. The popular kids at school were the football players. They got the pretty girls. A lot of famous rockers were high-school nerds." Similarly, Cyndi Lauper revealed her traumatic upbringing in Queens, New York: "I felt like such a loser when I was young. I had a lot of learning disabilities. And I was the one kids threw rocks at because I dressed funny, in thrift-shop clothing."

Meanwhile, Devo frontman Mark Mothersbaugh recalled the band's outsider status during the late-1970s in northeastern Ohio: "There were two places we could perform without fear of a fistfight or just being paid to quit. That was the Pirate's Cove in Cleveland, where 35 hardcore people would show up, and the Crypt in Akron, where we always had 20 friends and four guys wanting to beat us up. When you're that ostracized and disenfranchised in your peer group and in your local culture, you turn unfriendly back. I know we didn't appear to be friendly, but it was self-defense. It was part of our manifesto to separate ourselves out; we were more like aliens making satirical comments on the culture. We took pleasure in being lightning rods for hostility and freaking people out."

NARCISSISTS / BIG EGOS

Many rock stars have reputations for being overly confident, notoriously cocky and self-absorbed narcissists who will tell you, at the drop of a guitar pick, that they're the most talented, creative and gifted artist in the world. Psychiatrist Mark Ettensohn described clinical narcissism as displaying "behaviors and attitudes that include a grandiose sense of self, little empathy for others, and a persistent need to be admired." Ettensohn must have been watching the Grammy Awards ceremony when he made that statement.

Performing in a rock and roll band is a narcissist's dream job. Typically, a rock star appears on a massive, brightly lit stage with laser shows, fog machines and booming explosions. On the side of the stage, there are stacks of oversized, throbbing speakers. Above him are a pair of giant video monitors that capture close-ups of the action on the stage. Simultaneously, thousands of pairs of eyes will watch a lead singer's every move, devour his every statement and sing along to every lyric. Read a magazine or internet blog and these artists are the subjects of endless praise. And everywhere they go, they are bombarded by over-excited strangers who shout, "I'm your biggest fan."

Jim Morrison biographer Patricia Butler chronicled the singer's behavior while he was a film student at UCLA: "Jim often went to great lengths to draw attention to himself, just as he had at his previous schools, if only in a negative way. He still liked to do outrageous things, then gauge the reaction he got, filing the situations away in his brain for use at another time. He truly seemed to enjoy manipulating the emotions and behavior of those around him."

At the height of his career in the 1980s, R&B singer Terence Trent D'Arby admitted: "The reason I got into a band was I wanted attention, I wanted to get laid, and I wanted to *pose*. I want to be up on that stage, in effect saying, 'You're looking and you're listening to me now. What do you think of *this?*' And no matter what anybody says, that's no different from the reason Bob Dylan or Keith Richard or Pete Townshend got into this: they wanted to play guitar because it looked cool, and that's what rock and roll is about. Rock and roll was built around posers and boasters."

However, much of a rock artist's buildup is manufactured. It's the job of a promotion department at a record company to hype up an artist. On advertisements and press releases, professional writers employ superlatives such as "the greatest," "the most exciting," "breathtaking" and "legendary." And to achieve success the music business requires performers to aggressively promote themselves in order to attract fans, sell downloads and fill concert venues.

But a problem arises when a performer starts believing his own prefabricated myth. Before his Grammy was taken away, Milli Vanilli member Rob Pilatus told the press in 1990: "Musically, we are more talented than any Bob Dylan. Musically, we are more talented than Paul McCartney. Mick Jagger, his lines are not clear. He don't know how he should produce a sound. I'm the new modern rock 'n' roll. I'm the new Elvis." Likewise, Ian McCulloch of Echo and the Bunnymen once stated: "Let's be honest, there's only been two *really great singers* – me and Frank [Sinatra]."

The members of the British band Oasis – led by brothers Noel and Liam Gallagher – were notoriously boastful in interviews. In 1996, Noel proclaimed: "If it was 1965, and we'd just put out our second album, we'd absolutely be the pop kings of the world. It would be the Beatles, the Rolling Stones, Oasis, and then the Who. I firmly believe that."

Roger Karshner, the former vice president of Capitol Records, observed: "Some great artists are extreme ego nuts. They primp and rearrange themselves constantly. Every car window, store front, all reflective surfaces become their vanity mirrors. One particular guy even carried a small compact and was forever checking himself out in cars, on the street, in elevators and in restaurants.... Some concentrate on drawing flattery out of others. They ask, 'How do I look?' 'What do you think of my new shoes?' 'What do you think of my latest record?' 'I've just lost twenty-five pounds. Can't you tell?' 'Would you believe that I have a daughter [who's] twenty-three?'"

Not surprisingly, a number of musical acts have given themselves their own self-aggrandizing nicknames. While Little Richard has pontificated about being "The Architect of Rock and Roll," the Rolling Stones billed themselves as "The World's Greatest Rock and Roll Band" and Michael Jackson named himself "The King of Pop."

However, one of Jackson's mentors noted: "What most corrupted the life and career of Michael Jackson was his belief that he was different from ordinary folks – more elevated, more sensitive, more long suffering – and thus not subject to the rigid rules of right and wrong. His hubris knew no bounds. If you thought he was having too much plastic surgery, well, you could never understand the imaging needs of a superstar. And if you thought that sharing a bed with a child, however platonic, was morally deplorable, well, that too was because seeing it from your mortal vantage point could never enlighten you as how the self-proclaimed 'voice of the voiceless' saw it." But as a star in the spotlight from early in his childhood until his death, Jackson was a complex and troubled individual who battled a host of demons and unresolved emotional issues.

Similarly, in the early-1970s, Sly Stone – the leader of Sly and the Family Stone – was atop the musical world. But his career would soon spiral out of control. As his ex-manager explained: "Drugs hurt him, but the real villain was ego. It got blown way out of proportion. When Sly and the Family Stone first played at the Electric Circus [in New York City], Cynthia, Larry Carlton, Freddie, sister Rose, all would do solos. But as Sly became more prominent he started cutting down solos. At the end it was nothing but Sly performing. His ego got more distorted. He needed more and more of his glory. He believed in his own worthiness, and yet simultaneously to that, the self-destruction began. Unless someone is profoundly convinced or assured of that worthiness, as their success gets bigger and bigger, there is that small inner voice that says, 'You're full of shit.' The voice started to tear him down."

A few artists have recognized they had a problem with their bloated self-image. In a 2016 online post, rapper Kanye West admitted: "My number one enemy has been my ego." Similarly, singer John Mayer revealed in a 2015 interview that he was obsessed with reading Twitter comments about himself because of the pleasure it gave him. Admitting he had a problem, Mayer said, "So, I'm a recovered ego addict."

BATTLING PSYCHOLOGICAL PROBLEMS

After placing a hit song on the pop charts, a musician becomes a public figure. Quickly, every aspect of his personal life is examined under a microscope. On a daily basis, he is interacting with intrusive and demanding fans, traveling from show to show with little rest, abusing alcohol and drugs (often provided by complete strangers), struggling with the demands of fame and worrying about selling tickets to the next concert.

The pressures of a career in music can take a toll on even the most mentally stable performer. However, whether suffering from a mild neurosis or full-blown psychosis, there seems to be a far greater prevalence of mental illness in the world of music than in any other profession. And with the copious amounts of available drugs on the concert trail, pre-existing psychological maladies are often amplified and made more severe.

In 2005, Bono of U2 admitted: "little has been written about the performer's psychology." However, reading through the pages of *Rolling Stone* or *Billboard*, there are hundreds of musical artists who have *admitted* to undergoing psychological counseling for a myriad of issues. But due to the stigma of receiving mental health care, many performers choose not to publicly air their personal struggles.

British singer Adam Ant – who donned pirate attire and American Indian-inspired face paint at the height of his career – was diagnosed with bipolar disorder in 1995. Prescribed anti-depressants, he was unable to perform for the next 17 years. Ant later explained: "In this business, mental health is the last great taboo. If you're a junkie – whatever. If you're drunk, well, that's part and parcel. If you're just difficult, a diva, fine. But if you are nuts? Well, you're in trouble because you are not bankable then. And people don't want to talk about that. They certainly don't want to employ you."

Additionally, many musical performers suffer from Attention Deficit-Hyperactivity Disorder – more commonly known as ADHD – according to clinical psychologist Lara Honos-Webb. Black Eyed Peas member Will.i.am admitted: "If you listen to the songs I write, they are the most ADHD songs ever. They have five hooks in one and it all happens in three minutes."

*   *   *   *   *   *

Bebe Buell – the girlfriend of a series of notable singers, including Steven Tyler, Mick Jagger and Elvis Costello – was an "It Girl" on the rock and roll scene during the 1970s. She admitted: "I always chose rock stars as boyfriends because I liked their temperaments – all the nervousness, unstableness, and uncertainty. It was dangerous, and fun. It made life interesting to wake up in the morning with somebody who was always in a different mood, but it certainly didn't represent much sanity or security."

And in 2015, Todd Rundgren revealed the method Ringo Starr used to select the guest artists for his annual All-Starr Band tour: "The only requirement is that you had three hit singles at some point in your career.... Sometimes there should have been a psychological evaluation before that person was invited to join the band, which never happens."

Meanwhile, David Bowie, the Chamaeleon of Rock and Roll, was a creative genius. However, throughout his life, he was fearful of going insane – just like his psychotic half-brother, Terry Burns, and three of his mother's sisters. (The lyrics of Bowie's 1971 track, "All You Pretty Things," referenced one of Terry's psychotic episodes.) Bowie was tortured by the question of why he became a massive success while his sibling was in and out of mental institutions until 1985, when he finally killed himself.

Similarly, in 2018, heartland rocker Bruce Springsteen shocked fans when he confessed: "I have come close enough to [mental illness] where I know I am not completely well myself. I've had to deal with a lot of it over the years, and I'm on a variety of medications that keep me on an even keel; otherwise I can swing rather dramatically and... the wheels can come off a little bit. So we have to watch, in our family. I have to watch my kids, and I've been lucky there. It ran in my family going way before my dad."

Likewise, Joey Ramone suffered from a number of serious psychological issues. According to *Rolling Stone:* "When he was in his teens, Joey began behaving oddly – climbing in and out of bed repeatedly before he was ready for sleep, leaving food out of the refrigerator at night, becoming hostile with his mother when she asked him why he was acting strangely. Once, he pulled a knife on her. He started to hear voices, and could burst into inexplicable anger. In 1972, he voluntarily entered St. Vincent's Hospital for an evaluation and was kept for a month. The doctors diagnosed him as paranoid schizophrenic, 'with minimal brain damage.' Another psychiatrist told his mother, 'He'll most likely be a vegetable.' Not long after, his mother moved into a smaller apartment in the same building but didn't take him along; instead, he slept on the floor of her gallery." Later, he was also diagnosed with Obsessive Compulsive Disorder. However, bandmate Dee Dee Ramone insisted: "People who join a band like the Ramones don't come from stable backgrounds, because it's not that civilized an art form. Punk rock comes from angry kids who feel like being creative. I guess that's why members of the Ramones were known to throw TV sets from the roofs of apartment buildings at people below on the street."

Similarly, Irish singer Sinead O'Connor has struggled with multiple bouts of mental health problems. From public breakdowns, drug abuse and frequent attacks against the Catholic church, her antics were well documented in the media. In 2017, she infamously discussed her psychological battles during a streamed Facebook post, while holed away in a New Jersey motel room.

And Marilyn Manson admitted in 2015, "What I can say is that mental illness runs in the family." Likewise, according to *Mojo* magazine, singer Ian McCulloch of Echo and the Bunnymen "describes his life as 'hermit-like... like Howard Hughes without the billions'.... He lives alone, and because he has Obsessive Compulsive Disorder and various psychosomatic conditions, [and] a small group of friends... look after him and do his shopping for him, delivering it in blue plastic bags from the local late-night convenience store."

And in 2018, pop singer Lady Gaga admitted that for years she suffered from Post-Traumatic Stress Disorder (PTSD) and other related maladies: "I began to notice that I would stare off into space and black out for seconds or minutes" which "later morphed into physical chronic pain, fibromyalgia, panic attacks, acute trauma responses, and debilitating mental spirals that have included suicidal ideation and masochistic behavior."

Similarly, few music fans realized that pioneering rocker Bill Haley – whose chart-topping hit "Rock Around The Clock" ushered in the rock era – suffered cognitive problems and succumbed to a premature death at age 55 due to acute alcoholism.

*   *   *   *   *   *

Some rockers are legendary for their outrageous antics, whether Ozzy Osbourne biting the heads off a pair of doves, Keith Richards snorting his dead father's ashes, Alice Cooper throwing a live chicken into a frenzied crowd or R&B star Screamin' Jay Hawkins emerging from a coffin at his concerts.

However, rock journalist Dylan Jones contends that drummer Keith Moon – nicknamed Moon the Loon – set the bar for audacious behavior in rock and roll: "The Who's perpetual-motion machine of a drummer was long established as the quintessential rock 'n' roll reprobate, a man who would go out drinking on a Friday night, come back the following Wednesday and then ask his long-suffering girlfriend, 'Why didn't you pay the ransom?' This is the man who once drove his car through the glass doors of a hotel, who then drove all the way up to the reception desk, got out and asked for his room key. His antics were considered so outrageous that he made Keith Richards, Jim Morrison and Ozzy

Osbourne all seem like mischievous altar boys." However, Moon's bandmate Roger Daltrey explained: "Keith lived his entire life as a fantasy. He was the funniest man I've ever known, but he was also the saddest; I've seen Keith in some terrible times. I saw him at his height, but then I saw him at his lowest. Keith is someone I love deeply, but who was a deeply troubled character. I think he was possibly autistic, maybe even with a touch of Asperger's. He had an incredible talent but was completely uncontrollable. Not just a little bit uncontrollable, completely uncontrollable."

Additionally, there have been a number of legendary self-mutilators in rock and roll who would cut themselves onstage. Whether intended as performance art or a sign of mental illness, sometimes it is hard to differentiate between the two. A shirtless Sid Vicious was often photographed bleeding from numerous open wounds on his chest. And Richey Edwards of the Manic Street Preacher – who battled anorexia and depression – frequently cut himself. While talking to a music writer from *NME* in 1991, Edwards used a razorblade to carve "4Real" on his forearm. (The wound would require 18 stitches.) Conversely, Iggy Pop's legendary acts of self-mutilation during performances were more likely exercises in anti-social behavior.

However, Stiv Bator of the Dead Boys out-punked his fellow punk rockers when he literally died onstage during a concert. While executing his infamous "hanging trick" during a 1985 performance in Palo Alto, California, something went terribly wrong. Dead for more than a minute, he was brought back to life after paramedics used a defibrillator to restart his heart. Amazingly, he got back up and finished the concert. Bator later commented: "When you die on stage, how are you gonna follow that one up?"

Offstage, some rockers enjoyed engaging in disruptive behavior, even if it resulted in violence. When the Sex Pistols toured across the U.S. in 1978, the group was a lightning rod for controversy. Sid Vicious, who was fighting heroin withdrawal at the time, was in a particularly foul mood during the entire tour, which included several stops in the Deep South. As bandmate Johnny Rotten recalled, "[Sid] loved to approach these Dolly Parton look-alikes and their trucker boyfriends with their big cowboy hats.... There would be some fights in the redneck truck stops. They would stand up and say, 'I think you insulted my wife!' Sid, of course, didn't have the common sense to back down and say, 'No, I didn't, and sorry if you think so.' He'd say something daft like, 'I think your wig is an insult enough.' To Sid it was all just fashion statements. He didn't realize these people lived and died by their hairdos. Just like

Sid himself."

Oftentimes in the arts, a fine line separated genius from insanity. In the 1960s, Phil Spector was a talented producer who invented the Wall of Sound recording technique, as he churned out dozens of pop classics including "Be My Baby" and "You've Lost That Lovin' Feelin'." However, he was also renowned for his bizarre behavior – he kept his wife, Ronnie Spector, a prisoner in their home; he pointed a loaded gun at a number of rockers including John Lennon and Leonard Cohen; and he held the Ramones at gunpoint until they recorded the Ronettes' classic, "Baby, I Love You." Ron Weisner, co-founder of Buddah Records, recalled: "Phil was, as advertised, completely out of his mind, and every day or two, we'd be treated to the sound of a woman screaming, and the sight of said woman being chased to the elevator by a gun-toting Spector. And I sure as hell can understand why those women screamed the way they did. Whenever I was in a confined space with Phil, specifically the elevator, I was scared shitless, especially when he'd go into one of his rants."

However, Spector defended his eccentric behavior: "Even when the music business became big, I never felt like I fitted in. I never did all the drugs and the parties. I didn't feel comfortable. I always preferred the studio. Going out was always the big ordeal. Too hard. It was like being front of an audience. I just felt I didn't fit in. I was different. So I had to make my own world. And it made life complicated for me, but it made it justifiable. I look strange, I act strange, I made these strange records. So there's a reason to hate my guts – because I felt hated."

Tragically, a number of notable recording artists have been psychologically harmed by the pressures of the music industry, including Syd Barrett and Britney Spears. And in December 1964, on a flight from Los Angeles to a concert in Houston, Beach Boys co-founder Brian Wilson suffered the first of three nervous breakdowns. He subsequently stopped touring with the group for more than a decade. (Wilson was initially replaced in the Beach Boys by future country star Glen Campbell.) With the deterioration of Wilson's mental state, he became a recluse and began abusing drugs such as LSD. Eventually, Wilson became a patient of psychotherapist Dr. Eugene Landy, who would notoriously control every aspect of the musician's life.

INSECURITY

Not all rock stars are egotistical narcissists. Many musicians lack confidence and have an innate need for validation and positive reinforcement from audiences. Others, however, are overly self-conscious and have fragile egos. And oftentimes, choosing to go on a stage in front of an audience is an attempt to alleviate a sense of low self-esteem and to heal from past failures, broken relationships or a dysfunctional home life.

British pop singer Robbie Williams admitted in 2019 that he spent his entire career riddled with insecurity, social anxiety and self-doubt, which led to a three-year period during which he refused to leave his home. And in 1979, singer Ian Curtis of the British rock group Joy Division was overcome by insecurity and took his own life on the day before the band was scheduled to launch their first U.S. tour. Likewise, David Byrne of Talking Heads admitted: "Years ago when I started, I was very shy offstage. And when I got onstage, I felt this was my opportunity to let people know what I'm about. And soon as it's over, it's like, 'Can I go back to my room?'"

And Don Henley revealed in 1994, "I had a really rough time when the Eagles got successful; I got really confused for a while. I always go back to that song by Paul Simon called 'Fakin' In.' Everybody in the rock 'n' roll business or the movies has that fear of being found out. Deep down inside, they think or know they're not really as good as everybody thinks they are, because there's no logic to the starmaking machinery in this country."

Similarly, Shirley Manson, the leader of the alternative rock group Garbage, enjoyed several radio hits in the 1990s, including "Only Happy When It Rains" and "Stupid Girl." However, at the height of her career she suffered from acute anxiety: "In the middle of a European tour in support of the second Garbage album.... I was under immense physical and mental pressure. I was a media 'it' girl, and as a result I was lucky enough to be invited to grace the covers of newspapers and fashion magazines all over the world. Perversely, the downside of attracting so much attention was that I began to develop a self-consciousness about myself, the intensity of which I hadn't experienced since I was a young woman in the throes of puberty. I was suffering from extreme 'impostor syndrome,' constantly measuring myself against my peers, sincerely believing that they had gotten everything right and I had gotten everything so very wrong. The mental anguish I was inflicting on myself was extreme and drove me half out of my mind."

Even rock superstars wrestle with insecurity. Bono of U2 admitted in a 1987 interview: "There's a side of me I can't work out. I can't really work out why anyone would buy a U2 record. When I listen to it I just hear all the mistakes. It's a shame because we've made a few good records. But I just can't listen to them.... I think the instrumentation is

159

good or the way the group has played is good. But I don't like the way I've sung on any of the records. I don't think I'm a good singer, but I think I'm getting to *be* a good singer."

Pete Townshend stated in 2012: "It might surprise people to hear this, but the only guy I know that doesn't have any self-doubt is Sting. And we all find him difficult because of that. There are people I know pretty well – Mick [Jagger], Paul Simon, David Bowie, Ray Davies – that would have no difficulty agreeing with me when I said there were times when I felt out of step and very lost. They felt it, too. They might not admit it in public, but I can."

Similarly, Brian Jones of the Rolling Stones could be confident one moment and insecure the next. As his bandmate Bill Wyman recalled: "There were at least two sides to Brian's personality. One Brian was introverted, shy, sensitive, deep-thinking. The other was a preening peacock, gregarious, artistic, desperately needing assurance from his peers."

And Kurt Cobain was notoriously riddled with insecurities and believed he was not deserving of his fame and success. When he performed with Nirvana at an MTV Unplugged session in 1993, he was a nervous wreck, unsure how he would fare. Fearful of how the audience would react to his acoustic performance, Cobain asked an MTV employee: "Could you please make sure that this whole front row is just my friends?"

Johnny Cash expressed similar fears: "I can understand why Cobain felt that way, but he wasn't justified in thinking he was a fraud. He was successful because he was speaking honestly from his gut, but we all worry about whether we deserve the attention. In the early years, I felt guilty about it all. I had come from a real poor background and I didn't feel like I deserved all this money and attention. I kept thinking, 'I'm not what they think I am. I don't have all the answers. I'm not magic.' But then you grow with it and you learn that it really doesn't matter what other people think of you. You're just one human being, and you're doing the best you can. But it's not easy. It almost destroyed me."

And Neil Strauss, a rock critic for *The New York Times*, said of rock stardom: "Many celebrities who work hard for their success believe that celebrity and money will resolve their feelings of insignificance, insecurity, worthlessness, or disconnection. But, like Eric Clapton and Brian Wilson, they soon learn that rather than fixing one's flaws, fame... magnifies them. Especially when the drugs are free."

▶ CHAPTER 16
THE ROCK CONCERT

In 1964, a 21-year-old reporter named Larry Kane reluctantly agreed to join the Beatles press entourage for their first U.S. tour. Chronicling the rise of Beatlemania, Kane recalled a concert in Philadelphia: "During that show, I also found that the conduct and behavior of the fans was getting more of my attention than the music. Moving back from the corridor into the main hall, I surveyed the situation: Girls and some boys close together, standing, screaming, moaning, groaning, ripping at their hair, pushing, shoving, falling on the floor and crying, real tears streaming down hundreds of faces, smearing their mascara and lipstick, and mothers and fathers hiding in the back, some of them dancing to the music. For the first time, I started wondering whether their kids were in a state of trance. What was making them go?"

Likewise, Marianne Faithfull, who dated Mick Jagger for four years beginning in 1966, described the fanatical behavior she observed at one of her first Rolling Stone concerts: "Almost from the first notes of 'I'm A King Bee' an unearthly howl went up from thousands of possessed teenagers. Girls began pulling their hair out, standing on the back of their seats, pupils dilated, shaking uncontrollably. It was as if they were on some strange drug that propelled and synchronized them. Snake-handling frenzy buzzed through the hall. Dionysian mass hysteria was breaking out everywhere. Mick effortlessly reached inside them and snapped that twig."

$$*\qquad *\qquad *\qquad *\qquad *\qquad *$$

Is a rock concert just a concert – an aggregate of experienced musicians on an elevated stage, playing their hits for an assembled crowd? Jim Morrison insisted that concerts should be "spectacles." Likewise, Freddie Mercury once proclaimed: "A concert is not a live rendition of our album. It's a theatrical event."

In modern society, the rock concert has taken on many diverse functions – it is a media event, a social happening, an evening out, a forum to let loose, an escapist fantasy, an excuse to drink, a chance to take your girlfriend out on a date or to have a night out with your buddies. It is also a crucial component of youth self-exploration and personal growth.

If you're a fan of an artist, there is also an unwritten duty to attend the concert and to later brag "I was there." Oftentimes, it's also necessary to purchase and then wear a souvenir t-shirt just to emphasize the point. A concert also satisfies the human need to belong and identify with like-minded individuals as part of a musical community. In the case of the serious, hardcore music fan, a concert is an essential part of the rock and roll lifestyle. But most importantly, a rock concert is an opportunity to see the musical artist you enjoy and cherish.

And if the lead singer and musicians have properly done their jobs, they will connect with the audience in an ethereal manner. Singer Louise Wener of the '90s Britpop band Sleeper described the mindset of performing in front of a large, enthusiastic crowd: "I always imagined when you're on stage you'd be very self-conscious, all these thousands of people looking directly at you. But it's a strange thing where you actually forget yourself. It sounds really pretentious but you're locked into this sort of 'oneness of the experience.' You're having this gigantic party but you aren't aware of your part in it. You utterly let go. You play a chord and you see them move and you let go of everything, the nerves disappear, the insecurities disappear. And that *is* addictive." Similarly, Tom Petty once declared: "If you're not getting some kind of buzz from 20,000 people losing their minds, you've got a bad 'tude. Or else something's just not hooked up."

Playing songs in a certain order can also enhance the concert experience. As Roger Daltrey revealed: "I have an instinct for getting the songs in a sequence where the musical senses in the body are taken on a journey. If you put songs in the wrong place, you break the journey... In the early days, we knew so many songs, we didn't have a set list. I just used to shout them out and they'd go into the next song. I'd get the feel for which song needed to follow the one we were doing while we were doing it. I'd think where was I in my head, what was I was feeling, and then how could I take that feeling and emotion to another level without breaking the link. It was intense, a whole other level from just banging out one hit after another."

Similarly, during the mid-1960s when John Fogerty began playing in a small nightclub in Berkeley, he learned how to stage, orchestrate and pace a concert. He later explained: "Throughout my two or three years at the Monkey Inn, I was learning an awful lot about how to play in front of a live audience. How to talk to a crowd. How the music affects the mood and energy of the audience. If you played the wrong song, it could really deflate the atmosphere, But if you chose the *right* songs, it would make the place soar, and the feeling would be magical. I learned how to string songs together, to 'take a journey with the music.' Ah, man, the power of rock and roll."

And as artists become popular, their fans will memorize the lyrics to their songs. Oftentimes, certain hits become audience sing-alongs. Brian May of Queen first witnessed this phenomenon at the group's post "Bohemian Rhapsody" concerts in 1977: "When people started singing along, we found it kind of annoying at first. Then there was an enormous realization, at Bingley Hall, in the Midlands. They sang every note of every song. Freddie and I looked at each other and went: 'Something's happening here. We've been fighting it, and we should be embracing it.' That's where 'We Will Rock You' and 'We Are The Champions' came from."

Of course, every rock band will experience off-kilter nights. U2 frontman Bono admitted: "When I go onstage and a song is not connecting, I can feel it. You can feel people going to the bathroom or to buy a t-shirt, and you're annoyed." And when Led Zeppelin reunited for the Live Aid concert in 1985 – their first performance since John Bonham's death in 1980 – singer Robert Plant struggled to hit the high notes, Jimmy Page was handed a guitar that wasn't properly tuned and drummer Phil Collins was clearly unfamiliar with the group's songs.

THE HISTORY OF THE ROCK CONCERT

During the early years of rock and roll, concerts were organized by small, part-time promoters. Oftentimes, a radio deejay or record store owner would rent a venue, print up tickets and posters, and hire a local or regional act. The concert would be staged in a VFW hall, small amusement park, skating rink, teen club or rundown movie theater. Tickets would be priced at around a dollar. Remarkably, the cost to see a star like Elvis Presley in 1956 was $1.50. (The U.S. minimum wage that year was $1.00 an hour.)

There were a handful of notable concert promoters during the early years of rock and roll. Starting in the late-1940s, Los Angeles-based bandleader Johnny Otis led a series of traveling caravans of blues and R&B stars – including Johnny Ace, Etta James and Big Mama Thornton – across the country, mostly through the Deep South. Then after deejay Alan Freed had great success with his concerts in northeastern Ohio during the early-1950s, he took his Moondog revues on the road. And by the early-1960s, both *American Bandstand* host Dick Clark and New York City deejay Murray The K established their own caravan-style tours of pop, rock and R&B acts.

During this period, touring was a means of promoting your record and getting exposure – and was not considered a lucrative venture. Additionally, emerging acts would often perform for free at radio station events in exchange for precious airplay.

Even major acts earned little or nothing from touring. As the Rolling Stones' business accountant Prince Rupert Loewenstein explained: "In the early days the Stones had undertaken a number of tours, the first few organized by Andrew Oldham, the later tour under the control of Allen Klein after he had come on board. The remarkable thing about these tours was that, although people loved going to the show and the band gained an enormous amount of publicity and goodwill from touring – and the girls screaming and shouting were undoubtedly highly ego-enhancing for the band – no money ever came into their pockets."

Additionally, rock concerts were initially rudimentary affairs, with basic sound systems, unsophisticated lighting, inadequate security and few roadies. Scotty Moore, an early member of Elvis Presley's backing band, recalled: "We didn't have roadies back then. I was with Keith Richard in the studio, and he asked me how many guitars I used to take on the road back then. I told him *one*. I had to carry a guitar in my left hand, and an amp in my right hand – in and out of every show we played! He got a big kick out of that."

In 1964, when the Beatles performed for 8,000 fans in Washington, D.C., the arena was unequipped for rock concerts as evidenced by the terrible acoustics. On a tiny stage, the Fab Four employed just two microphones and three small Vox amplifiers. By 1966, the Beatles had stopped performing in public for two reasons. With the increasing complexity of their music, it became difficult to perform their songs in live settings. But more significantly, the band could not be heard above the constant cacophony of screaming young fans.

With the growing popularity of rock music, concerts became lucrative ventures in the late-1960s. Instead of playing in nightclubs that could seat a few hundred or theaters that could hold a couple thousand, rock acts began performing in large sports arenas. And when Madison Square Garden in New York City opened in 1969, it permitted seating for 20,000 – a far cry from smaller venues like the Fillmore East. As a result, a hit artist could earn $50,000 from a single performance at the Garden compared to just $20,000 for four shows over a two-day period at the 2,800-capacity Fillmore.

And then concerts got even bigger. Starting with the Monterey International Pop Festival in 1967 – which drew a crowd of 50,000 – rock festivals became the rage. Over the next three years, a series of legendary gatherings were staged, including the Newport Pop Festival, the Miami Pop Festival, the Atlanta Pop Festival and, of course, Woodstock. However, it was the disastrous Altamont Free Festival in 1969 that for a time tarnished the allure of such events.

The first major concert promoter of the rock era was San Francisco-based impresario Bill Graham. Initially booking shows at both the Fillmore Auditorium and the Winterland Arena, he was also instrumental in the careers of numerous local acts such as Janis Joplin, Jefferson Airplane and the Grateful Dead. Eventually, Graham would take his shows on a national stage. Transforming what had been an amateur enterprise, he established a rock promoter's formal role, which included band transportation, sound production, catering, security, the distribution of tickets and all of the logistics that it takes to oversee a concert by a major artist at a large venue. In the Bill Graham era, a number of competing concert promoters began carving out their own territories around the country.

The rise of arena rock also meant that major acts could demand guaranteed minimums or a percentage of ticket sales. While Led Zeppelin would play a gig for as little as $200 in 1968, their minimum per show reached $25,000 just two years later. By 1973, their concerts typically grossed hundreds of thousands of dollars. The group's improved financial position was due to their aggressive manager, Peter Grant, who in 1972 demanded a 90/10-percent division of the gate receipts between the band and promoter instead of the traditional 50/50 split. By the 1980s, rock concerts were significant money-making machines. Amazingly, the members of the Rolling Stones earned more from their 1981 tour, alone, than they had previously earned, *in total*, up to that point in their careers.

Meanwhile, larger outdoor venues were forced to employ visual effects on a grand scale in order to satisfy the fans sitting in the last rows. While Pink Floyd flew a 40-foot inflatable pig over audiences, ELO constructed an oversized, five-ton, 525,000-watt onstage spaceship with lasers and various effects. Additionally, Sony introduced its giant Jumbotron screen, which offered close-up shots of the onstage action.

The method of buying concert tickets has also evolved. In the days before the internet, snaring good seats was considered a rite of passage for rock fans. The process involved camping out in front of the venue, several hours before the tickets were scheduled to go on sale. Invariably, this meant that those at the front of the line were rewarded with excellent seats. But as a concert ticket became a commodity that was bought and re-sold, standing at the front of the line at the box office no longer guaranteed a good seat. Eventually, the best seats were siphoned off by promoters, record labels, fan clubs, radio stations, credit card companies, scalpers and others in the concert industry food-chain.

And in the digital era, there was a major paradigm shift in the music industry as concerts became far more profitable than selling physical products – whether vinyl records or CDs. Consequently, the majority of rock acts were earning almost all of their income from touring.

Additionally, by 2017, the U.S. concert industry reported annual sales of more than $3 billion in tour merchandise. From t-shirts and caps to posters and programs, these items were often bigger moneymakers than the actual concerts themselves. This new business model was especially bankable for established artists who rarely released new material but had cultivated a large, loyal fanbase. Consequently, acts like U2, Fleetwood Mac and Bruce Springsteen could guarantee sell-out crowds at large arenas by simply performing their classic songbooks of hits.

PRE-CONCERT EXCITEMENT

Whether you're sitting in the front row or the cheap seats, there's an atmosphere of festive anticipation before a concert. Although the audience is obviously excited to see their favorite group, the musicians who are about to hit the stage frequently battle episodes of pre-concert jitters.

Clem Burke, the drummer for Blondie, admitted: "I enjoy the tension and pressure that builds up around the day of the gig when you know you've just got to go and play, you do the sound check and you leave. The best time is like the couple hours in between the sound check and the actual gig, your body starts pumping adrenaline. It's a really good feeling, you feel sort of like Superman for a little while. If you could package that and sell it, you'd be all right."

Many musicians go through pre-show rituals before they take the stage. Keith Richards won't perform until he's eaten a plate of traditional Shepherd's Pie. Members of Weezer throw a Frisbee backstage. Pop singer Selena Gomez drinks some olive oil. The Foo Fighters dance to Michael Jackson songs and knock back some Jägermeister. And Leonard Cohen would guzzle a shot of whiskey and sing a verse of traditional Latin music.

And according to Elvis Presley insider Jerry Schilling, before a concert, "Elvis was like a panther in a cage, waiting to be let out. He never went backstage early, because when he put his jumpsuit on, he said, 'My adrenalin starts burning.' He was like Muhammad Ali before a fight. You could feel the intensity of Elvis right before going on stage, and if you were one of the four or five people backstage with him, you'd start to get nervous, too. He was never relaxed before a show."

Finally, as Beatles insider Ken Mansfield observed, "There is that unique moment for entertainers when they are told 'It's time,' and they journey that strange distance from the dressing room out onto the stage. Until you know you've connected with the audience, there is that deep-down indescribable fear of not pulling it off no matter who you are."

When the band hits the stage, they are greeted with a loud roar of approval. Stan Lynch, the original drummer of Tom Petty and the Heartbreakers, described the moment: "That's a real twilight zone, when you walk on the stage and the lights are down and it's 'Ladies and Gentlemen' time. I don't know what happens at that point, if I'm five years old or 50. I'm literally lost on that stage before they turn the lights on. It's like, 'How did I end up here? What's going on? How come there's only five of us and 20,000 of them?' This music stuff, it's really cool."

Similarly, Tom Petty admitted: "The energy of the crowd is insane. Twenty thousand people. It's the biggest jolt of adrenaline. It's very hard to explain. You know the old story about the woman lifting the car off her kid? It's in that realm. You can actually hurt yourself and not know it. If you're phony, they will feel it in the farthest row of the arena. You have to really care. And you have to make yourself care, time and time again."

Likewise, Sting observed: "How could you replace the feeling of walking out into a stage in front of thousands of people and all of them basically saying as one, 'We like you. We approve of you.' That's not something you could do without really."

PLAYING THEIR HITS

When attending a concert, a paying audience expects to hear most or all of the artist's biggest hits. Every musician understands they have an implicit responsibility to play those familiar songs. However, many acts choose to ignore that duty. David Thomas, the outspoken lead singer of the veteran art-rock group Pere Ubu, said of concertgoers: "I have never been concerned by what an audience wants or is interested in. Who the hell even asked them? And, more to the point, what the hell do they know?"

In 2010, Tom Petty was asked about the audience reaction to a mini-set of blues songs during the Mojo Tour: "I have a feeling that they'll stay in their seats and enjoy it, but I don't give a damn if everyone goes to the bathroom. I'm not going to be just a song-and-dance man. I'm gonna play what I want to play. I know I should always give people a good dose of what they came to hear, because I'm not playing at the corner bar, and it's quite an effort to go into an arena... and sit way up high and watch. But we also refused to become one of those groups that only live in the past. I can come out and play two hours of hits and everyone will be happy and it'll go great. But if I do that too much, I'm only feeding the nostalgia crowd. I love it when I see people and they play the hits, but I also want to see what they're doing at the moment.... If I had all this great new stuff in my back pocket and didn't pull it out, it would be criminal. If we don't do that, what are we? They've seen us play 'American Girl' a hundred times."

Some acts have legitimate reasons for not playing their past hits. Paul McCartney rarely performed Beatles songs when he initially launched his solo career in the early-1970s. He later explained: "The only reason I didn't want to do them right after the Beatles was I had just started Wings, and I thought, there's no way I can start Wings and still keep playing Beatles songs. So I kind of put an embargo on them, and all the promoters were quite upset. But then eventually we got well known. Right about 1976, Wings had a big American tour. And then I started to think, you know what, it's O.K. now. Now that we've established ourselves, I can now acknowledge my other group."

A number of notable acts dislike having to play their biggest hits at every show. Late in his career, Dylan preferred to play mostly newer material instead of his classic hits, which he called "that package of heavy, rotting meat." Similarly, Robert Plant has referred to the Led Zeppelin rock standard "Stairway To Heaven" as "that bloody wedding song." And Mike Score, the lead singer of the 1980s New Wave band A Flock Seagulls, told VH1 that he hated playing the group's most famous hit: "Every time I perform live, everyone just wants to hear 'I Ran.' I'm sick of it."

Fortunately, most artists want to accommodate audiences. In 2016, Mike Love of the Beach Boys admitted, "I've probably sung 'Fun, Fun, Fun' live close to 6,000 times." Likewise, Pat Benatar performs her biggest hits – which she has dubbed "The Holy 14" – at every concert. And Sting explained: "I've sung ['Roxanne'] on most of the nights of my life since [1977], and it's my job to sing it with the same freshness and enthusiasm as if I'd written it that afternoon and not thirty years previously. I always manage to find something new in it and I'm still grateful." Likewise, Pete Townshend proclaimed: "If I get tired of playing a song, I grab my guitar and find a quiet place. Then I play it over and over again until I get back to the mental state I was in when I first wrote the song. I find that same fire again and it reconnects me." However, some major artists with a long string of hits will perform just a verse or two of their best-known songs as part of an extended medley.

GETTING SICK: THE SHOW MUST GO ON

Rock stars are expected to be superhuman, so it's unsettling when they fall sick and can't perform. That was the case in July 2011, when three separate tours had to be postponed: Taylor Swift was stricken with bronchitis, Katy Perry had a bout of food poisoning and Adele suffered from laryngitis. And when a performer catches a cold or the flu, it's not a matter of simply calling off sick. The venue has been booked, the roadies have set up the stage, the promoter has paid for radio and newspaper advertisements and thousands of fans have bought tickets and are enroute to the concert.

Instead, most performers live by the adage that the show must go on. During a concert in the mid-1970s, James Brown stepped on a metal nail, which went completely through his foot and caused his boot to fill with blood. Despite suffering intense pain, he finished the show. Likewise, in 2015 when Dave Grohl of the Foo Fighters broke his leg during the middle of a concert in Sweden, he announced to the audience that he was heading to the hospital, but would return. Keeping his promise, an hour later he resumed the show – while sitting in a wheelchair with a bulky cast on his leg. Similarly, in 1991 when Rob Halford rode his trademark Harley-Davidson onto the stage, he collided with a malfunctioning drum riser. Falling off the bike, he broke his nose and was knocked unconscious. After he was revived, an angry and bloodied Halford finished the concert. And in 2020, Elton John performed a show in New Zealand, despite suffering from walking pneumonia. Halfway through the concert, the teary-eyed Rocket Man told the audience, "I've just completely lost my voice. I can't sing, I've got to go." He was escorted off the stage by a medic.

Some artists pay a huge price for going on the road despite serious health problems. Adam Ant revealed: "My body gave out before my mind did. I was on tour and my knees gave way. I think if I'd been handled properly, I might have had a chance. I never had a month off, even when I was plainly ill. I was a slave to my record label." And Michael Jackson was in frail health when he announced his This Is It farewell tour in 2009. Eager to pay off his mounting debts, he agreed to go on a grueling, 50-date tour. But after weeks of strenuous rehearsals, he passed away before the start of the tour.

Amazingly, several infamous tours were not cancelled – even in the face of tragedy. In February 1959, after the trio of Buddy Holly, Ritchie Valens and the Big Bopper perished in a plane crash at the edge of a corn field outside of Clear Lake, Iowa, the tour continued as planned. At the next stop in Moorhead, Minnesota, a number of replacement acts were added to the lineup, including a then-unknown 15-year-old singer named Bobby Vee. Similarly, when eleven fans were killed at a Who concert in Cincinnati, the band did not cancel the rest of the dates on the tour and performed in Buffalo on the following night. Likewise, after guitarist Randy Rhoads died in a freak plane crash while on the road with Ozzy Osbourne, the tour continued. As Osbourne later explained: "I honestly don't know how we did any of those gigs after Randy died. We were all in a state of shock." And, in 1987, on the second stop of a Bob Dylan and Grateful Dead co-headlining stadium tour, Jerry Garcia lapsed into a life-threatening diabetic coma for five days. Nonetheless, the tour went ahead as planned.

STAGE FRIGHT

When a veteran singer is performing on a concert stage – and is captivating tens of thousands of fans – it is hard to imagine that he or she could possibly suffer from stage fright. And yet, Barbra Streisand's stage fright kept her from performing in front of an audience for 27 years. Singer-songwriter Janis Ian suffered from the same fear and would tour only sporadically. And in 1970, Genesis co-founder Anthony Phillips quit the progressive-rock band over the issue of stage fright. And amazingly, a painfully shy Jim Morrison performed with his back to the audience when the Doors first appeared at the legendary Whisky A Go-Go nightclub in early-1967. Not once during the entire show did he turn around and face the crowd.

Likewise, guitarist Vivian Campbell of Def Leppard never felt comfortable on a stage. As bandmate Joe Elliott recalled: "I remember the night before one tour started, he was trying to smash his knuckles on the sink so he wouldn't have to play, because he was scared to death of getting up on stage. And then we did the gig and he was like: 'I'm fine.' With bruises everywhere."

And although the White Stripes – which consisted of guitarist Jack White and drummer Meg White – were on top of the musical world in 2007, the blues-rock act cancelled a heavily-anticipated tour. Offering an explanation, the duo issued a formal statement: "Meg White is suffering from acute anxiety and is unable to travel at this time." Painfully shy for much of her life, she was clearly uncomfortable on the stage. Subsequently, the White Stripes disbanded in 2011, and Jack White continued as a solo act.

Even experienced rockers can be stricken with the condition. Despite a long, fruitful career as the head of the Heartbreakers and a member of the Traveling Wilburys, Tom Petty suddenly had trouble performing in front of audiences in 1990. He recounted: "For the first time in my career, I developed stage fright. After a whole career in which I was very happy to take the stage, all of a sudden I went through a period of being terrified, puking, the whole thing."

It took some simple psychology for Roy Orbison to get over his insecurities. As he explained: "I used to be more frightened than I should have been. But I pulled in this parking lot at this concert, and the marquee said, ROY ORBISON, SOLD OUT. And there were no other names, and it sort of dawned on me that everybody came to see me and that they'd probably heard of me and they might even like me beforehand. So I went on that night, years and years ago, not so afraid."

Oftentimes, rock acts experience bouts of stage fright when they progress from playing clubs and small theaters to performing in front of large crowds in cavernous stadiums. In 2010, the Black Keys released their breakthrough top-10 album, *Brothers*, a project that would earn two Grammys. That same year, the group graduated to playing for larger audiences. Patrick Carney, the duo's drummer, told *Spin*: "The thing that really made me realize things were different was at Lollapalooza. There were, like, 50,000 people watching us, and I went through this weird panic mode that lasted through the middle of September. I melted down.... The whole time I felt like I was going to pass out. For six weeks after, I stopped picking up my phone and had this really weird stage fright every time we played." Similarly, hours after singer-songwriter James Arthur performed at the Monte Verde Festival in 2018, he revealed: "I had an anxiety attack on stage in front of 12,000 people tonight and no one would've known but I thought I was gonna die on stage which is maybe the scariest thing I've ever experienced in my life."

Some artists use alcohol to battle stage fright. In 2014, country star Tim McGraw admitted: "I used to have to have a few drinks to get on stage, because I'm sort of an innately shy person. To step out on stage and to sing and be in front of people was nerve-wracking for me in a lot of ways. That was the way I got my courage – some liquid courage – with a little Jack Daniel's." Similarly, following the sudden death of Prince in 2016, fans were shocked to discover that he took drugs before concerts to battle stage fright.

HECKLERS

Hecklers have been around for as long as there have been performers and audiences. Whether the masked actors at the amphitheaters of ancient Greece, the brutal gladiators at the Roman Coliseum, the sword swallowers at P.T. Barnum's three-ring circus or a rival team at an NFL game – hecklers will shout, scream and throw things during the middle of a concert, sporting event or play.

But does buying a ticket entitle someone to be disruptive at a public event? A loud heckler has the power to disrupt the vibe and flow of a concert by shouting something inane or insulting. Although yelling "Free Bird" at a concert may be considered harmless and amusing, screaming "you suck" is a far different matter.

Over the years, audiences at rock concerts have become increasingly hostile, belligerent and prone to violence. Meat Loaf was viciously heckled in 1977 when he opened for Cheap Trick in Chicago, shortly after the release of his breakthrough album, *Bat Out Of Hell*. As he recalled in his autobiography: "Times had changed, and this was typical of the seventies. In the sixties, nobody booed anybody. You might not get such big applause, but you had acts of very different stripes all playing together. Richie Havens playing with the Who, you had Ravi Shankar sitting there playing the sitar with Blue Cheer! People didn't even boo *Yoko*. In the sixties, you just didn't go there. It didn't make any difference what the band was playing, people would just sit and enjoy the music."

Veteran performers have learned how to handle hecklers. Most have a quick one-line response they use to shut down the troublemakers. But the method is not foolproof. At the 2003 Farm Aid concert in Columbus, Ohio, a visibly angry John Mellencamp lost his temper, put his hand over the microphone and exchanged angry insults with an audience member.

On occasion, a performer will physically confront a heckler. In 1970, at Pete Townshend's first-ever solo concert, a drunken fan who was sitting near the stage kept shouting for the Who guitarist to play the track "Underture" from *Tommy*. Townshend recalled: "He was persistent, and irritating. When he shouted his request once too often I leapt from the stage, got hold of him by the neck and was about to punch him." It took a friend of the drunk to diffuse the situation and prevent a beating.

Similarly, in 2018, veteran punk singer Mike Ness was performing with his band Social Distortion when he decided he wouldn't take any more verbal abuse from an audience member. After handing off his electric guitar to a roadie, he jumped off the stage and threw multiple punches. A few seconds later, members of security helped Ness back onto the stage, where he finished the concert. The heckler got the message and immediately left the venue.

Pioneering rocker Jerry Lee Lewis frequently encountered violent trouble-makers throughout the 1960s. In the wake of his scandalous marriage to his 13-year-old cousin, the Killer was relegated to county fairs and small clubs for most of the decade. At many of these venues, rabble-rousers showed up with the intention of getting into a fight with Lewis or a member of his band. Never one to avoid confrontations, Lewis frequently brawled at his concerts, even using his metal microphone stand as a weapon.

Similarly, Alice Cooper spent much of the early-1970s battling hecklers who came to his shows for the sole purpose of disrupting his performances. Instead of confronting the agitators, Cooper simply viewed the disturbances as a routine part of the show.

And in 1983, INXS launched their first-ever U.S. tour, after MTV began playing the video for their track, "The One Thing." But the audiences were not always appreciative of the Aussie band's New Wave-style dance rock. As the group's guitarist Andrew Farriss recalled: "In Texas, someone threw a pistol onstage. There was a note tied to the barrel: YOU'RE GONNA NEED THIS."

And in 2002, singer-songwriter Ryan Adams famously halted a concert at Nashville's Ryman Auditorium when a fan kept yelling out "Summer Of '69" – a reference to a hit by the similarly named Canadian singer Bryan Adams. About 15 years after the incident, Ryan Adams explained his actions: "As I approached the heckler's wooden pew, I was shocked. He was only a few years older than me. Unshaven, bleary-eyed. He had on a baseball hat and seemed so drunk that his limbs hung from his sides like a broken doll. His eyes were like two poached eggs waiting to break. The anger left me, and I instantly felt bad. No one was there for this man. No one stopped him. I said, 'Hey man, if you were trying to ruin the show you succeeded, but I need to try and finish this – it's my job.' I pulled out two $20 bills and said: 'Here is your money, please take a taxi and leave here. Go home and take an aspirin. Please. Leave.'

I walked back to the stage. People applauded."

The most infamous heckler in the history of rock and roll shouted "Judas" at Bob Dylan in 1966. Angry that the Voice of a Generation had started infusing electric rock into his traditional folk stylings, 22-year-old John Cordwell spoke for many in attendance when he heckled Dylan at a concert in Manchester, England. Visibly rattled by the incident, Dylan answered the heckler, "I don't believe you. You're a liar!," and then led his band on a blistering, electric rendition of "Like A Rolling Stone."

MANAGING CROWDS AT CONCERTS

When the Beatles toured across the U.S. in the mid-1960s, there were numerous breaches of security that could have easily injured members of the group. At the time, few police departments were trained in the logistics of handling large mobs of screaming teenage concertgoers. In August 1966, hundreds of shrieking fans broke through a police cordon at an outdoor performance by the Fab Four. As Beatles insider Tony Barrow recalled: "One of the wildest shows took place at the Municipal Stadium in Cleveland – where the crowd broke loose, crashed through a flimsy, four-foot security fence and invaded the field during 'Day Tripper.' Hopelessly outnumbered and overwhelmed, the local police simply gave up and stood back while hordes of fans took control of the stage and the 'secure' grassy area around it. The boys rushed off to their makeshift dressing room... and the concert was stopped for 30 minutes while private guards and police reinforcements restored order. At the end of that show roadie Mal Evans had to stop fans from stealing the boys' instruments from the stage as souvenirs."

By the 1970s, crowd control become a crucial concern at large, public events – especially after the security fiasco at the Altamont Festival, where one spectator was murdered and one of the performers, Marty Balin, was knocked out by a Hells Angel. An angry or overexcited mob can do serious harm. Although trained members of security are tasked with keeping order, a number of concerts have been marred by tragedy: in 2003, at least 100 people perished and 230 were injured at the Station nightclub fire in Rhode Island; more than 1,000 attendees were injured at Woodstock '99; and in 2017, 58 people were killed and 869 injured during an outdoor music festival in Las Vegas.

*   *   *   *   *   *

Providing security in the music industry eventually became big business. In 1989, *Rolling Stone* magazine reported that "some rockers spend an estimated $500,000 every year for personal security while on tour. A bodyguard working on a major concert tour can earn between $750 and $1,250 a week, with specialists who provide full-time home security and other services raking in much more."

The most important function of security guards at a rock concert is to protect the artist at all costs. Michael Francis, a veteran chief of concert security, revealed his strategy: "I study the audience on all sides, looking for anything out of the ordinary: someone who is standing up but not enjoying themselves, not singing along to the songs. Members of my security staff are positioned around the stage looking to see what these people are up to. Two experienced guys do nothing else all night but patrol the front twenty rows. Over the years, you develop a sixth sense that helps you spot the odd ones, the ones that could mean trouble."

Oftentimes, an over-exuberant fan will rush the stage during the middle of a concert. Although they're rarely a threat to the artist, they have no business being on that stage, and their mere presence can ruin a performance for the rest of the paying audience. They are also a risk to themselves on a stage that's overloaded with instruments, wires and high-voltage electrical equipment.

Most performers wait for the muscle-bound members of security to deal with stage runners. While female crashers tend to kiss or clutch onto their targets, male stage crashers tend to hug the object of their fandom. And while females are walked off the stage, their male counterparts are usually made to physically pay for their intrusions.

On a rare occasion, musicians will take care of the problem on their own. Reacting to a Rolling Stones fan who had rushed onto the stage during a performance of "Satisfaction" at a 1996 concert in Hampton, Virginia, an angry Keith Richards walloped the man in the head with a guitar and then pushed him away. The injured fan was subsequently carried off the stage by security guards. And at a 2014 concert by California-based punk band NOFX in Sydney, Australia, an enthusiastic male fan jumped onto the stage and hugged singer "Fat Mike" Burkett. Before security was able to remove the intruder, Burkett knocked down and then kicked the man in the face. (Burkett would later apologize to the stage runner.)

Although most artists manage to avert calamity, some performers were not as fortunate. On December 30, 1978, at the Winterland Ballroom in San Francisco, Tom Petty barely avoided serious bodily harm. During the middle of a performance, he was pulled into the audience. It took four fast-acting roadies to yank a dazed and shaken Petty out of the frenzied crowd and push him back onto the stage. In a matter of seconds, Petty had suffered a number of injuries: "I have a real heavy vest and they ripped that, my whole shirt went, I had a neckerchief tied real tight around my neck and... it's hanging down to my chest because it had been pulled and twisted. I lost handfuls of hair and my whole lip was busted. It was this weird sensation of falling and never hitting the ground and people diving in. They're crazy people when they're that worked up." Several years after the incident, Petty observed: "I've noticed that I can't get near an audience as Bruce Springsteen does. They rip me up. Bruce can walk through them. I think they look at him as their buddy. With me, there seems to be some violent or sexual vibes. I'm the last guy on earth to be violent."

Similarly, Roger Daltrey was dragged into an audience in 1965. During a concert in the town of Salisbury, England, Daltrey saw a fan pull a microphone stand off the stage. While attempting to retrieve the piece of equipment, Daltrey was yanked into the overly animated crowd. Unlike Petty, who suffered only superficial injuries, Daltrey seriously injured his back. And at a 1980 concert in Cincinnati, John Waite was wrestled into the audience and suffered a severe knee injury. After attempting to perform the following night, Waite was forced to cancel the rest of the tour.

*   *   *   *   *   *

Concertgoers often throw objects onto the stage, from bouquets of flowers to dangerous projectiles. The variety of things lobbed at performers is endless. When the Scorpions performed in St. Louis in 1982, a fan threw an open jar of live scorpions onto the stage. And at a Keith Urban concert, someone once threw a prosthetic leg onto the stage. After Urban autographed it, he asked the audience to "crowd surf" the leg back to the fan.

Pop singer Tom Jones explained how he learned to deal with objects thrown onto the stage: "I have years of experience in theaters and dance halls and now nightclubs. I've not come in for much abuse in that time, but I still like to think I've had most things thrown at me that an audience is likely to throw. It's a fairly limited repertoire of objects, after all. Mostly glassware. And you learn the techniques. If someone chucks a bottle, you try to catch it, or you pick it up and drink from it, or you say, 'Are you sure [you're] finished with that?' – something to defuse the situation, may even turn the moment to your advantage." Later, Jones had to contend with the frequent bombardments of women's undergarments.

Other artists weren't as fortunate as Tom Jones. In 2004, David Bowie was struck in the face by a small object during a concert in Oslo, Norway. The object – a lollipop – landed in Bowie's eye and got stuck in place. Luckily, he was unhurt and managed to finish the concert.

Similarly, after bassist Duff McKagan was struck by a projectile during a Guns N' Roses show in Sacramento, Axl Rose announced to the audience: "I hate to ruin your fun – and I'm fun – but somebody just hit Duff in the head with a bottle, and now he's not able to play. So we're sorry. Have a good night. And if you find the asshole, kill him." Similarly, bassist Geezer Butler was struck in the head with a bottle at a 1980 Black Sabbath concert in Milwaukee. The incident occurred during the middle of the concert, while the stage lights were briefly turned off. As Butler later recalled: "I was knocked out, and the band was busy getting me off the stage and to a hospital. When the lights came back up, there was no band on stage. And of course, the crowd freaked out. Someone should have gone out and explained – the promoter or someone. I mean, the band was worrying about getting me to the hospital, you know? So the crowd freaked out because there was suddenly no band on stage, and things got worse from there." A violent riot ensued, resulting in 80 arrests.

Disturbingly, concertgoers often toss fireworks onto the stage. Kiss drummer Peter Criss recalled an incident during a 1976 concert in Memphis: "One minute I'm playing and the next thing I know, I'm in an ambulance. Some kid threw a huge firecracker, an M-80, onstage and blew me right off the drums. I woke up in an ambulance and couldn't hear for six months. I was really pissed; it could have blown my head off. Actually, I was more angry about the fact that I was up there to give this kid a good time, and he was tryin' to hurt me." Similarly, in 1977, an M-80 landed onstage during an Aerosmith concert at the Spectrum in Philadelphia. While Joe Perry had to be treated for hand injuries, Steven Tyler suffered a damaged cornea.

And on December 4, 1971, Frank Zappa and the Mothers of Invention were performing at the Montreux Casino in Switzerland when a member of the audience fired a flare gun into the ceiling. The venue quickly caught on fire and completely burned to the ground. The incident was the impetus for the Deep Purple hit, "Smoke On The Water."

One performer employed a novel method to deal with items thrown onto the stage. At a 2018 concert in Australia, rapper Lil Wayne angrily threatened to have his bodyguards shoot their guns into the audience if any objects were heaved in his direction.

Some musical genres tend to draw more riotous crowds. Punk acts like Black Flag and the Clash were far more likely to attract boisterous, violent and drunken concertgoers than Elton John or Hall & Oates. As Dave Alvin of the Blasters explained: "The front of my 1964 Fender Mustang guitar has many shards of glass permanently embedded in it from beer bottles thrown at us by pissed-off audience members at punk shows. These wounds were badges of honor to me back then. One is a long gash from a beer bottle thrown at me by a dissatisfied patron at one early 1980 show with the Angry Samoans at the Shark Club in San Diego, while another is an almost delicate spray of tiny brown fragments from a beer bottle hurled at the stage when we played with the Weirdos about a month later at West LA's Club 88. The deepest, most dramatic slash running across the front of my guitar was from when we opened in late 1979 for Orange County heroes, the Crowd... The kid who threw that bottle had a pretty damn good arm and great aim, but I was fast enough and lucky enough to see it coming, so I had a split second to raise my guitar in the front of my face and deflect the projectile."

Similarly, booking agent John Giddens described the violent anarchy that typically occurred at Ramones concerts: "The fans used to get so carried away. It was like they're trying to injure themselves. It was an excuse for people to hurt each other. It was kids being able to take out their aggressions. You could come to a gig and behave in this aggressive nature and it was acceptable. You couldn't do that in the streets, could you? You couldn't do it at home. Your mum would shoot you. They played some free festival in Holland for 100,000 people. I was standing there watching the band and this kid turned around and hit another kid in the head with a bicycle chain. I remember... this blood came pouring down from under his hairline. It was disgusting."

The emergence of the mosh pit brought a new facet of aggression and violence to rock concerts. Evolving from the "slam dance" craze of the late-1970s, moshing became a common activity at punk, metal and alternative-rock shows. Tragically, there have been thousands of injuries and dozens of deaths around the world from moshing. Consequently, a number of venues have banned the activity.

HOSTILE PERFORMERS: TREATING FANS POORLY

James Brown proclaimed in his autobiography: "When you're on stage, the people who paid money to get in are the boss, even if it cost them only a quarter. You're working for them." However, not all performers choose to heed Brown's advice. In fact, some artists are outright hostile toward their audiences.

When fronting the Sex Pistols, Johnny Rotten routinely abused concertgoers with vulgar insults. Also, some major acts refuse to acknowledge their audiences at concerts and won't utter a single word between songs. Veteran artists like Bob Dylan and Van Morrison both reached the stage in their careers when they couldn't be bothered with audience interaction. Dylan argued: "It just doesn't seem relevant anymore. It's not stand-up comedy or a stage play. Also, it breaks my concentration to have to think of things to say or to respond to the crowd. The songs themselves do the talking. My songs do anyway."

Some performers will even scold their audiences. In 1983, an agitated David Crosby stopped a song, midway, and admonished the audience at an upscale cabaret in Ohio: "Stop ordering drinks from your waitress. Pay attention, this song is important." And at a 2019 solo show by Aaron Lewis, he repeatedly warned concertgoers to stay silent during his performance of an acoustic song. After refusing to heed his warnings, Lewis shouted a profanity at the audience and then walked off the stage. Likewise, at a 2008 Tori Amos concert in San Diego, she cursed out a pair of fans for talking during a performance of her track, "Code Red," and then ordered them out of the venue; she shouted: "It's a privilege to sit in the front row and I reserve those seats for people who appreciate music."

Not surprisingly, Jim Morrison was often confrontational with concertgoers. He once explained his relationship with audiences: "You've got to make them believe you're doing them a favor by being onstage. The more abusive you are, the more they love it." At an infamous show at the Dinner Key Auditorium in Miami in 1969, Morrison frequently berated and goaded the crowd: "How long are you going to let them push you around? How long? Maybe you like it? Maybe you like being pushed around? Maybe you love it? Maybe you love getting you face stuck in shit? Come on, you love it, don't you?"

Some artists enjoy pranking their audiences. One of Aerosmith's sound technicians recalled: "There was always a bottle of Jack Daniel's on the drum riser, as well as a bottle of 150-proof white rum.... Steven [Tyler's] little joke was to take one hit off this bottle and pass it down to the teenage kids in the first row. Five minutes later they'd all be vomiting because they weren't used to the overproof firewater. Nothing more hilarious than a row of puking fans."

And in his autobiography, punk rocker Johnny Ramone admitted: "At one point in the early nineties, I came into possession of a canister of police-issue mace, compliments of a former New York City cop. In fact, he was with us working as part of the crew at this show in Washington, D.C. It was a sturdy can, big enough that your whole hand went around the cannister, not one of those things that women carry. I figured he knew how to handle the mace, so I told him to get ready and fire it into the crowd at some point during the show. So he got behind a PA column and let go. It was terrific, like a bomb went off, with everybody running and pouring beer on their faces. That was a Ramones show."

Although mace could be considered a normal part of the show at a Ramones performance, the same could not be said of a concert by a Heartland rocker at the Fillmore Auditorium in San Francisco. In 1997, when someone unleashed a can of pepper spray during the middle of a concert by Tom Petty and the Heartbreakers, members of the audience struggled to breathe. The show was stopped and fans were treated by paramedics.

*   *   *   *   *   *

When Gene Simmons of Kiss was spitting blood onstage in the 1970s, it was fake blood and he didn't target members of the audience. However, some musical artists had no qualms about spewing their own bodily fluids onto concertgoers.

During her 2014 Bangerz tour, pop singer Miley Cyrus engaged in an unusual practice. She would fill her mouth with water and then spit the liquid onto the spectators in the first few rows – usually repeating the stunt several times during a single show. Similarly, during a 2014 performance by Lady Gaga at the annual SXSW music festival in Austin, the singer was joined onstage by a "vomit artist." During the performance of the track "Swine," Lady Gaga was the recipient of the artist's regurgitation.

And when Blind Melon performed in Vancouver on Halloween in 1993, singer Shannon Hoon removed all of his clothing and urinated on the audience. Later, according to the local media, the "police blocked the bus from going anywhere after the concert. Hoon climbed out a bus window on to the roof of the bus, where he screamed at police before the other members of his band talked him into getting off the roof." He was subsequently arrested and charged with public nudity and committing an indecent act.

Worse yet, punk rocker GG Allin was infamous for his signature stage move, which often resulted in physical brawls with fans. He would drop his pants, defecate and then heave his excrement into the audience.

Some musical acts have a penchant for starting their concerts hours late and keeping fans anxiously waiting in their seats. Venue operators are aware that if an act goes on later than scheduled, the patrons will spend more money and buy more drinks. It's a simple but abused strategy. Nonetheless, an artist risks the ire of concertgoers if they're kept waiting too long.

There have been a number of infamous instances of performers taking the stage hours past their scheduled start times. In 2005 at London's Coliseum, singer Lauryn Hill hit the stage two hours late because she was unable to decide which outfit to wear. And after Madonna started a Philadelphia concert two-and-a-half-hours late in 2017, she announced to the audience: "I want to apologize for being late. We had many changes to make from Europe to America, and I wanted the show to be perfect for you because my fans deserve it and quite frankly I deserve it."

Meanwhile, Guns N' Roses – who saw riots break out at their concerts in Montreal, St. Louis and Vancouver – often did not take the stage until after midnight. In 2006, the group's frontman Axl Rose almost caused another rampage in Newcastle, England, after he insisted on finishing his extravagant dinner – which included roast lamb and Yorkshire pudding – before belatedly taking the stage.

Some artists were legendary for missing scheduled concerts altogether. In the country music field, hard-drinking, honky-tonk singers like Hank Williams, Sr. and George Jones were both habitual no-shows. In 1979 alone, Jones skipped 54 concerts!

AUDIENCES VARY BY COUNTRY

Fan behavior at concerts varies around the world. As Andy Summers of the Police observed: "As overworked as it sounds, music is universal. The only differences are what happens around a show. In America, there's no tradition of little girls screaming and shouting as in England. In Japan they follow you to your hotel with autograph books. It Italy they're just crazy; we had a riot every night, with tear gas and police all the time."

British bass player Guy Pratt – who has worked with Pink Floyd, Roxy Music and Icehouse – explained: "American crowds make the most noise usually, but that doesn't mean they're the best crowds. Half their energy is being expelled on whooping and high-fiving each other and generally reveling in the shared experience of being at the gig with their mates rather than experiencing it."

In Japan, visiting American and European rock acts are surprised by the subdued reactions of polite fans who stay in their seats during the entire concert. Concertgoers tend to be reserved and are eerily quiet between songs.

And at a British music festival, Semisonic drummer Jacob Slichter recalled what happened when he walked into the massive crowd: "I was moved by the reverent silence of the listeners. It was a welcome contrast to the moshing and mud throwing we had seen at U.S. festivals." Conversely, British punk fans often engage in a less than reverent practice – spitting on musicians as an expression of approval and respect. Because of this unusual custom, the Ramones despised touring in the U.K.

Meanwhile, performing behind the Iron Curtain before the fall of the Soviet Union in 1991 was a grueling task for Western rock acts. When Elton John staged a tour of Russia in 1979, he was shocked by the poor hotel accommodations and lousy food. Additionally, most of the tickets had been set aside for KGB members, local police and various Communist party chiefs. Similarly, Uriah Heep singer Bernie Shaw remembered the difficulties of performing at the Olympic Stadium in Moscow: "It wasn't until we hit the stage on the first night that we realized the audience was not allowed to stand in front of us – they had to be seated. There was about 100 meters between us and the first pair of eyeballs. And around the perimeter of the audience were 300 armed soldiers – AK47s, fur hats, trench coats – with their backs to us. We were playing to the back of their heads.... I was able to push through the line of soldiers because they didn't know what to do. I'd stick the mic in their faces and try to get a bit of conversation out of them – they were under orders to shut up and keep control."

*   *   *   *   *   *

When asked to describe "the best feeling in the world," blues rock guitarist Joe Bonamassa stated, "The last note of the gig... when everyone's standing up and going crazy. The big finale after a job well done."

When a rock group finishes the last song of the night, the house lights are turned on. The audience realizes there will be no more encores and that it's time to go. The roadies storm the stage to pack up the gear and to get ready for another show on the following day in a town 250-miles away. The members of the band, meanwhile, take a victory walk to their dressing rooms, where a lively party awaits.

▶ CHAPTER 17
LIFE ON THE ROAD

The logistics of staging a concert are a massive undertaking for the artist – as well as for the venue, the promoter, the roadies and members of security. From the t-shirt vendor to the parking lot attendant to the sound engineer behind the mixing board, everyone has a specific job that must be done correctly. As for the band, just getting to a show in a distant city, unpacking in a hotel room, finding a decent meal and adjusting to a new environment can be both emotionally and physically taxing. For emerging bands, the members are forced to oversee all the details on their own, often without the aid of a manager. But for established acts, it's a well-practiced routine. Doors drummer John Densmore recalled: "With stardom, someone else dealt with the tedious part of traveling. It was easy to become spoiled and act like a child, because all the responsibilities were taken care of."

In the 1950s and most of the '60s, large entourages of musical acts usually traveled together in old school buses. When Buddy Holly, the Big Bopper and Ritchie Valens decided to splurge on an airplane ride to their next gig in Moorhead, Minnesota, it was to avoid another freezing ride in their dilapidated bus with a broken heater. Likewise, Jimmy Bowen, a rockabilly singer who later became a powerful record executive, chronicled his experience as a performer on Irving Field's "The Biggest Show of Stars" tour in 1957: "Altogether we must have had eight or nine acts on these buses. And these seats didn't have dividers. It was more crammed than a school bus. We used to hoist [Paul] Anka up and let him stretch out and sleep on the overhead luggage rack."

*   *   *   *   *   *

When young musicians initially form a band, transportation is a major concern. Countless budding artists have received help from a sympathetic parent who volunteered to haul both the gear and band members to youth clubs, school dances and the occasional club dates. If the band is fortunate, one of the members owns a station wagon or a rusty, dented van.

In their early days, the members of the Black Keys toured across the country in an older minivan, a 1994 Plymouth Grand Voyager. After arriving at their destination, they carried their own equipment and set up their gear on stage. Similarly, a superstar act like the Police initially toured the U.S. on the cheap. As drummer Stewart Copeland recalled: "We had four people, needed two hotel rooms and traveled in a station wagon. All we needed to make was $200 a show. We'd play anywhere.... We'd play gigs that did not show up on any agent's manual. We had to."

The next step after a station wagon or van is a tour bus. Unfortunately, some bands, no matter how well known, are never able to graduate to a decked-out tour bus with bunks and a bathroom. Monte Melnick, the manager of the Ramones, recalled an incident while traveling in the group's van: "We had been driving for hours and the guys were stiff from sitting all day. You can imagine what they looked like, piling out of the van, all stinky and stiff. They were wandering around the gas station in a zombie-like state, like something out of *Night of the Living Dead*, when the attendant turns to me and says, 'It's so nice of you to take care of these retarded boys.' I cracked up. The band was oblivious."

While most successful rockers eventually buy or rent a full-size tour bus, some did not enjoy the experience. Frank Black of alternative-rock group the Pixies stated: "If you've been on a tour bus, after a while it's kind of like being on a submarine. Everything kinda turns into *Das Boot*. Whether there's dialogue, or lack of dialogue, there's a tension — because it's not natural."

With rock becoming big business, more and more acts could afford to fly between their gigs. Some acts leased or purchased their own airplanes. Many of these crafts were converted into flying hotels with all the amenities. In 1974, Elton John toured on a private Boeing jet that was fitted with a piano bar.

STAYING IN HOTELS

When bands are first starting out, they typically share one room in a cheap motel. Later, if they start selling out clubs and theaters, the lead singer might get his own room. When emerging artists are unable to afford even a cheap room, they often depend on the generosity of local musicians or charitable fans, who would provide a couch and a simple meal. In the late-1960s, the members of Pink Floyd ran out of money during a West Coast tour and were forced to ask Alice Cooper for a place to stay. For a full week, the two bands lived together in the same cramped house.

Not surprisingly, rock acts have unusual relationships with hotels. And the bigger the band, the nicer the hotel. It's that simple. However, some hotel chains have banned certain rock groups for fear of upsetting their other guests. Subsequently, Aerosmith's touring manager resorted to reserving blocks of rooms under names such as the Globe Theater Company or the Shakespearean Players.

Conversely, some hotels specifically catered to touring rockers, as was the case with the Continental Hyatt House in Los Angeles. Additionally, many hotels looked forward to hosting rock and roll entourages. By placing musicians into the oldest rooms, they could charge for damages – real and otherwise – and have the rooms redecorated, courtesy of Keith Moon or Joe Walsh. A hotel owner in Cleveland recalled, "I loved Led Zeppelin, because they always traveled with their accountant. Whatever damage they did to their rooms, the accountant always took out his checkbook and paid for everything down to the penny. I didn't mind because I always got new stuff for whatever rooms they stayed in after they left."

A number of rockers were legendary for their violent and destructive antics while on the road. One infamous incident took place in 1967 at a Holiday Inn in Flint, Michigan. Celebrating his 21st birthday, the Who's drummer Keith Moon drove a Lincoln Continental into the hotel's outdoor swimming pool. As the opening act for Herman's Hermits, the Who were not liable for the financial cost of the mayhem, which totaled $25,000. (Ironically, in 1990, when Keith Moon's daughter, Mandy, inducted her father into the Rock and Roll Hall of Fame as a member of the Who, the ceremony was staged at New York's famed Waldorf Astoria Hotel, from which the elder Moon had been notoriously banned in 1968.)

Similarly, drummer Skip Alan of the Pretty Things recalled an incident in 1975: "[Led Zeppelin] have got the top floor and we're underneath. Now, everything you've heard about Zeppelin, if you quadruple it, that's what it was like. Total lunacy. I stayed in [John Bonham's] room one night, and you hear about him breaking up rooms? I'm talking to him and all of a sudden he gets up and starts systematically wrecking all the furniture. All the flat pack wardrobes, he's whacking them down, kicking and smashing them. Then, when he's flattened everything, he moves it into a big pile in the middle, and phones down to [tour manager Richard] Cole to get him another room.

It was unbelievable, really. It was like he felt he had a job to do."

And in 1989, Billy Idol spent a three-week period partying in Thailand. Even after reportedly causing extensive damage and racking up huge bills, he refused to leave his hotel room. In desperation, the hotel manager requested assistance from the military. The "Rebel Yell" singer was carried out of his room on a gurney by four armed soldiers and then banished from the country. As Idol later recalled, "I remember seeing them in one blurry moment of consciousness before I blacked out again to wake up puking at the airport."

However, some artists spend little time in their hotel rooms while touring. Bob Dylan has been known to take lengthy walks – without members of his security team – before concerts. Likewise, Alice Cooper admitted: "Every city I go to, as soon as I hit town I put my bags in the hotel and hit the shopping streets to get the feel of a town. That, to me, is where the city lives. I can't stand sitting in a hotel room. In London... I just like to wander around for eight hours."

*   *   *   *   *   *

In the 1970s, veteran rock journalist Lisa Robinson described what it was like to be in a rocker's hotel room. She recounted: "The [Rolling] Stones might have been considered the greatest rock and roll band in the world, but the general ambience and disarray in this [room] resembled what I would discover in time was the norm for a group of guys on the road. There was that musty smell, a combination of pachouli or musk and cigarette smoke; half-filled glasses of alcohol, half empty bottles of beer, dirty clothes. To this day, you can walk into any musician's hotel room or dressing room, or be in a van or a car or a limousine or a plane and there is still that smell. It was not unlike the smell of stale cigarettes and beer in a bar around closing time... and when you could smoke in a bar."

TOUR RIDERS

When the Beatles toured across America in the mid-1960s, their rider demands were simple. They asked for a backstage black-and-white television and some bottles of Coca-Cola. Similarly, Elvis Presley requested just four cups of water and ten soft drinks. By the 1970s, as rock tours became big business with massive profit potential, musical acts were better pampered. And pampered artists often make sizable demands from promoters and venues.

Veteran tour manager Noel E. Monk worked with everyone from James Taylor and Bonnie Raitt to Van Halen and the Sex Pistols. He noted the difference between emerging and established acts: "Part of the beauty – and fun – of taking a new band out on the road is that everyone tends to be very low-maintenance." The same could not be said of an artist with a few hit albums under his belt.

Tour riders during the arena-rock era could range from the basic to the outrageous. While Barbra Streisand, Led Zeppelin, Madonna, Diana Ross and Prince expected – and got – backstage amenities suitable for royalty, the members of the Ramones were happy with a workingman's meal of pizza and beer.

Tour demands often change during the span of a career. A rock star and his entourage know what they can get away with and will ask for all sorts of extravagances, such as obscure brands of scotch, beer, tea or bottled water. A mid-tier veteran group will ask for basics, like a few cases of beer, liquor, soft drinks and some snacks. However, an emerging act will more likely be happy with any extra cash instead of the backstage booze or food. One music industry insider reported that liquor "demands have ranged from warm beer (for Meat Loaf, whose manager denied it though several promoters mentioned it) to 17 different kinds of wine for one well-known anti-nuke balladeer (who also suggested temperatures at which they should be chilled)."

Robert "Nitebob" Czaykowski, who joined Aerosmith's road crew in 1975, recalled: "There were constant caterer freak-outs because their contract rider specified turkey on the bone; if they saw turkey loaf or turkey roll, they'd go ballistic." Steven Tyler would destroy the food table if the promoter decided to cut corners and fail to deliver a traditional roasted turkey.

According to a rider that was leaked onto the internet, the rock group Korn once demanded the backstage services of a "rock friendly" attorney as well as a doctor, dentist, masseuse and/or chiropractor. And according to Sharon Osbourne, who briefly managed the Smashing Pumpkins, the group's lead singer Billy Corgan had a rider demand that instructed "the promoter [to] find the ten ugliest people in each city to be in the audience."

The most notorious item in a tour rider was made by the members of Van Halen. The group requested bowls of M&M candies in their dressing rooms – with the brown ones removed. As the group's road manager Noel E. Monk later explained: "The intent of this portion of the rider wasn't to create more silly and degrading work for some poor promoter's assistant or unpaid intern – although that was an unintended by-product – but instead acted as a sort of insurance clause that proved that the things that really did matter in our contract (safety measures and the like) had to be given proper weight and consideration. We figured that if a promoter took the time to remove all the brown M&M's from the bowl before putting them in our dressing room, it was far less likely he'd screw up any of the other, really important stuff." But in the end, the negative publicity over the M&M's lasted for many years and came to represent the bloated excess of the rock star world.

Conversely, a number of recording artists do not abuse the tour rider system. Country music veteran Willie Nelson once stated: "I haven't really seen one on my contracts lately, but I know that I don't have any ridiculous riders on there. In the first place, I didn't know anything about that kind of backstage service – about having drinks and food and catering – when I was on the road playing out of Nashville before. We didn't have anything like that. It was unheard of for promoters to even think of anything like that. In fact, promoters today, in some of the shows that I've been around, *still* don't do that. I mean, they still promote the same old way. They don't furnish anything."

And Ray Davies of the Kinks revealed: "It's funny. When we did the Storyteller tour in '98 we didn't even have our own rider. We used to buy our own six-pack of beers each day. It was so far away from the Kinks." And in 2005, Tom Petty explained his rider requirements: "We've cut it down so much. There's not any drinkers in the band. All we ask is a hot meal, really, and in my room I think I have a couple of Cokes and some protein bars.... No deli trays; we don't like all that. I think people would laugh if they saw our rider, it's so simple."

*   *   *   *   *   *

The pampering of rock stars sometimes occurred in the recording studio as well. Major stars would book premium studios at the best times – usually evenings – which left mornings or late nights to newer artists. Most studios were sterile, cement block buildings with basic amenities – a bathroom, a small kitchen and a lounge area. Others resembled luxury suites. The Record Plant in Sausalito, near San Francisco, was geared toward big stars. Among the artists who recorded at the studio were Stevie Wonder, Prince and Fleetwood Mac. The facility included a Jacuzzi, basketball courts, a conference room with a water bed on the floor and even a kitchen staffed with chefs. Two guest houses and a speedboat were also available.

Chris Stone, one of the Record Plant's owners, recalled the

debauchery that took place over the several months it took for Fleetwood Mac to record *Rumours*: "That was excess at its most excessive. The band would come in at 7 at night, have a big feast, party till 1 or 2 in the morning, and then when they were so whacked-out they couldn't do anything, they'd start recording."

The group continued their extravagant ways during the recording of their followup album, *Tusk*. Christine McVie revealed: "Recording *Tusk* was quite absurd. The studio contract rider for refreshments was like a telephone directory. Exotic food delivered to the studio, crates of champagne. And it had to be the best, with no thought of what it cost. Stupid. Really stupid. Somebody once said that with the money we spent on champagne on one night, they could have made an entire album. And it's probably true."

*   *   *   *   *   *

No matter how fancy the hotel, concert venue or catering table, performers get tired and homesick. The first few tours in your 20s might be fun and exciting, but later ones are viewed as a job – a physically punishing and emotionally draining job.

Singer Aimee Mann recalled: "I was touring with 'Til Tuesday, things were going well but we'd been on the road for months. I was getting incredibly exhausted; along with exhaustion comes this weird zombie-state. There was one particular moment where I remember getting out my Swiss army knife and trying to calculate where I could cut my hand – so it wouldn't permanently damage me but it would make it impossible to play, so I could get myself off the tour. I knew the promoters would come down on me, I knew the band would come down on me, and I knew the record company would think I was a major-league asshole – and in fact, all those things happened. But I had my knife out and for a few seconds it didn't even enter my mind that this would be an irrational, problematic solution. Then I suddenly see this picture of myself and I say, 'Hold on. What am I thinking?'"

*   *   *   *   *   *

In the music business, a successful band is essentially a small company or corporation. The bigger the band, the more tasks that need to be performed. Ironically, some veteran artists feel they have a responsibility to go on the road, simply for the sake of their employees.

In 2014, Charlie Daniels was asked to identify the "high point" of his career. He responded, "That's easy: Keeping 30-plus people gainfully employed for over 30 years. I've got people working for me that it's the only real job they've ever had. They've got health insurance, 401(k) accounts, the works. I try to take care of my people." Similarly, when the Grateful Dead's leader Jerry Garcia passed away in 1995, the band had around 200 people on its payroll.

▶ CHAPTER 18
THE PARTIES, BOOZE AND DRUGS

On October 30, 1976, Bob Dylan's former backing group, the Band, was scheduled to appear as the musical guests on *Saturday Night Live*. Following a midweek rehearsal, the members of the group returned to their hotel rooms and were joined by *SNL* cast member John Belushi. Robbie Robertson, the group's guitarist, recalled the encounter: "I don't think John knew how to turn off his wit, quickness, his impersonations – it was truly mind-boggling. Then, suddenly, he went quiet and pulled me aside. 'Who's got the blow' he whispered. 'I mean, you're musicians, right? The musicians always got cocaine – is what I've been told. Please, don't burst my bubble.... So who's got the blow?'"

For many musicians, rock and roll is a non-stop party. Consequently, overindulgence is a common work-related hazard. Some rockers can tolerate large doses of alcohol or drugs and still be able to function, write music or perform on a concert stage. It was Keith Richards who set the bar for heavy drug use without succumbing to premature death. However, some of his acquaintances, like Gram Parsons and Keith Moon, attempted to keep up and paid the ultimate price.

Additionally, there can be major financial costs associated with maintaining a habit. Countless rockers have blown their entire fortunes on drugs. In 2015, Stevie Nicks revealed that she had spent over $1 million on cocaine before finally quitting: "There was no way to get off the white horse and I didn't want to." Likewise, Aerosmith frontman Steven Tyler admitted to wasting $2 million on cocaine, and once told a talk show host, "I snorted half of Peru."

The history of popular music is littered with accounts of careers cut short and lives ruined by substance addiction. But recreational drug use did not begin with rock and roll. Since the start of time, people have consumed conscious-altering herbs, fermented alcoholic beverages and various exotic concoctions for social, recreational and even religious purposes.

The United States has experienced waves of drug use throughout its history. In the 19th century, railroad companies hired Chinese migrants to lay tracks at half the standard pay rate in exchange for supplying the workers with opium. Opium's popularity quickly spread from the Chinese community in San Francisco to working-class cities on the East Coast.

During this period, the opium trade became a lucrative business. As chronicled by writer Luc Sante: "By 1840 an estimated 24,000 pounds were coming into the country every year, and a duty was imposed by the government which raised the price to $1.40 per pound. By 1860 the amount had grown to 105,000 pounds and the price had risen to $4.50. In 1870 half a million pounds were coming in, and the duty alone was $2.50 per pound. The period immediately after the Civil War brought drug use and its perfectly legal new avenues of enterprise." By the 1880s, opium dens were commonplace in the slums of urban centers, with 25,000 addicts in New York City alone.

Other hard drugs soon appeared across the American landscape. In the late-19th century, Coca-Cola contained cocaine, and Bayer Pharmaceuticals in its pre-aspirin period openly sold heroin. Developed in 1898 by a researcher at Bayer, heroin was initially marketed as an over-the-counter pain reliever and as a treatment for coughs.

Another common method of peddling drugs was the traveling medicine show, where alcoholic and narcotic preparations were sold as health tonics. Medicine shows often included musical entertainment, and many pop stars of the 20th century began their careers in these troupes, including Ray Acuff, Roy Rogers, Jimmy Rodgers and even Little Richard.

Illicit drug use came under attack at the start of the 20th century as Progressive Era reforms targeted the regulation of drugs, food safety, the education of children and safe working conditions. *The Pure Food and Drug Act of 1906* required the listing of ingredients in consumer products and medicines. A subsequent act in 1909 decreed that many previously legal substances were harmful to the mind and body. Soon after, cocaine and opiates were regulated by *The Harrison Act of 1914*, a revenue bill that taxed and limited the ability of doctors to prescribe certain drugs. Additionally, Congress passed *The Volstead Act* in 1920, which banned the manufacture and sale of alcoholic beverages. (The ban would be lifted in 1933.)

But while cocaine had nearly disappeared from the American landscape in the 1930s, heroin and marijuana became the domains of radical writers and jazz musicians. Heroin – or "smack" as it was called – came into vogue in the jazz community due to the influence of musical prodigy Charlie "Bird" Parker.

Meanwhile, amphetamines – or speed – were first marketed in the

1930s for a variety of ailments, and were given to members of the American, British and Germany military during World War II to battle fatigue. But after the war's end, many veterans continued to use the drug.

Marijuana use was rare in the U.S. before the Mexican Revolution of 1910, when thousands of Mexican immigrants brought the drug into the country. In the 1930s, marijuana was initially embraced in the jazz community, with jazzman Milton "Mezz" Mezzrow responsible for much of its popularity among his peers. However, in 1937, the U.S. Congress effectively banned the drug by imposing heavy fines for the possession of untaxed marijuana.

After a lull in drug use, in the early-1950s Turkish heroin was illegally smuggled into the U.S. via France. And in 1955, singing idol Frank Sinatra shocked his fans when he appeared as a crazed heroin addict in the film, *The Man With The Golden Arm*.

Marijuana would experience newfound popularity during the rock era. Although the 1958 rock film, *High School Confidential*, depicted marijuana dealing in high school, the drug was still primarily used by jazz musicians and those in the beatnik communities.

Soon, the Beatles and several other leading rock acts were at the forefront of embracing recreational drugs in popular culture. After using amphetamines to cope with the grueling schedule of their Hamburg days in the early-1960s, the members of the Fab Four initially tried marijuana in August 1964 at the invitation of Bob Dylan. A hipster who was wise to the ways of the world, Dylan rolled a joint for each Beatle inside a New York City hotel room when the two star acts met each other for the very first time.

During the rise of the counterculture movement in the 1960s, San Francisco became the epicenter of recreational drug use, as the consumption of mind-altering substances was considered a sign of legitimacy in the rock world. With the rise of psychedelia and drug culture, the Grateful Dead – along with writers Timothy Leary and Ken Kesey – openly advocated the use of LSD, which until 1966 was still legal. During this period, songs with drug-oriented lyrics began appearing on the rock charts. While the Association's "Along Came Mary" and the Byrds' "Eight Miles High" were accused of harboring hidden pro-drug messages, a number of hit songs openly addressed drug use, including Velvet Underground's "Heroin" and Jefferson Airplane's "White Rabbit." (Conversely, only a few songs in rock history have dared to criticize drug use. Those include "The No No Song" by Ringo Starr, "The Pusher" by Steppenwolf and "Master Of Puppets" by Metallica.)

DRUG USE & CREATIVITY

In the book, *Talking Smack: Honest Conversations About Drugs*, author Andrew McMillen wrote: "We tend to perceive creative people – musicians, painters, actors, writers and the like – as living 'on the edge,' outside the social norms and expectations that come with nine-to-five, salaried jobs. It's on the edge, we're led to believe, that 'the magic happens:' that by pushing the boundaries of the human mind and body, great work is created. Drug use is a natural fit with that ideal. Who wants to hear about a musician who treats the creative process like a job, with the regimented hours and routines familiar to so many of the rest of us? That's mundane. We'd rather hear about how a hit song was written on the tail-end of a five-day bender in Ibiza, its creators torn and frayed after a non-stop cocaine- and booze-fest. Whether or not this type of debauchery ever happens is irrelevant: it's the idea that's potent."

As a result, countless musicians have tried to enhance the creative process by dabbling with various mind-expanding substances. Sting stated: "I certainly wouldn't advocate that you have to take drugs to make art, but then you can't nullify the work of the Beatles. They took LSD and they made fantastic albums." Similarly, Gregg Allman wrote in his autobiography, "There's no question that taking psilocybin [psychedelic mushrooms] helped create so many spontaneous pieces of music." Likewise, John Taylor of Duran Duran insists that drugs play a central role in creativity: "Look, *Exile On Main Street* [by the Rolling Stones] wouldn't have happened without Keith Richards's heroin addiction. *Young Americans* wouldn't have happened without Bowie's cocaine addiction. Alcohol played a big part with Vincent Van Gogh. You need that edge. The trick is to find the edge without killing yourself." Not surprisingly, Duran Duran's 1997 album *Medazzaland* was named after Midazolam, a hypnotic sedative prescribed to Simon Le Bon following dental surgery.

And in the summer of 1993, just as Stone Temple Pilots had reached a career plateau, lead singer Scott Weiland yearned to try hard drugs. He explained: "I had never shot or snorted heroin before. But I studied heroin culture. The truth is that I loved heroin culture. I was intrigued by it. I had a friend in high school who was a junkie. I loved the work of William S. Burroughs and the brilliance of Charlie Parker. I loved the aesthetic of the Rolling Stones. I knew about John Lennon's heroin period. In the mid-eighties, I had been greatly influenced by Perry Farrell and Jane's Addiction. I associated heroin with romance, glamour, danger, and rock and roll excess. More than that, I was curious about the connection between heroin and creativity. At that point, I couldn't imagine my life, especially now that I was entering into the major leagues of alternative rock, without at least dabbling with the King of Drugs. So I put in my order." Weiland's drug use would later spiral out of control.

In his autobiography, pop-rock singer Tommy James revealed why he took drugs in the 1960s: "I used pills to write because they gave me some zany feeling that I felt I could channel into something creative. I used to find a magic topic to write about, but I usually would forget about it by the next day. I lost a lot of songs that way, forgetting what I had written."

Paul Simon offered a differing view on drug use and creative efforts: "There were times in the sixties and seventies when that stuff was ubiquitous. But I found most of the drugs, especially cocaine, were a waste of time. Cocaine made you want to party all night, and then you were exhausted and couldn't breathe the next day. Pot could make you dreamy and imaginative, but cocaine just made you want to run around. It was contemplative. I don't think I ever wrote anything on cocaine. It was also bad for your voice." And when Steven Tyler entered a drug rehab program, he feared that he would lose his ability to make music: "I thought they were trying to brainwash me. I thought I would lose my creativity."

Obviously, not everyone is convinced that drug use enhances creativity. According to British researcher Iain Smith, "The idea that drugs and alcohol give artists unique insights and powerful experiences is an illusion. When you try and capture the experiences [triggered by drugs or alcohol] they are often nonsense. These drugs often wipe your memory, so it's hard to remember how you were in that state of mind."

More commonly, rockers begin using drugs to get through long and arduous tours. At first, they take some amphetamines for the energy to perform, night after night, in city after city. But when those uppers keep them awake – and there's another show on the following night – they are forced to take something to put them to sleep. Soon, the drugs become just another instrument to be packed next to the guitar cases, microphone stands and amplifiers.

Some artists abused alcohol instead of illicit drugs. In 1968, Linda Ronstadt and her group the Stone Poneys toured as the opening act for the Doors. Ronstadt later recounted: "Jim [Morrison] was very soft spoken, quiet and very moody. When he was not drunk, he seemed nice enough but as soon as he began to drink, he really got very wild so quickly, which frightened me. I'd never been around that kind of heavy drinking, and seeing someone like Jim Morrison – who had such a personality change when he drank – was very frightening to me. It was scary to witness when someone seems one way and then they turn into someone else." Doors drummer John Densmore echoed the sentiment: "[Morrison] was an alcoholic. It's a bitch to be in a band with someone who is an alcoholic. It's a bitch to be in a family with an alcoholic. Or to be married to one. I tend to rebuke a lot of the mythology that has sprung up in the wake of his death. He had a disease. I want kids to understand that."

BAD PERFORMANCES WHILE ON DRUGS

Sometimes, rockers party *too* hard before a concert and are in no shape to perform. Instead of cancelling or postponing the show, most artists will simply hit the stage and hope that the audience won't notice or will be forgiving. But with the high price of concert tickets, audiences do notice and are usually unforgiving.

Some bands were notorious for their revelry. In the mid-1970s, the rock group Chicago toured with an onstage telephone booth – dubbed "the Snortitorium" – where members of the band could snort lines of cocaine during the concert without having to leave the stage. And Rod Stewart recalled touring with the Faces in the early-1970s: "We had the barman onstage, he had a proper bar and would bring us drinks on a tray."

During a Jefferson Starship tour across Europe in 1978, lead singer Grace Slick was sometimes too inebriated to perform. Consequently, the group's first scheduled show in Germany had to be cancelled. Then at the second show, a drunken Slick hurled abuse at the audience. Although the concert was filmed for the German television program *Rockpalast*, the episode never aired. (Soon after, Slick resigned from the group.)

Similarly, Danny Sugerman – the former manager of Iggy Pop – detailed one unfortunate episode from the early-1970s: "In Washington, D.C., five minutes before showtime, [Iggy] snorted a gram of THC. The announcer introduced the band, and Iggy walked right out of the dressing room, toward the stage, onto the stage, past the microphone stand, and straight off the stage, dropped ten feet, right into the audience, and passed out, face first in the cement."

And in 2003, ticket buyers felt shortchanged after a concert by Creed in Rosemont, Illinois, and later filed a lawsuit against the band. In the legal complaint, they claimed that lead singer Scott Stapp "was so intoxicated and/or medicated that he was unable to sing the lyrics of a single Creed song." Likewise, in 2004, singer Wes Scantlin of the group Puddle Of Mudd was pelted by cups of beer after informing an audience in Toledo, Ohio, that he was too high to perform. After his bandmates walked off the stage, Scantlin alternated between singing made-up songs and hurling insults at the few fans who remained. After the show, he was arrested on disorderly conduct charges.

And in one of rock history's most infamous incidents, a completely incapacitated Keith Moon collapsed during the middle of a Who concert at the Cow Palace in San Francisco after consuming large quantities of brandy and an animal tranquilizer. He passed out not once, but twice. With his bandmates unable to revive him a second time, an exasperated Pete Townshend asked if there was a drummer in the audience. A 19-year-old musician named Scott Halpin raised his hand and was pulled onto the stage. The Who managed to finish the rest of the concert with their replacement drummer.

Conversely, some artists were able to perform, even while self-medicated. At the peak of his drug use, Eric Clapton would snort a thick line of cocaine from a knife and finish off a bottle of cognac by the middle of the day. And at one concert in the early-1970s, he performed an *entire* show on his back. Clapton recalled that he laid on the floor of the stage "with the microphone stand lying beside me, and nobody batted an eyelid."

In 2007, a sober and clean Steven Tyler discussed his hard partying days: "In the late '70s, there were times when we'd actually pass out on stage. That's got nothing to do with rock 'n' roll rebellion. That's to do with selling the fans short. We know better now."

NOT TAKING DRUGS

Famed record producer Giorgio Moroder once admitted: "I'm probably the only guy in Los Angeles who never took coke. I'd come to the studio around noon, work until seven, then go home and have dinner. The second I was out the door, piles of coke would come out."

The short list full of notable rockers who chose not to use recreational drugs includes Bruce Springsteen, Gene Simmons and Paul Stanley of Kiss, Adam Ant, Ted Nugent, John Fogerty and Frank Zappa. Openly hostile toward drug use, Zappa was banned from *Saturday Night Live* after his appearance in 1978 for making the drug-friendly cast feel uncomfortable. And Simmons said in 2004: "Twenty years ago I stated... Peter Criss and Ace Frehley were drug addicts, but that Paul [Stanley] and I loved them and wanted them to stop using the stuff. The fans were furious. We were so un-rock 'n' roll, we were sons of bitches. But it was tough love."

Some artists avoid drugs due to the fear of harming their music careers. When Creedence Clearwater Revival emerged from the San Francisco area during the psychedelic '60s, they were mocked for their straightlaced ways. The group's drummer Doug "Cosmo" Clifford recalled: "Our peers laughed at us and called us the Boy Scouts of rock and roll. They said we would never make it, because we didn't smoke reefer and we were not jamming. We went to see the Grateful Dead one night. They were at the Fillmore, and we were really poor then, and it was a lot of money for us to buy a ticket. We went to see the local bands, and they were so stoned they weren't even in tune, and they were really terrible. This was our competition. They were whacked out, yet when they came off the stage they were giving each other high fives because they thought they sounded great. We made a pact on the floor of the Fillmore, right then, where we would do no drugs or no alcohol." And decades later, the CCR's vocalist John Fogerty continued to remain drug-free. MTV veejay Mark Goodman recalled an incident, inside a bathroom, backstage at the first Farm Aid concert in 1985: "I was standing at a urinal next to John Fogerty – both of us were peeing. I stretched out my arm to hand him the vial [of cocaine]. He said, 'I don't know what that is, but I don't want any of it.' I felt like the biggest schmuck in the world."

Some rock bands have come up with creative methods to separate those who drank or did drugs from those who did not. The British group, Madness, toured with two tour buses – one for drinkers and the other for abstainers. The Who didn't have that luxury as lead singer Roger Daltrey was the only member of the band in the 1970s who did not use drugs. Likewise, in AC-DC, guitarist Angus Young was the only non-user in the hard-partying metal group.

DRUG DEATHS

The rock and roll highway is littered with tragic drug deaths. In an industry that celebrates extreme alcohol and drug use, frequent overdoses are the norm. The roll call of drug overdose deaths includes Amy Winehouse, Michael Jackson, Whitney Houston, Bon Scott, John Entwistle, Scott Weiland and dozens more. Even a musical icon like Elvis Presley was hooked on multiple prescription drugs – which contributed to his untimely death at age 42 – despite his very public campaign against what he derisively referred to as "street drugs."

Danny Sugerman, a Doors insider, revealed how Jim Morrison would boast to his party friends: "First Jimi, Then Janis. You're drinking with number three." And Stan Lynch, the former drummer of Tom Petty and the Heartbreakers, lamented: "In almost every classic rock song I hear on the radio when I'm in my car there's someone I know that died from drugs. I love the music, but God, I want to pull the car over and cry. These are people I had a drink with, shared laughs with, and it hurts, it really hurts."

There have also been a number of near-fatal overdoses in the rock and roll community, including Nikki Sixx, Al Jourgensen of Ministry and Dave Gahan of Depeche Mode. And mirroring the lyrics of the 1978 hit by the Who, "Who Are You," Pete Townshend admitted: "One night in London I drank so much that I almost died. My driver found me lying in the gutter, unconscious, and rushed me to the emergency room. Fortunately, the hospital staff heard that Pete Townshend was in the ER, and they ran to help me. One of the privileges of being famous, I guess. But if I was just an average bloke, I'd probably be dead."

Similarly, at age 68 in 2017, Ozzy Osbourne addressed his past problem with booze: "I was saying to Sharon the other day, 'Every one of my bad drinking partners are all dead. No one's come back and said, 'Hi, Oz, it's cooler on the other side. Come and join us.' I want to be around for everyone. But more than that, I didn't love the way I felt after I got stoned or drunk or both."

QUITTING DRUGS

In the music business, seemingly everyone around you – bandmates, deejays, club owners and record company executives – is an enabler who encourages the use of drugs. If drugs are everywhere you work and are used by most of your friends and colleagues, then it's difficult to quit using without leaving your job as a musician. In fact, when a rocker quits taking drugs or stops drinking booze, it's a media event.

In 2015, when Paul McCartney admitted he no longer smoked marijuana, the news shocked his longtime fans. He told his hometown newspaper: "I don't do it any more. Why? The truth is that these days I don't really want to set an example to my kids and grandkids. It's now a parent thing. Back then I was just some guy around London having a ball, and the kids were little so I'd just try and keep it out of their faces. But now it's a question of not setting a bad example. So instead of smoking a spliff, I'll now have a glass of red wine or a nice margarita. The last time I smoked was a long time ago."

Similarly, singer-songwriter Bonnie Raitt admitted: "When I was young touring with a lot of these blues legends, well they could drink hard and I guess I believed that was something you needed to do. But it didn't really help them make better music and the negatives were many. When I looked around at friends of mine and went 'well John and Warren and Stevie Ray all just put out some of the best music of their careers since they sobered up.' So I did too."

And although heroin has taken the lives of numerous musicians, many former users have been able to bounce back from their addictions, including Anthony Kiedis, Dion DiMucci, Ray Charles and Keith Richards. In his autobiography, Three Dog Night member Chuck Negron – who provided the lead vocals on hits such as "One (Is The Loneliest Number)" and "Joy To The World" – revealed how heroin ruined his career and nearly took his life: "I enjoyed what Morrison, Joplin, and Hendrix did with their music. I had great respect for them all. But I never pursued friendships with any of them. In my heart I knew they were just like me, tormented by drugs and alcohol, and maybe even by their own success. I had no need to be close friends with people like me." Eventually, Negron spiraled into a life of addiction and poverty. Abandoning his music career, he sold off everything he owned – including his gold record awards – to fund his habit. And Sam Moore – half of the soul duo Sam & Dave – finally quit heroin in the mid-1980s after more than a decade as an addict. He later admitted: "You may not believe it, but this is true. I never thought I would *not* be a junkie. I *always* thought I would shoot dope. I always felt as though my life was going to be as a junkie or a drug dealer."

And in 2001, guitarist Slash of Guns N' Roses, a former heroin user, was diagnosed with an acute heart condition – cardiomyopathy – which was caused by decades of alcohol and drug use. He was given less than six-weeks to live. He survived by giving up both drugs and alcohol and by having a defibrillator implanted into his chest.

Some artists quit or avoid taking drugs for unusual reasons. Graham Nash revealed the event in 1984 that convinced him to stop using cocaine: "There was an end-of-tour party and everyone had these horrible cocaine smiles and I said 'Wow, I must look like that too,' and just stopped instantly." Similarly, Tommy Chong – of the rock comedy duo Cheech & Chong – stopped using LSD after he took his daughter to see a movie and began experiencing hallucinations. He recalled: "The entire theater was crawling with rats." And model Jerry Hall, the outspoken former wife of Mick Jagger, explained why her children never used drugs or alcohol: "I mean they spent their life looking at Keith Richards passed out on the couch."

▶ CHAPTER 19
SELLING OUT:
ACHIEVING MAINSTREAM SUCCESS

In 1992, when Nirvana appeared on the cover of *Rolling Stone*, Kurt Cobain wore a bulky sweater and a t-shirt that read "Corporate Magazines Still Suck." Nonetheless, Cobain had agreed to an interview and told the music magazine: "I don't blame the average seventeen-year-old punk-rock kid for calling me a sellout. I understand that. And maybe when they grow up a little bit, they'll realize there's more things to life than living out your rock and roll identity so righteously."

In the world of rock and roll, there is an ongoing battle between art and profit. Once a musician achieves mainstream success, he is accused of selling out. Some fans subscribe to the notion that remaining a starving artist who struggles to put food on his table is somehow more noble and deserving of respect than becoming a hit act who has amassed millions of followers on his Facebook page. A number of 1970s classic rock bands – like Styx, REO Speedwagon and Chicago – were also considered sellouts after taking a decidedly pop turn in the '80s.

In 1981, the Go-Go's emerged as music and media stars when their single, "Our Lips Are Sealed," became a major radio and MTV hit. But just a year earlier, the all-female group was playing for just a few hundred people in the dingy, underground punk clubs of Los Angeles. As the band's guitarist Jane Weidlin recalled, suddenly their old fans went ballistic: "We had become 'America's sweethearts.' People *literally* called us that. We weren't punk anymore. Now we were new wave, whatever that was. We didn't flip the bird at the Establishment – we *were* the establishment. The blowback from the kids still in Hollywood was swift, ugly, and final. The Go-Go's had *sold out*. Never mind that anyone who was in a band, punk or not, would've killed to be popular. To make a living making music. But we had abandoned ship. Like rats, but cuter. And it hurt to hear what our 'friends' back home now thought of us."

Likewise, singer-songwriter Jewel recalled an incident at one of her concerts in San Francisco, shortly after her debut album landed on the charts: "Tonight a boy was crying in the crowd. Not a boy. I think he was in his mid to late twenties. His eyes were red and his cheeks were smeared and wet. Then, between 'You Were Meant For Me' and 'Life Uncommon,' he yelled at me miserably, 'You sellout, You sellout.' He looked at me with sincere disappointment, like Achilles having realized his one weakness. 'I'm a sellout?' I said it back into the mike. He looked back at me pitifully. I did what I could to recover and come up with some light banter, but I couldn't help but consider his accusation. What had I done? What did he mean? I launched into the next song, but while I was singing I wondered what I could possibly have done to disappoint a total stranger so completely.... Then some girl yelled, 'Kick his ass, Jewel!' This was no consolation."

Like the Go-Go's and Jewel, the truth is that most musicians begin their careers with the long-term objective of scoring hits. Bruce Wooley – who co-wrote the New Wave classic "Video Killed The Radio Star – was a 26-year-old musician in 1980 when he proclaimed: "When all is said and done I'm in it to achieve some sort of success. Everybody that signs a record contract wants a record in the charts, if only to prove to themselves that they're not wasting their time. It's the most tangible proof that people like what you're doing."

Similarly, rapper and music mogul Jay-Z insisted: "That was the greatest trick in music that people ever pulled off, to convince artists that you can't be an act and make money. I think the people that were making the millions said that. It was shameful, especially in rock 'n' roll. Here you got these millionaire guys who had to pretend as if they weren't successful at all or it would be like a detriment to their career.... When you're in the studio you're an artist, you make music, and then after you finish, you market it to the world, I don't think anything is wrong with that. In fact, I know there's nothing wrong with that."

TOUR SPONSORSHIP & SONGS IN COMMERCIALS

During a low point in the career of British musician Gary Numan, he was beset with financial problems. As a result, his American Express credit card was canceled. However, a number of years later, American Express would pay Numan £100,000 for the use of his 1979 hit song, "Cars," in a television commercial.

There's great advertising value in hit songs, and corporations are eager to exploit memorable tunes to sell products. Nonetheless, a small number of major acts would not allow their music to be used in commercials for fear of cheapening their integrity as an artist. The short list of these performers includes Tom Petty, Beck, Radiohead, R.E.M. and the Beastie Boys. In 1967, Jim Morrison discovered that the other three members of the Doors had approved Buick's use of the group's groundbreaking hit "Light My Fire" in a television spot in exchange for a fee of $75,000. An enraged Morrison threatened to smash a Buick with a sledgehammer on live television if the automaker ever aired the commercial.

In the 1980s, there was still a great deal of opposition to using rock songs in commercials. Singer-songwriter Neil Young attacked the growing corporate influence in pop music with his caustic track, "This Note's For You." The song's video – which mocked Michael Jackson, Whitney Houston and especially Eric Clapton – was initially banned by MTV, but later won the prize for Video of the Year at the annual MTV Music Video Awards.

Likewise, there was grumbling in the music community when Nike used the Beatles classic "Revolution" in a 1987 television ad. The spot – which was sanctioned by Yoko Ono – featured sports celebrities such as Michael Jordan and John McEnroe. Nike had paid $250,000 each to EMI-Capitol Records and Michael Jackson, who owned the publishing rights to the song. In the end, the three surviving Beatles and Apple Records sued Nike to stop the commercial. An Apple attorney stated at the time: "The Beatles' position is that they don't sing jingles to peddle sneakers, beer, pantyhose or anything else."

But while Paul McCartney was protective of his own Fab Four compositions, he owned the publishing rights to numerous hit songs – including the Buddy Holly classic "Oh, Boy" – and had no qualms about licensing Holly's song to a carmaker for use in a television commercial. However, over the years a number of artists have softened their stance against allowing their music in advertisements. In 2002, Led Zeppelin relented and licensed the track "Rock And Roll" for use in a Cadillac spot. And suddenly, "Keep On Rolling" by REO Speedwagon was licensed by General Motors, the Who's "The Best I Ever Had" by Nissan and Bob Seger's "Like A Rock" by Chevy trucks. And not only did Bob Dylan allow Chrysler to use his composition "Forever Young," he also appeared in the commercial.

Similarly, John Mellencamp spent years attacking the corporate sponsorship of rock music. Then in 2006, he gave in and allowed his new track "My Country" to be used in an ad campaign by Chevrolet. Mellencamp even appeared in a commercial, strumming an acoustic guitar while sitting next to a classic Chevy pickup truck. Mellencamp attributed his change of heart to the realization that the music industry was ignoring older, veteran rockers. As *The New York Times* reported at the time: "[Mellencamp] said a turning point for him came last year, after he heard *Highway Companion*, the latest album by his contemporary Tom Petty. He liked it and thought the single 'Saving Grace' would be a hit, but then never heard the song on the radio or saw it on the video channels. Fearing a similar fate for his own music, Mr. Mellencamp said he decided to accept Chevrolet's offer."

Celebrities – whether musicians, actors or even politicians – can also earn a sizable payday by endorsing a product. R&B singer Sheila E. revealed: "What is rich? In truth, I have turned down more than I've made. In the early nineties, I was approached to participate in a TV infomercial about psychics. I declined, explaining that I didn't believe in their product. They assured me [it] didn't matter. They just needed my name, offering half a million up front and another half million once they filmed the ad. It was still easy to say no. All money is not good money.... I never would've imagined that turning down a million dollars in an instant would be such an easy choice." However, soul singer Dionne Warwick had no qualms about becoming the public face of the Psychic Friends Network. As she later explained: "It was during a period of time when I was not recording. You know, it kept the lights on in my house and food on my table. It was an earning power. I earned money that I normally would have earned if I was on the road. It's very simple."

Sheila E. wasn't the only celebrity who faced the predicament of disliking the product they were asked to endorse. According to Jermaine Jackson, his superstar brother Michael "didn't drink Pepsi because he didn't like it. Which was a potential problem when [we] lined up a $5 million Pepsi sponsorship deal, together with two television commercials that would rewrite 'Billie Jean' and use it as a jingle. When it was explained to Michael that he didn't need to drink Pepsi or be filmed drinking it, he was happier to compromise." (Infamously, while filming one of the commercials, Michael Jackson's hair caught on fire.)

In the 21st century, many artists have been forced to license their songs to advertisers as a matter of economics. In 2005, Madonna insisted, "I'm a businesswoman. The music industry has changed.... You must join forces with other brands and corporations. You're an idiot if you don't." Similarly, Devo's Mark Mothersbaugh defended the practice: "My feeling about that stuff is that it's a way to plant little tiny brain bombs, that will go off later in people's heads, in people's minds – people that would never listen to Devo, people that were like 'Oh, Devo is some bullshit art band.'" And in 1999, techno artist Moby raised eyebrows when he licensed all 18 tracks from his album, *Play*.

Additionally, musical artists often accept millions of dollars of corporate money in the form of tour sponsorships. Before the start of a Rolling Stones tour in 1981, the band's representatives contacted the head of a firm that matched sponsors with touring rock acts, and said: "We're going to mount this big tour. We have lots of production costs. Is there some way for us to offset some of that cost, so that we can still make our ticket prices reasonable?" While a deal with Schlitz beer fizzled, the tour was instead underwritten by another sponsor, Jovan Fragrances, which paid $500,000 for the right to publicize its brand on concert tickets, posters and print ads. The Stones never looked back and later inked deals with firms such as Radio Shack, Sprint and Ameriquest. And in 1988, when the British rock magazine *NME* confronted David Lee Roth about his sponsorship deal with Toshiba, the former Van Halen frontman responded: "That's just hippie bullshit from the '60s. If your message is not strong enough to transcend a soda-pop commercial, you got problems!"

However, with the high cost of using hit songs in television commercials, ad agencies began licensing music by emerging or unknown artists. As a result of the exposure, a number of TV spots spawned radio hits including "Days Go By" by Dirty Vegas, "Start The Commotion" by the Wiseguys and "We Are Young" by Fun.

And although Sting refused to allow a deodorant company to use the lyrics from the 1980 Police hit "Don't Stand So Close To Me," another of his compositions did make its way into a television spot. In 1995, Sting's solo album *Brand New Day* was meandering on the charts until the track "Desert Rose" was featured in an ad for Jaguar. Sting explained: "It wasn't a commercial for Jaguar originally. It was the video, and the director wanted us in a car, and he chose the new Jaguar. Then my manager at the time took our video to Jaguar and said, 'What do you think?' They flipped and said, 'We'd like to use that as our commercial.' They said, 'How much do you want?' We said, 'We don't really need any money, it's like promotion for our single.' So it was kind of a symbiotic, mutually beneficial kind of thing."

*   *   *   *   *   *

Since the dawn of the rock era, television programs have had the ability to create top-40 radio hits. On November 15, 1954, "Let Me Go, Lover" by pop singer Joan Weber aired on the CBS drama, *Studio One*. Rush-released due to consumer demand, the single topped the pop charts in January 1955.

Early television also proved it could create recording stars out of actors such as Ricky Nelson, Annette Funicello, Shelley Fabares and others. Soon after, television used its power to generate its own music stars like the Monkees, the Archies and the Partridge Family. Bass virtuoso Stu Hamm recalled watching Danny Partridge on *The Partridge Family*: "When I was a 14-year-old, chubby, little red-haired geek, so was he. I used to love that show. I loved the way he'd be playing these complicated bass lines and his hands wouldn't be moving. All the years of practicing I still haven't been able to accommodate that one. But I'm still working on it."

A few musical artists even had their own Saturday morning cartoon series, including the Beatles and the Jackson Five. And in the 1960s and '70s, a number of hit acts were given their own television variety series, including Sonny & Cher, Johnny Cash and Tony Orlando & Dawn. And with the advent of reality television, numerous classic rockers landed their own series, from Ozzy Osbourne and Tommy Lee to Gene Simmons and Bret Michaels.

Eventually, singing competitions such as *American Idol* and *The Voice* kickstarted the music careers of countless amateur performers. However, these types of programs were not a new phenomenon. Arthur Godfrey hosted a popular television show, *Talent Scouts*, from 1948 to 1958. Amazingly, both Buddy Holly and Elvis Presley auditioned for spots on Godfrey's show but were rejected.

▶ CHAPTER 20
A MUSIC CAREER ON THE DECLINE

Hit artists are subject to the fickle whims of ever-changing public tastes. As a result, fame and success can be fleeting and shortlived. There is no proven blueprint to remain on top. Some artists stay with the same formula during their entire careers, while others continually attempt to reinvent themselves. Ultimately, nearly all artists are eventually pushed aside for a new generation of innovators, trendsetters and hit makers.

PRESSURES OF FOLLOWUP ALBUMS

After an album explodes on the charts, record companies usually demand a stylistically identical followup album. After Meat Loaf set the sales charts on fire in the late-1970s with *Bat Out Of Hell*, Epic Records wanted a similar clone. Instead, Meat Loaf's next album, the underwhelming *Dead Ringer*, was a flop in the U.S. And after Fleetwood Mac reached superstar status with *Rumours*, the band purposely ignored calls from their label to record a similar pop-oriented album. Their followup, *Tusk*, was an experimental project that was viewed as a commercial failure.

During the making of the album, *Thriller* – which followed 1979's *Off The Wall* – Michael Jackson frequently declared, "We sold ten-million last time, and if we sell ten-million this time, we've failed." Released in 1982, *Thriller* would eventually sell more than 33-million copies in the U.S. alone, and a total of 65-million worldwide.

While making his next record, *Bad*, Jackson taped a piece of paper to his bathroom mirror which read, "100-million." But while working on the project, Jackson was an emotional wreck. As one of Jackson's assistants said at the time: "He's afraid to finish the record. The closer he gets to completing it, the more terrified he becomes of that confrontation with the public. [Producer] Quincy Jones could only keep him protected from it for so long, then he leaves the studio and it's there. He's reminded that everyone is waiting for this record and he gets into a shell, he's frightened." Although the album failed to sell 100-million copies, *Bad* would eventually top off at a whopping 45-million copies. Consequently, Jackson's next album, *Invincible*, took five years to record. Despite Sony's massive $25 million promotional budget, it was considered a flop, selling six-million copies worldwide.

THE DOWNFALL

In one of the cruelest moments in the history of music award shows, Michael Hutchence presented Oasis with a trophy at the 1996 Brit Awards. Instead of showing respect toward Hutchence – who had a very successful career in the 1980s and early '90s as the frontman for Australian rockers INXS – Oasis lead guitarist Noel Gallagher crudely remarked, "Has-beens shouldn't be presenting awards to gonna-bes."

In the world of rock and roll, you're only as popular and successful as your last single or album. It's the "what have you done for me lately" syndrome. One day, you're a rock star with your songs all over radio, your YouTube channel drawing millions of daily visitors and your sneering face plastered on the cover of *Rolling Stone*. Then suddenly, without warning, you realize that the rock press no longer hounds you, your new songs are no longer streamed and your fans are no longer wearing concert t-shirts adorned with your band's logo. And instead of sold-out shows in 20,000 seat arenas in large metropolises, promoters start booking you in three-thousand seat theaters in second-tier towns. Pretty soon you're playing county fairs. You then realize that you've become yesterday's flavor of the month.

Longevity in popular music is the rare exception rather than the rule. Amazingly, a number of major rock artists had very limited runs on the music charts. Creedence Clearwater Revival's top-40 hit streak lasted less than four-years, while Little Richard's hit run lasted a mere 18-months. And some hit acts released just one studio album, including Thunderclap Newman, Blind Faith and the Sex Pistols.

As part of the star-making machinery that drives the music industry, fads are quickly embraced and fully plundered. Consequently, the rock and roll cosmos is littered with artists who enjoyed a meteoric blast-off and then fell back to Earth. Frankie Goes To Hollywood was promoted as the Next Big Thing in 1984. But after scoring a pair of top-10 hits, two years later the band was all but forgotten in the U.S.

Similarly, the Monkees were pop-culture giants in the 1960s. Nicknamed the Pre-Fab Four, the quartet starred in a hit television show, and their debut album topped the charts for 13 weeks in 1966. Their followup, *More Of The Monkees*, spent 18 weeks in the number-one spot and sold more than five-million copies. But despite massive record sales, radio airplay and successful tours, the group disbanded in 1971. Musical tastes had changed and their young fans had grown up and moved on. Monkeemania was over.

And not long after Semisonic had scored a sizable radio hit in 1998 with the track "Closing Time," the alternative-rock group was dropped by its label. Band member Jacob Slichter recalled: "A year earlier, our faces had been on this huge billboard – but right then I just felt really small. It's a humbling experience. Absolutely. All our friends and family thought of us as big rock stars. And my expectations were out of control. I rented a second apartment. I got a second couch. A second color TV. I bought expensive clothes."

Similarly, jazz vocalist Nancy Wilson recalled an unsettling encounter in the 1990s: "I was performing in Cleveland and staying at the Sheraton. While my manager checked me in, I was waiting in the lobby when, only a few feet away, an elevator opened. I quickly glanced at the operator. *I know that man*, I said to myself. His uniform, two sizes too large, hung on his thin frame. His demeanor was especially friendly and sweet. Then I realized who it was – *Little Jimmy Scott!* I was about to say something, but I just couldn't. I felt heartbroken. My idol, the man who taught me the art of singing, the most brilliant singer I'd ever heard, was running an elevator."

On occasion an entire genre loses its luster and popularity. If you're riding on the wrong bandwagon of the musical popularity contest, your career takes a big hit. Usually the change in public tastes is gradual; other times it seems as if the shift occurs overnight. On rare occasions, a single artist can change the musical landscape, as was the case with both Elvis Presley and the Beatles.

In the early-1990s, hard rock and hair-metal bands became casualties when Kurt Cobain and Nirvana brought the Seattle sound and grunge-style rock to the forefront. Steve Gorman, the drummer of the Southern rock band the Black Crowes, recalled the moment in 1994 when he noticed the change in musical tastes: "We were in London for about a week [to promote a new album] .... We actually agreed to do an in-store appearance for the release. We hadn't done one of those in years, but our UK label begged us, saying creating a mob scene at a local mega-store would go a long way toward creating buzz for the new album. Walking into the store, we were immediately dispossessed of that notion. There were, at most, three dozen fans waiting for us. We signed albums, took pics, and were walking back to the hotel within fifteen minutes. Sixteen months earlier, we had headlined Glastonbury and the Phoenix Festival. As far as we knew, we owned the UK in the summer of 1993. And now... that's it? I guess the rest of our fans were all at home listening to the new Nirvana record."

Similarly, before the Fab Four catapulted into the number-one spot on the U.S. charts in February 1964 with "I Want To Hold Your Hand," the top-40 was dominated by wholesome pop singers like Bobby Vinton, Ricky Nelson and Brenda Lee as well as a smattering of rock, R&B and surf acts. However, over the next twelve-months, the Beatles would score a remarkable seven number-one hits and would open the door for a flood of British Invasion acts including the Rolling Stones, the Animals and the Dave Clark Five.

Suddenly, American pop artists were considered passe and had a difficult time selling records and garnering airplay. Although Paul Anka had dominated the charts beginning in the late-1950s, he had to reinvent himself in the post-Beatles era as a songwriter and businessman. As Anka explained in his autobiography: "Doubt is debilitating for a performer, and once it enters your life, it's hard to recover from it. Once the media abandoned certain performers, they lost their nerve. And once the spirit disappears in your mind, you're gone. I saw that so many times with friends. And you don't know what to say."

Likewise, the music industry experienced an anti-disco backlash in 1979, punctuated by the infamous Disco Demolition Night at Comiskey Park in July of that year. Organized by local rock deejay Steve Dahl, thousands of disco records were blown up during the middle of a double-header between the Chicago White Sox and the Detroit Tigers. Organizers had expected a crowd of 20,000 fans at the ballpark, but more than twice as many showed up to vent their rage. The event quickly descended into a riot as thousands of anti-disco protestors stormed the field.

Over the next few months, hundreds of radio stations around the U.S. dropped their disco formats. And while there were 16 disco songs in the top-40 during the first week of May 1979, one year later the number would drop to just four. In the aftermath, only a handful of disco acts would ever return to the top-40. While the Bee Gees were on top of the world at the end of 1977, as the *Saturday Night Fever* soundtrack gave them four monster radio hits, including "Stayin' Alive" and "Night Fever," the group was suddenly considered toxic.

The Bee Gees were not alone. The rock era is full of stories of musical artists who fell from grace. When Milli Vanilli admitted they hadn't provided the vocals on any of their hits, they were forced to return their Grammy for Best New Artist. And while Three Dog Night had dominated the pop charts during the first half of the 1970s with 21 top-40 hits, by 1976 the band was considered out of fashion. One of the group's members recalled: "Our last concert that year was scheduled on a warm summer night at the Greek Theater in L.A. By then the various promoters and other insiders were well aware of the group's internal and drug problems. We had tried to hide this from the fans as well, but to no avail. When I arrived with [my wife] backstage at the Greek, the first thing I noticed was a complete lack of guests, media, or various other personnel. The final blow came when I walked into our dressing room and saw a couple cans of soda and a towel. No deli tray, no flowers, no notes, not one thing that had marked our glory days."

Some artists have avoided the post-fad slump by constantly reinventing themselves. Madonna has gone through a number of musical phases and public personas during her multi-decade career on the charts. Likewise, David Bowie was nicknamed the Chameleon of Rock as he assumed multiple stage personalities including Ziggy Stardust and the Thin White Duke. And in 1974, Ray Davies of the Kinks told a rock critic: "A lot of people think I'm completely on the wrong track these days. They think I should have never stopped writing three-minute story-songs.... But I've written so many of them, I mean, like, 18 or 20 hit singles. I've lost count. But you can't keep doing that. People are going to lose interest in you if you just keep doing the same thing, over and over, which is what I felt I was doing. The formula begins to reveal itself. The magic goes. It did for me, anyway."

Even the Beatles feared losing some of their popularity when they entered a studio in December 1966 to start recording their experimental masterpiece, *Sgt. Pepper's Lonely Hearts Club Band*. Paul McCartney told *Life* magazine at the time: "Sure, we're going to lose some fans. We lost them in Liverpool when we took off our leather jackets and put on suits. But there's no point in standing still."

Similarly, just three months before the untimely death of Kurt Cobain in 1994, the grunge star admitted: "I hate to actually even say it, but I can't see [Nirvana] lasting more than a couple more albums, unless we really work hard on experimenting. I mean, let's face it. When the same people are together doing the same job, they're limited. I'm really interested in studying different things.... I don't want to put out another record that sounds like the last three records."

However, veering too far from your core audience comes with risks. Alienating longtime fans in the hopes of remaining musically relevant can torpedo your career. In 1996, Def Leppard recorded a grunge album

Slang, which was poorly received. And when Dee Dee Ramone of the Ramones changed his name to Dee Dee King and released a solo rap album, reviewers called the project "terrible" and "bizarre." Likewise, when pop-rapper MC Hammer decided to release a gangsta rap album, he was ridiculed in the hip hop community. And when country superstar Garth Brooks recorded a rock album under the pseudonym Chris Gaines, the project was poorly received.

Some recording artists lose far more than their fame when their careers grind to a halt. Although the British rock act Dexys Midnight Runners had topped the charts with "Come On Eileen," became MTV stars and scored a total of eight top-40 hits in their native England, lead singer Kevin Rowland later found himself homeless for two years. Likewise, Gap Band lead singer Charlie Wilson, who filled dance floors in the '80s with hits such as "You Dropped A Bomb On Me" and "Party Train," was sleeping in alleys during the mid-1990s.

And Sly Stone, the leader of the hit R&B/pop act Sly and the Family Stone, once owned multiple homes and a Napa Valley vineyard. After his personal life and career both imploded, he lived out of a van in Los Angeles. In 1986, Stone lamented: "A lot of my money disappeared. One day, 13 cars and [an RV] were taken from me. I didn't manage my money enough myself. It goes very fast, it goes much faster than you can see it go. There's no need for one person to have 13 cars. That's stupid. I bought drugs. I'd give presents like all the money in the world was mine. I paid the tab for whatever alcohol, drugs, airplanes, clothes, housing, whatever, for myself and everybody around me."

*   *   *   *   *   *

A few musical artists have beaten the odds and managed to return to the charts after extended absences. Acts who enjoyed career comebacks include Tina Turner, Cher, Aretha Franklin, Roy Orbison and Santana. Similarly, Aerosmith had been a rock powerhouse in the 1970s but fell on hard times at the end of the decade. It took an unlikely rap-rock collaboration in 1986 with Run-DMC to revive the group's fortunes. The following year, Aerosmith returned to prominence with the hit album *Permanent Vacation*, which sold five million copies in the U.S. alone. Suddenly, the group was no longer considered a has-been and returned to headlining large arenas. Similarly, John Fogerty of Creedence Clearwater Revival spent many years in court battling Saul Zaentz, the owner of Fantasy Records, over an inequitable recording contract. Then after a 12-year career lull, Fogerty enjoyed a major comeback in 1985 with the solo album, *Centerfield*.

However, the vast majority of attempted comebacks have been failures. For every Aerosmith or John Fogerty, there have been a hundred former hit acts who were relegated to oldies and classic rock radio, and would never again grace contemporary playlists.

*   *   *   *   *   *

Some veteran musical artists feel they no longer have anything to prove, whether to themselves or the public. They have worked hard, they have tasted success and their musical output is on display for the world to hear and judge. Also, they have long tired of playing the chart game. Although they have no real financial needs, they continue to perform music for the pleasure and comradery.

▶ CHAPTER 21
ROCK IS YOUTH: BATTLING OLD AGE

Sporting a boyish smile and a full head of shaggy hair in 1967, Paul McCartney sang about reaching the age of 64. At around the same time, Roger Daltrey declared he wanted to die before getting to be an old man. And in 1984, vocalist Marian Gold of the New Wave group Alphaville pondered the notion of always remaining young. But all three men did in fact grow old, and reached the advanced, gray age of 64.

In 1992, the U.S. Postal Service held a rare competition. The agency was planning to issue a 29-cent Elvis Presley stamp and wanted to know if Americans preferred an image of a lanky, vibrant, 1950s-era Elvis or a plump, mature, Vegas-style Elvis. The country spoke and the young, skinny Elvis won by a landslide, drawing 75-percent of the vote.

A veteran rock star in his 40s will often struggle with the process of transforming from a virile and fresh-faced singing idol into a middle-aged mortal who has suffered the physical ravages of an unhealthy and taxing lifestyle. In a profession where youth is worshiped and exploited, musicians with fading looks, receding hair lines, expanding beer bellies and a myriad of other age-related health issues are forced to face the reality of not leaving behind a svelte and attractive corpse.

Michael Jackson once told an interviewer: "I think growing old is... the most, the ugliest thing. When the body breaks down and you start to wrinkle, I think it's bad.... And I never want to look in the mirror and see that. I don't understand it. I really don't. And people say that growing old is beautiful and it's this and that. I disagree. I totally do." And in 2014 at age 67, Bee Gees co-founder Barry Gibb revealed: "I still think of myself as a teenager. I keep my bathroom mirror dark, so I can imagine myself as a kid and not see myself as I am now. It helps."

*　　　*　　　*　　　*　　　*　　　*

Rock and roll has always been geared toward youth. In the blurry, black-and-white kinescope recordings of *American Bandstand* from the 1950s and early '60s, the audiences consisted exclusively of cheerful, gum-chewing teens – mostly girls – few of whom were over 16 or 17. Rock and roll music gave young people their own language, dance crazes, clothing styles and cultural norms. At the same time, *old* people had their own boring music. While teenagers played their 45rpm singles on cool-looking, pastel-colored, portable record players, adults reclined in their well-worn easy chairs while they listened to Mantovani or Lawrence Welk LPs on their oversized, wood-grained stereo consoles.

During his teenage years in the 1950s, future blues-rocker Al Kooper was a member of the pop-rock group, the Royal Teens. He later recalled: "In those days there were no Elton John albums to take home and share with your parents. Rock and roll was the line of demarcation, and the lifestyle attached to it had to be led surreptitiously. I embraced it all: black leather jacket (mine was actually brown – one of many such concessions), rolled-upped sleeves, greasy hair, and engineer boots. I would've had sideburns if I could've grown them.... Naturally my parents weren't buying any of this, so I was forced to keep a stash of contraband clothing in a friend's garage. I'd wake up in the morning and get dressed, bid my parents good-bye, and head directly for that garage, where I'd *really* get dressed for school."

In 1964, Jack Weinberg, a 24-year-old activist at Berkeley, would tell a reporter: "Don't trust anyone over 30." (The quotation has been misattributed over the years to Abbie Hoffman, Jerry Rubin, the Beatles and many others.) This rebellious, anti-establishment position was embraced by a restless generation that believed it was much wiser and more enlightened than its elders.

However, in the first decade of the rock era, few acts expected to spend the rest of their lives recording music and performing on stages. It was an unfathomable notion at the time. In 2005, Tom Petty told an interviewer: "When I started doing this, there weren't any 50-year-old rock stars."

At the height of their popularity, the Everly Brothers were constantly asked what they planned on doing after their music careers were over. And in 1987, Paul McCartney told *Rolling Stone* magazine: "You see old interviews with us now, and Ringo [would] say, 'Well, you know, I might get lucky and have a string of hairdressing salons.' That was the apex of his vision at the time. And John and I are talking nervously: 'There might be 10 years of this.' Remember, we were 18, 20, maybe, saying this. We couldn't see playing rock 'n' roll beyond 30." Likewise, in 2017, Bob Seger revealed: "I thought I'd be done by 30. My original plan was to do it for five years between the age of 25 and 30 and then buy a motorcycle and drive across Europe, and then get a real job. It didn't work out that way." Similarly, in 1992, actor and singer Mark Wahlberg – also known as rapper Marky Mark – told a reporter: "Hopefully, I can go on to college and do something afterwards. As much as I love what I'm doing, I don't feel that it will last forever."

*   *   *   *   *   *

Attending a concert by a middle-aged rocker – decades after their prime – can be a jolt to a fan's psyche. Former Monkees member Mike Nesmith has often discussed the shock on audiences' faces at the start of his concerts. They expect to see the grinning, wrinkle-free, boyish singer they remember watching on the 1960s hit television sitcom. Instead, they're forced to accept the hard reality that Nesmith isn't impervious to the ravages of time and has aged along with them.

And in 2005, there were reports about a possible ABBA reunion when the four members of the group appeared at the Swedish premiere of the stage musical, *Mamma Mia!* However, Benny Andersson squashed the rumors and explained: "People want to remember us as we were – youthful and energetic. Not four sixty-somethings." And at age 73, Bob Dylan mused: "Passion is a young man's game. Young people can be passionate. Older people gotta be more wise. I mean, you're around awhile, you leave certain things to the young. Don't try to act like you're young. You could really hurt yourself."

At age 66, legendary guitarist Ritchie Blackmore, a member of Deep Purple and Rainbow, stated: "I sometimes look at the audience – I always sneak a peek before we go onstage, always have done, because you get those pre-show nerves... But sometimes I look out and they're so old... and I'll suddenly realize they're probably younger than me." And one heavy metal singer admitted: "When I see these old metal guys on the road now, the first thing you do now is whip out your wallet and show photos of your kids."

And in 1996 when Ozzy Osbourne wanted to join the Lollapalooza tour, organizers informed him that he was musically passe and not a good fit for younger audiences. Prompted by the rejection, he launched the annual Ozzfest tour, which brought together strong lineups of heavy metal acts, both young and old.

Ozzy's age was again an issue in 2001 during a meeting at *Rolling Stone* magazine. Sharon Osbourne, his outspoken wife, recalled: "The summer before [our reality television program] was released I met with the magazine's editor about putting Ozzy on the cover. They wanted to put [the group] Staind on the cover, saying they were more relevant than

Ozzy. I didn't want to belittle them, but they were a faceless band. The editor didn't disagree. He just explained that Ozzy was too old. I was so sick and angry after that lunch meeting. A year later, who comes asking for Ozzy to be on the cover? But they didn't just want Ozzy, they wanted all of us."

Conversely, the concert industry has wisely learned not to snub gray-haired, Baby Boomer music lovers who, in many instances, are the only demographic group that can easily afford $100 concert tickets. For that same reason, the advertising industry continues to pay hundreds of millions of dollars every year for the use of classic pop and rock songs in television commercials in an effort to appeal to older, wealthier consumers.

RETIRING FROM THE STAGE

Many rock stars attempt to maintain their youthful appearances by any means necessary. That includes plastic surgery, Botox injections, personal trainers and expensive supplements. It also requires steering clear of the traditional trappings of the rock and roll lifestyle: booze, drugs and junk food. At age 74, singer Roger Daltrey of the Who admitted: "I'm just aware of the fact that if I want to carry on singing with any quality I have to keep doing it. Voices are just a different set of muscles in the body. If you stop using them for any length of time, it will disappear."

Some rockers simply choose to age gracefully. In 2015, Eddie Van Halen attacked his former bandmate David Lee Roth for not acting his age: "We're not in our 20s anymore. We're in our 60s. Act like you're 60. I stopped coloring my hair, because I know I'm not going to be young again." And 75-year-old funk star George Clinton admitted in 2016: "Having my long hair and braids was cool when I was younger but when I got older the braids would fall out here and there, I was worried about people snatching them out. If I'd have been running around New Jersey in the last five years with all that I would have been laughed out of town, so I cut it."

Nonetheless, the big question remains – at what age should a rock artist retire? At what point does a concert performance by a classic act on his last legs devolve into a mockery? And even after accumulating sufficient wealth to last multiple lifetimes, why do some artists continue to grind out more money by staying on the road instead of retreating to a carefree, tropical paradise? Instead of retiring, Paul McCartney and Ringo Starr continued to tour more than five-decades after the Beatles last performed together as a group on a windy London rooftop. However, at age 69 in 2017, Alice Cooper – who had just released the 27th album of his career – offered a compelling reason why he still tours and records: "I'm sure Dylan doesn't think he's written his best song yet, nor Paul McCartney."

Amazingly, a number of aging rockers have publicly announced that they don't intend to retire from the stage, no matter their physical state or diminished skills. In 1993, 62-year-old musical legend Ray Charles stated: "I've loved music ever since I come into the world, and that's why I'm never gonna retire.... God knows I have enough money to last me the rest of my life – I'm not bragging or trying to be forward, I'm just telling the truth – so it ain't about the money. I know how to play music, I know how to write music, I know how to try to sing songs. And I'm gonna do that 'til God says otherwise." Similarly, Keith Richards told an interviewer in 2010, "I can't retire until I croak. I don't think they quite understand what I get out of this. I'm not doing it just for the money or for you. I'm doing it for me." And Stevie Nicks said at age 68 in 2017: "I'll never retire. My friend Doug Morris, who's been president of, like, every record company, said to me once, 'When you retire, you just get small.' Stand up straight, put on your heels, and get out there and do stuff."

However, guitarist Rusty Young of Poco admitted in 2014: "I'm going to be 68 in February – 68 years old – and I think for me, it's kind of silly to carry on. People say, 'Well, look at Mick Jagger or Paul McCartney.' But the difference is, these guys have a private plane, a limo that takes them to the airport. They stay at a five-star hotel. They go down to the gig, and everything's set up for them. I have to load up all my gear, drive to the airport, get on a Southwest Airlines flight, drive all my gear to the hotel and then drag all my gear from the hotel to the stage, spend all day setting it up, play a show, tear down all the gear, drag it back to the hotel. If I lived the life that Mick Jagger lived, then I might consider playing further."

And in 2019, 82-year-old pioneering rocker Jerry Lee Lewis continued to tour despite his profound frailty. Typically, the concerts would begin with his backing band playing four or five songs – without their leader. An announcement would be made that the Killer will be hitting the stage "in a little while." Finally, a barely mobile Lewis would slowly amble toward the center of the stage, with a walking cane in hand. Greeted by a tidal wave of applause, the former Sun Records fireball would then carefully take a seat at his piano.

After a hard life of boozing, brawling and carousing, Lewis had not aged gracefully and looked older than his advanced years. However, once Lewis began pounding the keys of the piano, the appreciative and respectful audience would overlook his less-than-stellar playing and creaky voice because – after all – this is *the* Jerry Lee Lewis, the notorious, outlaw rock and roller. After playing for a mere 35-minutes, Lewis would bow to the audience and leave the stage without delivering an encore. With the possibility that the concert might be his last-ever performance, it was preferable for a hardcore fan to see Lewis well past his prime than never at all.

*   *   *   *   *   *

Not everyone is a fan of aging musicians who refuse to retire. In 2001, author John Strausbaugh argued: "Rock simply cannot be credibly played by 60-year-old men with triple chins and bad toupees, pretending still to be excited about songs they wrote 30 or 40 years ago and have played some thousands of times since." Similarly, in 2013, Brett Gurewitz, the guitarist of the veteran punk-rock band Bad Religion, explained: "Nobody wants a 50-year-old dude singing about beers, bongs and boobies." Likewise, John Lennon told an interviewer in 1980, "Who'd want to hear a croaking Beatle of 80?"

In 2006, Pete Townshend argued: "I don't think that the big Baby Boomer bands are going to be able to do this much longer. I really don't.... I don't want to go out and see Bob Dylan. I don't want to go out and see the Stones. I wouldn't pay money to go see the Who, not even with the new songs. I wouldn't pay money to go see Crosby, Stills and Nash. They... make me sick. When I say that, what I mean is, I'm an ageist about it. I don't want to look at these old guys in their self-congratulatory mode. Somebody gave me tickets for Marlene Dietrich's last concert in London, and apparently she came out and she looked fantastic under the lights, but you know she's an eighty-year-old woman held together by glue and string. Why would you want to do that?"

And realistically, as rockers grow older, many have been stricken with devastating old age maladies like Parkinson's and Alzheimer's Disease. Singer-songwriter Glenn Campbell battled dementia as have Neil Diamond, AC/DC guitarist Malcolm Young and Judas Priest guitarist Glenn Tipton. Even a former teen idol like David Cassidy of the Partridge Family was not immune from the ravages of the disease.

Additionally, numerous aging rockers also suffer from another malady – profound hearing loss caused by years of performing on stages next to stacks of eardrum-shattering speakers. Rockers such as Eric

Clapton, Pete Townshend and Neil Young have publicly discussed their acute hearing loss. Likewise, Ozzy Osbourne admitted in 2010: "I suffer from permanent tinnitus... which means I've got this constant ringing in my ears, which has also made me somewhat deaf (or 'conveniently deaf,' as Sharon calls it).... Should have worn earplugs, I guess."

Another common problem with older performers is the fact that many have trouble singing their hits, which were recorded decades earlier. Oftentimes their vocal cords have been damaged by years of drinking or smoking, or they simply can no longer reach the high notes. Some artists extend their careers by employing technological tricks – such as using a pitch-correcting device like Auto-Tune. And, sadly, some well-known veteran artists have been caught lip-syncing to pre-recorded vocal tracks.

BECOMING AN OLDIES ARTIST

When an artist stops appearing on the current music charts or top-40 radio, he is classified as an oldies act. As a result, his new material is rarely heard over the airwaves. And after a while, he's dropped by his record label. Pirkle Lee Moses – the lead singer of the 1950s hit doo-wop group, the El Dorados – described what happened when he tried to promote some new songs in the 1990s: "Forty years later, here we are, with a new record. I took it 'round to radio stations. They laughed at me."

In an often-told story, fans of Ricky Nelson had difficulty adjusting to the grown-up version of the youthful entertainer they remembered from the television show, *The Adventures of Ozzie and Harriet*. At age 21 in 1961, he had shortened his first name to "Rick" and tried to appeal to older audiences. Then, several years later, he wanted a complete break from his teen idol past. Taking a turn to country-rock, he formed the Stone Canyon Band. However, concert audiences were hostile to the changes and instead wanted to hear his old hits. He chronicled the situation in the lyrics of his 1972 hit song, "Garden Party."

Similarly, rock and roll pioneer Dion DiMucci – the former leader of Dion and the Belmonts – never stopped recording new material. Late in his career, he nearly regretted his return to the stage: "It wasn't easy. People kept asking me to sing the old songs, just one more time, and if I couldn't get around it, I'd knock off a verse or two, poking fun at the memories, making them laugh to hide my pain.... It was harder than you might think. I wrestled with a lot of old feelings.... Those songs, all they stood for, were a part of a life I'd turned away from a long time ago. To face it all again was painful and a little scary. I didn't want to start living in the past, to find that people liked me better then than they do now. Maybe it's something every entertainer goes through, but that didn't make it any easier."

And Ritchie Blackmore stated in 2011: "There's nothing wrong with nostalgia. I like to go out and see certain old bands when they reform, or when they come out and tour. But at the same time, I'd hate to be in that band." Conversely, Tom Petty argued in 1990, "I'm not interested in nostalgia. I don't want to wind up like the Beach Boys. They used to be an innovative group. Now they're almost vaudevillian."

*   *   *   *   *   *

In the 1990s, after PBS began airing a series of popular, oldies revival concerts, many previously forgotten acts were suddenly in demand. The problem with the resurgence of interest was, of course, that many of these artists were in their 60s and 70s, and were either uninterested in restarting their music careers or not healthy enough to perform on a stage.

However, where there's money to be made, there's always a way to revive an oldies act. Suddenly, doo-wop vocal groups from the 1950s began hitting the road with one original member and four or five replacement singers, many of whom were in their 20s or 30s. For instance, in 2001, there was a trio of oldies bands touring on the same bill – the Drifters, the Platters and the Coasters. However, out of the three groups, there was only one legitimate, classic member – Billy "Bip" Guy of the Coasters.

Likewise, in the early 21st century, few classic rock bands toured with all their original members, whether through attrition or death. When Dave Mason joined a struggling version of Fleetwood Mac in 1993, he was joined by two other replacement members, Billy Burnette and Bekka Bramlett. Missing from the touring group at the time were Stevie Nicks, Lindsey Buckingham and Christine McVie. Mason would later lament that it felt like he was in a "cover band."

And although the duo Sam and Dave dominated the pop and R&B charts in the late-1960s, members Sam Moore and Dave Prater later had a falling out and went their separate ways. While Moore performed as a solo act, Prater hit the concert road in the 1980s with a series of fake Sams, under the billing, "The Sam and Dave Revue." The wife of the real Sam recalled: "[Dave Prater] came up with every story. That Sam had cancer, that he was retired or locked up in rehab. That the fake Sam was actually the real, original Sam who had gone in the Army years earlier.... It took years for us to convince people that [my] Sam wasn't the fake Sam. To this day we have people coming up and telling him, 'Hey, I booked you in 1986' and, 'Boy you sure look different' or, 'You sure sound different.'"

Oftentimes, the names of oldies groups are bought and sold like commodities. An East Coast oldies promoter defended the practice of knowingly booking these counterfeit rock acts: "Nobody cares who the people are in the group. As long as somebody can present some legal right to the name, then as a promoter it's not my concern who's really in the group. All the audience wants is a good show."

And in 1998, *The New York Times* reported: "Chuck Blasco of the Vogues, whose 'Five O'Clock World' was one in a string of hits that lasted from 1965 to 1971, learned in 1975 that the group's name had been trademarked by strangers and another group was doing their songs after their record company sold the group's recording and management contracts. The new owner offered to sell the name back to the group members, but after making a few payments, the original Vogues balked. 'We said, 'Why are we doing this?'' Mr. Blasco said. 'Why do we have to buy something we created? It didn't make sense at that point, and it still doesn't.' Outside 14 counties in western Pennsylvania under the jurisdiction of the Federal Court in Pittsburgh, where he won the right to use the Vogues name, Mr. Blasco still may not advertise his current group as the Vogues. 'I don't know how these people can wake up in the morning and look themselves in the face,' he said." Fake rock groups became such a problem that some states passed legislation banning the practice.

The continued popularity of oldies and classic rock music gave rise to the tribute act. Amazingly, there's great earning potential in dressing up as Michael Jackson or Bruce Springsteen, learning their stage moves and mimicking their vocal styles. One Mariah Carey tribute singer from Connecticut has earned as much as $70,000 for a single performance. And one Beatles tribute act – appropriately named 1964: The Tribute – was formed as a part-time venture but eventually began playing in large venues all over the country, including prestigious stages like Carnegie Hall. And while veteran drummer Joe Vitale often backed Crosby, Stills & Nash on their tours, his son – Joe Vitale, Jr. – joined a Crosby, Stills, Nash & Young tribute act called Ohio.

Not surprisingly, tribute acts are often proficient at imitating hit artists. Cheap Trick guitarist Rick Nielsen once admitted: "We occasionally mangle our own stuff. But I've seen some Cheap Trick tribute bands that are actually a little better than we are."

▶ CHAPTER 22
THE END OF THE LINE

Some performers choose to walk away from the music industry at the height of their careers. They leave for a variety of reasons. In 2013, when Billy Joel was asked by *Rolling Stone* magazine why he hadn't recorded a "pop album" in 20 years, he replied: "Bruce has asked me. Pete Townshend backstage the other night asked me. A lot of people don't understand – why would you retire from rock stardom? When it becomes redundant, when it becomes more of a business, a lot of the motivation leaves. By the time I got to [1993's] *River Of Dreams* and that song 'Famous Last Words,' I felt like, 'OK, I've had my say.' I've given away a lot of my own life in these songs and now I want to have a little bit of my own life for me."

Similarly, in the mid-1980s, Journey was a hot commodity on both top-40 and album-rock radio. Calling a group meeting, singer Steve Perry announced he was leaving the group: "I can't go on, I can't do this. Guys we've done it. We can't get any bigger. If we keep going, we're going to end up being some classic rock nostalgia band. We'll end up being just a memory – a shadow of what we used to be.... I need my life back. I'm toast. I'm just toast." Looking back at his decision, in 2018 Perry revealed: "I had lost that deep passion in my heart for the inner joy of songwriting and singing. I sort of let it all go. If it came back great; if it didn't, so be it, because I'd already lived the dream of dreams.... As much as I missed the lights, as much as I missed the stage, the applause and the adoration of people who were loving the music I was participating in, I had to walk away from it to be emotionally on my own without it. And that took time. That doesn't mean I didn't miss it, it means I had to keep walking the other way. There was personal work to be done within myself."

Likewise, Charlotte Caffey of the Go-Go's explained why both she and Belinda Carlisle had walked away from the group in 1985: "We had reminded each other of the pact we had made when we first started the band in 1978: when it stops being fun we will break up. And it had definitely stopped being fun."

Some artists quit because of their negative experiences in the music industry. Such was the case with bassist Ron Blair, who quit Tom Petty and the Heartbreakers in 1982. As Petty explained: "When he first quit, he didn't quit the band, he quit the whole music thing. He was fed up." Likewise, pop singer George Michael essentially left the music industry in the early-1990s after several years of chart-topping hit singles as both a solo artist and a member of Wham. He explained at the time: "It's quite simple, really. I decided that the thing I really enjoy... the thing I really needed was my songwriting. I didn't need the celebrity.... I'm sure a lot of people are going to believe all this is just some sort of gimmick... just another way to stir interest. But I'm also sure that most people find it hard to believe that stardom can make you miserable. After all, everybody wants to be a star. I certainly did, and I worked hard to get it. But I was miserable, and I don't want to feel that way again.... The truth is, it all got much bigger than I ever imagined – and much harder to control. Ultimately, I wasn't comfortable with that kind of visibility and power. Once I became more confident as a writer, I realized I didn't need all that other bolstering."

Similarly, Tom Scholz, the founder of the classic rock group Boston, was quickly disillusioned by the music industry. He later explained: "We had gone on a horrible tour in 1978-79. It was long, and when I got off the road, I wasn't sure that I wanted to ever go on tour again. I was going to hang it up and just record. I took a little time after [the album] *Don't Look Back*. I was drained. I was demoralized. I wasn't sure I wanted to be in the music business. I didn't like what I had seen. Brad [Delp] and I had made a lot of money for a lot of people, and I didn't like what they were doing. I began to feel guilty about enabling people to do things that I didn't approve of. I considered leaving music altogether and going back to being an engineer [at Polaroid]."

A number of rockers have abandoned popular music for religious reasons. Little Richard, an ordained minister, distanced himself from the depravity-filled world of rock music at the height of his career in October 1957. But five-years later, when he returned to his rock and roll roots, he was relegated to oldies status. Similarly, guitarist Brian "Head" Welch of the metal band Korn walked away from a $23 million record contract in 2005 after he gained religious faith. He would return to the group in 2013. On the other hand, after Prince became a devout Jehovah's Witness in the late-1990s, he didn't leave music. Instead, he subsequently refrained from performing his more raunchy songs.

Some artists leave music for financial reasons. Soul singer Bill Withers quit in the mid-1970s after scoring a string of hits, including

"Lean On Me" and "Ain't No Sunshine." As Withers recalled: "They weren't paying me.... They looked at me and said, 'So, I owe you some money, so what?' I was socialized in the military. When some guy is smushing my face down, it doesn't go down well. Since I was self-contained and had no manager, my solution was to erase [a completed] album. I don't even know which one it was, but it's gone.... In hindsight, I have some regret and could probably have handled that differently." Then, five-years after winning a Grammy in 1980 for the hit single "Just The Two Of Us," Withers left the music industry for good.

Conversely, some artists retire after achieving their career and financial goals. As the lead guitarist and vocalist of Dire Straits, Mark Knopfler scored a breakthrough hit in 1978 with "Sultans Of Swing." By the mid-1980s, the group topped the charts with "Money For Nothing" and Knopfler became an early MTV star. A decade later, he left Dire Straits behind: "I never expected it to get that big. I don't really care about making more money at this point. What am I going to do with it? Buy a boat? I don't really want a boat. And I've got a lot of guitars."

Likewise, Ric Ocasek had tired of the public spotlight when he dissolved the Cars in 1988. He later revealed why he abandoned his music career: "I have no interest. I'd rather paint, or write, or do anything else. It's something that was already done, and those records are already locked away. I'm going into the future. As a rule, I'd rather live in the future than the past." (Ocasek reluctantly reformed the Cars in 2010 for an album and a short tour.)

*   *   *   *   *   *

Even after leaving the world of rock and roll, it is difficult to shed the fame and expect privacy – especially in the internet age. Former 1960s pop singer Marianne Faithfull was haunted by her persistent fame. In a 2013 interviewed, she stated: "[I] hate being recognized. I can't even say my own name in public. I've gone to fashion shows in New York and because I couldn't bring myself to say, 'My name is Marianne Faithfull and I have an invitation,' I've actually turned round at the door and left. To hear those words coming out of my mouth would be so vulgar."

Although some former hit acts remain in the music industry as session musicians, songwriters or producers, most choose to completely leave the chaotic scene. On the VH1 program *Bands Reunited*, former singers and musicians were captured in their various post-rock careers, many which were not very glamorous.

Terry Chimes, the drummer on the debut Clash album, became a chiropractor. After leaving Van Halen, David Lee Roth was briefly a paramedic in New York City. And while rapper Vanilla Ice bought and renovated houses, Anthrax guitarist Dan Spitz became a master watchmaker.

Some former rockers pursued professional or academic careers. After keyboardist Mark Avsec – of both Wild Cherry and Donnie Iris and the Cruisers – battled charges of copyright infringement, he became an attorney who specialized in music law and intellectual property. Similarly, bass player Jackie Fuchs of the 1970s rock group the Runaways became a lawyer and author and was also a three-day winner on the television quiz show, *Jeopardy!* And guitarist Jeff "Skunk" Baxter – of the Doobie Brothers and Steely Dan – emerged as a consultant in the field of mobile missile defense.

Meanwhile, Art Garfunkel decided to make a drastic career change in the early-1970s. Just a few years after enjoying a strong run of hits as a part of Simon & Garfunkel, he got married and took a job teaching math at a private school in Connecticut. He recalled: "It was a weird stage of my life, to leave Simon & Garfunkel at the height of our success and become a math teacher. I would talk them through a math problem and ask if anyone had any questions and they would say: 'What were the Beatles like?'" Not surprisingly, Garfunkel's career as an educator did not last, and he soon returned to music.

THE DEATH OF A ROCKER: FAMILY BATTLES

Following the death of a hit musical artist, there's often a mad scramble for control of the estate by spouses and family members. Often, wills are "located" and then "lost." Or there are multiple wills, with heirs banished at the last minute. Court battles ensue, sometimes taking years to settle. In one such lawsuit, former doo-wop singing star Frankie Lymon was found dead in 1968 on the floor of his grandmother's apartment with a needle in his arm. In 1986, Lymon's widow was forced to battle two other women – both of whom claimed to be his wives – for control of the singer's estate. The legal fight was chronicled in the film, *Why Do Fools Fall In Love.*

And when Prince died suddenly in 2016, he was survived by one full-sibling and five half-siblings. But as many as 700 people claimed to be related to the performer and inquired about taking a DNA test – all hoping to share a portion of his $200 million estate. In the end, the court determined there were no additional heirs beyond his six siblings.

The fortunes of some rockers seemingly disappear. After the sudden death of Michael Hutchence in a Sydney hotel room in 1997, little of his $27 million estate could be located. As the leader of INXS, he enjoyed a strong run of hit singles and albums, including *Kick*, which sold 20-million copies worldwide and spawned the chart-topping hit "I Need You Tonight." However, as *The Telegraph* reported: "An executor's report sent to his family eight years after his death stated that the 37-year-old had just $506 (Australian dollars) in cash at the time of his death, and his share of INXS's bank balance was $572." Twenty-years after Hutchence's death, his daughter Tiger Lily had yet to receive any of her father's millions.

Sometimes, legal fights drag on for so long that the performer's body remains in limbo. A full year after James Brown succumbed to complications from pneumonia in 2006, he remained uninterred as his family members battled for control of his estate. Sadly, his body would be moved at least 14 times before his eventual burial. A full decade after his death, members of his family were still mired in legal squabbles.

Conversely, Police frontman Sting announced in 2014 that he would not be leaving his massive fortune – estimated at more than $300 million – to his children. He explained: "They have this work ethic that makes them want to succeed on their own merit. People make assumptions, that they were born with a silver spoon in their mouth, but they have not been given a lot."

POST-DEATH CAREER SUCCESS

When a famous rocker dies, there's a buying frenzy on Amazon, Ebay and other online collector sites. Before Michael Jackson's sudden death in 2009, a used copy of his common, vinyl LP, *Thriller*, sold for less than $5. Then suddenly, the same piece of vinyl was trading for $50 to $75. And on Amazon, biographies of deceased artists suddenly jump in value. Other items like vintage concert t-shirts or used concert tickets also reach stratospheric prices. Additionally, the artist's record label will rush-release an album or two in order to satisfy public demand.

Amazingly, death is sometimes just a speed bump in an artist's career. Shortly after the demise of Elvis Presley in August 1977, his outspoken manager Col. Tom Parker made a bold statement: "Nothing has changed, this won't change anything.... It don't mean a damn thing. It's just like when he was in the army.... Elvis isn't dead. Just his body is gone."

As *People* magazine reported at the time: "On the streets of Memphis, vendors are hawking copies of Elvis' last will and testament for $4. In Columbus, Georgia, parts of a 1956 Cadillac Eldorado that Presley once owned are being melted down into $4.95 pendants. A shirt he wore in concert sells for $500. In Cincinnati riot police are put on alert to handle 4,500 memento collectors flocking to an Elvis convention. There are $573 gold medallions from West Germany, Elvis watches ($21.50) and choker chains ($14) from Britain, an entire tasteless line of geegaws from the licensed factota of the Presley estate itself.... An Oregon woman is baking ceramic statuettes of Presley ('You can grow little plants in the guitar') and one 'coffin rider' (as the exploiters are being called) showed up at the Cincinnati convention with 30,000 copies of the Memphis papers carrying stories of Presley's death. Asking price was $2 apiece. 'I hate people who try to capitalize on his death,' admits one 'obsessed' collector, Paul Dowling of Ruxton, Maryland. 'I'd never sell, but there's plenty of money to be made on Elvis. Everybody's getting into the act.'"

Meanwhile, Col. Tom Parker's prediction came true. When Elvis died, his estate was valued at a mere $4 million. Elvis had left everything to daughter Lisa Marie, with Elvis' father Vernon named the executor. After Vernon's death in 1979, Elvis' ex-wife Priscilla Presley took over as executor. The following year, she established Elvis Presley Enterprises (EPE). She opened up the Graceland mansion as a tourist site, which generated $20 million annually from admission fees. Eventually, EPE became a lucrative global industry that licensed hundreds and hundreds of Elvis-related products. In 2004, she sold the bulk of EPE – including the rights to Elvis' name and image – for approximately $100 million. Additionally, Elvis would continue to sell records after he left the earthly stage and even scored an international hit in 2002 with a remixed version of his 1968 track, "A Little Less Conversation."

Elvis wasn't the only rocker with a strong post-death career. A full decade after the demise of the Doors' frontman in 1971, he was featured on the cover of *Rolling Stone* magazine with the blaring headline: "Jim Morrison – he's hot, he's sexy and he's dead." An executive at Morrison's label said at the time, "The group is bigger now than when Morrison was alive. We've sold more Doors records this year than in any year since they were first released."

And shortly after Jimi Hendrix perished in a London apartment, there was a scheme to display his body at Madison Square Garden in a last-gasp attempt to milk his fame for a quick buck. Instead, his legacy was extended through a series of posthumous albums that were cobbled together from unfinished sessions and live performances. Although

Hendrix was working on just his fourth album at the time of his death, more than forty *new* studio and live Hendrix albums were later issued. On occasion, posthumous releases were carried out in a more respectful manner. Natalie Cole scored the biggest hit of her career in 1991, when she released a duet version of the pop standard, "Unforgettable," that featured the vocals of her late father, Nat King Cole.

However, there are times when desperate record companies lack a sufficient number of quality tracks and are forced to get creative. Such was the case in 2010 when Sony Records issued the posthumous Michael Jackson album, *Michael*. After a superfan questioned the authenticity of the project, he hired a forensic audiologist. In 2018, Sony admitted that Jackson "may not have sung" on three of the album's tracks.

Meanwhile, in what was described as a spectacular moment in television history, a three-dimensional hologram of Elvis Presley seemingly performed a duet of "If I Can Dream" with Celine Dion on a 2007 episode of *American Idol*. Elvis appeared to walk alongside the Canadian songstress before stopping at the front of the stage. In the digital age, just because you're dead doesn't mean you have to stop performing for live audiences.

Soon, other holograms made their debuts. A hologram of departed rapper Tupac Shakur appeared at the 2012 Coachella Valley Music and Arts Festival – on the same stage as his former musical partners Dr. Dre and Snoop Dogg. And just six-years after the death of Ronnie James Dio, a hologram of the heavy-metal rocker performed across Europe with his former bandmates on a tour billed as "Dio Returns."

And in 2018, a Roy Orbison hologram toured across North America – backed by a full band. A *Los Angeles Times* reviewer reported: "In the darkened Wiltern Theatre in Los Angeles, hundreds of people couldn't wait to see legendary rocker Roy Orbison. A live orchestra pumped up the crowd with a medley of his hits. Old photos of him flashed across a giant screen. Then, the crooner appeared to rise magically from the stage, wearing his signature light gray suit and black shades and jamming on a red Gibson guitar to his 1960 hit 'Only the Lonely.' Fans screamed as they quickly positioned their smartphones to record the spectral image. 'This is as good as seeing him in person as you'll ever get,' marveled [a fan], who paid about $200 for a pair of tickets to the Tuesday night show.... Still, there were some awkward moments during Tuesday night's performance. When a song finished and the hologram said 'Thank you,' some audience members laughed, unsure of the appropriate response to a programmed event."

Some enterprising rockers yearned to create their own touring holograms while they were still alive. Ahmet Zappa revealed how Frank Zappa was considering that option: "My father talked about wanting to create his own hologram company. He was a futurist and a brilliant creative mind. He'd talk about wanting to stay at home so he could keep making music while his hologram went out and performed." And in 2018, George Clinton admitted that he had filmed some hologram performances with his band: "I wanted to give something to my family."

But not everyone was a fan of the technology. When the father of Amy Winehouse announced in 2018 that he would be staging a hologram tour of his late daughter, her ex-husband protested the move. There are some obvious ethical issues concerning the technology. Is it appropriate to create a visual clone of a deceased performer without their permission? And who should have the legal authority to do so – the artist's heirs, record company or former bandmates?

▶ CLOSING TIME

The music industry – with its lure of money, power and fame – is a precarious career choice. Being a rock star may look like lots of fun, but there are endless drawbacks and considerable personal sacrifices which must be made. Late in his career, Joe Walsh admitted: "And here's the thing: What we do as rock and roll stars, everybody thinks that's a whole lifestyle that we live, and that it's glorious and extravagant and wonderful. And they think that 24 hours a day we're famous and wearing expensive clothes and riding around in limos. But that's not really true. We're really cool for about an hour and a half onstage. And the rest of the day we're taking out garbage and picking up dog crap and washing cars and sucking eggs like everybody else on the planet. We're ordinary average guys."

Singer Charlie Daniels lamented: "You work while everybody else plays. You travel while everyone else sleeps. You miss your family birthdays and anniversaries, and your kids grow and change while you're gone. Yes, there's a price to be paid. I've seen strong grown men come apart on the road." And Roy Orbison once declared: "Being a legend is a great thing. But it doesn't tune your guitar or change your tire."

And sadly, the late Robin Gibb of the Bee Gees believed that his famous family paid dearly for the group's enormous success. Shortly after he was diagnosed with cancer in 2013, he pondered: "I sometimes wonder if all the tragedies my family has suffered, like Andy and Maurice dying so young and everything that's happened to me recently, is a kind of karmic price we are paying for all the fame and fortune we've had."

* * * * * *

At age 66 in 2018, Chrissie Hynde looked back at her career and mused: "I can't think of anything better than playing in a rock 'n' roll band. This really is the most fun thing that I've ever found. To be on a tour bus with your gang is just fantastic. You do a show, you get to see the world, and just hang out and goof around. And you get paid for it."

Similarly, Tom Petty believed that creating music provides a universal benefit: "Johnny Cash said this to me one day: 'This is noble work.' I wasn't sure what he meant. 'Noble work?' He goes, 'Yeah, it makes a lot of people happy.' That hit me like a bolt to the brain. Why didn't I ever have that thought before? I was probably thinking about me being happy. This basic idea Johnny shared seemed revolutionary in some odd way. It makes millions happy. Then I went and played some shows and looked out as far as you can see [and] people are jumping up and down. They're happy. It helped me to see the value of it and what it meant in these people's lives, because, really, what it means to them is exactly what it meant to me. Music has always been my passport to a better place."

Conversely, Bob Geldof of the Boomtown Rats offered a more cynical perspective: "There's nothing great about singing pop songs. It's a pretty minor talent, at best, and it's ludicrously over-compensated by this society." Likewise, Gene Simmons told an NPR reporter: "When you really think about it, I'm not delusional enough to think that what I do is important to life as we know it on this planet. No. But neither is what you do. You know, the world can get along very well without us."

Similarly, Bono of U2 admitted that sometimes even he gets tired of hearing about himself: "I'm sick of Bono. And I am Bono. It's like, oh, man, shut up. But there it is." Likewise, John Lennon admitted in 1971: "We used to believe the Beatles myth just as much as the public, and we were in love with them in just the same way. But basically we were four individuals who eventually recovered our own individualities after being submerged in a myth. I know a lot of people were upset when we finished, but every circus has to come to an end. The Beatles were a monument that had to be either changed or scrapped. As it happens, it was scrapped. The Beatles were supposed to be this and supposed to be that, but really all we were was a band that got very big."

*   *   *   *   *   *

In the internet age, the music industry operates in a much different manner than during rock and roll's heyday in the last half of the 20th century. Instead of hundreds of record companies competing for a spot on the *Billboard* charts, by 2020, just three major labels controlled more than 90-percent of the airplay, downloads and streaming in the U.S.

Additionally, the music industry no longer nurtures its young acts, refuses to take risks and rarely celebrates artistry. In 2004, Jerry Wexler, a veteran producer and former co-owner of Atlantic Records, stated: "The industry is in an awful state, and that conglomeration... has certainly taken a lot of soul out of the business. And what with the problems of downloading and counterfeiting, things are in such terrible shape – witness the decimation of staffs [at record companies], the unbelievable firings. It's just a tragedy."

And with the consolidation of the broadcasting industry beginning in the 1990s, decisions at radio stations are increasingly made by consultants and bankers, which has resulted in bland and homogenized playlists. In the aftermath, gone were local and regional hits. And deejays – once stars in their own right – have been relegated to voice-tracking their shows with automated computer programs instead of interacting with listeners.

In 2016, an employee at an artist management company lamented: "A 'career' in music is a pretty rare thing.... We're in an industry where over 90% of releases never recoup the money spent on them. The industry underwrites failure as a necessary part of its operation and looks to the supercharged successes of a very small number of artists to cover the losses. That's pretty dysfunctional."

Not surprisingly, in the 21st century there were few emerging performers who enjoyed mass appeal and could be considered rock stars. Gone are the days of smash, superstar albums when the Eagles would sell 26-million copies of *Hotel California* or Michael Jackson could enjoy sales of 33-million copies of *Thriller*. As Elton John lamented: "[In] the late '60s and early '70s... there were 10 or 12 albums you had to have every week. Now, it's hard to find 10 or 12 albums a year." And at the end of 2019, *Lemonade* by Beyoncé was named the Top Album of the Decade despite the fact that only a small segment of the population could actually name a single track from the album.

Even making music was no longer a profitable venture. In 2011, Cinderella bassist Eric Brittingham explained why the metal band had not recorded a studio album since 1994: "In the musical climate these days and the way we like to do things, it's not really worth doing it anymore. Our last record cost $1.2 million to make and the cheapest record we've ever made was $400,000. You can't do that these days because no one even sells $400,000 worth of records, CDs or downloads. Everything's changed. Everyone makes records in their bedrooms basically for next to nothing and in my opinion, most of them sound like it. That's not what we're about."

Consequently, there is little financial incentive for an artist or label to spend millions of dollars in an attempt to create another *Sgt. Pepper* or *Dark Side Of The Moon*. As Jerry Cantrell of Alice In Chains observed, "It really sucks because there's probably a 12-year-old kid out there who could be the next Kurt Cobain, but he's never going to get the chance to be heard because there's no future or money in making music anymore."

And in 2014, John Mellencamp declared: "There'll never be another Beatles, Dylan or Johnny Cash. There's not gonna be another resurgence of something like punk or grunge to save the music business. It's all done. The record companies decided to turn their backs on established artists such as myself and started chasing girls in stretch dresses. Which is fine. Guys like me became trophies on a shelf; we were too expensive to operate."

▶ POSTSCRIPT

I worked on this book, on and off, for more than twenty-years. Although it was an enjoyable process to amass and then organize the information into readable chapters, it was no easy task. At one point, I considered sharing co-authorship with another writer because it looked as though the project would never be completed. Finally, a friend said to me: "You worked on it for this long, you might as well finish it – no matter how long it takes."

Ultimately, the central question of the book remains unanswered: knowing what we do about the extreme personal costs and sacrifices that are required to become a rock star – is it worth it? Is the act of achieving success worth the price of an unhealthy nomadic lifestyle with little privacy, astronomical rates of substance abuse and the likelihood of an early death? And should we encourage friends or family members to work in the music industry? Of course, not all performers engage in the hedonist behaviors described in this book, but the temptations certainly are omnipresent.

Additionally, many of the chapters could be expanded into their own books, and hopefully someone will attempt such a chore in the future. Lastly, some of the more controversial material in the book could have been omitted, but then the conversation would not have taken place. We must celebrate and encourage the free exchange of ideas.

► SELECTED BIBLIOGRAPHY

Aerosmith; & Davis, Stephen. (2003). *Walk This Way: The Autobiography of Aerosmith*. New York: HarperCollins.

Ant, Adam. (2006). *Stand & Deliver: The Autobiography*. London: Sidgwick & Jackson.

Boyd, William. (2016, January 12). How David Bowie and I hoaxed the art world. *The Guardian*.

Brodessar-Akner, Taffy. (2018, February 8). Jimmy Buffett does not live the Jimmy Buffett lifestyle. *The New York Times*.

Brody, Jane E. (1998, August 25). Researchers unravel the motives of stalkers. *The New York Times*.

Brown, Bobby. (2016). *Every Little Step: My Story*. New York: Dey Street Books.

Dannen, Frederic. (1990). *Hit Men: Power Brokers and Fast Money Inside the Music Business*. New York: Times Books.

Das, Lina. (2015, August 14). Sex, drugs and lots of Monkee business! As they prepare to play in the UK, Peter Tork and Micky Dolenz admit they weren't as innocent as they looked. *The Daily Mail*.

Davis, Stephen. (2018). *Hammer of the Gods: Led Zeppelin*. London: Pan Books.

Fekadu, Mesfin. (2019, December 15). Beyonce's 'Lemonade' named Associated Press album of the decade. *The Columbus Dispatch*.

Goddard, Simon. (2005, February). Blimy! It's Gary Numan on the blower. *Uncut*.

Guralnick, Peter. (2005). *Dream Boogie: The Triumph of Sam Cooke*. Boston: Little, Brown & Company.

Jones, Allan. (2016). *Can't Stand Up For Falling Down: Rock 'n' Roll War Stories*. London: Bloomsbury.

Kershaw, Andy. (2005, September 23). Bob Dylan: How I found the man who shouted 'Judas.' *The Independent*.

Mansfield, Ken; & Stoker, Brent. (2007). *The White Book*. Nashville: Thomas Nelson.

Monk, Noel E.; Layden, Joe. (2017). *Runnin' with the Devil*. New York: HarperCollins.

Richards, Keith; & Fox, James. (2010). *Life*. New York: Little, Brown and Company.

Richards, Matt; & Longthorne, Mark. (2016). *Somebody To Love: The Life, Death and Legacy of Freddie Mercury*. Richmond, CA: Weldon Owen.

Simpson, Dave. (2010, September 23). From pop star to chiropractor: musicians' post-musical careers. *The Guardian*.

Stewart, Dave. (2016). *Sweet Dreams are Made of This*. New York: New American Library.

Talevski, Nick. (2009). *Hang on Sloopy: The History of Rock and Roll in Ohio*. Green, OH: Guardian Express Media.

Talevski, Nick; & West, Robert D. (2009). *The Origins and Early History of Rock and Roll*. Green, OH: Guardian Express Media.

Thomas, Nick. (2014). *Tom Petty: An American Rock and Roll Story*. Green, OH: Guardian Express Media.

▶ NOTES

INTRODUCTION

1. "The whole point of being..." ~ Fortnam, Ian. (2019, July). Q&A: Bobbie Gillespie. *Classic Rock.*
2. "As you sign a record..." ~ Childs, Andy. (1975, July). Billy Joel, piano man. *ZigZag.*
3. "Take Nashville for example, we..." ~ Price, Deborah Evans. (1989, November). Bon Jovi: Opposite methods result in hit songs. *American Songwriter.*
4. "I think the other thing..." ~ The Editors of *Rolling Stone.* (2012). *Harrison.* New York: Simon and Schuster.
5. "It was so fast and..." ~ Fricke, David. (1994, January 27). Our man in Nirvana rages on (and on) about stardom, fatherhood, his feud with Pearl Jam, the death of grunge and why he's never been happier in his life. *Rolling Stone.*
6. "Like most unsigned young musicians..." ~ Hell, Richard. (2013). *I Dreamed I Was a Very Clean Tramp.* New York: Ecco.
7. "My goal had always been..." ~ Bono, Sonny. (1991). *And the Beat Goes On.* New York: Pocket Books.
8. "[In 1978] I was absolutely..." ~ Adams, Bret. (1998, May 7). Used 'Cars.' *(Cleveland) Scene.*
9. "All of a sudden everyone..." ~ Everley, Dave. (2017, November). Gary Numan. *Q.*
10. "The truth about the music..." ~ Daniels, Charlie. (2017). *Never Look at the Empty Seats: A Memoir.* New York: HarperCollins.
11. The man who would become... ~ Runtagh, Jordan. (2019, March 4). The unseen Freddie Mercury: Exploring the private man behind the Bohemian Rhapsody character. *People.*
12. "I didn't want to meet..." ~ Springsteen, Bruce. (2016). *Born to Run.* New York: Simon & Schuster.
13. "I would stab my mother..." ~ Strauss, Neil. (2011). *Everyone Loves You When You're Dead.* New York: HarperCollins.

CHAPTER 1: MOTIVATIONS FOR BECOMING A ROCK STAR

1. "I've been rich and I've..." ~ Hann, Michael. (2012 February 2). David Lee Roth: 'I've been rich and I've been poor. Rich is better.' *The Guardian.*
2. "I saw him on TV..." ~ Goldberg, Michael; Ressner, Jeffrey; & Pond, Steve [Compilers]. (1989, January 26). Tributes. *Rolling Stone.*
3. "We're a rock 'n' roll..." ~ Cummings, Sue. (1986, January). Asleep at the wheel. *Spin.*
4. "Every kid on every block..." ~ Tyler, Steven; & Dalton, David. (2012). *Does the Noise in My Head Bother You?* New York: HarperCollins.
5. "I didn't get into music..." ~ Fogerty, John. (2015). *Fortunate Song: My Life, My Music.* New York: Little, Brown and Company.
6. "As far back as I..." ~ Phantom, Slim Jim. (2016). *A Stray Cat Struts: My Life as a Rockabilly Rebel.* New York: Thomas Dunne Books.
7. "I was channeling even more..." ~ Stewart, Dave. (2016). *Sweet Dreams Are Made of This.* New York: New American Library.
8. "Since I was 14, my..." ~ Blake, Mark. (2017, April). The kick inside. *Q.*
9. "When I was a child..." ~ Hainey, Michael. (2019, Winter). Beneath the surface of Bruce Springsteen. *Esquire.*
10. "Somehow, even at the age..." ~ Ramone, Dee Dee. (2000). *Lobotomy: Surviving the Ramones.* Cambridge, MA: Da Capo Press.
11. "I had never thought of..." ~ Kiersh, Edward. (1986). *Where are You Now, Bo Diddley?* Garden City, NJ: Dolphin.
12. "Money is very important in..." ~ Lowell, Spencer. (2015, May 16). 'I'm probably the only guy in L.A. who never took coke.' *Billboard.*
13. "When we first decided to..." ~ Hughes, Rob. (2018, May). Anything you want. *Uncut.*
14. "I want the money just..." ~ Cleave, Maureen. (1963, March 4). How does a Beatle live?: John Lennon lives like this? *The (London) Evening Standard.*
15. "You can never have too..." ~ Ling. Dave. (2016, July). The gospel according to Gene Simmons. *Classic Rock.*

16. "I don't like to go..." ~ Oseary, Guy. (2004). *On the Record*. New York: Penguin.
17. "Hey! Come on you lazy..." ~ Atkins, Martyn (Director); & Pluta, James (Producer). (2014). *Mr. Blue Sky: The Story of Jeff Lynne & ELO* [DVD]. Eagle Rock.
18. "The idea of becoming a pop..." ~ Anka, Paul; & Dalton, David. (2013). *My Way: An Autobiography*. New York: St. Martin's Press.
19. "My husband and I thought..." ~ Levin, Angela. (2012, September 8). Exclusive interview: Freddie Mercury's mother on her 'dear boy.' *The Daily Telegraph*.
20. "You're wasting your time, listening..." ~ Cash, Johnny; & Carr, Patrick. (1997). *Cash: The Autobiography*. New York: Harper San Francisco.
21. "Good thing you're not..." ~ Hedegaard, Erik. (2018, February 8). The sound & the fury of Meat Loaf. *Rolling Stone*.
22. "The guitar's all right for..." ~ The Beatles. (2000). *Anthology*. San Francisco: Chronicle Books.
23. "You go do it, but..." ~ Harrison, George. (2002). *I, Me, Mine*. San Francisco: Chronicle Books.
24. "No! How could that happen?..." ~ Scaggs, Austin. (2007, October 4). Q&A: KT Tunstall. *Rolling Stone*.
25. "My mother thought I was..." ~ Flanagan, Bill. (1979, August). The Cars. *Trouser Press*.
26. "When the first check came..." ~ Shteamer, Hank. (2019, December). Ringo Starr & Dave Grohl. *Rolling Stone*.
27. "When I was in school..." ~ Cook, Richard. (2003). When does a dinosaur cut off its tail? A conversation with Neil Young. In Barney Hoskyns (Ed.), *The Sound and the Fury*. New York: Bloomsbury.
28. "I was told at school..." ~ "Hollywood star honour for Brighton rock drummer and Albion fan Steve Ferrone." (2014, February 3). *The Argus*.
29. "Popular music was looked down..." ~ Everly, Dave. (2019, May). Local hero. *Classic Rock*.
30. "I want to drop out..." ~ Grohl, Virginia Hanlon. (2017). *From Cradle to Stage*. Berkeley, CA: Seal Press.
31. "They were almost Buddhist in..." ~ Grohl, Virginia Hanlon. (2017). *From Cradle to Stage*. Berkeley, CA: Seal Press.
32. "I went to the factory..." ~ Woodmansey, Woody. (2016). *Spiders from Mars: My Life with Bowie*. New York: St. Martin's Press.
33. "I was still living in..." ~ Willman, Chris. (2014, June 8). Let's hear it for the boys. *Parade*.
34. "So it was funny because..." ~ Mason, Anthony. (2015, September 26). Bill Withers on Hall of Fame induction: "It's like a pre-obituary." *CBS This Morning*.
35. "I was driving a cab..." ~ Cohen, Scott. (1989, March). Kiss this. *Spin*.
36. "Buddy told us what the..." ~ DiMucci, Dion; & Aquilina, Mike. (2011). *Dion: The Wanderer Talks Truth*. Cincinnati: Servant Books.
37. "didn't go to the next..." ~ Weisner, Ron; & Goldsher, Alan. (2014). *Listen Out Loud*. Guilford, CT: Lyons Press.

CHAPTER 2: EARLY STRUGGLES
1. "It really came together after..." ~ Margolis, Lynne. (2013, February). John Fogerty: The bar room prophet looks back, & ahead. *American Songwriter*.
2. "The curtain opened and there..." ~ Catchpole, Chris. (2016, September). Cash for questions: ZZ Top. *Q*.
3. "Just seven people turned up..." ~ Bevan Bev. (1980). *The Electric Light Orchestra Story*. London: Mushroom Publishing Ltd.
4. "We play the Last Chance..." ~ Manna, Sal. (1981, February). Police get their bullets. *Trouser Press*.
5. "I didn't know they were..." ~ Nachman, Gerald. (2009). *Right Here on Our Stage Tonight!: Ed Sullivan's America*. Berkeley: University of California Press.
6. "The ZZ Top tour was..." ~ Oliver, Derek. (2012, Number 6). All you need is Loverboy. *Classic Rock Presents AOR*.
7. "We were in Kansas City; there..." ~ Wilson, Charlie. (2015). *I am Charlie Wilson*. New York: Atria.

CHAPTER 3: THE FIRST SUCCESS
1. "[I] remember doing an Elvis..." ~ Sheff, David; & Sheff, Victoria. (1982, May). The *Playboy* interview. *Playboy*.

2. "My prize was a transistor radio..." ~ Bono, Sonny. (1991). *And the Beat Goes On*. New York: Pocket Books.
3. "When I think about it..." ~ Tyler, Steven; & Dalton, David. (2012). *Does the Noise in My Head Bother You?* New York: HarperCollins.
4. "I was born to be..." ~ Bragg, Rick. (2014). *Jerry Lee Lewis: His Own Story*. New York: Harper.
5. "I used to say, 'Don't..." ~ The Beatles. (2000). *Anthology*. San Francisco: Chronicle Books.
6. "It was at summer camp..." ~ Kemp, Louie. (2019). *Dylan & Me: 51 Years of Adventures*. Los Angeles: Westrose Press.
7. "I remember saying it to..." ~ Anthony, Mason. (2014, May 25). Barry Gibb: Back on stage. *CBS Sunday Morning*.
8. "I went and saw this..." ~ Guerra, Tom. (2008, April). Runnin' down a dream: Mike Campbell. *Premier Guitar*.
9. "Los Angeles was a town..." ~ Pearcy, Stephen; & Benjamin, Sam. (2013). *Sex, Drugs, Ratt & Roll*. New York: Gallery.
10. "I remember one lady, Wanda..." ~ Wofford, Jerry. (2015, January 4). Garth Brooks' story of success follows him on comeback tour arriving in Tulsa. *Tulsa World*.
11. "He told me I'd need..." ~ Marshall, Max. (2018, June). Growing up with Steve Miller. *Texas Monthly*.
12. "When Carrie Underwood won Season..." ~ Yarborough, Chuck. (2018, December 8). Allie Collen shows she has 'it,' just like her famous dad, Garth Brooks. *The Cleveland Plain Dealer*.
13. "you learn the art of..." ~ Kessler, Ted (Ed.). *The 10 Commandments: In Their Own Words*. London: Corsair.
14. "I remember looking at them..." ~ Roberts, Randall. (2018, July 12). The art of de-evolution: Mark Mothersbaugh and Gerald Casale discuss two new books that celebrate punk band Devo's visual work. *The Los Angeles Times*.
15. "We had gone back to..." ~ Fricke, David. (2014, August 14). Tom Petty's rock & roll refuge. *Rolling Stone*.
16. "What a high: hearing one..." ~ Densmore, John. (1990). *Riders on the Storm: My Life with Jim Morrison and the Doors*. New York: Delacorte Press.
17. "Then the big moment came..." ~ Young, Neil. (2012). *Waging Heavy Peace: A Hippie Dream*. New York: Blue Ridge Press.
18. "I can't tell you how ..." ~ Zimmerman, Lee. (2103, November). Where are they now? *Goldmine*.
19. "I was wondering who they'd..." ~ Meat Loaf; & Dalton, David. (1999). *To Hell and Back*. New York: ReganBooks.
20. "When 'Lookin' After Number One'"... ~ Fallon, Andy. (2011, February). The *Mojo* interview: Bob Geldof. *Mojo*.
21. "Sleeping in my car and..." ~ Oseary, Guy. (2004). *On the Record*. New York: Penguin.
22. "When I taped the *Primetime*..." ~ Aiken, Clay. (2004). *Learning to Sing: Hearing the Music in Your Life*. New York: Random House.

CHAPTER 4: EARLY MONEY

1. "In the beginning, when we..." ~ Hedegaard, Erik. (2017, June 1). The last hair metal band. *Rolling Stone*.
2. "It was weird how it..." ~ Sullivan, Mary Lou. (2010). *Raisin' Cain: The Wild and Raucous Story of Johnny Winter*. New York: Backbeat Books.
3. "We played a lot of..." ~ Valentine, Gary. (2006). Touched by your presence. In *Punk: The Whole Story*. London: DK.
4. "Like lots of bands, we..." ~ Tyler, Steven; & Dalton, David. (2012). *Does the Noise in My Head Bother You?* New York: HarperCollins.
5. "Most of the liaisons with..." ~ Crosby, David; & Gottlieb, Carl. (1988). *Long Time Gone: The Autobiography of David Crosby*. New York: Doubleday.
6. "somebody from a record company..." ~ Ellefson, David. (1997). *Making Music Your Business: A Guide for Young Musicians*. San Francisco: Miller Freeman.
7. "When my mom used to..." ~ Hagar, Sammy; & Selvin, Joel. (2011). *Red: My Uncensored Life in Rock*. New York: HarperCollins.
8. "We went hungry a lot..." ~ White, Timothy. (1978, November). Looking back in anger. *Crawdaddy!*

9. "I'd never seen an indoor..." ~ Marshall, Ben. (2011, February). Ben Marshall meets... Jack Bruce. *Uncut*.

10. "I grew up in an..." ~ Fricke, David. (2016, June 2). Q&A: Eric Clapton. *Rolling Stone*.

11. "Going to the grocery store..." ~ Benatar, Pat; & Cox, Patsi Bale. (2010). *Between a Heart and a Rock Place*. New York: William Morrow.

12. "I had a shirt, one..." ~ Osbourne, Sharon; Osbourne, Ozzy; & Gold, Todd. (2003). *Ordinary People: Our Story*. New York: MTV Books / Pocket Books.

13. "Everything I'd ever wanted as..." ~ Osbourne, Ozzy; & Ayres, Chris. (2010). *I am Ozzy*. New York: Grand Central Publishing.

14. "I remember the cold. It..." ~ Jones, Quincy. (2001). *Q: The Autobiography of Quincy Jones*. New York: Doubleday.

15. "I've always coped extremely well... " ~ Sky, Rick. (1994). *The Show Must Go On: The Life of Freddie Mercury*. New York: Citadel.

16. "I really enjoy my money..." ~ Anders, Marcel. (2014, August). Partying: Elton John. *Classic Rock*.

17. "A 1965 baby blue Mustang..." ~ Cohen, Scott. (1994). *Yakety Yak*. New York: Fireside.

18. "We started off 1976 on..." ~ Wilde, Jon. (2006, March). Masters of the universe. *Uncut*.

19. "I used to work on..." ~ Iley, Chrissy. (2016, June 25). Billy Joel talks about his three divorces and the woman who saved him. *The Daily Mail*.

20. "I do think I approached..." ~ Phillips, Michelle. (1986). *California Dreamin'*. New York: Warner Books.

21. "For every Bono, who married..." ~ Hepworth, David. (2011, April). And another thing. *Word*.

22. "When the money started coming..." ~ Greenwald, Matthew. (2002). *Go Where You Wanna Go: The Oral History of the Mamas & the Papas*. New York: Cooper Square Press.

23. "I'd never seen anybody spend..." ~ Greenwald, Matthew. (2002). *Go Where You Wanna Go: The Oral History of the Mamas & the Papas*. New York: Cooper Square Press.

24. "I remember Nick [Rhodes] and..." ~ Odell, Michael. (2003, November 15). In their own words. *The Observer*.

25. "Bro, I was spending money..." ~ Hedegaard, Erik. (1997, October 30). The X-rated redemption of Mark Wahlberg. *Rolling Stone*.

26. "I had a forty-one-foot..." ~ Crosby, David; & Gottlieb, Carl. (1988). *Long Time Gone: The Autobiography of David Crosby*. New York: Doubleday.

27. "Steinman ordered the whole menu..." ~ Blackwood, Nina; Goodman, Mark; Hunter, Alan; Quinn, Martha; & Edwards, Gavin. (2013). *VJ: The Unplugged Adventures of MTV's First Wave*. New York: Atria.

28. "On a hot, lazy Las..." ~ Brown, Stacy. (2014, June 8). Michael Jackson's kids get $8M a year allowance. *The New York Post*.

29. "There's a stack of children's..." ~ Richardson, Terry. (2015, January 15). The vampire of the Hollywood Hills. *Rolling Stone*.

30. "When you first get your..." ~ Clarke, Alan. (2008, October). The *Spin* interview. *Spin*.

31. "I am embarrassed to admit..." ~ Cash, John Carter. (1987). *From the Heart*. New York: Prentice Hall.

32. "Watching the other artists on..." ~ Berry, Chuck. (1988). *The Autobiography*. New York: Fireside.

33. "I go around and turn..." ~ Wilson, Scott. (2005, April/May). On the record: A conversation with... Moby. *Magnet*.

34. "Don't buy stupid things like..." ~ Oseary, Guy. (2004). *On the Record*. New York: Penguin.

35. "I'm not very materially minded..." ~ Sweeting, Adam. (1987, July). The Cure. *Spin*.

36. "I don't need a big..." ~ Deevoy, Adrian. (2018, August 5). Still super-hip (and all lip) at 66, The Pretenders' Chrissie Hynde tells *Event* why she swears at fans, enrages sex abuse victims... and has swapped the wild life for walks in the park. *Event Magazine*.

37. "Rod doesn't carry money, doesn't..." ~ Naughton, John. (2010, June). 99% true: Rod Stewart. *Word*.

38. "You know what doesn't feel..." ~ Doyle, Tom. (2006. November). Paul McCartney: Beatle. *Q*.

39. "In the beginning of Zeppelin..." ~ Tolinski, Brad. (2006, February). Jimmy Page graces *Guitar World*. *Guitar World*.

40. "Elvis did not... become rich..." ~ Williamson, Joel. (2014). *Elvis Presley: A Southern Life*. New York: Oxford University Press.

CHAPTER 5: MUSICIANS AS BUSINESSMEN

1. "owing six figures in advance..." ~ Clooney, Rosemary; & Barthel, Joan. (1999). *Girl Singer: An Autobiography*. New York: Doubleday.
2. "A particular melodramatic moment..." ~ Pruter, Robert. (1991, November 1). Jackie Wilson: The most tragic figure in rhythm 'n' blues. *Goldmine*.
3. "Our lives turned upside down..." ~ Sterling, Bill. (2005, February 16). Rock Hall of Famer brings message to Shore. *Eastern Shore News*.
4. "They were paying us less..." ~ Garden, Joe. (1997, July). Mark Mothersbaugh. *The Onion*.
5. "and his managers tried to..." ~ Knight, Gladys. (1997). *Between Each Line of Pain and Glory: My Life Story*. New York: Hyperion.
6. "The exact words I remember..." ~ Cohen, Elliot Stephen. (2010, June). Not fade away. *Record Collector*.
7. "We thought we'd get rich..." ~ Wederhorn, Jon; & Turman, Katherine. (2013). *Louder Than Hell*. New York: itbooks.
8. "Sam owed me millions. He..." ~ Young, Charles M. (2006, October 19). The Killer reloaded. *Rolling Stone*.
9. "This is all supposition, but..." ~ Bahadur, Raj. (1984, February 23). Joey Molland: A true rock 'n' roll survivor. *(Cleveland) Scene*.
10. "We used to go in.." ~ Wiederhorn, Jon. (1995, March). The royalty scam. *Rolling Stone*.
11. "The company I was with..." ~ Pollock, Bruce. (1981). *When Rock was Young*. New York: Holt, Rinehart and Winston.
12. "In those days you never..." ~ Ritz, David. (2002). *Faith in Time: The Life of Jimmy Scott*. Cambridge, MA: Da Capo.
13. "When I started to ask..." ~ DeYoung, Bill. (2001, April 18). Bo Diddley: He's a M-A-N! *Goldmine*.
14. "It was indentured servitude, and..." ~ Sylvester, Bruce. (2006, August). Words and music of Don McLean. *Discoveries*.
15. "Artists are very vulnerable. They'll..." ~ Sylvester, Bruce. (2006, August). Words and music of Don McLean. *Discoveries*.
16. "'Trust Me' and 'just sign..." ~ McLagan, Ian "Mac." (2000). *All the Rage*. New York: Billboard.
17. "We signed a contract with..." ~ Fogerty, John. (2015). *Fortunate Song: My Life, My Music*. New York: Little, Brown and Company.
18. "We sat in Saul Zaentz's..." ~ Cavanagh, David. (2012, February). Bad blood rising. *Uncut*.
19. "We earned millions and millions..." ~ Lennon, John; & Ono, Yoko. (2018). *Imagine John Yoko*. New York: Grand Central Publishing.
20. "The essence of what he..." ~ Loewenstein, Prince Rubert. (2013). *A Prince Among Stones*. New York: Bloomsbury.
21. "They belonged to one of..." ~ Selvin, Joel. (2016). *Altamont: the Rolling Stones, the Hells Angels, and the Inside Story of Rock's Darkest Day*. New York: Dey Street Books.
22. "I own my own publishing..." ~ Ellefson, David. (1997). *Making Music Your Business: A Guide for Young Musicians*. San Francisco: Miller Freeman.
23. "One of the paragraphs stated.." ~ Shaw, Suzy; & Farren, Mick. (2007). *Bomp!: Saving the World One Record at a Time*. San Francisco: Ammo.
24. "We got all dressed up..." ~ Brown, James; & Tucker, Bruce. (1986). *James Brown: The Godfather of Soul*. New York: Macmillan.
25. "the practice of buying or..." ~ Clooney, Rosemary; & Barthel, Joan. (1999). *Girl Singer: An Autobiography*. New York: Doubleday.
26. "Aware of their rising status..." ~ DeMain, Bill. (2005, November). 100 years of payola. *Performing Songwriter*.
27. "a man said to me, 'If..." ~ "Now Don't Cry." (1959, December 7). *Time*.
28. "The going prices for air..." ~ "Pop records: Moguls, money & monsters." (1973, February 12). *Time*.
29. "It was number one on..." ~ Scott, Barry. (1994). *We Had Joy, We Had Fun*. Boston: Faber and Faber.

CHAPTER 6: DEVELOPING YOUR STAGE PRESENCE AND PUBLIC PERSONA

1. "I've always thought it would..." ~ Mathews, Garret. (2001). *They Came to Play: Stories from the Early Days of Rock*. Tampa: McGregor Publishing.
2. "I like some of the.." ~ White, Timothy. (1986, September). Gabriel. *Spin*.

3. "Today record companies don't even..." ~ Friedman, Bayta; & Lyons, Steve. (1986, November). Revolt against mediocrity. *The Progressive*.

4. "It is really quite important..." ~ Gabriel, Francis; & Baker Masand, Stacy. (2014). *The Rockstar Remedy*. New York: Harper Wave.

5. "I like to sit in..." ~ Berlin, Joey. (1996). *Toxic Fame: Celebrities Speak on Stardom*. Detroit: Visible Ink.

6. "Glenn [Frey] was always two..." ~ Heaton, Michael. (2013, July 7). Clevelander spent years flying with the Eagles. *The Cleveland Plain Dealer*.

7. "I was hanging out a..." ~ Mora, Anthony. (1980, July). Two faces has Alice: Or maybe three. *Trouser Press*.

8. "Sometimes I need to be reminded ..." ~ Jones, Allan. (2016). *Can't Stand Up For Falling Down: Rock 'n' Roll War Stories*. London: Bloomsbury.

9. "By 1973 the character Bowie..." ~ Sandford, Christopher. (1997). *Bowie: Loving the Alien*. Cambridge: Da Capo Press.

10. "wouldn't leave me alone for..." ~ Sandford, Christopher. (1997). *Bowie: Loving the Alien*. Cambridge: Da Capo Press.

11. "Eventually, the door opened and.." ~ Hilburn, Robert. (2009). *Corn flakes with John Lennon and Other Tales from a Rock 'n' Roll Life*. New York: Rodale.

12. "I'd walk out of my..." ~ Osbourne, Ozzy; & Ayres, Chris. (2010). *I am Ozzy*. New York: Grand Central Publishing.

13. "Ronnie Gilbert, one of the..." ~ Dylan, Bob, (2004). *Chronicles: Volume One*. New York: Simon & Schuster.

14. "A little like Pink Floyd..." ~ Watts, Peter. (2017, June). Take the long way home. *Uncut*.

15. "It was during 1977 that..." ~ Wilde, Jon. (2006, March). Masters of the universe. *Uncut*.

16. At concerts that averaged $8... ~ Lendt, C.K. (1997). *Kiss and Sell*. New York: Billboard Books.

17. From 1977 to 1979 alone... ~ Lendt, C.K. (1997). *Kiss and Sell*. New York: Billboard Books.

18. "Our licensing and merchandising dwarfs..." ~ Ryan, Patrick. (2017, September 12). Kiss' Gene Simmons to unveil 150 unreleased songs in career-spanning box set. *USA Today*.

19. "I saw an opportunity there..." ~ Cohen, Scott. (1986, November). Cry for love. *Spin*.

20. "Some people – you're born, you..." ~ Bob Dylan interview. (2004, December 5). *60 Minutes* (CBS).

21. "were born out of necessity. When..." ~ Weingarten, Marc. (2000). *Station to Station: The History of Rock 'n' Roll on Television*. New York: Pocket Books.

22. "You saw the scruffiness, the..." ~ Williams, Alex. (2016, November 9). How the Rolling Stones became fashion icons. *The New York Times*.

23. "When I used to go..." ~ Leaf, David; & Sharp, Ken. (2003). *Kiss: Behind the Mask*. New York: Warner Books.

24. "Our signature thrift-store style..." ~ Doe, John; & Tom DeSavia. (2019). *More Fun in the New World*. New York: De Capo Press.

25. "Why would anyone have stage..." ~ Frank, Josh; & Ganz, Caryn. (2006). *Fool the World: The Oral History of a Band Called Pixies*. New York: St. Martin's Griffin.

26. "I was in the center..." ~ Martinaug, Douglas. (2014, August 1). Manny Roth, 94, impresario of Cafe Wha?, is dead. *The New York Times*.

27. "Initially I was a drummer..." ~ Marks, Craig. (2012, April). Q&A: Soundgarden frontman Chris Cornell. *Details*.

28. "I took a guitar to..." ~ Diehl, Kenneth. (2009, April). As the mutton-chopped brains behind Motörhead, Lemmy has always rocked – and lived – by the credo "Everything louder than everything else." *Spin*.

29. "I had been noticing something..." ~ Greene, Bob. (2008). *When We Get to Surf City*. New York: St. Martin's Press.

30. "I remember walking through Dearborn..." ~ Anders, Marcel. (2017, December). Q&A: Robert Plant. *Classic Rock*.

31. "We loved dressing up and..." ~ Phantom, Slim Jim. (2016). *A Stray Cat Struts: My Life as a Rockabilly Rebel*. New York: Thomas Dunne Books.

CHAPTER 7: CRITICS VS. ROCKERS

1. "power and access came from..." ~ Cameron, Sue. (2018). *Hollywood Secrets and Scandals*. Albany, GA: BearManor Media.
2. "When I arrived at *The...*" ~ Almond, Steve. (2010). *Rock and Roll Will Save Your Life*. New York: Random House.
3. "I saw rock and roll..." ~ Landau, Jon. (1974, May 22). Growing young with rock and roll. *The Real Paper*.
4. "the poor quality of the..." ~ Landau, Jon. (1967, November 9). *Are You Experienced?*, the Jimi Hendrix Experience. *Rolling Stone*.
5. "The Beatles are not merely..." ~ Buckley, William F., Jr. (1968, August 24). How I discovered that rock is here to tay. *The Saturday Evening Post*.
6. "With their bizarre shrubbery, the..." ~ Schneider, Cary. (2014, February 9). What the critics wrote about the Beatles in 1964. *The Los Angeles Times*.
7. "The Beatles' vocal quality can..." ~ Strongin, Theodore. (1964, February 10). *The New York Times*.
8. "Remember this: An interview is..." ~ Heldenfels, Rich. (2015, October 8). The HeldenFiles: Chrissie Hynde, Nicki Minaj and difficult interviews. *The Akron Beacon Journal*.
9. "They get brutal. They (the..." ~ Liben, Michael P. (1979, February). Tom Petty – Heartbreaker at home & a broad. *New Wave Rock*.
10. "We sometimes felt incapable of..." ~ Redding, Noel; & Appleby, Carol. (1996). *Are You Experienced?* New York: Da Capo Press.
11. "Very few artists have done..." ~ Robertson, Robbie. (2016). *Testimony*. New York: Crown Archetype.
12. "The rhythm section is sloppy..." ~ Henke, Jim. (1981, June 11). Queen holds court in South America. *Rolling Stone*.
13. "No one mentions that, although..." ~ Francis, Connie. (1984). *Who's Sorry Now*. New York: St. Martin's Press.
14. "I do albums and, like..." ~ Fricke, David. (2016, August 25). Paul McCartney: The *Rolling Stone* interview. *Rolling Stone*.
15. "The things that hurt the..." ~ Jonze, Tim. (2017, March 25). John Lydon: 'Without punk I would have probably become a drug dealer.' *The Guardian*.
16. "He wanted no unnecessary people..." ~ German, Bill. (2009). *Under TheirThumb*. New York: Villiard.
17. "there should be no questions..." ~ Catlin, Roger. (2016, September 15). What's new, Tom Jones? The hitmaker is still finding more things to sing about. *The Washington Post*.
18. "It's been a long time..." ~ Jones, Allan. (2016). *Can't Stand Up For Falling Down: Rock 'n' Roll War Stories*. London: Bloomsbury.
19. "My only beef, one that..." ~ Hunter, Ian. (1996). *Diary of a Rock 'n' Roll Star*. Shropshire, UK: Independent Music Press.
20. "*The Sun* [newspaper] in England..." ~ Berlin, Joey. (1996). *Toxic Fame: Celebrities Speak on Stardom*. Detroit: Visible Ink.
21. "When 'Bat' came out there..." ~ La Rose, Lauren. (2016, May 16). Meat Loaf reminisces about 'Bat Out of Hell.' *The Hamilton Spectator*.
22. "The level of hostility was..." ~ Cowan, Andy. (2013, December). Rock 'n' roll confidential. *Mojo*.
23. "Billy Joel isn't talking. Anthony..." ~ Yarborough, Chuck. (2017, June 18). When stars snub the press, they snub the fans. *The Cleveland Plain Dealer*.
24. "Mystique is the greatest thing..." ~ Doyle, Patrick. (2019, December). Elton John & Lana Del Rey. *Rolling Stone*.
25. "threats and assaults by rappers..." ~ Williams, Monte. (1998, December 22). Irate rappers give journalists a combat beat; music press is a target of violence and threats. *The New York Times*.
26. "[It] takes night vision one..." ~ "Last word: Steven Tyler." (2014, June). *Q*.
27. "Britney drives like a rabbit..." ~ Gross, Michael Joseph. (2008, March). Road to ruin. *Blender*.
28. "There we were walking along..." ~ Cameron, Sue. (2018). *Hollywood Secrets and Scandals*. Albany, GA: BearManor Media.

CHAPTER 8: BAND POLITICS

1. "George [Harrison] came up to..." ~ Farndale, Nigel. (2015, May 24). Art Garfunkel on Paul Simon: 'I created a monster.' *The Telegraph*.
2. "If you've ever been..." ~ Furay, Richie; & Roberts, Michael. (2006). *Pickin' Up the Pieces*. Colorado Springs, CO: WaterBrook Press.
3. "Pete [Townshend] describes us as..." ~ Daltrey, Roger. (2018). *Thanks a Lot, Mr. Kibblewhite: My Story*. New York: Henry Holt and Company.
4. "I don't want to name..." ~ Greene, Andy. (2017, January 12). Petty's 'last big one?' *Rolling Stone*.
5. "A band can only be..." ~ Cohen, Scott. (1987, September). Treading Waters. *Spin*.
6. "I think it's important to..." ~ Sliwicki, Susan. (2013, Fall). Everything you ever wanted to know about the Beatles (but didn't know where to look). *Goldmine*.
7. "I would rather eat my..." ~ Morley, Paul. (2006, May). The last temptation of Morrissey. *Uncut*.
8. "We went into RCA studio..." ~ Mehr, Bob. (2013, June). John Fogerty: The *Mojo* interview. *Mojo*.
9. "They were crazy. They'd be..." ~ Fredericks, Bob. (2016, August 30). Talking Heads drummer relives the early days of CBGB, the Ramones and rise of punk rock. *The New York Post*.
10. "I'm going to kick your..." ~ Felder, Don. (2008). *Heaven and Hell: My Life in the Eagles (1974-2001)*. Hoboken, NJ: John Wiley & Sons.
11. "As the night progressed, we..." ~ Felder, Don. (2008). *Heaven and Hell: My Life in the Eagles (1974-2001)*. Hoboken, NJ: John Wiley & Sons.
12. "You never knew what to..." ~ Young, Neil. (2012). *Waging Heavy Peace: A Hippie Dream*. New York: Blue Ridge Press.
13. "I strongly request that I..." ~ Martens, Todd; & Roberts, Randall. (2012, April 12). Axl Rose says no to Rock Hall. *The Los Angeles Times*.
14. "expected to see more ego..." ~ "It all started with a phone call from Harry Belafonte.... to.... Ken Kragen." (1985, April 6). *Billboard*.
15. "You had five guys with..." ~ Heaton, Michael. (2013, July 7). Clevelander spent years flying with the Eagles. *The Cleveland Plain Dealer*.
16. "screamed at, beaten up, drugged..." ~ French, John "Drumbo." (2013). Dartford, England: Proper Music Publishing.
17. "We all drank, don't get me..." ~ Hann, Michael. (2018, August 8). "We had this inner demon of pop wanting to come out." *The Guardian*.
18. "For a split second, no..." ~ Ribowsky Mark. (2010). *Ain't Too Proud to Beg*. Hoboken, NJ: John Wiley & Sons.
19. "It's the one defining moment..." ~ Greene, Andy. (2010, January). The last word: Steven Van Zandt on the death of rock and the biggest mistake he ever made. *Rolling Stone*.
20. "Despite all the positivity, we..." ~ Downing, K.K.; & Eglington, Mark. (2018). Heavy Duty: Days and Nights in Judas Priest. New York: Da Capo.
21. "I agreed because I was..." ~ Nash, Jesse. (1989, November). Roy Orbison. *Music Express*.
22. "Some of the artists were..." ~ Graham, Bill; & Greenfield, Robert. (1992). *Bill Graham Presents: My Life Inside Rock and Out*. Boston: Da Capo Press.
23. "We are like night and..." ~ Diehl, Matt. (2010, April 22). It's a Joni Mitchell concert, sans Joni. *The Los Angeles Times*.
24. "[sleeping with] their whole bands..." ~ Diehl, Matt. (2010, April 22). It's a Joni Mitchell concert, sans Joni. *The Los Angeles Times*.

CHAPTER 9: THE RELATIONSHIP BETWEEN FANS AND MUSICIANS

1. "You are purposely trying to..." ~ Caulfield, Philip. (2012, June 26). Kenny Chesney fan booted from country star's 'Brothers of the Sun' show for looking too much like Kenny Chesney. *The New York Daily News*.
2. "Once Justin shot to fame..." ~ Monde, Chiderah. (2013, October 20). Justin Bieber fanatic undergoes plastic surgery to look like pop star. *The New York Daily News*.
3. "I'm a great Glasgow Celtic..." ~ Halpern, Jake. (2007). *Fame Junkies: The Hidden Truths Behind America's Favorite Addiction*. Boston: Houghton Mifflin Company.
4. "Rainbow waves of tie-dye..." ~ Barbieri, Susan M. (1991, April 8). Living for the Dead: The Grateful Dead's followers aren't just fans anymore – they qualify as a subculture. *The Orlando Sentinel*.
5. "He was riding an escalator..." ~ Winans, Bebe. (2012). *The Whitney I Knew*. Brentwood, TN: Worthy.

6. "The public property thing can..." ~ Powell, Fiona Russell. (1984, February). Duran Duran: Simon Le Bon. *The Face.*

7. "I've met a lot of..." ~ Pareles, Jon. (1992, April 8). At lunch with Marky Mark; The high priest of hot and now. *The New York Times.*

8. "Sometimes I say, 'I don't...'" ~ Dunn, Jancee. (April 20, 1995). Belly: Crowning moment. *Rolling Stone.*

9. "I'm sick of all these..." ~ Wenner, Jann S. (2000). *Lennon Remembers.* New York: Rolling Stone Press.

10. "I was never more in..." ~ Richards, Keith; & Fox, James. (2010). *Life.* New York: Little, Brown and Company.

11. "We had come down in..." ~ Niesel, Jeff. (2018, September 12). Still Monkeeing around. *[Cleveland] Scene.*

12. "The local police formed a..." ~ Yates, Henry. (2010, August). Ever meet Hendrix? *Classic Rock.*

13. "toured New Zealand and Australia..." ~ Aronowitz, Alfred G. (2014, February). From the archive: Beatles invasion. *The Saturday Evening Post.*

14. "Arriving for Ed Sullivan, we..." ~ Wright, James "Tappy;" & Weinberg, Rod. (2010). *Rock Roadie.* New York: Thomas Dunne Books.

15. "I would say that I've..." ~ Klosterman, Chuck. (2005). *Killing Yourself to Live.* New York: Scribner.

16. "I would feel embarrassed charging..." ~ Hiatt, Brian. (2005, August 11). *Rolling Stone.*

17. "What they do in terms..." ~ Lindquist, David. (2002, February 17). American dreamers. *The Indianapolis Star.*

18. "I always say to my..." ~ Kot, Greg. (2002, April 10). McCartney on the record about ticket prices, drugs and Harrison. *The Chicago Tribune.*

19. "People in the industry don't..." ~ Peisner, David. (2007, June). Kicks for free. *Spin.*

20. "The Stones played for two..." ~ Peisner, David. (2007, June). Kicks for free. *Spin.*

21. "or you could've paid $3,250..." ~ Knopper, Steve. (2014, June 5). Are VIPs ruining festivals? *Rolling Stone.*

22. "Joining an artist's online fan..." ~ Greene, Andy. (2007, April 19). The new fan club ticket scam. *Rolling Stone.*

23. "Buying really good tickets to..." ~ Dyer, Bob. Passing up the Stones concert. *The Akron Beacon Journal.*

24. "Fan clubs often don't even..." ~ Greene, Andy. (2007, April 19). The new fan club ticket scam. *Rolling Stone.*

25. "The first time somebody asked..." ~ Eliscu, Jenny. (2008, October 30). Elvis Costello & the attraction. *Rolling Stone.*

26. "I would stand by the..." ~ Reynolds, Debbie; & Columbia, David Patrick. (1988). New York: *Debbie: My Life.*

27. "I get used to it. 'It's...'" ~ Hutton, Jack, (2011). I'm dreading old age. *Uncut: Ultimate Music Guide.*

28. "Over the years, I've become..." ~ Knight, Gladys. (1997). *Between Each Line of Pain and Glory: My Life Story.* New York: Hyperion.

29. In his best year, he... ~ Costa, Brian. (2013, May 30). 4,256 hits, millions in autographs. *The Wall Street Journal.*

30. "Now when I arrive at..." ~ Young, Neil. (2012). *Waging Heavy Peace: A Hippie Dream.* New York: Blue Ridge Press.

31. "The real reward for me..." ~ Wright, Gary. (2014). *Dream Weaver.* New York: Penguin.

32. "One thing I've noticed is..." ~ Schlager, Ken. (2006, March 18). Henke on curating: Serious, fun and filled with spirit. *Billboard.*

33. "Eventually one of our crew..." ~ Benatar, Pat; & Cox, Patsi Bale. (2010). *Between a Heart and a Rock Place.* New York: William Morrow.

34. "The hardest part of the..." ~ Ant, Adam. (2006). *Stand & Deliver: The Autobiography.* London: Sidgwick & Jackson.

35. "[People] would steal my garbage..." ~ Goldberg, Michael. (1986, January 16). Back on the road. *Rolling Stone.*

36. "They go through your rubbish..." ~ Sawyer, Miranda. (2003, October 19). The Pet Shop Boys' Commandments. *The Observer.*

37. "After a good half-hour..." ~ Dreifus, Claudia. (1971, March 4). Bob Dylan in the Alley: The Alan J. Weberman Story. *Rolling Stone.*

CHAPTER 10: THE FAME AND THE POWER OF ROCK STARDOM

1. "Picture this. You wake up..." ~ Norment, Lynn. (1999, May). Whitney Houston talks about the men in her life – and the rumors, lies and insults that are the high price of fame. *Ebony*.

2. "30,000 screaming, waving New Yorkers..." ~ Cook, Fred J. (1962). *Entertaining the World: P.T. Barnum*. Chicago: Encyclopedia Britannica Press.

3. "the first blockbuster recording artist..." ~ Midgette, Anne. (2003, November 20). Caruso's tenor, a century later; memorabilia shown at the Metropolitan honors a legend. *The New York Times*.

4. "A lot of people who..." ~ Doyle, Patrick. (2019, July). Q&A: Jack White. *Rolling Stone*.

5. "I did want to be..." ~ Odell, Michael. (2009, February). The girl can't help it. *Spin*.

6. "We were in Detroit, playing..." ~ Fricke, David. (1994, January 27). Our man in Nirvana rages on (and on) about stardom, fatherhood, his feud with Pearl Jam, the death of grunge and why he's never been happier in his life. *Rolling Stone*.

7. "They're looking at you all..." ~ Hall, Russell. (2012, March/April). Q&A: Counting Crows. *Music & Musicians*.

8. "[I] can't get enough of..." ~ Jones, Tom. (2015). *Over the Top and Back: The Autobiography*. New York: Blue Rider Press.

9. "Elvis was not comfortable with..." ~ Orlando, Tony; & Cox, Patsi Bale. (2002). *Halfway to Paradise*. New York: St. Martin's Press.

10. "Adulation in particular sets you..." ~ Redding, Noel; & Appleby, Carol. (1996). *Are You Experienced?* New York: Da Capo.

11. "The first time I spoke..." ~ Klosterman, Chuck. (2001). *Fargo Rock City: A Heavy Metal Odyssey in Rural North Dakota*. New York: Scribner.

12. "Dick Clark was almost like..." ~ DiMucci, Dion; & Aquilina, Mike. (2011). *Dion: The Wanderer Talks Truth*. Cincinnati: Servant Books.

13. "Dave is not a rock..." ~ Zlozower, Neil. (2004, May). New world order. *Guitar World*.

14. "He had always been, as..." ~ Monk, Noel E.; & Layden, Joe. (2017). *Runnin' with the Devil*. New York: HarperCollins.

15. "I could be unbelievably horrible..." ~ Boshoff, Alison. (2004, October 6). What *is* wrong with Elton John? *The Daily Mail*.

16. "The sky was the limit..." ~ Escovedo, Sheila; & Holden, Wendy. (2014). *The Beat of My Own Drum*. New York: Atria.

17. "She would demand that people..." ~ Hoffmann, Bill. (1999, September 23). A flashback to her bad old diva days. *The New York Post*.

18. "When bands have a lead..." ~ Majewski, Lori; & Bernstein, Jonathan. (2015, February/March). Bow Wow Wow: Naked ambition. *Classic Pop*.

19. "In the '60s, he was..." ~ Ryan, Patrick. (2017, November 10). David Bowie: New HBO documentary gives an intimate look at icon's 'Last Five Years.' *USA Today*.

20. "Fame itself, of course, doesn't..." ~ DeMain Bill. (2011, May). David Bowie, one of the most consistently great British songwriters of all time, explains his creative process, and tells us why time and place matter. *Classic Rock*.

21. "was No. 1 every week..." ~ Kashner, Sam. (2007, Fall). Fever pitch. *Wired* supplement: *Movies Rock*.

22. "I have wrestled with a..." ~ Danton, Eric R. (2011, December). Q&A: The Fray. *Music & Musicians*.

23. "Somebody had made a transfusion..." ~ Sheff, David. (2000) *All We Are Saying: The Last Major Interview with John Lennon and Yoko Ono*. New York: St. Martin's Griffin.

24. "Imagine living like this. You..." ~ Ian, Janis. (2008). *Society's Child: My Autobiography*. New York: Jeremy P. Tarcher / Penguin.

25. "People are always trying to..." ~ Rowland, Mark. (1988, December). Guns N' Roses are outlaws, and everyone has Guns N' Roses. *Musician*.

26. "Being a rock star doesn't..." ~ Daniels, Charlie. (2007). *Growing Up Country*. New York: Flying Dolphin Books.

27. "Even in the nineties, when..." ~ Hendrickson, Matt. (2011, November). Q&A: Noel Gallagher. *Details*.

28. "The 51-year-old singer..." ~ Lawless, Jill. (2012, October 21). Susan Boyle's fairy tale dream tempered by reality. *The Philadelphia Inquirer*.

29. "In the Nineties, I started..." ~ Wenner, Jann S. (2005, September 3). Bono: The *Rolling Stone* interview. *Rolling Stone*.

30. Iggy [Pop] once said that..." ~ Scapelliti, Christopher. (2004, May). The house that Jack built. *Guitar World*.

31. I'm walking through the doors..." ~ Jones, Allan. (2016). *Can't Stand Up For Falling Down: Rock 'n' Roll War Stories*. London: Bloomsbury.

32. "The impact that Bob Dylan..." ~ Royko, Mike. (1982). *Sez Who? Sez Me*. New York: E.P. Dutton.

33. "I believe that my music..." ~ Dalton, David. (1970, May 28). Little Richard: Child of God. *Rolling Stone*.

34. "He wasn't God, but he..." ~ Jackson, LaToya. (2009, September 11). Interview on *20-20*. ABC.

35. "It was as if a..." ~ Aronowitz, Alfred G. (2014, February). From the archive: Beatles invasion. *The Saturday Evening Post*.

36. "Crippled people were constantly being..." ~ The Beatles. (2000). *Anthology*. San Francisco: Chronicle.

37. "Everywhere the Beatles turned, they..." ~ Brown, Peter; & Gaines, Steven. (1983). *The Love You Make: An Insider's Story of the Beatles*. New York: Macmillan.

38. "In Australia, a woman threw..." ~ Stark, Steven D. (2005). *Meet the Beatles*. New York: HarperEntertainment.

39. "We were only trying to..." ~ The Beatles. (2000). *Anthology*. San Francisco: Chronicle.

40. "I'm not claiming divinity. I've..." ~ Cott, Jonathan. (2010, December 23). The last interview. *Rolling Stone*.

41. "You know, for so long..." ~ Price, Mark J. (2014, September 15). Local history: Silver Lake girl had fab time meeting Beatles in 1964. *The Akron Beacon Journal*.

42. "Music is a real magic..." ~ Block, Melissa. (2014, August 4). Tom Petty on cheap speakers and George Harrison. *All Things Considered*. Philadelphia: NPR.

43. "There's an unwritten rule in..." ~ Connolly, Ray. (2018). *Being John Lennon: A Restless Life*. New York: Pegasus.

CHAPTER 11: ROCK STARS & PRIVACY

1. "On the back patio of..." ~ Pappademas, Alex. (2018, September 5). Steve Perry walked away from Journey. A promise finally ended his silence. *The New York Times*.

2. "the last place" that he... ~ Higginbotham, Adam. (2008, March). Ringo Starr. *Blender*.

3. "[Elvis] achieved the material riches..." ~ McKeen, William. (2007, August). What we talk about: We talk about Elvis. *American History*.

4. "You wouldn't see Elvis in..." ~ Anka, Paul; & Dalton, David. (2013). *My Way: An Autobiography*. New York: St. Martin's Press.

5. "At Graceland, he spent most..." ~ Connelly, Sherryl. (2014). Elvis Presley's fiancee Ginger Alden details the King's bad temper, secluded Graceland life, and luxurious gifts in new memoir. *The New York Post*.

6. "Sometimes you're in the gym..." ~ Greene, Andy. (2016, April 7). The last word: Steven Tyler. *Rolling Stone*.

7. "George grew tired of fame..." ~ Scott, Ken; & Owsinski, Bobby. (2012). *Abbey Road to Ziggy Stardust*. Los Angeles: Alfred Music Publishing.

8. "George once said that fame..." ~ Wilde, Jon. (2004, July). McCartney: My life in the shadow of the Beatles. *Uncut*.

9. "the last place' he 'visited'..." ~ Higginbotham, Adam. (2008, March). Ringo Starr. *Blender*,

10. "I see these hungry eyes..." ~ Lennon, John; & Ono, Yoko. (2018). *Imagine John Yoko*. New York: Grand Central Publishing.

11. "I just felt really sorry..." ~ Fricke, David. (1994, January 27). Our man in Nirvana rages on (and on) about stardom, fatherhood, his feud with Pearl Jam, the death of grunge and why he's never been happier in his life. *Rolling Stone*.

12. "Would I have liked to..." ~ Cole, Paul. (2014, March 13). ELO legend Jeff Lynne: I would not have liked being in The Beatles. *The Birmingham Mail*.

13. "I guess there are certain..." ~ Elliott, Paul. (2015, Summer). Heavy load. *Classic Rock*.

14. "I was well aware of..." ~ Cash, Johnny. (1975). *Man in Black*. New York: Warner Books.

15. "Everyone you work with, buy..." ~ Tyler, Steven; & Dalton, David. (2012). *Does the Noise in My Head Bother You?* New York: HarperCollins.

16. "I felt so bad for..." ~ Earls, John. (2015, October/November). Paper cuts. *Classic Pop*.

17. "In four months, I went..." ~ Kandell, Steve. (2010, September). All we got is his photograph. *Spin*.

18. "I noticed one older man..." ~ Ian, Janis. (2008). *Society's Child: My Autobiography*. New York: Jeremy P. Tarcher / Penguin.
19. "When we arrived at one..." ~ Duswalt, Craig. (2014). *Welcome to My Jungle*. Dallas: BenBella Books.
20. John Lennon complained that he... ~ John Lennon and Yoko Ono interview. (1971, September 11). *The Dick Cavett Show* (ABC).
21. "The minute we walked in..." ~ Simmons, Sylvie. (2009, September). The real slowhand. *Mojo*.
22. "No one bothers me. It's..." ~ Aydlette, Larry. (2017, May 15). Jimmy Buffett concert: Why he never gets recognized in Palm Beach. *The Palm Beach Post*.
23. "There were no photographs of..." ~ "Remembering the 'Passed.'" (2012, May). *Goldmine*.
24. "George Strait has discovered that..." ~ Sanneh, Kelefa. (2017, July 24). George Strait's long ride. *The New Yorker*.
25. "If I go to a..." ~ Markin, Carole. (1990). *Bad Dates*. New York: Citadel.
26. "I was waiting for the..." ~ Cross, Craig. (2006). *The Beatles: Day-by-Day, Song-by-Song, Record-by-Record*. Bloomington, IN: iUniverse.
27. "'I'm a singer, sir,' I..." ~ Francis, Connie. (1984). *Who's Sorry Now*. New York: St. Martin's Press.
28. Similarly, after playing a sold-out... ~ Hauff, Natalie Caula. (2014, June 6). No ID? No entry to Nashville bar for country super star Darius Rucker. *The Charleston Post and Courier*.
29. "The craziest it ever got..." ~ Cher; & Coplon, Jeff. (1998). *The First Time*. New York: Simon & Schuster.

CHAPTER 12: BAD AND ILLEGAL BEHAVIOR EXCUSED

1. "If you were in a..." ~ Uhelszki, Jaan. (2020, February). "I enjoyed every trip I had." *Uncut*.
2. "That song changed my relationship..." ~ Hagar, Sammy; & Selvin, Joel. (2011). *Red: My Uncensored Life in Rock*. New York: HarperCollins.
3. "Steven would come in with..." ~ Aerosmith; & Davis, Stephen. (1997). *Walk This Way: The Autobiography of Aerosmith*. New York: Avon Books.
4. "There are rules in life..." ~ Francis, Connie. (1984). *Who's Sorry Now*. New York: St. Martin's Press.
5. "It was my normal thing..." ~ Clapton, Eric. (2007). *Clapton: The Autobiography*. New York: Broadway.
6. "I was out of control..." ~ Meat Loaf; & Dalton, David. (1999). *To Hell and Back*. New York: ReganBooks.
7. "would get red carpet treatment..." ~ Cavanagh, David. (2011, March). House of the unholy. *Uncut*.
8. "Most evenings ended with us..." ~ Blake, Mark. (2014, March). Cash for questions: Prog wizard Rick Wakeman on Bowie, his dinner with Lennon and breaking poppadoms with his penis. *Q*.
9. "I don't have a lot..." ~ Grierson, Tim. (2007, December). Dear superstar: Simon LeBon. *Blender*.
10. "When stuff is going well..." ~ "10 questions for Yannis Philipakis." (2017, August). *Q*.
11. "The most important lesson I've..." ~ Stevens, Shakin'. (2018, no. 52). Who are ya? *Vive Le Rock*.
12. "The days of being a..." ~ Greene, Andy. (2016, October 6). Q&A: Matt Healy of the 1975. *Rolling Stone*.
13. "[Nike had] seen that we..." ~ Marsh, Dave. (1981, July). Tom Petty. *Musician*.
14. "I'll tell you how much..." ~ Davis, Stephen. (1985). *Hammer of the Gods*. London: Sidgwick & Jackson.
15. "That night we went into..." ~ Boyd, Pattie; & Junor, Penny. (2007). *Wonderful Tonight: George Harrison, Eric Clapton, and Me*. New York: Harmony.
16. "If you go out without..." ~ Mason, Nick. (2005). *Inside Out: A Personal History of Pink Floyd*. San Francisco: Chronicle Books.
17. "We didn't have any tickets..." ~ Thomson, Graeme. (2015). *George Harrison: Behind the Locked Door*. New York: Overlook Omnibus.
18. "The national promoters of the..." ~ "Jacksons want a free ride to play Philadelphia." (1984, June 30). *The Akron Beacon Journal*.
19. "I have never said, 'Do..." ~ Kessler, Ted (Ed.). *The 10 Commandments: In Their Own Words*. London: Corsair.
20. "It was very nice of..." ~ Scapelliti, Christopher. (2004, May). The house that Jack built. *Guitar World*.
21. "poked a hole in it..." ~ Rivera, Zayda. (2013, March 26). Jared Leto reveals fan once sent him an ear in the mail. *The New York Daily News*.

252

CHAPTER 13: THE SPECIAL FANS: THE GROUPIES

1. "a term coined by Bill.." ~ Wyman, Bill. (1997). *Stone Alone: The Story of a Rock 'n' Roll Band.* Cambridge, MA: Da Capo Press.
2. "It was interesting how playing..." ~ Hell, Richard. (2013). *I Dreamed I Was a Very Clean Tramp.* New York: Ecco.
3. "It seemed like women fell..." ~ Bragg, Rick. (2014). *Jerry Lee Lewis: His Own Story.* New York: Harper.
4. "Back in the day, I..." ~ Pearcy, Stephen; & Benjamin, Sam. (2013). *Sex, Drugs, Ratt & Roll.* New York: Gallery.
5. "Right away, I could tell..." ~ Simon, Carly. (2015). *Boys in the Trees: A Memoir.* New York: Flatiron.
6. "Even after our first album..." ~ Osbourne, Ozzy; & Ayres, Chris. (2010). *I am Ozzy.* New York: Grand Central Publishing.
7. "One time I was on..." ~ Jones, Amy. (2018, May 21). 'I wasn't led astray.' *The Sun.*
8. "We were sitting in the..." ~ Sounes, Howard. (2001). *Down the Highway: The Life of Bob Dylan.* New York: Grove Press.
9. "It seemed like the tour-bus..." ~ Knight, Gladys. (1997). *Between Each Line of Pain and Glory: My Life Story.* New York: Hyperion.
10. "I had it down to..." ~ Farndale, Nigel. (2015, May 23). Art Garfunkel on Paul Simon: 'I created a monster.' *The Telegraph.*
11. "I have male fans. I..." ~ Wexler, Erica Bettina. (1986, January). Tuesday's child. *Spin.*
12. "[We were] very cloistered.... Christine..." ~ Lennon, Christine. (2011, May). Stevie Nicks: Wild at heart. *Harper's Bizarre.*
13. "That house was like the..." ~ Williamson, Nigel. (2003, May). Fleetwood Mac: 'Everybody was pretty weirded out' – the story of Rumours. *Uncut.*
14. "It doesn't work like that..." ~ Deevoy, Adrian. (2018, August 5). Still super-hip (and all lip) at 66, The Pretenders' Chrissie Hynde tells Event why she swears at fans, enrages sex abuse victims... and has swapped the wild life for walks in the park. *Event Magazine.*
15. "As a young, attractive member..." ~ Monk, Noel E.; & Layden, Joe. (2017). *Runnin' with the Devil.* New York: HarperCollins.
16. "Why would any rock star..." ~ Deevoy, Adrian. (2018, May 19). Look who's back... Yes, it's rock legend Roger Daltrey talking 'bout... his open marriage, his life-threatening illness and why – at 74 – he's definitely NOT going to f-f-fade away. *Event Magazine.*
17. "Imagine three or four girls..." ~ Sears, Neil. (2012, September 28). What I did was insane. *The Daily Mail.*
18. "out of the corner of..." ~ Wright, James "Tappy;" & Weinberg, Rod. (2010). *Rock Roadie.* New York: Thomas Dunne Books.
19. "I, for one, had overdosed..." ~ Redding, Noel; & Appleby, Carol. (1996). *Are You Experienced?* New York: Da Capo Press.
20. "My take on groupies had..." ~ Townshend, Pete. (2012). *Who I Am.* New York: HarperCollins.
21. "Groupies were fun, especially at..." ~ Mora, Anthony. (1980, July). Two faces has Alice: Or maybe three. *Trouser Press.*
22. "Those girls seemed, after a..." ~ Bevan Bev. (1980). *The Electric Light Orchestra Story.* London: Mushroom Publishing Ltd.
23. "Some of the girls were..." ~ DiLorenzo, Kris. (1978, February). Syd Barrett: Careening through life. *Trouser Press.*
24. "Some guys in bands still..." ~ Kapranos, Alex. (2018, May). 10 commandments: Alex Kapranis. *Q.*
25. "You're always getting people trying..." ~ Spurrier, Jeff. (1985, July). A private conversation with General Public. *Spin.*
26. "As we became famous, people..." ~ Redding, Noel; & Appleby, Carol. (1996). *Are You Experienced?* Da Capo: New York.
27. "Avoid people who just want..." ~ Oseary, Guy. (2004). *On the Record.* New York: Penguin.
28. "He had about a hundred..." ~ Sounes, Howard. (2001). *Down the Highway: The Life of Bob Dylan.* New York: Grove Press.
29. "I have never surrounded myself..." ~ di Perna, Alan. (1999, April). Tom Petty: American boy. *Pulse.*
30. "We talked about music and..." ~ Williams, Andy. (2009). *Moon River and Me.* New York: Viking.
31. "A lot of times it..." ~ Phillips, Michelle. (1986). *California Dreamin'.* New York: Warner Books.

32. "had all of these people..." ~ Dollar, Steve. (2017, April 15). Inside the unauthorized Whitney Houston doc that her estate tried to shut down. *Billboard.*
33. "If you're not famous, you..." ~ Johnston, Jenny. (2011, April 18). Fame stole his sanity: So why is Adam Ant risking everything for one last moment in the spotlight? *The Daily Mail.*
34. "She told me that the..." ~ Ant, Adam. (2006). *Stand & Deliver: The Autobiography.* London: Sidgwick & Jackson.
35. "According to Michael, 'Billy Jean'..." ~ Howe, Rupert. (2009, August). Freak out! *Q.*
36. "obsessed with ABBA in general..." ~ Hoffmann, Bill. (2000, April 16). ABBA pop queen lives in terror of fan from hell. *The New York Post.*
37. "The way he was harassing..." ~ Dunn, Jancee. (April 20, 1995). Belly: Crowning moment. *Rolling Stone.*

CHAPTER 14: HOMELIFE: FAMILY AND FRIENDS OF ROCK STARS

1. "If you're a musician I..." ~ Carr, Roy. (2011). We really didn't care about anybody. *Uncut: Ultimate Music Guide.*
2. "You've got to always remember..." ~ Balfour, Victoria. (1986). *Rock Wives.* New York: Beech Tree Books.
3. "After being on the road..." ~ Leaf, David; & Sharp, Ken. (2003). *Kiss: Behind the Mask.* New York: Warner Books.
4. "For each step that you ..." ~ Runtagh, Jordan. (2019, March 4). The unseen Freddie Mercury: Exploring the private man behind the Bohemian Rhapsody character. *People.*
5. "Leaving [home] was the worst..." ~ Langley, William. (2015, May 23). Why Shirley Bassey is horrified by today's pop stars. *The Telegraph.*
6. "One day in 1960, they..." ~ Edmonds, Ben. (2016, No. 8). Marvin Isley. *Mojo.*
7. "we got a check from..." ~ Nash, Graham. (2013), *Wild Tales: A Rock & Roll Life.* New York: Crown Archetype.
8. "I say to him, 'Well..." ~ Jones, Tom. (2015). *Over the Top and Back: The Autobiography.* New York: Blue Rider Press.
9. "As my success increased, life..." ~ Thomas, B.J.; & Thomas, Gloria. (1983). *In Tune: Finding How Good Life Can Be.* Old Tappan, NJ: Fleming H. Revell Company.
10. "I gave a lot of my..." ~ Das, Lina. (2015, August 14). Sex, drugs and lots of Monkee business! As they prepare to play in the UK, Peter Tork and Micky Dolenz admit they weren't as innocent as they looked. *The Daily Mail.*
11. "All of a sudden, in..." ~ Hilburn, Robert. (2018). *Paul Simon: The Life.* New York: Simon & Schuster.
12. "Toby, you just don't know..." ~ Thompson, Toby. (2008). *Positively Main Street* (Rev. ed.). Minneapolis: University of Minnesota.
13. "My mother was a nice..." ~ The Beatles. (2000). *Anthology.* San Francisco: Chronicle.
14. "It was just a feeling..." ~ Holt, Georgia; Quinn, Phyllis; & Russell, Sue. (1988). *Star Mothers.* New York: Simon & Schuster.
15. "I suppose part of my..." ~ McKenna, Kristine. (1980, February 7). The Police: Making New Wave safe for America. *Rolling Stone.*
16. "She found it hard to..." ~ Duerden, Nick. (2015, September 6). Aimee Osbourne interview: How reality TV changed her family, and why she's finally ready to launch her own music career. *The Independent.*
17. "The first thing I did..." ~ Osbourne, Sharon; & Dening, Penelope. (2005). *Extreme: My Autobiography.* New York: Springboard Press.
18. "People are fascinated by me..." ~ Brown, Laura. (2008, March). High School Musical starring Frances Bean Cobain: Kurt and Courtney's daughter is ready to hit the spotlight. *Harper's Bazaar.*
19. "My father was always surrounded..." ~ Phillips, Mackenzie; & Liftin, Hilary. (2009). *High on Arrival.* New York: Simon Spotlight Entertainment.
20. "While I believe that marriage..." ~ Elliott, Paul. (2014, August). Mick Jones: The Foreigner man knows what love is. *Classic Rock.*
21. "By far the hardest things..." ~ Daniels, Charlie. (2017). *Never Look at the Empty Seats: A Memoir.* New York: HarperCollins.

22. "My family acknowledges I'm sort..." ~ Goldberg, Michael. (1986, January 16). Back on the road. *Rolling Stone.*
23. "I wouldn't see dad in..." ~ Rees, Paul. (2017, December). The not so quiet one. *Classic Rock.*
24. "People said, 'How could you..." ~ Jordan, Julie. (2015, April 20). Garth Brooks: Why I chose family over fame. *People.*
25. "I don't anticipate making any..." ~ Sellers, John. (2010, September). Tough questions for Phil Collins. *Spin.*
26. "When I was going to..." ~ Fricke, David. (1998, June 11. The *Rolling Stone* interview: Sean Lennon. *Rolling Stone.*
27. "In my situation, people are..." ~ Mehr, Bob. (2012, May 13). Lisa Marie Presley at peace with her music legacy. *The (Memphis) Commercial Appeal.*
28. "What am I going to..." ~ Fricke, David. (2014, May 22). Out of the shadow. *Rolling Stone.*
29. "When I was at school..." ~ Odell, Michael. (2019, May 7). What life is like when your dad's Rod Stewart. *The Times of London.*
30. "It spooked me, really. It..." ~ Boucher, Geoff. (2006, December 31). Happily not retired. *The Los Angeles Times.*
31. "found it strange that although..." ~ Lennon, Cynthia. (2005). *John.* New York: Three Rivers Press.
32. "The hardest part of our..." ~ Carlisle, Belinda. (2010). *Lips Unsealed.* New York: Crown.
33. "As soon as he walked..." ~ Thompson, Toby. (2008). *Positively Main Street* (Rev. ed.). Minneapolis: University of Minnesota.
34. "I had a very cool..." ~ Patterson, Sylvia. (2013, February). Cash for questions: Marianne Faithfull. *Q.*
35. "During our lovemaking, I caught..." ~ Lipton, Peggy; Dalton, David; & Dalton, Coco. (2005). *Breathing Out.* New York: St. Martin's Press.
36. "To date somebody in the..." ~ Dyer, Bob. (2013, February 23). Springsteen's former girlfriend was student at KSU. *The Akron Beacon Journal.*
37. "There was one guy in... ~ Lee, Tommy. (2005). *Tommyland.* New York: Simon & Schuster.
38. "I've gotten more attention from..." ~ Doyle, Patrick. (2015, October 8). Q&A: Ed Sheeran. *Rolling Stone.*
39. "I am flypaper for damaged..." ~ Richardson, Terry. (2015, January 15). The vampire of the Hollywood Hills. *Rolling Stone.*
40. "Every woman I've ever had..." ~ Allman, Gregg; & Light, Alan. (2012). *My Cross to Bear.* New York: William Morrow.
41. "Meeting new people, especially women..." ~ Ant, Adam. (2006). *Stand & Deliver: The Autobiography.* London: Sidgwick & Jackson.
42. "Like, I'm gonna go to..." ~ Yuan, Jada. (2013, June 17). Stevie Nicks, the fairy godmother of rock. *New York Magazine.*
43. "Hi! My name is Stevie..." ~ Yuan, Jada. (2013, June 17). Stevie Nicks, the fairy godmother of rock. *New York Magazine.*
44. "When I was younger, I'd..." ~ Collen, Phil; & Epting, Chris. (2019). *Adrenalized: Life, Def Leppard, and Beyond.* New York: Atria Books.
45. "I used to hear them..." ~ Norman, Philip. (2012, September 28). I thought Mick and I would be together for ever. *The Daily Mail.*
46. "People are just interested in..." ~ Goldman, Andrew. (2013, May 26). Billy Joel on not working and not giving up drinking. *The New York Times.*
47. "Rock stars like them because..." ~ Cohen, Scott; & Start, Annette. (1985, October). Models & rockstars. *Spin.*
48. "Models go out with them..." ~ Cohen, Scott; & Start, Annette. (1985, October). Models & rockstars. *Spin.*
49. "I didn't choose to, you..." ~ "Interview with Madonna." (2001, January 12). *20/20.* ABC television network.
50. "I've received some nasty 'fan'..." ~ Springfield, Rick. (2010). *Late, Late at Night.* New York: Touchstone.
51. "stated that she and Jim..." ~ Butler, Patricia. (1998). *Angels Dance and Angels Die.* New York: Simon & Schuster.
52. "I was still a secret..." ~ Lennon, Cynthia. (2005). *John.* New York: Three Rivers Press.
53. "Someone asked me recently whether.." ~ Lennon, Cynthia. (2005). *John.* New York: Three Rivers Press.

54. "I had reporters waiting for..." ~ Heatley, Michael. (2010). *The Girl in the Song*. Chicago: Chicago Press Review.

55. "For the next couple of..." ~ Womack, Kenneth. (2018). *Sound Pictures: The Life of Beatles Producer George Martin (The Later Years: 1966-2016)*. Leominster, England: Orphans Publishing.

56. "I find the concept of..." ~ "Taylor Swift interviews rock 'n' roll icon Pattie Boyd on songwriting, Beatlemania, & the power of being a muse." (2018, August). *Harper's Bazaar*.

57. "We were very happy for..." ~ Williamson, Nigel. (2003, May). Fleetwood Mac: 'Everybody was pretty weirded out' – the story of Rumours. *Uncut*.

CHAPTER 15: THE MIND OF A ROCK AND ROLL

1. "I think some people are..." ~ Shteamer, Hank. (2019, December). Ringo Starr & Dave Grohl. *Rolling Stone*.

2. "Without a doubt, I'd be..." ~ Furnish, David. (1996, July). Rock's Bach. *Interview*.

3. "She was just another one..." ~ Everley, Dave. (2018, December). California Dreaming. *Classic Rock*.

4. "I felt like such a..." ~ Solomon, Deborah. (2006, April 16). Girls just want to sing Weill. *The New York Times*.

5. "There were two place we..." ~ Willman, Chris. (2010, August). The secret history of Devo. *Spin*.

6. "behaviors and attitudes that include..." ~ Ettensohn, Mark. (2016). *Unmasking Narcissism: A Guide to Understanding the Narcissist in Your Life*. Berkeley, CA: Athea Press.

7. "Jim often went to great..." ~ Butler, Patricia. (1998). *Angels Dance and Angels Die*. New York: Simon & Schuster.

8. "The reason I got into..." ~ Gilmore, Mikal. (1988, June 16). Can Terence Trent D'Arby be as good as he thinks he is. *Rolling Stone*.

9. "Musically, we are more talented..." ~ Cocks, Jay. (1990, March 5). Music: Two scoops of Vanilli. *Time*.

10. "Let's be honest, there's only..." ~ Tonge, David. (2018, August). A perfect storm? *Mojo*.

11. "If it was 1965, and..." ~ Strauss, Neil. (1996, February). Beat the Beatles. *Spin*.

12. "Some great artists are extreme..." ~ Karshner, Roger. (1971). *The Music Machine*. Los Angeles: Nash Publishing.

13. "What most corrupted the life..." ~ Boteach, Rabbi Shmuley. (2009). *The Michael Jackson Tapes*. New York: Vanguard.

14. "Drugs hurt him, but the..." ~ Kiersh, Edward. (1985, December). Sly Stone's heart of darkness. *Spin*.

15. "So, I'm a recovered ego..." ~ Mayer, John, (2015, March 6). Interview with Ronan Farrow. *The Today Show* (NBC).

16. "Very little has been written..." ~ Wenner, Jann S. (2005, September 3). Bono: The *Rolling Stone* interview. *Rolling Stone*.

17. "In this business, mental health..." ~ Johnston, Jenny. (2011, April 18). Fame stole his sanity. So why is Adam Ant risking everything for one last moment in the spotlight? *The Daily Mail*.

18. Clinical psychologist Lara Honos-Webb... ~ Honos-Webb, Lara. (2016 April 15). ADHD and the rock star gene. PsychologyToday.com.

19. "I always chose rock stars..." ~ Buell, Bebe; & Bockris, Victor. (2001). *Rebel Heart: An American Rock 'n' Roll Journey*. New York: St. Martin's Press.

20. "The only requirement is that..." ~ Abram, Malcom X. (2015, April 22). Todd Rundgren refuses to atrophy with Sunday's show at Hard Rock Rocksino. *The Akron Beacon Journal*.

21. "If you listen to the..." ~ Edwards, Natalie. (2013, April 23). *The Voice* judge tells of his battle with ADHA. *The Mirror*.

22. "I have come close enough..." ~ Hainey, Michael. (2019, Winter). Beneath the surface of Bruce Springsteen. *Esquire*.

23. "When he was in his..." ~ Gillmore, Mikal. (2016, April 21). The curse of the Ramones. *Rolling Stone*.

24. "People who join a band..." ~ Ramone, Dee Dee; & Kofman, Veronica. (2000). *Lobotomy: Surviving the Ramones*. New York: Thunder's Mouth Press.

25. "What I can say is..." ~ Richardson, Terry. (2015, January 15). The Vampire of the Hollywood Hills. *Rolling Stone*.

26. "describes his life as 'hermit-like..." ~ Tonge, David. (2018, August). A perfect storm? *Mojo*.

27. "I began to notice that..." ~ Lady Gaga. (2018, November 8). Speech at the SAG-AFTRA Foundation's Patron of the Artists Awards.

28. "The Who's perpetual-motion machine..." ~ Jones, Dylan. (2018, July). Roger Daltrey: 'Keith Moon lived his entire life as a fantasy.' *GQ*.
29. "Keith lived his entire life..." ~ Jones, Dylan. (2018, July). Roger Daltrey: 'Keith Moon lived his entire life as a fantasy.' *GQ*.
30. "When you die on stage..." ~ Pfeiffer, Bob. (1987, February 6). Night of the living Dead Boys. *The Washington Post*.
31. "[Sid] loved to approach these..." ~ Lydon, John; Zimmerman, Keith; & Zimmerman, Kent. (1994). *Rotten: No Irish, No Blacks, No Dogs*. London: Hodder and Stoughton.
32. "Phil was, as advertised, completely..." ~ Weisner, Ron; & Goldsher, Alan. (2014). *Listen Out Loud*. Guilford, CT: Lyons Press.
33. "Even when the music business..." ~ Lennon, John; & Ono, Yoko. (2018). *Imagine John Yoko*. New York: Grand Central Publishing.
34. "Years ago when I started..." ~ Browne, David. (2019, December). David Byrne & Tierra Whack. *Rolling Stone*.
35. "I had a really rough..." ~ White, Timothy. (1994, November 19). Farewell to a good day in hell. *Billboard*.
36. "In the middle of a..." ~ Manson, Shirley. (2018, July 3). Shirley Manson: The first time I cut myself. *The New York Times*.
37. "There's a side of me..." ~ Irwin, Colin. (1987, June). Glory days. *Spin*.
38. "It might surprise people to..." ~ Blake, Mark. (2012, December). The *Mojo* interview. *Mojo*.
39. "There were at least two..." ~ Wyman, Bill; & Coleman, Ray. (1997). *Stone Alone: The Story of a Rock 'n' Roll Band*. New York: DaCapo Press.
40. "Could you please make sure..." ~ Sutherland, Mark. (2013, December). Nirvana: MTV Unplugged 20 years on. *Q*.
41. "I can understand why Cobain..." ~ Hilburn, Robert. (2013). *Johnny Cash: The Life*. New York: Little, Brown and Company.
42. "Many celebrities who work hard..." ~ Strauss, Neil. (2011). *Everyone Loves You When You're Dead*. New York: HarperCollins.

CHAPTER 16: THE ROCK CONCERT

1. "During that show, I also..." ~ Kane, Larry. (2003). *Ticket to Ride: Inside the Beatles' 1964 Tour That Changed the World*. Philadelphia: Running Press.
2. "Almost from the first notes of..." ~ Faithfull, Marianne; & Dalton, David. (2000). *Faithfull*. New York: Cooper Square Press.
3. "A concert is not a live..." ~ Weeks, Isaac. (2018, November 5). Wrangler's 'Bohemian Rhapsody' collection puts Queen lyrics on jeans, jackets & shirts. *Billboard*.
4. "I always imagined when you're..." ~ Ellen, Mark. (2010, July). Britpop was a singing ship: Louise Wener was 'in steerage without a lifeboat.' *The Word*.
5. "If you're not getting some..." ~ Wolfe, Alexandra. (2016, April 15). Tom Petty won't back down. *The Wall Street Journal*.
6. "I have an instinct for..." ~ Daltrey, Roger. (2018). *Thanks a Lot, Mr. Kibblewhite: My Story*. New York: Henry Holt and Company.
7. "Throughout my two or three..." ~ Fogerty, John. (2015). *Fortunate Song: My Life, My Music*. New York: Little, Brown and Company.
8. "When people started singing along..." ~ Yates, Henry. (2015, December). Queen: *Classic Rock's* Living Legends 2015. *Classic Rock*.
9. "When I go onstage and..." ~ Wenner, Jann S. (2005, September 3). Bono: The *Rolling Stone* interview. *Rolling Stone*.
10. "In the early days the..." ~ Loewenstein, Prince Rubert. (2013). *A Prince Among Stones*. New York: Bloomsbury.
11. "We didn't have roadies back..." ~ Dickerson, Deke, (2009, January). Scotty Moore. *Guitar Player*.
12. "I enjoy the tension and..." ~ Robinson, Richard. (1980, November). Blondie's Clem Burke breathes to the beat. *Hit Parader*.
13. "Elvis was like a panther..." ~ McPherson, Douglas. (2019, September-October). The King's Schilling. *Vintage Rock*.

14. "There is that unique moment..." ~ Mansfield, Ken; & Stoker, Brent. (2007). *The White Book*. Nashville: Thomas Nelson.
15. "That's a real twilight zone..." ~ DeYoung, Bill. (1984 July 20). Stan Lynch, the homebody Heartbreaker. *The Gainesville Sun*.
16. "The energy of the crowd..." ~ Petty, Tom. (2006, August). What I've learned. *Esquire*.
17. "How could you replace the..." ~ Berlin, Joey. (1996). *Toxic Fame: Celebrities Speak on Stardom*. Detroit: Visible Ink.
18. "I have never been concerned..." ~ Gallucci, Michael. (2011, April 6). The idiot diaries. *Scene*.
19. "I have a feeling that..." ~ Willman, Chris. (2010, September-October). The great wide open. *M Music & Musicians*.
20. "The only reason I didn't..." ~ Ganz, Caryn. (2016, August 10). Sir Paul on fans, the Beatles and himself. *The New York Times*.
21. "I've probably sung "Fun, Fun..." ~ Hedegaard, Erik. (2016, February 25). Mike Love's cosmic journey. *Rolling Stone*.
22. "I've sung ['Roxanne'] on most..." ~ Sting. (2007). *Lyrics by Sting*. New York: Dial Press.
23. "If I get tired of.." ~ Phillips, Beau. (2014). *I Killed Pink Floyd's Pig*. Seattle: Peanut Butter Publishing.
24. Despite the pain and a... ~ Dougherty, Steve. (2014 July 24). James Brown and the making of "Get on Up." *The Wall Street Journal*.
25. "My body gave out before..." ~ Johnston, Jenny. (2011, April 18). Fame stole his sanity: So why is Adam Ant risking everything for one last moment in the spotlight? *The Daily Mail*.
26. "I honestly don't know how..." ~ Wederhorn, Jon; & Turman, Katherine. (2013). *Louder Than Hell*. New York: itbooks.
27. "I remember the night before..." ~ Hann, Michael. (2018, August 8). "We had this inner demon of pop wanting to come out." *The Guardian*.
28. "For the first time in..." ~ Wild, David. (1991, August 8). Over the hump. *Rolling Stone*.
29. "I used to be more..." ~ Pond, Steve. (1989, January 26). Roy Orbison: 1936-1988. *Rolling Stone*.
30. "The thing that really made..." ~ Petrusich, Amanda. (2011, January). Artist of the year: The Black Keys. *Spin*.
31. "I had an anxiety attack..." ~ Giles, Kayleigh. (2018, August 11). James' pain: James Arthur suffers anxiety attack on stage in front of 12,000 people as he admits he thought he was going to die. *The Sun*.
32. "I used to have to ..." ~ "Tim McGraw." (2014, June 8). *Oprah's Master Class* (OWN).
33. "Times had changed, and this..." ~ Meat Loaf; & Dalton, David. (1999). *To Hell and Back*. New York: HarperCollins.
34. "He was persistent, and irritating..." ~ Townshend, Pete. (2012). *Who I Am*. New York: HarperCollins.
35. "In Texas, someone threw a..." ~ Sheffield, Rob. (2008, October). INXS: Need you tonight. *Blender*.
36. "As I approached the heckler's..." ~ Adams, Ryan. (2017, February 9). The first time I was rattled by a heckler. *The New York Times*.
37. "One of the wildest shows..." ~ Barrow, Tony. (2005) *John, Paul, George, Ringo & Me*. London: Andre Deutsch.
38. "some rockers spend an estimated..." ~ Ressner, Jeffrey. (1989, April 6). Stand by me: Inside the world of rock & roll bodyguards. *Rolling Stone*.
39. "I study the audience on..." ~ Francis, Michael. (2003). *Star Man: The Right Hand of Rock 'n' Roll*. London: Simon & Schuster.
40. "I have a real heavy..." ~ Marsh, Dave. (1981, July). Tom Petty. *Musician*.
41. "I've noticed that I can't..." ~ Rensin, David. (1982, September). 20 questions: Tom Petty. *Playboy*.
42. "I have years of experience..." ~ Jones, Tom. (2015). *Over the Top and Back: The Autobiography*. New York: Blue Rider Press.
43. "I was knocked out, and..." ~ Muendel, Jeff. (2007, April). Heaven and hell. *Maximum Ink*.
44. "one minute I'm playing and..." ~ Leaf, David; & Sharp, Ken. (2003). *Kiss: Behind the Mask*. New York: Warner Books.
45. "The front of my 1964..." ~ Doe, John. (2016). *Under the Big Black Sun: A Personal History of Punk*. Boston: Da Capo Press.
46. "When you're on stage, the..." ~ Brown, James; & Tucker, Bruce. (1986). *James Brown: The Godfather of Soul*. New York: Macmillan.

47. "The fans used to get..." ~ Melnick, Monte A.; & Meyer, Frank. (2003). *On the Road with the Ramones*. New York: MJF Books.

48. "You've got to make them..." ~ Farley, Robert. (2005, September 25). Mary and Jim to the end. *The St. Petersburg Times*.

49. "It just doesn't seem relevant..." ~ Gunderson, Edna. (1989, September 29). Bob Dylan offers 'Mercy' to a new generation of fans. *The San Bernardino County Sun*.

50. "There was always a bottle..." ~ Aerosmith; & Davis, Stephen. (1997). *Walk This Way: The Autobiography of Aerosmith*. New York: Avon Books.

51. "At one point in the..." ~ Ramone, Johnny. (2012). Commando: *The Autobiography of Johnny Ramone*. New York: Abrams.

52. "police blocked the bus from..." ~ Fayerman, Pamela. (1993, November 2). Promoter tears strip off naked rocker. *The Vancouver Sun*.

53. "As overworked as it sounds..." ~ Manna, Sal. (1981, February). Police get their bullets. *Trouser Press*.

54. "American crowds make the most..." ~ Pratt, Guy. (2012, April). Crowd control. *The Word*.

55. "I was moved by the..." ~ Slichter, Jacob. (2004). *So You Wanna Be a Rock & Roll Star*. Broadway Books: New York.

56. "It wasn't until we hit..." ~ Black, Johnny. (2013, June). Uriah Heep help end the Cold War. *Classic Rock*.

57. "The last note of the..." ~ Elliott, Paul. (2012, Summer). Heavy load. *Classic Rock*.

CHAPTER 17: LIFE ON THE ROAD

1. "With stardom, someone else dealt..." ~ Densmore, John. (1990). *Riders on the Storm: My Life With Jim Morrison and the Doors*. New York: Delacorte Press.

2. "Altogether we must have had..." ~ Bowen, Jimmy; & Jerome, Jim. (1997). *Rough Mix*. New York: Simon & Schuster.

3. "We had four people, needed..." ~ Manna, Sal. (1981, February). Police get their bullets. *Trouser Press*.

4. "We had been driving for..." ~ Melnick, Monte A.; & Meyer, Frank. (2003). *On the Road with the Ramones*. New York: MJF Books.

5. "I loved Led Zeppelin, because..." ~ Heaton, Michael. (2013, November 1). Famed hotel owner Jim Swingos takes a long look back on the glory days. *The Cleveland Plain Dealer*.

6. "If you've been on a..." ~ Barton, Laura. (2005, August 20). Misfits that fit. *The Guardian*.

7. "Zeppelin have got the top..." ~ Cavanagh, David. (2011, March). House of the unholy. *Uncut*.

8. "I remember seeing them in..." ~ Idol, Billy. *Dancing with Myself*. New York. Touchstone.

9. "Every city I go to..." ~ Lewis, John. (2008, August). An audience with... Alice Cooper. *Uncut*.

10. "The Stones might have been..." ~ Robinson, Lisa. (2014). *There Goes Gravity*. New York: Riverhead Books.

11. "Part of the beauty – and..." ~ Monk, Noel E.; & Layden, Joe. (2017). *Runnin' with the Devil*. New York: HarperCollins.

12. "demands gave ranged from warm..." ~ Harrington, Richard. (1980, September 20). Bands' demands are stranger than fiction. *The Sarasota Herald-Tribune*.

13. "There were constant caterer freak-outs..." ~ Aerosmith; & Davis, Stephen. (1997). *Walk this Way: The Autobiography of Aerosmith*. New York: Avon Books.

14. "the promoter... find the ten..." ~ Osbourne, Sharon; & Dening, Penelope. (2005). *Extreme: My Autobiography*. New York: Springboard Press.

15. "The intent of this portion..." ~ Monk, Noel E.; & Layden, Joe. (2017). *Runnin' with the Devil*. New York: HarperCollins.

16. "I haven't really seen one..." ~ Harris, Stacy. (1978, July). Willie Nelson: On picnics and things. *Country Music Roundup*.

17. "It's funny. When we did..." ~ Moody, Paul. (2011, April). A round with Ray Davies. *Q*.

18. "We've cut it down so..." ~ Waddell, Ray. (2005, August 13). Veteran Petty production team keeps focus on music. *Billboard*.

19. "That was excess at its..." ~ Verna, Paul (1997, November 8). Bay area's Plant marks 25 Years. *Billboard*.

20. "Recording Tusk was quite absurd..." ~ Williamson, Nigel. (2003, May). Fleetwood Mac: 'Everybody was pretty weirded out' – the story of *Rumours*. *Uncut*.

21. "I was touring with 'Til ..." ~ Milano Brett. (1996, February). Life after new wave: A former MTV queen rehabilitated into a singer-songwriter, Aimee Mann doesn't suffer fools – she writes songs about them. *Pulse.*
22. "That's easy: Keeping 30-plus..." ~ Greenblatt, Mike. (2014, May). The devil and Mr. Daniels. *Goldmine.*

CHAPTER 18: THE PARTIES, BOOZE AND DRUGS

1. "I don't think John knew..." ~ Robertson, Robbie. (2016). *Testimony.* New York: Crown Archetype.
2. "There was no way to..." ~ Howe, Zoe. (2105). *Stevie Nicks: Visions, Dreams & Rumors.* New York: Overlook-Omnibus.
3. "By 1840 an estimated 24,000..." ~ Sante, Luc. (1991). *Low Life: Lures and Snares of Old New York.* New York: Macmillan.
4. "reported that high school students..." ~ Palladino, Grace. (1996). *Teenagers: An American History.* New York: BasicBooks.
5. Medicine shows often included musical... ~ Shapiro, Harry. (1999). *Waiting for the Man: The Story of Drugs and Popular Culture* (Rev. ed.). London: Helter Skelter.
6. Marijuana use was rare in.. ~ Shapiro, Harry. (1999). *Waiting for the Man: The Story of Drugs and Popular Culture* (Rev. ed.). London: Helter Skelter.
7. "We tend to perceive creative..." ~ McMillen, Andrew. (2014). *Talking Smack: Honest Conversations About Drugs.* Queensland, Australia: University of Queensland Press.
8. "I certainly wouldn't advocate..." ~ Greig, Geordie. (2014 June 21). Why my children will not be inheriting my £180million fortune. *The Daily Mail.*
9. "There's no question, that taking..." ~ Allman, Gregg; & Light, Alan. (2012). *My Cross to Bear.* New York: William Morrow.
10. "Look, *Exile On Main Street...*" ~ Odell, Michael. (2003, November 15). In their own words. *The Observer.*
11. "I had never shot or..." ~ Weiland, Scott; & Ritz, David (2011). *Not Dead & Not for Sale.* New York: Scribner.
12. "I used pills to write because..." ~ James, Tommy; & Fitzpatrick, Martin. (2010). *Me, the Mob, and the Music.* New York: Scribner.
13. "There were times in the..." ~ Hilburn, Robert. (2018). *Paul Simon: The Life.* New York: Simon & Schuster.
14. "I thought they were trying..." ~ Heath, Chris. (2019, February 19). Clean: 9 sober musicians on how they thrive creatively without booze or drugs. *GQ.*
15. "The idea that drugs and..." ~ von Radowitz, John. (2010, June 25). Drunk writers were better sober, says psychiatrists. *The Independent.*
16. "Jim [Morrison] was very spoken..." ~ Sharp, Ken. (2013, November). Life with Linda. *Goldmine.*
17. "[Morrison] was an alcoholic. It's..." ~ Greenblatt, Mike. (2014, May). Rock and roll doorman. *Goldmine.*
18. "In Washington, D.C., five minutes..." ~ Sugerman, Danny. (1989). *Wonderland Avenue.* New York: William Morrow and Company.
19. "with the microphone stand lying..." ~ Clapton, Eric. (2007). *Clapton: The Autobiography.* New York: Broadway.
20. "We had the barman onstage..." ~ Kessler, Ted (Ed.). *The 10 Commandments: In Their Own Words.* London: Corsair.
21. "In the late '70s, there..." ~ Wilde, Jon, (2007, February). An audience with... Aerosmith. *Uncut.*
22. "I'm probably the only guy..." ~ Lowell, Spencer. (2015, May 16). 'I'm probably the only guy in L.A. who never took coke.' *Billboard.*
23. "Twenty years ago I stated..." ~ Ling, Dave. (2004, July). Face off: Gene Simmons. *Classic Rock.*
24. "Our peers laughed at us..." ~ Wright, Jeb. (2013, June). Keeping the faith. *Goldmine.*
25. "I was standing at a..." ~ Blackwood, Nina; Goodman, Mark; Hunter, Alan; Quinn, Martha; & Edwards, Gavin. (2013). *VJ: The Unplugged Adventures of MTV's First Wave.* New York: Atria.
26. "In almost every classic rock..." ~ Troyanek, Madelyn. (2005, April 10). Former rock and roll star lives the quiet life on the beach, finds success as hit song writer. *The St. Augustine Record.*
27. "First Jimi, Then Janis. You're..." ~ Sugerman, Danny. (1989). *Wonderland Avenue.* New York: William Morrow and Company.

28. "One night in London I..." ~ Phillips, Beau. (2014). *I Killed Pink Floyd's Pig*. Seattle: Peanut Butter Publishing.
29. "I was saying to Sharon..." ~ Grow, Kory. (2017, September 21). The last word: Ozzy Osbourne. *Rolling Stone*.
30. "I don't do it any..." ~ Moodie, Clemmie. (2015, May 29). Paul McCartney: "I gave up weed for my grandkids." *The Liverpool Echo*.
31. "When I was young touring..." ~ Derdeyn, Stuart. (2017, June 10). Living legend Bonnie Raitt slides into Vancouver. *The Vancouver Sun*.
32. "I enjoyed what Morrison, Joplin..." ~ Negron, Chuck; & Blatchford, Chris. (1999). *Three Dog Nightmare*. Los Angeles: Renaissance Books.
33. "You may not believe it..." ~ Mehr, Bob. (2000, August 17). Song of salvation. *Phoenix New Times*.
34. "There was an end-of-tour..." ~ Deevoy, Adrian. (2018, July 22). Graham Nash reveals why he's dating a woman half his age after turning his back on his wife, drugs AND his former bandmates. *Event Magazine*.
35. "The entire theater was crawling..." ~ Chong, Tommy. (2006). *The I Chong*. New York: Simon Spotlight Entertainment.
36. "I mean they spent their..." ~ Marsh, Stefanie. (2015, November 15). Jerry Hall on life with Mick. *The Times of London*.

CHAPTER 19: SELLING OUT: ACHIEVING MAINSTREAM SUCCESS

1. "I don't blame the average..." ~ Azerrad, Michael. (1992, April 16). Nirvana: Inside the heart and mind of Kurt Cobain. *Rolling Stone*.
2. "We had become 'America's sweethearts.'"... ~ Doe, John; & Tom DeSavia. (2019). *More Fun in the New World*. New York: De Capo Press.
3. "Tonight a boy was crying..." ~ Kilcher, Jewel. (2000). *Chasing Down the Dawn*. New York: HarperEntertainment.
4. "When all is said and..." ~ Young, Jon. (1980, May). Bruce Wooley: Music not just for money. *Trouser Press*.
5. "That was the greatest trick in..." ~ Baker, Ben. (2010, October 11). Their message. *Forbes*.
6. "The Beatles' position is that..." ~ Arango, Tim. (2006, December 11). Happiness is a warm iPod. *Fortune Magazine*.
7. "[Mellencamp] said a turning point..." ~ Light, Alan. (2007, January 22). Changes in Mellencamp country. *The New York Times*.
8. "What is rich? In truth..." ~ Escovedo, Sheila; & Holden, Wendy. (2014). *The Beat of My Own Drum*. New York: Atria.
9. "It was during a period... ~ Fleming, Amy. (2020, March 23). Dionne Warwick on singing, psychics and the hell of segregation: 'We all bleed red blood.' *The Guardian*.
10. "Michael [Jackson] didn't drink Pepsi..." ~ Jackson, Jermaine. (2011). *You Are Not Alone: Michael, Through a Brother's Eyes*. New York: Touchstone.
11. "I'm a businesswoman. The music..." ~ Paolette, Michael. (2005, November 12). Dancing queen. *Billboard*.
12. "My feeling about that stuff..." ~ Schlansky, Evan. (2010, September-October). Devo. *American Songwriter*.
13. "We're going to mount this..." ~ Grabowy, Greg. (2006, November 11). Q&A: Jay Coleman. *Billboard*.
14. "That's just hippy bullshit from..." ~ Swift, David. (December 3, 1988). "I laugh to win." *NME*.
15. "It wasn't a commercial for..." ~ "Sting Q&A." (2003, December 13). *Billboard*.
16. "When I was a 14-year-old..." ~ Black, Judy. (1990, December 5). The Milli Vanilli scandal. *(Cleveland) Scene*.

CHAPTER 20: A MUSIC CAREER ON THE DECLINE

1. "We sold ten million last..." ~ Weisner, Ron; & Goldsher, Alan. (2014). *Listen Out Loud*. Guilford, CT: Lyons Press.
2. "He's afraid to finish the..." ~ Troupe, Quincy. (1987, June). The pressure to beat it. *Spin*.
3. "I have these bad dreams..." ~ Hedges, Dan. (1988, July). Choose your Poison. *Spin*.
4. "A year earlier, our faces..." ~ Collis, Clark. (2004, November). You're fired! *Blender*.

261

5. "I was performing in Cleveland..." ~ Ritz, David. (2002). *Faith in Time: The Life of Jimmy Scott.* Cambridge, MA: Da Capo.

6. "We were in London for..." ~ Gorman, Steve; & Hyden, Steven. (2019). *Hard to Handle: The Life and Death of the Black Crowes.* New York: Da Capo Press.

7. "Doubt is debilitating for a..." ~ Anka, Paul; & Dalton, David. (2013). *My Way: An Autobiography.* New York: St. Martin's Press.

8. "Our last concert that year..." ~ Greenspoon, Jimmy; & Bego, Mark. (1991). *One is the Loneliest Number.* New York: Pharos.

9. "A lot of people think..." ~ Jones, Allan. (2016). *Can't Stand Up For Falling Down: Rock 'n' Roll War Stories.* London: Bloomsbury.

10. "Sure, we're going to lose..." ~ Thompson, Thomas. (1967, June 16). The new far-out Beatles. *Life.*

11. "I hate to actually even ..." ~ Fricke, David. (1994, January 27). Our man in Nirvana rages on (and on) about stardom, fatherhood, his feud with Pearl Jam, the death of grunge and why he's never been happier in his life. *Rolling Stone.*

12. "A lot of my money..." ~ Kiersh, Edward. (1985, December). Sly Stone's heart of darkness. *Spin.*

CHAPTER 21: ROCK IS YOUTH: BATTLING OLD AGE

1. "I think growing old is..." ~ Boteach, Rabbi Shmuley. (2009). *The Michael Jackson Tapes.* New York: Vanguard.

2. "I still think of myself..." ~ Eells, Josh. (2014, June 5). The last brother. *Rolling Stone.*

3. "In those days there were..." ~ Kooper, Al. (2008). *Backstage Passes & Backstabbing Bastards.* New York: Backbeat Books.

4. "When I started doing this..." ~ Schlenker, Dave. (2005, December). Grapevine: Tom Petty takes it home. *Gainesville Magazine.*

5. "You see old interviews with..." ~ DeCurtis, Anthony. (2006, May). You say it's my birthday. *AARP Magazine.*

6. "I thought I'd be done..." ~ Greene, Andy. (2018, January 2). Bob Seger. *Rolling Stone.*

7. "Hopefully, I can go on..." ~ Pareles, Jon. (1992, April 8). At lunch with Marky Mark; The high priest of hot and now. *The New York Times.*

8. "People want to remember us..." ~ Born, Matt. (2005, February 14). Super troupers reunite for ABBA musical. *The Telegraph.*

9. "Passion is a young man's..." ~ Love, Robert. (2015, February/March). Bob Dylan does the American standards his way. *AARP Magazine.*

10. "I sometimes look at the..." ~ Thompson, Dave. (2011, June). From Deep Purple to Blackmore's Night. *Goldmine.*

11. "When I see these old..." ~ Kane, Dan. (2006, July 9). Heavy metal screamer is Mr. Mom at home. *The Canton Repository.*

12. "The summer before [our television..." ~ Osbourne, Sharon; Osbourne, Ozzy; & Gold, Todd. (2003). *Ordinary People: Our Story.* New York: MTV Books / Pocket Books.

13. "I'm just aware of the..." ~ Vaziri, Aidin. (2018, March 7). Pop Quiz: The Who's Roger Daltrey on why singing "Baba O'Riley" is good for the spirit. *The San Francisco Chronicle.*

14. "We're not in our 20s..." ~ Klosterman, Chuck. (2015, June 27). The last guitar god. *Billboard.*

15. "Having my long hair and..." ~ Clinton, George. (2016, October). 10 commandments. *Q.*

16. "I'm sure Dylan doesn't think..." ~ Chick, Stevie. (2017, August). The *Mojo* interview. *Mojo.*

17. "I've loved music ever since..." ~ White, Timothy. (1993, March 6). Ray Charles's brave new world. *Billboard.*

18. "I can't retire until I..." ~ Fricke, David. (2010, October 28). Keith by Keith. *Rolling Stone.*

19. "I'll never retire. My friend..." ~ Greene, Andy. (2017, March 23). The last word: Stevie Nicks. *Rolling Stone.*

20. "I'm going to be 68..." ~ Zimmerman, Lee. (2014, April). Looking at life after 'Crazy Love.' *Goldmine.*

21. "Rock simply cannot be credibly..." ~ Strausbaugh, John. (2001, September 17). Dinosaur Rock. *Forbes.*

22. "Who'd want to hear a..." ~ "John Lennon answers 40 intimate questions." (1964, June). *16 Magazine.*

23. "Nobody wants a 50-year-old..." ~ "Welcome back: Bad Religion." (2013, April). *Classic Rock.*

24. "I don't think that the..." ~ Eliscu, Jenny. (2006, November 2). Dr. Who. *Rolling Stone*.
25. "I suffer from permanent tinnitus..." ~ Osbourne, Ozzy. (2010, July 25) Ask Dr. Ozzy. *Times of London*.
26. "Forty years later, here we..." ~ Jancik, Wayne. (1998). *The Billboard Book of One-Hit Wonders*. New York: Billboard.
27. "It wasn't easy. People kept..." ~ DiMucci, Dion; & Seay, Davin. (1988). *The Wanderer: Dion's Story*. New York: Beech Tree Books.
28. "There's nothing wrong with nostalgia..." ~ Thompson, Dave. (2011, June). From Deep Purple to Blackmore's Night. *Goldmine*.
29. "I'm not interested in nostalgia..." ~ Gundersen, Edna. (1990, February 9). Petty at his peak. *USA Today*.
30. Mason would later lament that... ~ DeRiso, Nick. (2014, February 12). Dave Mason on Traffic, Fleetwood Mac and going his own way. SomethingElse.com.
31. "They came up with every..." ~ Mehr, Bob. (2000, August 17). Song of salvation. *Phoenix New Times*.
32. "Nobody cares who the people..." ~ Miller, Chuck. (2001, June 15). Doo-wop "hall of fame" concert draws protest from artists, fans. *Goldmine*.
33. "Chuck Blasco of the Vogues..." ~ Pareles, Jon; & McKinley, Jesse. (1998, May 28). Great pretenders: Pop imitators sing the same old song; but nothing like the real thing, some oldies performers complain. *The New York Times*.
34. "We occasionally mangle our own..." ~ Yarborough, Chuck. (2019, September 16). Cheap Trick's Rick Nielsen doesn't need a lot words to say how much he loves playing. *The Cleveland Plain Dealer*.

CHAPTER 22: THE END OF THE LINE
1. "Bruce has asked me. Pete..." ~ Hiatt, Brian. (2013, February 14). Q&A: Billy Joel. *Rolling Stone*.
2. "I can't go on, I..." ~ Cain, Jonathan. (2018). *Don't Stop Believin': The Man, the Band, and the Songs that Inspired Generations*. Grand Rapids, MI: Zondervan.
3. "I had lost that deep..." ~ Elliott, Paul. (2018, November). Never say never again. *Classic Rock*.
4. "We had reminded each other..." ~ Doe, John; & Tom DeSavia. (2019). *More Fun in the New World*. New York: De Capo Press.
5. "When he first quit, he..." ~ Strauss, Neil. (2006, July 13). Tom Petty's last dance. *Rolling Stone*.
6. "It's quite simple, really. I..." ~ Hilburn, Robert. (1990, September 9). George Michael's case against fame. *The Los Angeles Times*.
7. "We had gone on a..." ~ Wright, Jeb. (2008, August 1). The journey continues. *Goldmine*.
8. "They weren't paying me.... They..." ~ Greene, Andy. (2015, March 27). 10 things we learned spending two days with Bill Withers. *Rolling Stone*.
9. "I never expected it to..." ~ Spencer, Scott. (2008, August 7). Mark Knopfler's second act. *Rolling Stone*.
10. "I have no interest. I'd..." ~ Colon, Suzan. (1997, April 17). Ric Ocasek on working with Billy Corgan for new album, how he invented himself. *Rolling Stone*.
11. "[I] hate being recognized..." ~ Patterson, Sylvia. (2013, February). Cash for questions: Marianne Faithfull. *Q*.
12. "It was a weird stage..." ~ Farndale, Nigel. (2015, May 24). Art Garfunkel on Paul Simon: 'I created a monster.' *The Telegraph*.
13. "An executor's report sent to..." ~ Hall, James. (2019, December 28). The Michael Hutchence mystery: where did all his money go? *The Telegraph*.
14. "have this work ethic that..." ~ Greig, Geordie. (2014 June 21). Why my children will not be inheriting my £180million fortune. *The Daily Mail*.
15. "Nothing has changed, this won't..." ~ Bertrand, Michael. (2011). How much does it cost if it's free?: The selling (out) of Elvis Presley. In Elizabeth Barfoot Christian (Ed.), *Rock Brands*. Lanham, MD: Lexington Books.
16. "On the streets of Memphis..." ~ "Everything Elvis." (1977, October 10). *People*.
17. "Jim Morrison – he's hot, he's..." ~ Breslin, Rosemary. (1981, September 17). Jim Morrison – he's hot, he's sexy and he's dead. *Rolling Stone*.
18. "In the darkened Wiltern Theatre..." ~ Lee, Wendy. (2018, October 6). Roy Orbison hologram concert in L.A. invites awe and debate. *The Los Angeles Times*.

19. "My father talked about wanting..." ~ Uhelszki, Jaan. (2018). I don't think I'm that much of a control freak any more. *Uncut.*
20. "I wanted to give something to my family." ~ Hiatt, Brian. (2018, March 8). The last word: George Clinton. *Rolling Stone.*

CLOSING TIME

1. "And here's the thing: What..." ~ Bienstock, Richard. (2016, May 19). Joe Walsh: My life in 15 songs. *Rolling Stone.*
2. "You work while everybody else..." ~ Daniels, Charlie. (2017). *Never Look at the Empty Seats: A Memoir.* New York: HarperCollins.
3. "Being a legend is a..." ~ Kruth, John. (2013). *Rhapsody in Black: The Life and Music of Roy Orbison.* Milwaukee, WI: Backbeat Books.
4. "I sometimes wonder if all..." ~ Meyer, David N. (2013). *The Bee Gees: The Biography.* Cambridge, MA: Da Capo Press.
5. "I can't think of anything..." ~ Deevoy, Adrian. (2018, August 5). Still super-hip (and all lip) at 66, The Pretenders' Chrissie Hynde tells Event why she swears at fans, enrages sex abuse victims... and has swapped the wild life for walks in the park. *Event Magazine.*
6. "Johnny Cash said this to..." ~ Bogdanovich, Peter. (2007). *Runnin' Down A Dream: Tom Petty and the Heartbreakers.* San Francisco: Chronicle Books.
7. "There's nothing great about singing..." ~ "It all started with a phone call from Harry Belafonte.... to... Ken Kragen." (1985, April 6). *Billboard.*
8. "When you really think about..." ~ Gross, Terry. (2002, February 4). Interview with Gene Simmons. *Fresh Air* (NPR).
9. "I'm sick of Bono. And..." ~ Wenner, Jann S. (2005, September 3). Bono: The *Rolling Stone* interview. *Rolling Stone.*
10. "We used to believe the..." ~ Connelly, Ray. (2009, September 6). Exclusive: John Lennon, the lost interviews. *The Times of London.*
11. "The [music] industry is in..." ~ Holland, Bill. (2004, November 27). The last word: A Q&A with Jerry Wexler. *Billboard.*
12. "A 'career' in music is..." ~ Burrows, Marc. (2016, January 30). The long, hard road to rock 'n' roll success: 'We're essentially skint.' *The Guardian.*
13. "[In] the late '60s and..." ~ Stransky, Tanner. (2010, October 15). Q&A: Elton John. *Entertainment Weekly.*
14. "In the musical climate these..." ~ Hammer, Adam. (2011, July 21). Cinderella celebrates 25th anniversary world tour. *The St. Cloud Times.*
15. "It really sucks because there's..." ~ McIntyre, Ken. (2013, June). The hollow men. *Classic Rock.*
16. "There'll never be another Beatles..." ~ Rees, Paul. (2014, August). John Mellencamp: From Little Bastard to cranky old man to footnote? *Classic Rock.*

OTHER BOOKS
BY NICK THOMAS

Tom Petty: A Rock and Roll Life

The Traveling Wilburys: The Biography

CPSIA information can be obtained
at www.ICGtesting.com
Printed in the USA
LVHW012353140920
666035LV00015B/1093